LASER

LASER

A. W. STRAWSBURG

LASER

iUniverse books may be ordered through booksellers or by contacting:

iUniverse
1663 Liberty Drive
Bloomington, IN 47403
www.iuniverse.com
1-800-Authors (1-800-288-4677)

ISBN: 978-1-5320-5319-1 (sc)
ISBN: 978-1-5320-5320-7 (e)

Library of Congress Control Number: 2018909045

Print information available on the last page.

iUniverse rev. date: 09/12/2018

Chapter   1

The old rusty van rolled past row after row and mile after mile of corn. Far ahead on the horizon a city appears to float like an island in an ocean of corn.

Dr. Jase Brick's mind was preoccupied with his schedule. "I need to be at the university lab in forty five minutes. If this old van keeps running, I should make it. This has been a busy day already, and it doesn't seem to be slowing down."

He looked over at his wife as he drove. "She has been by my side from the day that we met. When my cancer took away my chance to father a child, she was there for me."

"Jill, are you all right? You are being very quiet."

"Yes, I was just thinking about that little boy at the adoption agency. He was so sweet. I can't believe that he might be coming home with us in two days. Are we ready?"

Jase took her by the hand, "No one is more ready than we are. Would you like me to drop you off at the house?"

"Are you kidding? This project is as much mine as it is yours." Jill smiled, "But I can't get that little boy out of my head. After waiting all these months to adopt a baby, now it happens at the same time as the University presents your research project."

"Jill, this day could change our lives on so many levels."

"We are almost there Jill, are you ready?"

"Let's do it. Let's show these corporate white collars......"

"Settle down, Jill," he laughed. "We will show them things that have never been seen before."

As they turned by the stream and went up the hill to the parking lot for the old science building, they noticed several cars that were new to the campus. One of the cars had US Government on the license plates.

Jill looked at the plates and frowned. "Who invited the Government?"

"I don't know. I didn't invite them," replied Jase.

He parked the van close to the main door, but before they could get the van door opened, one of the staff came running out.

"Jase, boy I am glad you are here. All the corporate representatives are here, but I didn't know you invited the government."

"I didn't, what do you think they want?" he asked.

When they got out of the van, Jase grabbed his brief case and followed Jill into the building.

The old science building was not much to look at and it had not been updated since it was built in the 1950s. But it had been a good place for Jase to go forward with his cancer research.

The Dean of the university met them at the door. Jase looked at Jill and whispered, "Now this is scary, he never smiles."

Jill laughed, "No I don't think that I have ever seen him smile before either."

Dean Charles opened the door for them. "Jase, Jill we have been waiting for you. Please come in, I want to introduce you to some of our guests. Or better yet, I will let them introduce themselves to you."

Dean Charles entered the room first. "Gentlemen, may I introduce Dr Jase Brick and his wife Jill."

"There must be at least ten people here," Jase whispered to Jill. Both of them were shocked. They would never remember all their names and who they represented.

One by one, the guest introduced themselves.

A tall man in an impressively tailored suit walked forward. "Dr. Brick, it is a pleasure to meet you at last. My name is Michael Greyger. I am very much interested in your research."

As Dr. Brick shook hands with Mr. Greyger, he asked, "Is that your Government car parked outside?"

"Why yes, it is. I work for an agency that is part of the US Government."

The Dean waved his hands and shouted, "Now everyone, let's go into Dr. Brick's lab."

Jase and Jill walked in first.

Jase addressed the audience. "I hope after our presentation you will be just as excited about this project as my wife and I are. Shall we begin?"

He walked over to the display. "I am a cancer survivor. Ever since that day when I was given a clean bill of health, I have dedicated my life to cancer research."

"I was fortunate enough for Dean Charles to offer me a position at the University. My work here has not been cheap, and the University needs financial help to keep our research going. We think we are at the beginning of the end of cancer. Now, let me prove it."

"Your body is under constant attack from cancer cells. Normally, your body can fight and win this battle, but sometimes your body needs a little help. I have developed a compound that can seek out cancer cells and destroy them."

"I also am working on a new laser that can remove cancerous tumors from your body without the need for surgery."

One of the men attending interrupted, "Dr. Brick, you think that you can cure a person that has a tumor inside of their body without making an incision. How can this be?"

"Mr...? I'm sorry, I didn't get your name."

"Dr. Brick, my name is Allan Smith. I represent the industrialist, Blake Canond."

Everyone in the room turned to look at the man after hearing the name of his employer.

Jase replied, "To answer your question, yes. I think, that with your help, I can cure just about any kind of cancer."

After a murmur of skepticism from the guests, Dr. Brick continued.

With a confident smile, Jase looked at the group. "Gentlemen, this chelating compound will attach to the cancer cells and destroy them, even on a microscopic level. Then they can be removed through the bowls."

"Dr. Brick," a voice came from the back of the room, "How do you destroy a tumor that has already become too large for the compound to remove?"

"Good question, Mr. Greyger. That is when we use the laser."

"Dr. Brick, does this laser exist only in theory?"

"I have a small working prototype here in the lab."

Jase walked over to the laser. "Go get them, Jase." Jill said in a low voice to herself.

"Now bear in mind, this laser has two beams. Let me show you. The two laser beams are the same until I put the source into the CPU. One beam is positive, and one beam is negative. They can go from the size of a micro dot to almost any size, if you have enough power. The two laser units are connected by this cable."

Mr. Greyger looked straight at Jase. "Really, Dr. Brick, any size?"

Jase nodded yes.

"Let me show you how it works. I still have some issues with power, but with your financial help, we can overcome those issues. Now watch!"

"Jill, would you pass out the special safety glasses for our guests?"

She smiled as she handed each one a set of glasses.

All eyes watched as Dr. Brick turned the laser on.

"The positive beam is green. Watch while I put my hand in front of the beam. The beam passes through with no harm to my hand." Jase held up his hand for all to see.

"Now, over here is the other laser and this one is negative. Let me energize it."

Jase walked over to the other side of the table. "When I turn the power on, you will hear a high pitch sound. The sound only lasts a few seconds until the laser warms up."

"Now, as you can see, this beam is red." Jase put his hand in front of the laser, and the red beam passed through his hand. No one said a word.

"Would you please remove your glasses? Notice that you cannot see the beams without your glasses."

"Dr Brick, how can two lasers that pass though your hand cure cancer?" asked one of the guests.

"I'm glad you asked." Jase smiled and went on talking. "Watch while I put up this thin sheet of plywood."

Jill helped him slide the sheet of plywood into its frame on the table. She then turned and looked at their guests. "Dr. Brick is pointing the negative laser at the plywood. Gentlemen, you might want to come closer for a better look."

The entire group stood up. "Come closer, the laser will not hurt you. Don't be shy."

"But would you please put your glasses back on," Dr Brick requested. "Now watch. Jill, please turn on the positive charged laser."

"Gentlemen, you see both the lasers have beams passing through the wood and the wood is unharmed. Now watch when the tip of the two laser beams touch on the other side of the plywood."

All eyes in the room were on the red and green beams.

"Would you turn the lights off for a moment, Jill?" Jill walked over to the door and turned off the switch to the lights.

"As you can see, I have a frozen pea hanging by a thread behind the plywood."

You could have heard a pin drop.

"Now, I will adjust the two beams so that they touch on the side of the pea."

When the beams touched, there was a little electric arc.

"You see gentlemen, when the beams touch, only the edge of the pea is destroyed upon contact. No other part of the pea is harmed."

"Now watch as I enlarge the size of the beams and adjust the power."

As Jill looked around the room, she could feel the excitement. Jase had everyone's attention including Dean Charles.

"Gentlemen, as the size of the beams increases, so does the disintegration of the pea until there is nothing left of it."

"Jill, turn the lights on please and help me shut down the lasers."

"Gentleman, I believe that you just have witnessed the largest breakthrough in the history of cancer research," Dean Charles said.

The room was flooded with questions.

Jase held up his hand. "Gentlemen, I will answer all your questions, but please just one at a time. Jase pointed to one of the men, "Your question?"

"Have you used this laser on live tissue, and, Dr. Brick, how close are you in releasing the chelating compound for use?"

"Let me answer your question by introducing you to our dog, Rex."

Jill brought Rex into the room. His tail was wagging slowly as he entered.

"We think Rex is about six years old. When he was brought to us, he was almost dead. He had cancer throughout his body. We were told there was no hope for him by the local veterinarian. He could not even stand under his own power."

"We started Rex on an IV of our compound and nourishment. As you can see, he has completely recovered."

"Dr. Brick, do you have proof that this dog had cancer?"

"Yes, copies of all the documents will be given to each of you upon conclusion of the meeting."

"Dr. Brick, what makes your chelating compound different from the type that was developed around WW II?"

"That compound was designed to remove lead. This one is designed to remove cancer. I think you will be impressed as you look through the research papers."

"Jill, would you pass out the folders?"

"This University needs your support. Please help us keep this project moving at a rapid pace. Everyday people are dying of cancer and this could change their lives."

Dean Charles spoke up. "Well, this concludes our demonstration. Thank you, Dr. Brick. Gentlemen, if you would follow me, I would like to show you some of the other projects we are involved in."

Jill and Jase stood at the door saying goodbye to the guests.

"Jill, I think that went all right, don't you?" Jase grinned at her.

She punched him. "You had them eating out of your hand, and you know it!"

Just then Michael Greyger walked back in. "Dr. Brick, can I stop and see you tomorrow? I would like to look over these folders first."

"Tomorrow might be a bad day. Jill and I are right in the middle of adopting a child, so we don't know what our schedule will be. Could you call before you come?"

"Yes, I see that I have your cell phone number on the project folder. Until tomorrow then."

"We will look forward to it," answered Jase. He shook hands with Michael as he left.

"Jase, I like Michael, he seems like a really nice person."

"I get the same feeling. I wonder what the US Government wants with our project?"

Jill and Jase cleaned up the lab. They took the laser apart and locked it away. Jase put the main part of the laser in his case. He walked outside of the lab, where a stocky man with a scruffy appearance was waiting.

"Would you put this somewhere in a safe place?" The man nodded. He took the case and disappeared.

As Jase opened the door to the van for Jill, she grabbed him around the neck. "I'm so proud of you." Then she jumped into the van.

Jase closed the door after Jill got in. The door didn't close right, so he used a little more effort the second time. Finally satisfied, he walked to the other side of the vehicle grumbling. Some day he would have a better one.

Jase and his wife started home to their small apartment.

When they arrived home, they pulled up in front of their building. All of the units in the complex looked the same. "Jill, I wonder what would happen if we switched all the numbers on the apartments. Do you think anyone could find their way home?"

"You couldn't. Sometimes you have so much on your mind, I don't know how you find your way home now."

They went into their home. There was not much to look at, a small kitchen, dining / living area, two bedrooms and a bath.

"Jill, it is almost five o'clock. I think if the adoption agency was going to call, they would have done it by now. There is no sense sitting around waiting for the phone to ring. Would you like to go out to eat?"

"Oh, why not, and let's go to the new baby store that just opened next to the mall."

Jase smiled, "That would be fine."

That night Michael Greyger was on the phone talking to his people in Virginia. "You find out what adoption agency the Brick's are using. I want to know everything that is going on. This is a first priority. Call me back as soon as you have some answers, and I don't mean tomorrow, understood?"

"Yes sir," answered the voice on the other end. Michael hung up.

Close to 9:00 pm, Michael's phone rang.

"This is Michael."

"The adoption was approved! The baby is less than a week old, and he is African American, according to the administer Martha Woods."

"You get back on the phone and tell that woman she will be out of a job if that adoption goes through. The last thing the Brick family needs right now, is to take care of some little kid. If you have to, send an agent to her house and scare the fucking shit out of her!"

Michael ended the call not waiting for an answer.

Chapter 2

The next morning the Bricks were having a cup of coffee. Jase reached over and grabbed Jill's hand. "If we don't hear anything within the hour, I will call her myself."

"Jase, I don't like it, something is wrong. I can just feel it."

"Now Jill, let's not make something out of nothing."

"Jase, you said that if anything went wrong, you would take that teaching job for a year, so we could get our family going."

"I know I said that, but…"

"No buts, Jase, you promised." Jill was trying to hold back tears, but it was not working.

Jase's cell phone started to ring. Jill held on to Jase, her eyes were open wide and full of tears.

"Hello, this is Jase." he answered.

"Dr. Brick, hi this is Michael Greyer. I hope this is a good time to call. Did you get your son, Michael caught himself or daughter yet? I hope everything went well."

"Hi Michael," he answered as he looked at Jill and shook his head no. "It really is not a good time. Jill and I are waiting to hear from the agency now."

"I'm only a block away, and it would mean so much to me if you had a few moments."

"Alright Michael, but we have a lot going right now."

"I understand, and I will be right there. I promise I won't take up much of your time. See you in a few minutes."

"Sorry Jill, Michael was just a block away. Let's see what he has to say."

Jill was trying to wipe the tears away as she went to the bedroom.

Michael walked up to the door, but before he could knock, Jase opened it.

"Hi Michael, come in we are waiting for the phone call now. We thought it was Mrs. Woods from the adoption agency when you called."

"Well, I hope everything turns out alright for you two."

"Thanks Michael, we appreciate your thoughts."

Just then the phone started to ring. "Jill, it's Martha Woods," he yelled. "Hello, this is Jase."

"Hello Dr. Brick, this is Martha. There has been a change. The mother has decided she would rather have a black family adopt her son. We already have a family chosen. I'm so sorry, I think you and Jill would be the perfect parents." She sounded like she was going to cry. "Dr. Brick, I have to go. I wish you the best, goodbye."

Jase hung up. Jill was looking right at Jase and without him saying a word, she knew.

"Jill, the mother picked another family. Mrs. Woods was crying. I think she really wanted us to get the child."

Jill left the room crying.

"Michael, as you can see this is a bad time."

Michael sat there for a moment. "Dr. Brick, if I could just have a moment of your time. I will be short."

"Michael, my wife and I decided that if the adoption fell through, we would just take some time off. As of right now, my project is on hold."

"Dr. Brick, what will you do?" asked Michael.

"I have been offered a teaching job. I told Jill that I would take it for a while until we get over this. We really want a family. I am sorry, but I must go to Jill. I hope that you understand."

"Dr. Brick, if I can do anything, please let me know."

Jase walked Michael to the door and they shook hands.

"Michael, I will call you. Thanks for coming over, it means a lot to Jill and me."

With a caring smile, Michael said, "Dr. Brick, let me see what I can do on my end."
Then he turned and walked to his car.

Jase went to the bedroom, where Jill was crying on the bed.

"Jill, I told Michael that the project is on hold for now. Our family is more important."

Jill came over to Jase and put her arms around him. "Jase, I love that little boy so much."

"I do too, Jill. I do too."

Chapter   3

Michael Greyger opened his car door and got in. He pushed the speed-dial on his cell phone.

"This is Michael. It did not work out the way we planned. We are going to have to find Dr. Brick a child. You find him a white child and make it a girl."

Michael listened at the response.

"No, don't worry, they want a child so bad they will take anything short of a puppy. Make sure that this child is healthy. I don't want any time wasted on a sick child. Do I make myself clear?"

Michael paused, as he listened.

"Good, I want this to happen now. When you find one, call me. Now move."

Michael hung up. Then he dialed again.

"This is Michael. Get the team together. We need to pay a visit to a University. I will call with the details." Michael hung up and dialed again.

"This is Michael again. I also will need an agent, and she must look like a grandmother."

"Michael, a grandmother?" the voice asked.

"Yes, that right, some one's grandmother. Dr. Brick is going to need a nanny. Call me as soon as you find one."

Michael hung up. He smiled and drove back to the motel. He parked the car and went inside to the lobby.

"You know this is about the nicest town I have ever been to," he said to the young lady at the desk.

"Why thank you, Mr. Greyger," she said. "This is a nice place to live."

"Really, tell me more. Do you have much crime?"

"Well, once in a while one of the students from the university may get into trouble, but that's about it." Michael watched the desk clerk as she talked.

"Is there a good place to eat around here? I'm so tired of fast food. Do you know what I mean?"

"Yes, Mr. Greyger, I do. There is a nice restaurant just down the street. It is a little pricey, but it is very good. Here is one of their cards."

"Thank you, I feel like I'm at home already. You have been a lot of help. By the way, when was the last time you were there?"

"Mr. Greyger, I make minimum wage and I have a family," she smiled.
"You enjoy yourself, Mr. Greyger."

"Thank you, I will," he answered.

Michael went up to his room, opened the door and sat down. His phone rang.

"This is Michael. Good, no I don't want to know what you had to do to get the child. Is it white, healthy and a girl?"

"Yes Sir," the caller answered.

"Good. Now have the same agency call Dr. Brick with the good news. Wait until you hear from me to make the call. Call me when you have everything set up. One more thing, don't let that Martha person call, do it yourself."

Michael hung up and smiled. Then he picked up the phone and called Dr. Brick's house.

"Dr. Brick, this is Michael. I was very upset when I left your home. I have been on the phone all afternoon trying to be of some help to you. Would you like to have dinner with me tonight? The nice lady at the desk here said there is a good place to eat right down the road. I know Jill is upset and maybe I can help. I promise we will not talk shop, just adoption."

"I have to ask Jill, may I call you back?"

"Yes. I will be leaving tomorrow, so if you can't come, I understand. If you change your mind, you have my number. Jase, can I call you Jase, it has been good talking to you. Thanks for your time, goodnight." Michael hung up and looked pleased.

Chapter 4

"Jill, that was Michael. He said he would like to buy dinner for us tonight, and that he might be able to help us."

"Jase, how can he help?"

"I don't know, but if we don't go, we will never know. He is leaving tomorrow. He also said that he would not talk shop."

"Call him, Jase, call him right now!" Jill handed Jase the phone.

Jase dialed Michael's number. "Michael, this is Jase. Jill and I would very much like to have dinner with you."

"Good, about 7:00 then."

"About 7:00 would be fine. We will see you there." Jase hung up.

"Now Jill, don't look at me like that!"

She ran to Jase, screaming and tackled him. "Now what good would I be if you hurt my back and we could not go out to dinner?" said Jase.

She put her finger on Jase's lips, and grinned, "I would rather not talk about it right now."

"Jill, it is almost 6:00 and we must meet Michael at 7:00, I think we should get up, don't you?"

At five till seven they pulled up to the restaurant and parked between two cars that that they could not even think about owning.

They walked in. "Hi my name is----," he did not get to finish.

"Dr. Brick, your table is ready. Mr. Greyger has already arrived and is waiting." The couple smiled at each other and followed the host to the table.

Michael stood up as they approached. "Jase, Jill, I am so glad you could make it. Please have a seat and remember this is my treat." Michael smiled as they sat down.

"Michael, what is this all about?" asked Jill.

"Let's order first." He waved his hand, and the waiter came right over.

Michael spoke, "We would like to order. This dinner is on me."

Jill and Jase ordered, and then Michael ordered a steak. He told the waiter, "Just bring me the best one you have, and it will be fine."

"Yes sir," answered the waiter.

"Now folks, I was so upset when I left you home, that I have been on the phone all afternoon. I can't even imagine how you feel. That was the worst news I think I have ever heard. I pulled in some favors that people owe me, and here is what I found out."

"You two have been moved to the front of the list at your adoption agency. I know you wanted a little boy, but we can't do anything about that. I can't tell you if it will be a boy or a girl, but you will be getting a child."

"I don't care and neither does Jase," Jill said breathlessly.

"And I don't know what race the child will be. Did I overstep my bounds?" Michael looked right at Jill.

"No! No!" answered Jill. "Michael, how can we ever thank you. You have made us the happiest people on earth." They talked for over an hour after they had eaten, like old friends.

Then Michael spoke, "I'm afraid I have to get going. I must leave early tomorrow. Jase, I will call you in the morning before I leave to check on you two."

"Thank you, Michael."

"Jill, this is one of the best meals I have ever eaten and I don't even remember what I had." Jase said. Jill gave him a loving gaze.

The waiter came over. "How was the meal and will there be anything else for you?"

"This was one of the best meals I have ever had, and I think my wife would say the same." Jase answered.

Jill said, "Everything was great."

The waiter looked at Michael, "Anything else for you, sir?"

"Yes, one more thing, I would like to have a gift certificate for two of your most expensive meals. Also, would you send it to the young lady at the desk at my motel? Her name is Linda. I know that it is not something you do all the time."

"Yes sir, I will take care of it myself."

"I would do it myself, but I don't want the lady to think I am making a pass at her and getting the wrong impression." Then Michael stood up and shook hands with Jase and Jill.

"Doctor, Jill until tomorrow."

They left the restaurant. Michael got into his car and the Bricks drove off in their van.

"What a night, it is like a fairy tale come true. Let's go home." Jill smiled at Jase

Michael drove away slowly. He waved at Jase and Jill at the same time as he was talking on the phone. "Make the adoption happen tomorrow. Give them the phone call about 10:00 am. No screw ups, understand? Good."

Michael hung up. He drove his car onto the university campus and stopped next to the small stream at the bottom of the drive to Dr. Brick's lab. Michael was on the phone again. "This is Michael, is your team ready? Good. Tonight is the night. I want you to take all the info on the chelating compound also."

"That's right; I don't want Dr. Brick to know what we really want."

Chapter   5

The next morning they almost ran into each other racing to the phone as it rang.

"Hello," Jill said. "Oh hi, Michael."

"Have you heard anything yet?" asked Michael.

"No, not yet. Michael, we cannot ever thank you enough for your help."

"I have a little time before I leave. Do you have coffee or should I pick some up?" Michael asked.

"I just put a fresh pot of coffee on. We would love to see you."

"Jase, Michael is on his way to the airport. He is going to stop for a cup of coffee and say goodbye."

"That would be nice," he smiled.

Jill looked out the window. "Michael is here!" Jill yelled as she ran to the door.

"Good morning Michael. Come on in, the coffee is ready."

Michael smiled and came in. He grabbed Jase's hand. "Jase, if there is anything I can do for you and Jill, just give me a call. Do you still have my card?"

"Yes, we do, somewhere," said Jase.

"Here is another one. It is my private number, so don't give it to anyone,"

"Don't worry, I won't. What time does your plane leave, Michael?"

"About 11:30 am, so I can't stay long. I have to be back to DC for work."

"Michael, just what part of the government do you work for?" asked Jase.

"It is no more that a glorified PR job. If something is going on that will benefit the country, then they send me to check it out."

"Well regardless, we are glad you came."

Michael looked at his watch. "Well, it is about 10:00, so I will get on the move. Now we are still interested in you program, so when you are ready, please give me a call."

Before Michael could say anything else, the phone rang.

Jill ran to answer the phone. "Yes, this is Jill. We can be there in about an hour. Thank you!"

"Jase, they have a baby, and they need a family A.S.A.P. The mother was killed in a car crash last night, and there is no other family. They want us to come right now!"

"Jill, how far do you have to go?" Michael look concerned.

"The office is about 25 miles away."

"We can take my car," Michael said.

"But Michael, you have a flight to catch."

"There will be other flights, but this is something I may never see again for the rest of my life."

They grabbed a few things and jumped into Michael's car. They were at the agency in no time.

As Michael drove, he forced a smile for the entire trip. Suddenly, Jase's phone rang with the sound of steel drums.

"Is that your cell phone?" asked Michael.

"Jase wanted the phone to remind him of the islands," answered Jill.

"Hello, this is Jase. When? No, I will call you back as soon as I get back in town."

"Jase, what is going on?" Jill asked him.

"Someone broke into the lab last night. There is nothing we can do until we get back."

Jill and Jase stared at each other, but did not speak.

Michael's cell rang.

"This is Michael, may I help you?"

"Not right now, can I call you in a little bit? Yes I'm driving, would not want to have an accident." Michael hung up. His smile was gone.

"Dr. Brick, was your lab vandalized?"

"Maybe, there was nothing there of any value. Jill and I removed all the important stuff right after our meeting at the lab," explained Jase.

"We always do. Better safe than sorry," replied Jill.

"Michael, just ahead is the agency." said Jase.

"There is no place to park. I will let you two out and wait for you in the car."

"No Michael, you are as much a part of this as we are. Please come in with us," Jill answered.

Michael nodded, "I will be right there." He let Jase and Jill out in front of the building.

"Jill, let's try not to run into the building." Trying to control their excitement, they walked up the sidewalk to the building.

Martha Woods was watching for them as they arrived. She ran out to meet them with tears in her eyes. As she reached out to hug Jase, he didn't realize that she put something into his pocket.

"I am so happy for you." Then she went down the side walk in the other direction.

Michael was watching as Martha Woods walked away. "Who was that, Jase?" he asked.

"That was Martha Woods. She works here and has done so much for us in the past."

"What did she say to you?" Michael inquired.

"She said that she was so happy for us."

"That was nice of her." Michael looked puzzled.

Jill said, "Well she is a nice person."

Chapter   6

The Bricks walked up the steps to the adoption agency. As Jase opened the door, he watched Jill. Her face was full of excitement.

When they walk into the office, there was a new girl at the desk.

"You must be Dr. and Mrs. Brick."

"Yes," Jase answered.

"We have been expecting you two. My name is Ann. Please come this way."

They walked back to the nurse's office. Ann opened the door. There was a nurse sitting in the rocker. In her arms was the most beautiful little girl they had ever seen.

The nurse smiled at Jill. "Would you like to hold your daughter?"

Jill rushed over, as the nurse calmly stood up.

"Now, have a seat, and I will put you new daughter in your arms."

Jase watched Jill take the child.

"Jase, look at her eyes, they are blue like yours," Jill started to cry.

Although the baby was very quiet, she watched each move that Jill made.

"Jase, look at how smart she is. What color hair does she have?"

Jase could not answer. He was so happy he thought he was going to cry himself.

Finally Jase spoke. "Thank you Ann, what do we have to do now?"

"Just sign a few papers. Everything else is done. You must know some very important people. This is the quickest adoption I have ever seen. But for now, you two sit and get to know your new baby. The rest of us will wait outside."

Michael, Ann and the nurse walked out.

Michael looked at Ann. "Don't you think 'you must know someone bull shit' was a little much."

A moment of fear flashed across Ann's face, but she recovered.

Ann smiled. "Michael, I did not lie. This is the only adoption I have ever done, so it is the quickest. This is Nurse Linda Peach. She was going to retire this month, but decided to stay on for one more job."

"Thank you, Miss Peach. Now Ann, you did a good job, but did you have to rub out the mother?"

"Believe me, Michael, this baby is much better off with those two than that whore mother of hers."

"Whatever." Michael walked away.

"Friendly person, that Michael, I have heard about him. He could charm the fangs out of a snake and then bite his head off," Miss Peach said.

Ann warned Miss Peach, "Don't ever let him hear you say that or you might find yourself floating in a river."

Nurse Peach nodded her head.

Linda Peach was in her fifties. Her hair was not yet grey, but had started to lighten. She did not have the body that Ann did, but she was still very attractive for her age. And she could snap your neck in a heartbeat.

Michael came back.

"Ann, what happened at the lab? Did you find anything?"

"Just a lot of nothing, they must have taken anything to do with the laser somewhere else."

"Damn it, what could he have done with the rest of it that fast. Stay close, I will call you when I get back to the university. I don't want you to go back to the school and blow your cover."

"Michael, put on your happy face, I think that the family has bonded enough. Let's go back in," Ann said.

Chapter   7

Jill and Jase had lost track of time. When the door opened, Michael, Ann and the nurse came back in. They were all smiling.

"Jill, how is the new family doing?" asked Ann.

Jill gave the baby to Jase very carefully, and then she ran over to Michael.

"Michael, we can never thank you enough. We will raise this child with more love than anyone can imagine."

"I know you will, Jill. Now Ann, what do we have to do to get this family on the road?"

Ann said, "Michael, isn't it?"

Michael nodded with no smile this time.

"All the paperwork is in the office, and most of it is done. Just a few places to sign, and you're ready to go home."

"Ann, is there anything else for our new family?" Michael glared at her.

Ann looked at Michael, puzzled. Then she said, "Mr. and Mrs. Brick, this is Nurse Linda Peach. She will, for the first week or so, drop over to see if you need any help with the new child. This is a big change for all of you."

"Jase, I don't think we need any help, do you?" asked Jill.

Before Jase could answer, Ann interrupted.

"Jill, with the speed of this adoption, you really don't have a choice. This is standard procedure. You would not want me to get in trouble, would you?"

"It will be all right, Jill, and until we find out what happened at the lab, we might want a little help."

"All right, Jase, but just for a week."

A few minutes later, they were walking down the steps with their new daughter. "Thanks again Michael. Jill and I will always be in your debt," Jase said.

"You are welcome, Jase. I will go get the car and be right back."

Instinctively, Jase put his hand in his pocket to retrieve his car key. He pulled out a folded piece of paper that was from Martha Woods. It read, "Dr. Brick, call me when you can, but please do not tell anyone about this note."

"Jase, what is that?" Jill asked.

"Oh nothing, here comes Michael."

The car came to a stop, and Jase opened the door for Jill and the baby. By this time, Michael was at their side.

"Would you like to sit with your family, Jase?"

"That would be nice, thanks."

Most of the trip back, Jill watched the baby. "You know, Jase, we are going to have to name this little girl. What do you think if her middle name was Michelle?"

"That would be fine."

Michael drove up to the door, and then he helped bring all the clothes and baby things in.

"Dr. Brick, I think I'll let you two enjoy your night. Call if you need anything. It looks like I will be here for another day, and I would not want it any other way."

"Thanks, Michael, I will call you tomorrow." They watched Michael as he walked back to the car.

"What a nice man, Jase. He sure has gone out his way to help us."

Just then Jase remembered the note from Martha Woods. Slowly he pulled it from his pants pocket as Jill took the baby to the bedroom.

As Jase wondered what Martha wanted, the steel drums of his cell phone rang.

"Hello, this is Jase. Right now? We just brought out new daughter home. Okay, I will be right there."

He turned the phone off. "Jill, I have to go to the lab. Dean Charles is waiting for me."

Jill looked up. "Well Jase, hurry back, your daughter and I would like to talk about her name." Jill gave Jase a hug as he left.

It only took few minutes to get to the lab. When he arrived, there was yellow tape across the parking lot. Dean Charles was at the door.

"Jase, they destroyed your lab. Come in and look."

The police were just wrapping up. Jase knew most of them. One of them asked, "Well, how is the new baby? I bet Jill is happy?"

"They are doing just fine. It has been a long day, but a good one. Now, what happened here?"

Dean Charles and Jase stood and watched as the police started to walk out. Then one of them, a friend of Jase's, pulled him aside.

"Jase, would you come inside? I want to show you something."

"As they entered the lab, he said, "Jase, they were after something, but all of the equipment is still intact. Nothing was taken, just ransacked. If they wanted something that they could sell quickly, they would have taken all this." He pointed to the printers, copiers and other things that could be sold.

"Whatever they were looking for, they did not find it. They will be back. Watch over your shoulder, Jase. And be careful."

Jase watched Dean Charles as he walked around the lab.

"Jase, we have never had anything like this happen at the University. Do you see anything missing?"

The file folder for the chelating formula was opened. "That file is in my brief case, and there are only two backups, one in Florida and one in Ohio. Let's go into the other room."

The two lasers were there. "They are no good without the power pack and source material, and they would also need the CPU. I think that they wanted the chelating compound. In the right hands, it would be worth a lot of money."

Jase put his hand on the Dean's shoulder. "This is not as bad as it looks.

Jill and I will have this place back in business in just a few hours."

He turned sharply, "You mean we are still in business?"

"Absolutely, now I have to go home to my family. Sounds kind of good doesn't it."

He turned and started to walk out. When he put his hand in his pocket, he remembered the note Martha had given him.

"Dean, will you excuse me, I have to make a phone call." With a nod, he walked into the other room.

He cleared a place at his desk, sat down in the chaos and called Martha.

He dialed the number to Martha's cell phone, it rang, and then voicemail took over. "Martha, this is Jase Brick, just wanted to thank you for everything."

As soon as he hung up, the phone rang. "Dr Brick, this is Martha."

"Hi,---"

"Dr. Brick, I don't have much time. I'm calling you from a pay phone. If you tell anyone about this conversation, I will say it never happened. First, our phones are being tapped. Be careful what you say. Next write down this number."

"Martha, whose number is this?"

"It is the number of the mother of the little boy you wanted to adopt."

"You told me she did not want us to have her son."

"Dr. Brick, please let me talk. By just calling you, I have put my life in danger. Please don't tell anyone that I told you this. Call the woman, ok?"

"Yes, of course -----" the phone went dead.

He thought a lot of things have happened today, but this one took the cake. He started to call Jill, and then he remembered what Martha said. He closed the phone and walked out of the office. He waved at Dean Charles and walked to the van.

He started to drive home. As he came to the stop light, he noticed a pay phone next to a convenience store. He pulled in and parked right in front of the pay phone. He looked around to see if anyone was watching, then dropped the coins in the phone and dialed the number that Martha had given him.

The phone rang.

"Hello, my name is Dr. Brick; I was given this number to call."

A very excited voice of the young mother answered. "Dr. Brick, I'm so happy you called. Why did you change your mind about adopting my son?"

"Hold on, I thought you did not want us to adopt your son?"

"Yes, I still do. I can't take care of him. You are my only hope."

"May I call you back tomorrow, I know someone who can help."

"Thank you, Dr. Brick, I know you will be a good father to my son."

"Good, I will call you first thing the morning."

Jase jumped into the van. As he started to drive home again, he thought, "Jill will not believe this. One day no children, the next day we have two."

Across the street from the pay phone, a man sat in his car talking on his phone.

"Tell Michael that Dr. Brick made a phone call from the pay phone."

Chapter   8

He drove straight home and parked the van in front of the apartment. When he jumped out, the van continued to run. Jase stopped and turned around. Giving the van a dirty look was enough for the motor to stop.

As he opened the door, he could hear the baby and Jill.

"Jase, look at her, she is so beautiful," she said.

"Jill, I have something to tell you, and I don't know where to start."

Jill stopped, turned and looked at him. She raised one eye brow and said, "Go on."

"When we were at the agency, Martha Woods put a piece of paper in my pocket with her phone number on it, with instructions not to tell anyone about the note. She said her life would be in danger if anyone found out that she had given out her number."

"And did you call her?"

"Yes. Jill, she gave me the number of the woman that has the little baby boy. The one we were going to adopt."

Now he had Jill's full attention.

"She still wants us to adopt her son!"

Jill sat there staring at Jase.

"Jill, did you hear me? She wants us to have her son."

"Can we do it, Jase?"

"I think so, but we are going to need some help."

Jill smiled, "You mean Michael?"

"Yes, I hate to ask him, but if anyone can do it, he can."

Jill looked at the baby girl. "Would you like to have a baby brother? Jase, I almost forgot. How was the lab? Did they get anything?"

"Not really, just made a mess. I'll clean it up in the morning."

Jill raised her eye brow again. "You mean after you call Michael?"

"I will call him right now. I put his number on the cell." Jase picked up his phone and made the call.

"Michael, this is Jase. I wanted to call and thank you again and also ask another favor."

"Jase, if I can do it, I will, but how was the lab? Was there much damage?"

"No, the lab was just messed up a little. Whoever did it was probably looking for something they could sell very quickly."

"Well, I'm glad," answered Michael.

"Thanks, but that is not what I called about."

"What can I do for you?"

"Do you remember the little boy that we were going to adopt?"

"Sure, that was one of the worst days of my life."

"I just spoke to his mother, and there was some kind of mix-up. She still wants us to adopt her son. Can you help?"

"Well Jase, I didn't see that one coming. Are you sure you want two children?"

"Yes, Jill and I want him very much."

"That is a big order, but I will see if I can do anything."

"Thank you, Michael, I will call you in the morning." Jase hung up the phone and turned to Jill.

"Michael will make a few calls in the morning. If I don't hear from him by 10:00, I will call his cell."

"Jase, this is the best day of my life. Now come here and see your daughter. Do you like the name Eva?"

Chapter 9

Michael ended his phone call. He was stunned. "What the hell happened? He thought he had this under control. He sat there for a minute, then picked up his phone and calmly entered a number.

"This is Michael, get your team together. When Dr. Brick and his new fucking family leave their house I want it bugged. No more fuck-ups understand?"

Michael slammed the phone down on the seat only to pick it up again.

"Ann, this is Michael. We have a problem. No, let me rephrase that, you have a problem."

"Yes Michael," answered Ann.

"Dr Brick found out that the mother of the little black kid still wants him to be adopted."

"How did he find out?"

"How the fuck should I know, but Dr. Brick knows. Now he wants to adopt him too. The nanny is now going to be full time."

"You want Miss Peach day and night? They did not want her to start with."

"That's right, day and night. You let me worry about it.

I will call you in the morning."

Michael's mind was already churning up a new plan. He was awake most of the night, but by morning, his plan was in place.

Michael was up early. He went down to the lobby at the motel.

"Good morning, Mr. Greyger." The girl at the desk gave him an appreciative grin. "Thank you for the free dinner. I can't believe you did that for me." Then she looked both ways to make sure no one was looking and ran around the desk to give Michael a hug.

Michael smiled, "Now you and your husband can have dinner on me, ok?"

She smiled back, brushed herself off and walked back behind the desk. "Mr. Greyger, have a very nice day."

"And you too." With that Michael left.

As he walked to his car, Michael dialed Ann's number.

"Ann, would you like to have breakfast with me? Meet me down at the restaurant in about half an hour." Without saying goodbye, he hung up.

As he drove, he was on the phone to his boss. "Good morning, sir, this is Michael. I would like to move the Brick family back to Virginia."

"Do you think they will come?"

"Yes sir, I will make them an offer that they can't turn down."

"Do what you have to do."

"Yes, I will keep you up-to-date."

"Good, we need the weapon."

"I will take care of it, goodbye."

Michael pulled into the parking lot at the restaurant. Ann pulled in behind him. He got out of his car and walked to the door, then stopped and turned to see where Ann was.

As if Michael put on a mask, he greeted Ann with a smile. "Good morning, Ann, it is good that you could meet me on so little notice."

Ann looked at him with a smirk. "Why Mr. Greyger, I would not have missed it for my life."

Michael smiled, as if she was right, and opened the door for her.

When they were inside, Ann whispered to Michael. "You know you could have made it in Hollywood, you have a gift."

Michael gave her a sigh as if the remark was not worth a comeback.

"How many this morning for breakfast?" the waitress asked.

Michael answered, "Just the two of us, thank you. Can you give us a table where we can talk privately? Perhaps that corner would be suitable."

Ann could not believe how the woman was charmed by Michael. Then she remembered the first time she had met him. She said to herself, "I fell in love with Satan's son."

The waitress took them over to a table in the corner. "Your server will be right with you, coffee?" Michael and Ann both said yes.

"Michael, you are good. Now what are you up to?"

Ann could open just as many doors with her looks as Michael could with his charm. She was not quite as evil, but she had not done this as long as Michael.

"Dr. Brick is going to call me in a little while. He wants me to help him adopt the little black kid."

"Go on Michael." Ann was clearly shocked.

"So now we have two kids to slow us down. Take care of it, even if you have to use that Martha bitch."

"Michael, I have never seen you give in. What are the rules?"

"First, say that the agency will not let them adopt unless they have a full time nurse. Ms. Peach will do fine."

"She was supposed to retire soon. How long will this job last?"

"Don't worry about it."

"Well, that will be the first thing she will ask?"

Michael just kept talking. "Next, Dr. Brick will need a larger house, but on his income that will not happen."

"Michael, he will smell a rat if you offer him a job." Now Ann was concerned.

"I have the team ready to strike again. This time I want them to look professional. We might want to offer the Bricks a safer place to stay until the project is finished."

"Now that's the Michael I have come to know," laughed Ann.

The waitress came with the coffee and took their order. Michael was as charming as always.

"I think we will both have the special. He turned and looked at Ann, "Is that alright, Ann?"

"I was just going to ask for the special. My how on earth did you know? It is as if you read my mind."

Michael raised his hand so Ann would stop talking. "And this will be on me, I insist."

Ann gave him a phony smile and watched the waitress walked away. "Michael, is any one going to get hurt?"

Michael glared at Ann.

"You just answered my question. You know it does not have to be like that," pleaded Ann.

For the first time, and only for a minute, Michael let his guard down. His face went red with anger for a moment, then back to normal.

A chill went down Ann's back. She knew she had pushed a little too hard.

"Okay Michael, I will start the wheels in motion. You don't have to worry about my end."

Ann got up and walked out. She was almost to her car, when she could feel Michael staring at her. As she turned her eyes met Michael's. He was on the phone talking.

Ann was scared. Michael put his phone down, and Ann called his number to try and smooth things over. He looked at his phone and saw that it was Ann. He turned to the window and stared at her. The call went right to voice mail.

Ann drove to the adoption agency. When she walked in, Martha Woods was standing inside the door.

"Martha, could we go somewhere and talk?"

Martha was a little surprised to see Ann. "Come into my office." Ann followed Martha into her office.

"Now what is this about, Ann, or whatever your name is? Why do I have the honor of this visit?" Martha sat there waiting for a response.

Ann shut the door slowly behind her. "Martha, you do not have to like me, but if you value your life, you will do as I say."

"What do you want now, Ann?"

"Somehow Dr. Brick found out about the boy. The government thinks that he would be a great father. We will even have Nurse Peach be a full time nanny. Uncle Sam will take care of everything."

"Ann, what's going on? How are Jase and Jill involved in this?"

"Martha, make this adoption happen or you will be shut down. The less you say, the better off you will be. We have a file on you and your son. All I have to do is make a call and he is gone. Do you understand?"

Ann looked at Martha. They both knew what she had said was true.

"What do you want?" sighed Martha.

"Dr. Brick will call you sometime today. You need to inform him that a full time nurse will be required for the adoption to go through. And, I hope for your sake, it was not you who told him about the little boy."

"Who do you think you are? You have no right telling me what to do," fired back Martha.

"Martha, if you have not figured it out already, we are not nice people. Anyone who gets in our way is removed. Now shall we start?"

Ann got up and looked at Martha. "I hope that this has been an informative visit for you. If all goes right, we will not meet again." Ann smiled and walked out, thinking to herself, "I have become Michael."

Martha sat there looking down at her hands. She was holding a pen, and her hands were shaking so hard the pen dropped to her desk.

Chapter   10

"Jase, what time will you call Michael?"

"In a little while, before I go to the lab."

"Will you put the car seat in the van? Eva and I have some shopping to do while you are at work."

"It would be my pleasure to help out you two ladies. Where are you going on your first trip?"

"We just need a few things and, who knows, maybe we will visit some friends."

He had never seen Jill so happy. Jase grabbed the car seat and went out to the van, unaware of the black van parked across the street.

As he walked toward his van, his phone rang.

"Hello, this is Dr. Brick."

"Jase, this is Michael."

"Good morning Michael, do you have any news for us? Jill, Michael is on the phone."

"How is the new baby?" asked Michael.

"The baby is just fine. Or should I say, Eva is just fine."

"What a beautiful name, and I do have some news. Can I come over?"

"We will be right here, and the coffee is fresh. See you in a few minutes."

"Jill, Michael is on his way over, and he said he has some information for us."

"Is it good or bad information, Jase?"

"It must not be too bad. He sounded all right."

"Well, hold Eva and I will make that fresh coffee you told Michael I had."

Jase was holding Eva and looking out the window, when Michael pulled up.

"Look Eva, Michael is here." Jase walked over and opened the door.

"Welcome, come in, the coffee is ready."

"Hi Michael," a voice came from the kitchen.

"Hi Jill, how is the new mother?"

Jill came out of the kitchen. "Michael, how can we ever thank you?" She gave Michael a hug. "Now sit down, the coffee is on the way. I will be right back, and you can tell us what you found out."

"Jase, you were right. I called the agency this morning. There was some kind of misunderstanding, and the little boy needs a home."

Jill was becoming impatient. "Michael, can we still have him?"

"Yes and no," Michael answered slowly.

They sat there waiting anxiously for Michael to continue.

"We need to address two issues. Is your home big enough for another child, and can you afford him? And one more thing, with two children the agency requires you to have a full time nurse for a while."

"Michael, we can't afford all that. Not on what we make," Jill answered.

"That is what I thought. Would you consider taking your work to a government lab, say in Virginia? The government is very interested in your chelating compound for cancer."

"I don't know, Dean Charles has been very good to us," said Jase.

"Well, it was just a thought. Let me see what I can do?"

"Michael, it is as if Jill and I have known you forever. Thank you."

"Well, I should be leaving. I have a lot to do, and it looks like you two are both leaving also."

"I am going into the lab, and Jill and Eva are going on their first shopping trip."

Jill jumped up. "Michael, let me get you that coffee I promised. It's ready, and it only takes a minute."

"Oh, that reminds me." Michael pulled out an envelope from his pocket. "Jill, here is a little something for the baby. It is a gift certificate from the new baby store on the other side of town. I was supposed to give it to you yesterday, but I forgot. They have a big sale going on today."

Jill looked at the envelope. "Michael, that is one of the places I was going to go. Thank you." She gave him another hug.

LASER
By A.W.STRAWSBURG

Michael finished drinking his coffee. "Well got to go. As soon as I find something out, I will call." Michael shook hands with them and walked out.

"What a nice man," Jill said.

Jase nodded. "Yes he is."

Michael reached his car and got in. He looked into the rear view mirror. When he saw the van parked across the street, he picked up his phone and called the driver.

"They are all leaving in a short time. You have thirty minutes." He watched as the men nod their heads, and then Michael drove away smiling.

Chapter   11

"Jill, the car seat is in the van. Is there anything else you need?"

Jill was coming out the door with the baby, as the proud new father watched.

"No Jase, I think that is everything. I'll drive and let you out."

They both got into the van and turned to see if Eva was all right. After checking out the back seat cargo, Jill backed out of the lot. She drove very carefully to the lab and let Jase out.

Jase opened the back door and gave Eva a kiss then went to see Jill.

"You are so beautiful, I love you." He gave her a kiss, waved at Eva, then watched as they drove off.

Dean Charles was at the lab, and he had some of the maintenance men there.

"Jase, how is the family?"

"Great, Dean, just great."

"I have asked security to watch the lab more closely. We have never had anything happen like this before. The news people have been calling me all day."

"What have you been telling them?"

"That the lab was probably ransacked by some kids looking for drug money."

Jase shook his head, "I agree, whoever did this did not know what they were looking for. They might try some of the other offices next."

"You may be right. I'll have security keep a close watch."

Jase walked over to the files on the floor. As he started to pick them up, he noticed some of the data files were missing.

"Now that is odd, why would some of the files be missing?"

"Maybe they are in this mess on the floor," said Dean Charles.

He shook his head, "I don't think so, Dean," and he continued looking for the missing files.

The office secretary came into the lab. "Dean Charles, there is a Mr. Greyger on the phone for you."

"Wasn't he one of the men who were here for the demonstration at the lab?" Dean Charles was puzzled.

"Yes," Jase said. "Jill and I really like him, long story, which I will tell you later."

Dean Charles went to answer the phone call.

"Something does not add up here, but what is it? What am I missing?" Jase walked over to the desk. When he walked over to the laser, there was nothing out of place. "Why did they not even check out the laser equipment? Also there is a lot of money sitting around here." Jase kept working at cleaning up the mess. In a very short time, all was back in order.

The door opened and Dean Charles walked in. "Well, that was a different call. It seems that the government is very interested in your chelating compound project. They have offered the university a grant to expedite your progress, and it looks like you got a raise too. Mr. Greyger thought that you would be better off if you lived closer to your work. If it is all right with you, Jase, I will see if there is anything on the university property that will work for you and your family."

Jase was stunned.

"Jase, is that all right with you?" Dean Charles repeated.

"I don't know what to say."

"Say yes, Jase. Just say yes."

"Yes. I think that Jill would like that very much and that would be better than moving to Virginia," said Jase.

"What was that, Jase?" Dean Charles looked somewhat confused.

"Well, Mr. Greyger offered to move me to Virginia to a government lab."

Dean Charles' eye brows shot up. "What!"

Jase laughed, "Dean, I told him no."

Jase could see the surprised look leave Dean Charles' face. "We don't want to leave. Your offer is much better. Wait until I tell Jill."

Jase grinned, "I don't know if I can take any more good news today. I had better get back to work, before someone pulls the rug out from underneath me."

"Jase, I will keep you informed. One of the staff was thinking of taking some time off to do research down in the Keys. Maybe his place will be available. I will check on it."

As Dean Charles walked out, Jase started to check all the equipment. "Why is everything out of place except the laser? Am I reading too much into this? Surely whoever broke in saw that there was another room with more equipment in it." By this time, it was getting late. He had spent the entire day looking for something that was not there.

Jase walked out into the hall as Jill drove up. He could see her smile even before she stopped. He walked out of the door and over to the van.

"Jill, all I have to do is lock up, and I will be right back," he said.

He walked back to the lab, looked around again and locked up. "What is going on? What am I missing?" he wondered.

Michael's phone rang. "It is done, new record, 19 minutes. We bugged every room."

"You perverts didn't use video did you?"

The men in the van looked at each other and then smiled.

"No Michael, what do you take us for?"

"Good, now let me know if you hear anything, and I don't care what time it is."

"Yes sir."

Chapter 12

Jill was waiting in the van. Jase hopped into the front passenger seat.

"Jill, something is not right here, and I cannot figure out what it is. Everything in the main room was torn apart, but very little was touched in the laser room, and nothing was missing. And another thing, Martha Woods said not to tell anyone she had talked to us, or her life would be in danger. What if someone asked how we found out about the boy? What will we say?"

"Say nothing, Jase."

"Martha also said that our phones are tapped. What if our apartment is also?"

"Now Jase, I think that you are putting more into this than you should."

"Just in case, I think that I will make a little stop on the way home."

Jill drove to the other side of the campus, and they stopped at another lab. "I will only be a minute. Keep the motor running."

The lab door was still unlocked. "Good, someone might still be here," he thought.

Jase walked in just as a man in his late fifties was coming out. He looked like he has not trimmed his beard in a long time.

"Jase, what are you doing here. Don't you have enough to do?" He laughed.

"Professor, do you have a minute?"

"Sure Jase, come in. You look worried. What can I do for you?"

"Do you have anything that will tell me if my lab has been bugged?"

"You are serious, aren't you?" Jase nodded his head yes.

"Stop by tomorrow, and I will have something ready for you."

"Professor, keep this between us."

"Sure Jase, don't worry. Just like Watergate."

Jase shook his head. "You will never change."

The Professor locked the door to the lab, and they walked to the Professor's car.

Jase smiled and asked, "Professor, just how much have you spent on cars in your life time?"

The Professor looked offended. "This one cost me over $600, and I have three more at home just like it for parts. Look at my new radio."

Jase looked at the dash, "There is a hole in the dash with the wires coming out."

"Jase, look in the back seat." A boom box sat in the back seat with a $3 sales tag on it.

"I got it at of a yard sale. Nice right?" The Professor looked over at Jase's van, and Jill waved at him. When they walked over to the van, Jase opened the back door.

"Hi Jill, I just came out to see the new girl. Oh my, she is just about the prettiest thing I have ever seen. Now what is your name little girl?"

Jill spoke up, "Her name is Eva."

"Well, I'm happy to meet you Eva. I look forward to seeing you again. Jase, I will talk to you tomorrow."

Eva took one look at the Professor and started to cry.

"Well, sometimes I affect girls that way. He grinned showing a few missing teeth."

Jase shut the door, and thanked the Professor. As he drove away, a car in the lot across the road was watching.

"Michael, he just stopped to show off the baby to one of the staff. I think that they are on the way home now. We will follow them, but not to close."

"Jill, please don't say anything about the apartment being bugged, at least not until I get it checked."

"Jase," Jill was laughing.

"Just humor me, please?"

"Ok Jase, but I will not let you live this down."

They went home, and the rest of the night they were careful not to say or do anything that might relate to the lab.

Jill put Eva to sleep and walked out to the living room. "I am going to take a bath. Will you listen for the baby?"

Jase smiled and nodded his head. "Don't worry, she is in good hands."

The apartment was small with only one bath, so Jill could hear if the baby was awake. She drew the bath water and walked back into the bedroom to undress and get her robe. She came back and tested the water, closed the door and lit some candles. She took off her robe slipped into the tub and sank into a wave of bubbles. With a happy sigh, she closed her eyes and smiled.

Across the street in a parked van, two men sat very carefully watching their video screen.

"She is a fox, no wonder Michael didn't want us to use video."

The next day, Jase was up and out of the house early. When he arrived at the lab, there was a government car sitting in the lot. He walked in to see Michael and Dean Charles sitting at a desk.

"Jase, great you're here. Michael and I have some news for you. There is a three bedroom house on campus that is in need of repair, but we just did not have the funds to fix at this time. Mr. Greyger has offered to remodel the house using his own people. There is no charge to the school, as long as your research progresses. I have already taken Mr. Greyger over to the house and showed him around. What do you think, Jase?"

Jase stood there for a moment. "Dean, how long do you think that will take?"

Michael spoke up. "Jase, I hope that I have not overstepped my bounds. I can have my people in there today, and have you in by the end of the week."

Dean Charles spoke up. "And Jase, he has offered to fund your project. We are back in business. I have no doubt you will be one of the most famous people in the world for cancer research. And your research has helped this University beyond anything that I could have ever dreamed. Thank you, Michael and Dr. Brick. Speak up man, what do you say?"

"What can I say? I say yes. Michael, how can I ever thank you."

"Dr. Brick, you just keep that research going, and together, we will find a cure. Now, if you gentleman will excuse me, I have a house to take care of." Michael shook hands with them and went out the door.

"How could we ever have been so lucky? I have never met a nicer man. The first thing I want you to do is make a list of everything that you need. Bring it to my office, and I will take care of it myself." Dean Charles jumped up to leave.

"Dean, I don't think that I have ever seen you this excited before."

"Jase, just keep up the good work."

Suddenly, Jase could hear a dog bark.

"Well it sounds like Rex will have a new home. I had better go and feed him."

Jase heard the steel drums of his phone, he picked up his cell. It was Jill.

"Jase, I just spoke to Michael, and we got a house. Not just any house, a three bedroom house. And as soon as we have the house, we will have a son. The adoption was approved. Jase, did you hear me? We will have a son!"

Jase grinned, "I heard you. I think most of the people on campus heard you. Jill, I love you. As soon as I can wrap up, I will be home."

He spent the rest of the day making a list of improvements and materials that the lab needed. He was about to take the list to the Dean's office, when someone opened the door.

"Jase, I've got something for you." It was the Professor, and he was holding a small case.

"It took me most of the day, and I had to make a few calls, but I think that this will do the job. Now let me show you how to use it."

The Professor opened the lid. "All you have to do is turn it on like this."

Jase watched him.

With a surprised look, the Professor closed the box. "Well this doesn't help much, back to the drawing board. Jase, let me do some more work on this answering machine. I will just have to bring it back."

He looked at Jase. "Let me show you a book of some more machines in the car, and I don't have to put them together."

Jase started to say something, but the Professor put his finger to his lips and grabbed him by the arm. In a happy but stern voice the Professor said, "Oh come on, you have time. Besides, I want to show you the pictures we took at the football game."

Jase knew something was up. They had never been to a game at the same time this year. The Professor wanted him to get out of the lab.

They walked out of the building to the Professor's car and got in. "Close the door Jase. Sorry about that. This thing went off the chart. Your lab is bugged."

"So that is why nothing is missing." Jase shook his head. "They just wanted to bug the place."

"Jase, keep smiling like there nothing is wrong. Now listen, take this home with you. Open the lid and push this switch to turn it on. This arrow will point in the direction of the bug. When I turned it on in your lab, the arrow went nuts. Your entire lab is bugged. I don't know what is going on, but someone has gone to a lot of trouble for some reason. You know you might have industrial spies. Stranger things have happened. Let me know how it turns out."

Jase closed up the lab and thought, "The secretary should be back tomorrow. Should I tell her anything? I think someone wants the chelating compound. This is bigger than I had expected. First thing I should do is to go home and check it out."

Not far away in a car, a man sat watching the lab. He picked up his cell phone and made a call.

"Michael, I'm in the lot overlooking Dr. Bricks lab. The man that Dr. Brick talked too yesterday just left. Would you like someone to talk to him?"

Chapter   13

Michael was at the new house with a small army of his people. Everything was going on schedule when his phone rang.

"This is Michael, can I help you?"

"Michael, we found out that the man Dr. Brick was talking to is Professor Williams. Are you sure you don't want us to talk to him?"

"No, let the Professor go for now, but we might talk to him later." Michael ended the call as one of the university students walked up to him.

Michael smiled, "Well, thank you for calling. I look forward to talking to you in the future."

He looked over at the young man. "Hello, do you go to school here?"

"Yes sir, my first year. Do you need any help? I could use the work?"

Michael responded, "Well, you just never know." He put his hand out and shook the young man's hand. "If you give me your name and number, I can call you if I need you."

"Yes sir." He took out a pen and paper from his back pack and gave Michael all his information.

Michael said, "If things keep going as slow as they are now, I will be calling you next week."

The young man thanked Michael and walked off. Michael folded the paper very carefully and walked over to a trash can and threw it in.

Jase was about home. As he turned into the drive that led up to his apartment, he noticed a van across the street. He thought that he had seen it there before. Jase wondered about the van for a minute, but all he could think about now was Jill and Eva. He could not wait to see them. Jill opened the door even before he reached it.

"Well hello, Dr. Brick. Did you come home to see your family?" Jill grinned.

He was happy to be home. He set the box that the Professor had given him on the table. Eva was sleeping, and Jase went quietly over to see her.

"How was your day?" asked Jill.

"Glad you asked. It was great, and I have a little surprise for you."

Jill sensed something was wrong by the look on her husband's face. She watched Jase walk over to the box. He opened it and turned it on. The needle went crazy.

"Well, that's not good," he said as he closed the box.

"Jase, what is going on?"

"Jill, may I use your cell phone, my battery is low?"

"Yes, it is here somewhere."

"Could you please go get it?"

After a couple of minutes, Jill came back from the bedroom with her phone. "I don't know if it will work, I haven't charged it today."

Jase took the phone and went outside the back door. He called the Professor's number. "There is only one way to find out." He said to himself.

"Professor, when I turned on the box, it went off the chart. There is a van across the street, and it has been there for at least two days. Would you come over?"

"Can you read the plates on the van?"

"No."

"Say no more Brick, I am on the way."

"Good, I will be watching for you." Jase went back in the apartment.

"Jase, you didn't answer me, what is going on?"

"Oh nothing," he smiled at Jill and whispered in her ear. "The house and the office are bugged. Do not say anything, just act as if nothing is wrong. The Professor is coming over to check the van in the parking lot across the street."

Jill's eyes shot open. She went over to the baby and started to dress her in case they suddenly had to leave.

It was not long before the Professor came down the road. His shaggy exterior did not reflect the lethal ex-Marine underneath it.

Jill and Jase sat looking out the window. Jase whispered to Jill, "When the Professor gets here, if there is any sign of trouble call 911."

Jill nodded, and her hands were shaking. She had her cell phone in her hand.

The Professor drove by the van. He turned into the far end of the lot, and then slowly came up behind the van and stopped. He flashed the lights. At first he thought that the van was empty.

Suddenly the backup lights on the van came on. The Professor said, "Oh shit," and tried to get out of the way. The van rammed the 86

Chevy before he could move it. Parts flew everywhere. Some of them were only held on with duct tape. The passenger door was gone. The Professor jumped out.

As Jill called 911, Jase was on his way out the door. The van tried to ram the car again. This time, the impact put the car on its side as the Professor jumped out of the way.

Jase was about to cross the street, when the van went forward and jumped the curb. It hit two parked cars and took off up the street.

By this time people, were coming from everywhere. The Professor walked over to Jase.

"That's the last time I come to one of your parties. Look at this Jase, where will I find another 86 Chevy in that condition? This is going to cost you Jase, that $600 car had a new radio."

As they were talking, they could hear the police sirens coming closer. When the police arrived, Jase was surprised to see Michael behind them. He jumped out of the car. "Jase, are you all right? I have scanner in the car."

A policeman came over to Michael. "Sir, you are going to have to move your car."

Jill came running over, and she had Eva in her arms. They were both crying. "Jase, are you all right?"

Before Jase could answer, the Professor said, "I'm alright, Jill, but my $600 car is shot and my new radio is toast."

Jill tried to laugh. "Jase, what is going on?"

Michael was talking to the police. He showed him some kind of ID. The officer got on his radio as Michael started walking toward Jase.

The Professor saw Michael coming. "Jase, I have a bad feeling about that guy."

"No, he is all right. He is one of the good guys," Jase said.

"If you say so," said the Professor.

"Jase, what the hell happened?"

"Michael, it is a long story. This is my friend, Bill Williams. We just call him Professor."

Michael shook the Professor's hand. "Is that your car?"

"It was my brand new $600 car. If Jase invites you to a party, don't go."

The Professor looked at Jill. "Let's go over to your apartment, I want to check something out. Come on Michael, you might like this."

The three of them started to walk back to the apartment as the policeman yelled, "What do you want us to do with this car?"

The Professor looked at the officer, "Your guess is as good as mine."

Back at the apartment, the Professor picked up the box as he started into the living room. "Jase, you have two cameras and a mic." He pointed at the light in the ceiling. "This is some high tech shit. Do you have any needle nose pliers? I left mine in the car."

Jill said, "I think so." She went into the kitchen and returned with a pair of pliers.

"I didn't know we had those, Jill." Jase gave her a surprised look.

"Who do you think fixes things around here?" Jill replied.

The Professor took the tool, grabbed a chair and pulled something off the light. "Here is another mic, and it's a good one." he said. Next he went to the crown trim at the ceiling. "Camera, this is also real good one." He walked into the kitchen and discovered another mic. He continued on into the bedrooms. Jill grabbed Jase's arm.

He called from the master bedroom, "Mic and camera." Next he went in to Eva's room. "Mic," he called out. As he went into the bath, you could hear a pin drop. "Mic and a camera." Michael could hardly hide his anger.

"Jase, I don't know what they were looking for, but this is some very high tech equipment. This was not some run of the mill job. Tomorrow, I will go down and check the lab. Jill, your apartment is clean. No one is watching you now."

"Brick, this is the worst party I have ever been to. I can't wait for the next one. Michael, how would you like to give this old man a ride home?"

Michael didn't want to leave, but nodded his head yes. "I would be glad to, Professor," he said.

"Jase, the sooner we get you into the other house, the better," the Professor said.

"And I will be glad to check it out for you every week, but it will cost you. You know how many margaritas this is going to be? How about you, Michael, want to stop for a drink?"

"Not this time, Professor, give me a rain check."

"Ok, see you Brick." The Professor followed Michael out the door, quickly giving Jase a knowing smirk.

The baby was awake now, and Jill was feeding her.

"Jase, I have never been so scared in my life. Why would someone bug our home? What are we going to do?"

Jase shook his head and answered, "Jill, I don't know."

Michael and the Professor walked toward his car as the tow truck was flipping it over.

"Professor, may I call you by your first name?" Michael was trying to find out more about the Professor.

"If you had a name like William Williams, would you like it? Just keep it Professor. Besides no one would know who you were talking about if you used anything other than Professor."

Michael forced a laugh as they walked to his car. "What are you a Professor of?"

"Electronics and stuff, until my other job kicks in."

"What would that be?"

"Sailing to some place that is warm all year around."

They were in the car now. "Where would you like to go, Professor?"

"Why don't you drop off me at the VFW? It is right on your way. Would you like to come in and have one for the road?"

Michael looked at the Professor, "Maybe I will."

"Well hell, Michael, that would be fine," laughed the Professor. It's just ahead on the right, and the drinks are on me."

They entered the small brick building and started to go toward the bar.

"Professor, let's take the table by the wall. I don't want anyone to see me. You understand."

"Well hell, you are no fun." They walked over to the table and sat down. The Professor ordered drinks, by raising his hand and holding two fingers up.

"The drinks are cheap and the service is good here. This is my kind of place." The Professor lost his smile long enough to ask. "So Michael, are you government, political or military?"

"What do you think?"

"You don't act like a politician, so it has to be government or military. If you were working for the government, you probably would not have so much clout. You seem to be able to pick up the phone and get whatever you want. If you are military, you would have to be on a mission."

The bartender brought over two drinks. "Here you go Professor. Are you running a tab?"

"Hell yes, you don't expect me to keep track do you?"

The bartender smiled and said, "You never change," and then he went back to the bar.

The Professor looked at Michael and grinned. "So what is your mission? Those bugs in Brick's apartment were military. They must be pretty new stuff too, because I've never seen them before. I try to keep up on that shit."

Michael was not used to anyone trying to get information from him. "Professor, we are very interested in anything that will stop cancer, and that is the only reason that I am here. And I am not military. I work for a research facility in Virginia, but I cannot disclose anything else. The agency I work for is very discrete."

"How do you like your drink Michael, its gin and Squirt? If they can't mix a good Margareta, it works for me."

"The drink is fine, Professor. Now let me ask you something. What do you think is going on? Do you have a theory?"

"I have two or three, and you are involved in one of them. Why are you so interested in a chelation compound for curing cancer?"

At this point, Michael finished his drink not answering the Professor's question. "Professor, here is my card. If you can figure out what is going on, call me."

Michael got up and started to leave. "Professor, would you do me a favor?"

"Probably," he replied.

"The Bricks will be moving into a house on campus. Would you check it out for bugs before they move in?"

"Hell yes, just let someone try and stop me."

Michael put out his hand. "I find you to be a very interesting person. What branch of service were you in and what did you do?"

"Marines, and the agency that I was in, is also very discrete."

As Michael walked out, the Professor went up to the bar and sat down.

"How is your night, Professor?" asked the bartender.

"Well hell, I just wrecked my new $600 car," and he started to tell his story again.

Chapter 14

Michael walked out of the VFW, and even before he was to his car, he was on the phone.

"Ann, this is Michael. I need the Brick's house to go into overtime.

Tell the contractor no bugs. And Ann, don't let yourself be seen on the job site."

"No bugs, Michael?" Ann was surprised

"That's right. Dr. Brick's friend found every one of the bugs at his place, including the video cameras, and it only took him 8 minutes. Take care of this. I have some business with our stake-out people."

"Video, I thought you said no video?"

"That's right, video. And yes, I did tell those to two perverts not to use it."

Michael hung up, took in a deep breath and then called the stake out van. "Are you in a safe place?"

One of the men in the van answered. "Yes Michael."

"Good, now for the next question. Why do you think that cameras were installed in the Brick's apartment? I know that you two would not challenge my orders, would you?"

The two men in the van went silent. This time Michael used a threatening voice. "I'm going to ask you two perverts a question, and you had better answer as if your life depends on it."

The two men knew they were in trouble. One tried to give the phone to the other, but he would not take it. Then, with sweat running down his face, he answered.

"We had already installed the video cameras before you called, and there was not enough time to go back and remove them. I am sorry we did not tell you, but we did not use the video." The men looked at each other in shock.

It was hard for Michael to control his anger. "Now you two perverts get that van out of sight. Make arrangements for a truck to pick up the van and get it out of here. Be sure no one sees you two getting rid of it, then go back to Virginia. I will deal with you there when I get back".

"Yes Sir, consider it done. Is there anything else we can do for you?"

Michael did not respond. When he was truly upset, he wasn't in control of himself. He would be up all night trying to straighten this out.

The Bricks were also up all night. They were scared and unsure of their next step.

"Jase, what are they after? It does not make sense. Are we safe?"

"I don't know, Jill. We can't get out of this place fast enough for me. I think that you and Eva should go to work with me today."

Jill nodded her head yes and started to get ready. In the bedroom and bathroom, she could not help staring at the holes in the wall and ceiling where the cameras had been. "How did they get in, and when did they do it?" Jill thought. She got into the shower before she took off her robe, then she turned the water on. When she was done, she carefully reached out to grab a towel to dry, then put on her robe before she stepped out. When she was back in the bedroom, she left the robe on as long as she could only to drop it at the last possible second before dressing. "That was the quickest I ever got dressed," she thought as she walked out of the room.

Jase was sitting in deep thought. "I think that I will give Michael a call, what do you think?" he asked Jill.

"That might be a good idea. I think that we could use some help."

Jase pushed the speed dial on his phone. "Michael, this is Jase."

"Jase, I was up all night trying to make some sense of this mess."

"We were too. Would you like to come into the lab this morning? We are scared, and we think we could use some help."

"Under the circumstances, I think it would be a good idea. I will be there as soon as I get something to eat"

"Michael, Jill and I can never thank you enough."

Michael hung up, looked forward and smiled. He went down to the lobby. When he arrived, the girl at the desk smiled.

"Good morning, Mr. Greyger. How was your night?"

"It was a long one, but now the day is starting to look better. How was your night?"

"Well, my husband and I really enjoyed our dinners, and everyone treated us so nice. How can I ever thank you?"

"You already have. It is nice to see your smile, when I come down to the lobby each morning."

"Mr. Greyger, have a nice day."

LASER
By A.W.STRAWSBURG

Michael walked out of the motel. He had his game face back on. He went to his car, looked around and got in. This had the making of a very good day. He drove to the restaurant.

By this time, Jase and Jill were also ready to leave. They stopped at a fast food restaurant and purchased two meals to go. The Professor was waiting for them when they arrived at the lab. "Look Jase, we have company," said Jill.

Jase helped get Eva's things, and the three of them went inside with the Professor.

"Brick, I will make this quick. I want to be out of here if Michael arrives."

"Why is that?" Jase looked surprised.

"I don't know yet, but I'm working on it. See how fast you can get moved into the new house. Don't tell Michael anything about the lab, including anything that has to do with me. And another thing, I took all the bugs out of the lab. It was bugged everywhere, and they used the same kind of equipment that was in your place. I think that it is better if I stay your silent partner for now. I'm on my way to your new house, and I'm leaving by the back door of the lab."

Jill stared at Jase. Her eyes said it all. He could see she was frightened. Jase came over and took her hands in his. "Jill, as soon as we finish this project, all of us are going on a vacation. You think of a place that you would like to go, and I hope that it is someplace warm."

Jill looked at Eva. "Would you like to play in the sand under a palm tree?" The baby smiled, as if she knew what her new mother had said.

Chapter   15

Michael was about finished eating. He looked at his watch and thought he had let the Bricks worry long enough.

"How was your meal, Mr. Greyger?" asked the waitress as the she handed him the check.

He handed her the bill back with his credit card. She tried not to look at the check, but Michael had given her such a nice tip, it was hard not to. "Thank you, Mr. Greyger! Please have a nice day, and come back again."

In a few minutes, Michael was going up the hill to the lab. He parked next to the handicap space. "That is a waste of time," he thought. "Most of the people with handicap signs in their cars don't need them."

When he walked into the lab, Jase was working at his desk. He lifted his head. "Good to see you, Michael." A voice from the other room said. "Hi Michael"

"Hi Jill," Michael said in a soft voice. "Boy, what a night, I did not get any sleep. How about you guys?" By now Jill had walked in.

"Michael, the only one who got any sleep was this little one." Eva was resting in her arms.

"Jill, have you put that little girl down yet?" Michael smiled. The ice was broken. Michael had only been there a few minutes, and everyone was more relaxed.

"How is the house coming, Michael?" asked Jase.

"The house is almost done. I will feel much better when you are in it."

"We will too, Michael," said Jill.

"In the meantime, why don't we ask the Dean if he could have campus security watch your apartment for you?" Michael knew what the answer was even before he asked.

Jase answered, "They cannot go off campus."

"Well, how about the local police?" Michael came back.

"We can ask, but don't hold your breath. This small town prides itself on having no crime. If the newspaper found out, there would be some unhappy people on the campus board."

Michael paused, "I could call my people, if you want me to."

Jill was about to answer, when the steel drums on Jase's phone went off. Jase answered, "Hi Professor, what is going on?"

"Hell Brick, your house will not be ready for a couple of days. As much as I don't want company, you guys will just have to stay with me. I already have some of the students cleaning up my house. I will talk to you this afternoon. I'm sure Michael is there. Tell him I said hello," and then he hung up.

Jase looked puzzled. "That was the Professor. He said he was at the house, and it was going to be a couple of days before it was going to be ready. He wants us to stay with him until then."

Jill looked surprised. "Jase, have you ever been in the Professor's house? Does it look as bad on the inside as it does on the outside?"

Jase stopped her. "I'm sure it will fine, and yes, I have been in his home."

"What do you think, Michael?" asked Jill.

"Where is his house?"

"Just off campus, that way no one can tell him how to take care of his house."

Michael was at a loss for words. When he recovered, he said, "That might be your only option for now. One more thing, Jase," said Michael. "We don't want anyone to know about this. If the adoption agency would get wind of this, they might not like it."

Jill watched Michael as he spoke. "Well Michael, I guess they will not find out then, will they?"

Michael smiled at Jill. "If you would like, I can have a crew pack all your things and take them over to the Professor's house." He was hoping to get a good look at their possessions. "That way, you will not have to go back to your apartment."

"No Michael, Jill and I will pack. But it would be nice if your people were there to help with the move."

Michael answered, "Consider it done."

Chapter 16

"Jill, would you mind being in charge of the move? I have so much to do here, and I will be just a call a way."

"If it means that I never have to go back to that apartment and stay another night, yes."

Michael made a call to his people. "The Bricks are moving, and they need some help. Have some of the crew get a van and packing material. Meet me at their place." Michael looked up to see Jase and Jill staring at him.

Quickly, Michael said, "When you are ready, call me and I will give you the address and the time to be there. Thanks again for all your help." On the other end of the conversation a man said, "Michael must be with someone, he was not his usual asshole self."

"Jill, can I give you and the baby a lift?"

"Thanks Michael, I'll be ready in just a moment."

In the other room, a dog was barking. Jill looked at Jase. "Do you think Rex could come with us when we get in the new house?"

"Of course, he is part of the Brick family."

Michael said, "Jill, I will be out in the car. Whenever you are ready, come out."

"Ok Michael, I will be there in just a minute." Michael walked out.

"Jase, did you hear Michael when he was on the phone?"

"Don't read too much into it. Remember, Michael is the one who is helping with the other adoption. Let's just concentrate on getting into the new house."

"I guess you are right. But there has been so much happen the last few days, I'm a little paranoid."

Jase walked over and gave her and Ava a kiss. "Now go get packed. I will see you after I finish here."

Jill packed the baby up and waved as she left.

Michael was waiting. He jumped out to help her put the baby in the back seat.

"Michael, how can we ever thank you?"

Michael smiled and opened the door for Jill. "Jill, you and your husband could help me by getting your project in full operation. That is the only thanks I need," he said as they drove away.

As soon as Jill and Michael had gone, Jase called the Professor. "Professor, where are you?"

"I'm over at my house. Are you coming over? You can buy lunch."

"Be there in a little while. There are a couple of things that I want to finish."

Jase went over to his files and checked them one more time. He went into the laser lab and everything looked right, but he couldn't stop feeling that he was missing something.

The cleanup crew was about done. "Lock up when you are finished. I am going to lunch." Jase shouted as he left.

Jase drove up to the Professor's house. It was an older two story in need of paint. There were some students working on the porch cleaning up the trash.

As Jase walked onto the porch, the Professor was coming out the front door. Jase grinned, "I have never seen your porch this clean before. It is usually full of aluminum cans."

"Hell Brick, you cost me this time. The price of aluminum is not very high, but because it's you, I had the kids take them to the scrap yard and get whatever they could. Are you hungry? Let's go to the VFW. They serve a mean ham and cheese. Why don't you drive, my car is a little run down."

As they got into the van, the Professor said, "Jase, I haven't got this mess figured out yet. I don't like Greyger, and I think he is up to something. For right, now let's not tell him anything. Here, I got you something." The Professor reached into his pocket and pulled out a cell phone. "Now the only time you use it is to call me, OK?" Jase took the phone.

"Your cell phone is tapped, but don't let on that you know it. Also, tell Jill not to say anything either."

Jase and the Professor went straight to the bar when they went into the club.

"What will you have, Professor, do you need a menu?" asked the bartender as he handed the Professor a gin and squirt.

"You see Brick, this is why I come here, the service. Bartender, put this on Bricks tab. He is the one who cost me my $600 car." As soon as he heard this, the bartender put his hands in the air and started to walk away. "I've heard this one before," he said.

"Hell, come back here, we are hungry."

After they ordered lunch, Jase asked, "Why do you feel that way about Michael, Professor?"

The Professor turned, and in a soft but serious voice, answered. "Brick, you and your wife are in over your heads. I have not figured out why yet, but I will. For now, you and Jill stay with me until the house is ready. After that, we will play it by ear, OK Brick?" Jase nodded.

The food came and they ate in silence. The bartender came up and asked, "Is there anything else I can do for you guys?"

"No thank you," Jase answered.

"Who was your friend the other night, Professor?" asked the bartender. The Professor looked up over his glasses. In a slow calm voice, he answered, "That is what we want to know."

Jase paid for the meal. When they got up to leave, he said, "Professor, I don't have the same feeling about Michael that you do, but I respect what you are saying."

"Good, thank you."

When they were in the van, the Professor started to look around. He held up his finger so Jase would know not to speak. He checked out the van, front to rear.

"Do you have your detector with you?" Jase asked.

"I'm not checking for bugs, even though I should. How much do you want for the van? My insurance company is going to give me twice what I had in my car. Are you interested?"

Jase started to laugh. "You drove that car for a long time, and you only had $600 in it. Now you are making money on it? Only you could do it."

The Professor was still looking at Jase. Then he said, "Well, what you think, are you interested?"

Still laughing, Jase said, "I will keep it in mind. Where are you going, Professor?"

"With you, we better go help Jill pack."

When they arrived, there was a moving van sitting in the drive, and people were loading furniture. "Come on Professor, let's see what we can do to help."

Once inside, they found that Jill was trying to watch the baby and pack. "Jase, thank goodness you are here. Watch Eva while I pack." She started to walk away, then stopped and turned. "Hi Professor, glad you could make it."

"Jill, what can I do while Jase takes care of the little one?"

"Come this way Professor and I will show you."

Jase watched over Eva. "All seems good in the world at this minute, but better not push it," he thought.

It was an easy move, since there was not much to pack. They did not have anything new except for the baby furniture.

Jill came over to Jase smiling. "Jase, by the end of the week we will be in our new house. Do you know what that means? Eva will have a brother, and we can thank Michael for that." With everything that was going on, Jase hadn't thought about the adoption.

The Professor overheard what Jill said and growled.

With everyone's help, it did not take long to pack, and soon they were on their way to the Professor's home.

The Professor sat with Eva in the back of the van. "Now Eva, tell your Dad and Mom that they should sell their van to me. And another thing, you can call me Uncle Bill." When Jill and Jase heard this, they turned to look at each other and grinned.

When they pulled up to the Professor's home, Jill looked amazed. "Are we at the right house?" She turned around to look at the Professor.

"Well hell, Jill, I don't clean up this place for just anyone." Then he looked at Eva. "You don't think Uncle Bill would let you stay in a dirty house, do you?"

Jase parked in front of the house and the moving van pulled up behind.

The Bricks got out and stared at the house. "Professor, how did you -- I mean the last time I saw your house, you had to turn sideways just to walk through the door."

"Jill, I want Eva to have a good first impression."

They took Eva out of her car seat and went in. The old Victorian still had its charm. It had wide wood trim and high ceilings with dark crown molding.

"Professor, the house looks great! I had no idea that it was in such good condition. I bet you neighbors are happy," said Jase.

"Yeah Brick, some of them even waved at me this afternoon. Sent a chill right down my spine."

Jill asked, "What did you do with all your stuff?"

"All I can say is don't go into the last bedroom, you may never come out. We would have to send in a search party. And Brick, do you know how long it will take me to put everything back? It will take me weeks to get everything back to normal."

The movers came in with some of the Brick's belongings.

The Professor said, "Jill, go up the steps. The first room on the right is yours."

Jill waved to the men, "Gentlemen, this way please." They followed her up the steps. "Just put all the boxes in here. Professor," Jill yelled, "Do you think that we should put the big things over at the new house?"

"That would be a good idea," he answered.

Jase was holding Eva. With all the things going on, he did not want to let her out of his sight.

Jill came down the steps. "Professor, are you sure this is the right house?"

"Hell, Jill, the next time you go up the steps look in the last room, but don't go in. It is far too dangerous. Make sure you close the door. I don't want anything to get out."

"Professor, I think I will wait until Jase is with me."

"Smart girl," he said.

Jase shook his head. "You two will be at it all night. I can see it already."

One of the movers came in and went up to Jill. "All of the boxes are in. Where do you want the furniture?"

The Professor spoke up. "Do you know where the house is on campus that Dr. Brick is going to move into?"

"Yes sir, we do." He answered.

The Professor raised an eyebrow. "Would you mind taking the rest over there and putting it in the living room? We will sort it out later."

"Yes sir," and he left.

The Professor watched as the moving van left. "Now how do you suppose they knew where to go?"

Jase answered. "You are getting too paranoid."

The Professor walked over to Jase. "You are going to spoil that little girl. Let Uncle Bill hold her while you two get unpacked."

Jill put her arm into Jase's arm and squeezed. They both looked amazed.

"Now go on, I can only hold her until she starts to cry or something worse. If that happens, I will call you. At that time, it would be in your best interest to be quick. Now Eva, let Uncle Bill tell you a story about my life at sea." Jase and Jill left them and went up the steps.

"Jase, let's peek in the last room, how bad can it be?" They walked down the hall and stopped at the door. They opened the door slowly, as if something on the other side would grab them.

The room was dark. Jase reached his hand over to find the light switch. When the light came on, the room transformed itself from a bedroom to what looked like the back stage of an old theater. It was filled to the ceiling. There was just enough room for the door to open. The Professor never threw anything out, and the room was proof.

"Whatever you do Jase, don't touch anything. If one thing falls, we will never get the door closed." Jase held the door open for Jill and then slowly closed it behind her. "Wow, I don't think that I have ever seen so much stuff in one room. Come on Jase, let's unpack before Uncle Bill has his hands full."

"Hey Brick, you daughter is leaking," came the voice from downstairs.

Jill walked down the steps. The Professor was setting with Eva. She had thrown up on him, but he was enjoying every minute of the small disaster.

"Would you like some help, Professor?" Jill asked.

"I would, sometimes I have this affect on girls." Jill took the baby and handed a towel to the Professor.

After they had settled in at the Professor's house, Jill said, "We have some food that should be used up. Tonight is my treat."

"This just gets better and better," said the Professor.

Jill was out in the kitchen, and Jase and the Professor were in the living room talking.

"Jase, you haven't said anything about my involvement in your project, have you?"

"No," Jase answered.

"Good, for now, let's keep it that way." Jase nodded yes.

Chapter 17

Michael pulled up to the house on campus, rolled down his window and motioned for one of the men to come over to his car. "Get in," he said.

The man promptly opened the door and got in. "Everything is going very smoothly and the house will be ready tomorrow. Michael, why are we not bugging the house?"

Michael turned to look at him. "The bugs in the last place were detected, and I don't want it to happen again. I will call the Bricks and tell them they can move in tomorrow. If anything goes wrong, call me, and call me when you are finished." The man nodded and got out.

Michael called Ann. "This is Michael. I want the other adoption to go forward ASAP. Have Miss Woods call the Bricks."

"Why her?" asked Ann.

"They trust her."

"Michael, how soon do you want this to happen?"

"Now, and make sure Nurse Peach is ready."

"You know Peach is ready to retire? This job might last for a while."

"You tell Nurse Peach--" Michael stopped himself. "Ann, would you have Nurse Peach give me a call? I would appreciate it."

"Yes Michael, I will give the message to her. Will there be anything else?"

"Not right now." As he drove off, his phone rang.

"Hello, this is Michael."

"This is Linda Peach."

"Linda, how would you like to have lunch with me?"

"That would be fine."

Michael told Linda about the diner near his motel. "I will see you there in a little while."
She felt a chill go down her back. "I'm getting to old for the crap," she thought.

Before long, Linda arrived at the restaurant. She parked next to Michael's car. Michael was already in the restaurant. He watched Linda as she walked in, trying to size her up. She was in her fifties, long hair with a tint of grey and very attractive.

Linda came inside and looked around for Michael. The waitress came over. "Mr. Greyger is waiting for you over here." Linda thanked her and walked over to Michael's table.

"Linda, please have a seat. It is good to finally talk with you. Have you eaten yet?"

"Michael, let's not get to cozy. First, I would like to know what you want."

The waitress came over. "What can I get you?" she said with a smile.

"BLT and a salad, and please make it to go." The waitress took her order, and thanked her.

"Michael, you know that this is my last month with the agency. I've paid my dues and I'm ready to retire."

"Linda, you are going to have to put your retirement on hold for a little while longer. You are the perfect person for this job, please hear me out."

"This had better be good."

"As you know, the Bricks would like to adopt another child. They are going to need some help, and you are going to be that help. As soon as they move into the new house on campus, they will need your services. All you have to do is take the pressure off the Bricks long enough for them to finish their project."

"That's all you want Michael? What are you not telling me?"

"That is all, you can trust me."

"I wish I could Michael, but I have heard too much about you. I'll give you a couple of weeks and that is it, agreed?"

Michael smiled, "Thank you Linda, you won't be sorry." Michael raised his hand for the waitress to come over.

"Yes, Mr. Greyger."

"Miss Peach will be staying for lunch, would you take care of it?"

Linda forced a smile. "Now that I'm staying for lunch, Michael, tell me what is so important about the Bricks?"

"His research is vital to the country."

"I'm surprised that you are so interested in a cure for cancer. I heard that you are taking orders from Richard on this. If Richard is involved, this is big."

Michael answered in a stern voice, "Linda, I never want to hear you say Richard's name again. Is that clear?"

"So I was right."

"I like you Linda, so don't do anything that will change that."

Linda sighed, "So what is the next step?"

"There is a newborn that the Bricks want to adopt. I can't figure out why, but they will not finish the project until it happens. The adoption agency has told them that they need a nurse to stay with them full time for a while. That is where you come in. You are going to be my eyes and ears in that house. As soon as the project is done, you can leave, any questions?"

"Then I can retire?"

"Yes Linda, then you can do whatever you want for the rest of your life."

Linda was thinking about what Michael had said. "And Michael, I will never have to see you again?"

"Yes."

"Michael, it is a deal. Let's get this show on the road."

The waitress came over with their food. "Will there be anything else, Mr. Greyger?"

"Not right now, thank you."

Michael picked up his phone. "Ann, this is Michael. Linda is on board. Get things rolling on your end, and call me when you are ready."

After a quiet lunch, Michael walked Linda to her car. He opened the door for her and held his hand out. "Linda your country thanks you."

"Michael, these are nice people, don't hurt them."

When Linda was sure Michael couldn't see her, she pulled out a bottle of hand sanitizer and cleaned her hands. "I feel like I have been pissed on," she thought.

Michael was already on his way back to the motel. As he walked in, he was greeted by all the staff. He waved and went up to his room.

Michael sat on his bed and called Richard. "This is Michael, everything is back on track. They move into the new house tomorrow. I still don't know where the plans for the laser are, but they have to be on campus somewhere. I will let you know as soon as I find out."

Michael ended the phone call. "Now, Dr. Brick, where are the plans and how does this thing work?" he said to himself.

Michael drove over to the Dean's office and parked in front of the building. He put on a smile and walked in.

"Hello, is Dean Charles in? My name is Michael Greyger."

The lady at the desk was more than happy to help. She picked up the phone and called the Dean. "Mr. Greyger is here to see you. Shall I send him in?"

She laid the phone down gently. "Dean Charles will be right out, Mr. Greyger. Please have a seat. It should not be very long. I have been looking forward to meeting you. I have heard nothing but good things about you, and what you are doing for Dr. Brick and his family."

"Thank you, and you can call me Michael."

"Mr. Greyger,"-

Michael stopped her, "Just Michael."

"Michael, my name is Joyce."

"Joyce, have I come at a good time? I hope I am not inconveniencing Dean Charles."

"You are fine. He should be right out. He is on the phone."

Michael looked around and noticed that there were many antiques in the office. "Does Dean Charles collect antiques?"

Joyce answered, "He does, and some of them are quite rare."

"These are really beautiful. I'm sure he must be very proud of them," Michael said.

"You are so right. These pieces are like part of his family. He won't let anyone dust them. He does it himself."

Just then the door opened. "Michael, please come in, I just got off the phone with our director of maintenance. He said the house is ready to go. We could not have done it without your help. How can we ever thank you?"

"Dean, without your vision for Dr. Brick, none of this would be possible. I believe that all the credit belongs to you. All I did was give you a little help. And if I was not here, you would have found some other way of getting it done." At this point, Michael had Dean Charles eating out of his hand.

"So Michael, what can I do for you?" asked Dean Charles.

"Well, Dean Charles, I will be leaving tomorrow, and I wanted to leave my card with you. If there is anything that I can do for you or the Bricks, please let me know."

"I'm sorry that you have to go, but you will always be welcome here at the school and in my home. I appreciate your generous funding and the help you given us with the house."

Michael stopped him. "Dean Charles, it was my pleasure. Now, let's finish this project." He stood and handed the Dean his card. They shook hands, and Michael left the room.

On his way out he said, "Joyce, it has been a pleasure. I hope to see you again."

"Goodbye, Michael, have a good day."

When Michael got into his car, his phone rang. "Michael, this is Ann, the adoption is set. Do you want me to call the Bricks?"

"No, I told you that Martha Woods needs to take care of it, but make sure that she is never alone with the Bricks. If she gets out of control, get her out of the room."

"When do you want her to call?"

"This afternoon," he said. "They can have the baby tomorrow, but Nurse Peach is part of the deal. Don't give them any time to find another nurse."

"Yes Michael."

"Good, and get me a plane ticket for tomorrow to get out of this place."

"Michael, are you leaving?" Ann's voice perked up.

"Don't get too excited, Ann. It is just for show. I will keep you informed." Michael hung up.

"What an asshole, he did not even say goodbye." thought Ann.

Chapter   18

The Bricks were sitting at the Professor's house, when Jase's phone started to ring.

"Jase, the steel drums are calling," Jill said.

He looked at the caller ID, and then answered. "Hello Dean Charles, what is the good news?"

"The good news is that your house is ready. Michael's men worked around the clock. Would you like to go check it out? I can meet you there."

"How soon do you want us there?" Jase was excited.

"When you get there, give me a call. I will be there in five minutes."

"Great, we will see you in a little while."

"Jill, the house is ready. Do you want to go for a peek?"

"I do but Eva just went down for a nap. You go and tell me all about it."

"OK, come on Professor and bring your bug detector."

"Already got it. Let's take your van. I don't have a car right now."

Jase laughed, "Let's go, Professor. Maybe I will let you drive, just so you don't forget how to."

The Professor pulled up to the house as the workers were walking out the door.

"Are you Dr. Brick?" One of the workers asked.

"Yes," Jase answered.

"I have a set of keys for you. If you want, I can show you what we did to the house."

"That would be great."

They followed the man back into the house. "As you can see, the outside of the house received a new coat of paint. We sandblasted the brick and sidewalk. Looks a lot better, don't you think?"

"It looks good. I can't wait to see the inside."

"We cleaned up the porch and were able to get all the windows to work. This place was in pretty bad shape."

Jase nodded. The Professor never said a word, but he had his detector out as he walked into the house.

"Dr. Brick, what is your friend doing?" asked the man.

"Oh, the Professor is kind of an exterminator. He is looking for bugs," replied Jase.

The man looked puzzled but kept walking. "As you can see, there are all new floor coverings and paint. It is clean from top to bottom. This place was really run down."

They walked into the kitchen. "We replaced almost the entire kitchen."

The Professor spoke up, "Who paid for all of this?"

"All I can tell you is Michael Greyger was in charge of paying the bills. Would you like to see the upstairs?"

They walked up the steps. "It looks like a new house," Jase said.

"We installed all new smoke and carbon dioxide detectors, so you should not have to worry about that. All of the bedrooms are freshly painted and ready to go. One more thing, there is a master bath and a main bath, but Michael wanted us to put a bath in the last bedroom. Plus you have a half bath down stairs. Do you have any questions?"

"No, not really, how is the furnace and air?"

"We went over everything and changed the filter. There was not much else to check."

"I don't know what to say. This place is far better than I ever expected. Will you thank all of the people for a great job? My wife will never believe it. If she was here, she would be in tears."

"I will relay the message. You have a nice day."

He turned toward the Professor and asked, "Did you find any bugs crawling around?"

The Professor stopped and looked at the man. "Hell no, should I have?" The man did not know how to answer, so he just waved and walked out the door.

Jase and the Professor watched him as he walked back toward them.

"Dr Brick, I guess you would like to have these." He handed him two sets of door keys.
As he walked away, he turned and yelled, "If you need anything, just call."

Jase yelled back, "Thanks for everything."

"Well, Professor, did you find anything?"

"I found nothing Brick, not a damn thing."

"Well, let's lock up and go back."

Jill was waiting at the door for them. "Well, how does it look?"

Before Jase could say anything, the Professor spoke. "Jill, it is nothing like my place, but I think you will like it."

Jill would not take that as an answer. "Jase, tell me how does it look?"

"It is just about the nicest house I have ever seen. I hope the shock is not too much for us."

"I want to know everything."

Before he could say anything the phone rang. "Dr. Brick, this is Martha Woods. How are you?"

"Very good Martha, how are you?"

"Just fine. I guess you know there was some kind of mix up with the little boy that you wanted to adopt. The mother still wants you to adopt her son. We need to place him very quickly. Have you looked into a larger home yet?"

"We will be moving into a new place tomorrow. It has four bedrooms, and it is on campus."

"Dr. Brick, do you want me to start the paperwork?"

"Yes, of course," Jase answered.

"Now, the agency might want you to get a nurse to help for--" Martha stopped.
Ann was standing on the other side of her desk.

In a soft but stern voice, Ann said, "You will send a nurse or there will not be an adoption."

"Sorry, Dr. Brick, I was interrupted. The only way we will allow another adoption to close is if we send our nurse to help with the baby until you adjust to your new family."

"Well, if that is the only way, then that is what we will do. But I don't know if I can afford to pay much."

"We will discuss that when we finish the paper work."

"Martha, thank you so much. I will tell Jill, and I will call you tomorrow."

"Thank you, Dr. Brick, until then." She ended the call.

Ann was sitting across the desk from Martha. "I don't want you to talk to the Bricks unless I'm with you. Do you understand?"

"Ann, what do you want with the Bricks? They are nice people, and they are not stupid. Sooner or later, they will know something is going on."

"Martha, all you need to know is to keep your mouth shut or you could end up like that little girl's mother. Sometime accidents happen. You would not like your child to grow up without a mother, would you?"

Martha was mad and scared at the same time. "Just do what you are going to do and get out of here."

"And one more thing, Martha, we will be watching you and your child for a long time, so don't get any ideas. I think we have an understanding." Ann got up from her chair. "I will be back tomorrow." She walked out of the room.

As soon as Ann left the room, Martha started to cry.

Chapter 19

Jase closed his phone. Jill watched, waiting for him to say something. He looked over at her, "Well, what are we going to eat tonight?"

Jill could not take it anymore. "Mister, if you know what is good for you, you will tell me what Martha said."

"We could have the boy as soon as tomorrow, if we still want to."

"Tomorrow, is that what you said?"

"I told her we would call tomorrow, after we have moved into the new house. She said she would have all the paperwork ready. Now there is one catch, Jill."

"The nurse?" asked Jill.

"Yes, at least for a little while until we are settled in. Personally, I think that it is a good idea."

"Are they going to send the nurse that was at the agency?"

"I don't know, but I liked her. I'm sure Martha would not send anyone she didn't approve of."

"You are probably right, and I could use some help for a little while."

The Professor spoke up. "How about I go out and bring back supper. Tomorrow is going to be a long day."

Jase watched him, "I suppose you want to drive the van?"

"Well hell, Brick, that is if you want supper." Jase handed him the keys.

"What do you two want to eat? It is on me."

"Professor, you pick. We are just glad to be here. Do you want Jase to go with you?" said Jill.

"No, that is all right. I'm going to stop at the lab to pick up a few things, and then I will be right back."

The Professor got into the van and started driving toward the campus. As he drove, he looked into the rear view mirror. There was a car behind him with no lights on. He decided to drive around for a while to see if he was being followed. As he turned, he noticed that the car went straight. It was a black Ford. He kept watching, and the car's lights turn on.

"Probably just forgot to turn his lights on," he thought, as he turned into a pizza and sub shop. He walked in.

"Hello Professor, what will it be tonight?"

"Give me the special, two salads and a two liter of cola."

With a grin, the boy at the counter said, "I don't think I have ever seen you get a salad before. What is going on?"

"Maybe I have some lady friends staying over."

The young man smiled, "There is a first time for everything."

"Well, there went your tip." The Professor said.

"Professor, you never tip."

"I might have tonight, you never know."

"Here you go Professor. See you tomorrow night."

The Professor took the food. When he started to get into the van, he noticed the same black Ford across the street in a parking lot. He put the food into the van and walked over to the Ford. A man in his late twenties was sitting in the car. The Professor motioned for him to roll the window down.

"I have been watching you drive around all night. Are you lost?" asked the Professor.

"No," replied the man. "I have been looking for my girlfriend. I think she has been running around on me."

The Professor laughed, "Well, I wish you luck." He started to walk away, and then Professor stopped and turned. "Did you know that sometimes your lights don't work? You might want to tell Michael to get them fixed."

He went back to the van humming a tune, as the car drove away. He decided not to go back to the lab, and instead, returned to the house.

The Professor walked in and put the food on the table in the kitchen. Jill was feeding the baby.

"I think that we should get the white dishes out for this special event. Jase, they are up in the cabinet on the right above the sink."

Jase walked over to the cabinet and opened it. "Professor, all I see is paper plates."

"That's the ones, good job, Brick."

The Professor and Jase filled their plates. "Can I get you something, Jill?" asked Jase.

"No, I will be there in a little bit."

The Professor nodded to Jase to follow him to the other room. "I was followed, so I did not go to the lab."

"Are you sure?"

"I asked the driver to have Michael get his lights fixed."

Jase said, "You don't think he had anything to do with it, do you?"

"No harm done, Brick. If he is not with Greyger, he will not know what I am talking about. If he is, well, that is another story. Anyway you look at it, when your van moves, someone is watching. I will have someone run the plates tomorrow."

"Don't say anything to Jill, Professor."

"Don't worry, I won't."

Jill walked in holding Eva. "Sorry we won't be staying very long, Professor," she said.

"Because of you, I got my house cleaned up. But before you leave, you must sign a paper that you saw it clean. I will date it and have it framed. It might be worth something someday. Now, let Uncle Bill hold that girl, so her mom can eat."

"Why Professor, I don't think I have ever seen this side of you," said Jill.

"Don't tell anyone. I wouldn't want that information to get out."

Jill was eating pizza while watching the Professor as he held Eva. "Professor, why do you live the way you do?"

The Professor smiled. "I don't have any brothers and sisters, but I do have few relatives who I can't stand. They all think that I don't have any money, so they leave me alone. And I like it that way. I paid my dues. Now, I have my sailboat and a life. I leave when I want to, and I don't answer to anyone. As soon as I get you two settled in, I'm heading for the Keys. Jase, you should go with me. My boat is at the Chesapeake bay waiting to sail."

"I would like that, but I don't see it happening in the near future."

"You never know, Jase, you never know."

Jill spoke up. "Jase, I think that you should do it as soon as you can. Just make sure you come back."

"Maybe Jill, but that is that last thing on my mind right now."

"Well hell, Brick, it's a plan then."

The next morning they were all up early. There was a knock at the door, and the Professor opened it. It was the movers.

"Are you sure that you have the right house?" asked the Professor.

"We were hired to move the Brick family, and that job is not done until they are in the new house," came the reply.

"Well, come on in guys. The party is just getting started." The Professor yelled upstairs, "The movers are here."

Jill and Jase looked at each other. "The movers are here?" After a moment they said, "Come on up." Four hours later they were in their new house.

"Jase, call Martha. We are ready."

Before Jase could get his phone out, it rang.

"Jase, this is Michael."

"Michael, we were just going to call the adoption agency. We are in our new house. How can we ever thank you?"

"Just keep the research in high gear, and call me if I can help in any way. I will be leaving in a few hours, but we must keep in touch."

"I'm sorry to see you leave. We should be up and running at the lab as soon as the new baby gets settled in."

The Professor was listening. When he heard that Michael was leaving, he started to do a dance. Then he stopped. "Ask him what flight he is on."

Jase nodded. "Michael, what time does your flight leave?"

Michael responded, "4:10 pm with one stop in Chicago, then arriving in Virginia by midnight."

"That is a long layover. Is that the best you could do?"

"I don't have much of a choice. I have a meeting first thing in the morning."

"Well Michael, we will miss you. Have a safe trip and please stay in touch. Goodbye."

As Jase put his phone in his pocket, the Professor has his finger in his mouth trying to gag, while still doing his little dance.

This time Jill asked, "Professor, I take it you don't care for Michael?"

"There is something that does not quite click about him. No, I don't care for him, but I have been wrong before."

"I think that you are wrong this time Professor. If it wasn't for him----"

Jase stopped her before she said anything else. "Jill, the Professor is just a little concerned about his newly adopted niece." Upon hearing that, Jill backed down, to the Professors relief.

"Now, let's call Martha." Jase took the phone from his pocket and put the numbers in.

When someone answered, Jase said, "Hi, this is Dr. Brick. Is Martha Woods in?"

"Hi Dr. Brick, this is Ann."

Chapter 20

"Hello Ann, can I please talk to Martha?"

"As a matter of fact, Dr. Brick, she was hoping that you would call today. That little boy still needs a home. Let me get Mrs. Woods on the line."

Ann put the phone on hold and walked into Martha's office. "Dr. Brick is on the phone, line one. You know what to tell him, and I will be right here if you need me." Ann glared at her.

Martha picked up the phone. "Dr. Brick, it is good to hear from you. Have you moved into your new house?"

"We are in the house as we speak."

"Good, I need to send Ann over to perform an inspection of the house. If it meets her approval, the adoption can go forward tomorrow. I think she can come right now. Would that be all right?"

"That will be fine."

"Also, Nurse Peach would like to ride over with Ann, since she will be helping you out for a little while."

"Martha, are you also coming?"

"Not this time, Dr. Brick, but maybe in the future. I will tell Ann that she can leave anytime. I will talk to you later." Martha hung up.

"You are never to go over to the Brick's house, Martha. Stay away from them, unless I am with you, understand?"

Martha nodded.

"Good." Ann got up and walked out of the office.

Martha stared at the door. "I hope that someone gets that bitch someday," she said in a soft vengeful voice.

Ann walked back to the nursery. Linda Peach sat at a table going over the paperwork for the assignment.

"Linda, it is time we go to see your new home."

"Not for very long, Ann, so don't you forget that."

"It will be for as long as we say," Ann fired back.

"Listen you little blond bitch, this is my last job. You stay out of my way, or I will drop you where you stand."

"I'm perfectly aware of you defense skills. We don't have time for this, so put your nanny face on and let's go." They walked out the back door and got into Ann's car.

"It is people like you that make me thankful I am retiring."

Ann answered without taking her eyes off the road. "You are just like me, Linda, and you know it."

Linda snapped back, "I was never like you, and I never will be."

They were quiet as they drove though the countryside. Ann remembered when she was twenty-one, and Michael came to the school to offer her a job. "The chance of a life time," he said. "Help your country and have an exciting job at the same time." Michael also said, "The job is so good, hardly anyone ever quits." What he should have said was, "Hardly any one quits and lives." She glanced at Linda sitting in the other seat. "Is this what I have to look forward to in a few years?" she thought.

Soon they could see the buildings of the university on the horizon. "Well, Linda, this will be you new home for awhile."

Linda turned to look out the window. "You know, Ann, your personal life was over when you signed up for this job. Even if by some miracle you survive until you are my age, your chances of being a mother and having a family of your own is very slim. You can play hardball for now, but you have given up everything."

Ann did not answer. She knew Linda was right. They continued the drive to the campus and pulled up in front of Dr. Brick's house. "Look at the house, Michael does good work when he wants to." said Linda.

Ann started to get out, when Linda grabbed her arm. "Listen Ann, I have forgotten more than you will ever know. I have turned down promotions that you will never see. You might think you are in charge of me, but the best thing I can say is stay out of my way." Linda opened the door and got out. Stunned by Linda's remark, Ann sat there for a moment, then she got out of the car.

"I will do the talking, Linda."

"I would not have it any other way," Linda answered. "Smile Ann, they are watching through the front window." Ann waved as they start up the walk.

"Jase, they are here," called Jill. Jill opened the door. "Hi Ann, hi Linda, come on in."

Linda quickly looked around the room. She stopped when she saw Jase holding his little girl. "Dr. Brick, you make the perfect picture. That baby was meant for you two."

Linda walked over to Jase. "Can I hold her? Jill, she looks just like you." Linda hugged the little girl as Eva smiled. "Now Jill, where is the baby's room?"

Linda and Jill hit it off right away. "Come on Linda, I'll show you," Jill said.

Linda stopped and turned. "Ann, you probably should come too. After all, this is your inspection."

Ann was pissed, but she did not show it. "I'm right behind you."

Jase and the Professor were left standing in the living room. "Well hell, Brick, that went good."

The girls were upstairs in the baby's room. "For now, we are going to put both of the babies in the same room. What do you think, Linda?" asked Jill.

"I think that would be fine. You have plenty of room. Now where will I be staying?"

"Right next door, come on let me show you. You know this seems funny, two days ago I did not know what this house looked like, and now I'm showing you around."

They walked into Linda's room. The room was large with plenty of light. "Is this new furniture? I was not expecting that, Jill."

"Michael must have ordered it, but I really don't know. Everything was here when we moved in."

"Who is Michael?" Linda asked. Ann jerked her head toward Linda.

Jill answered, "He is the one who made all of this possible. I don't know what we would have done without him."

"Well, maybe I will get to meet him sometime. He sounds like a nice person. Don't you think so, Ann?" Linda smiled. Ann could have killed her right on the spot.

Jill answered, "Both of you have met him. He was with us the day we picked up Eva."

"That's right, you remember him don't you, Ann." Linda was having a really good time.

"Well, how do you like your room, Linda?" asked Jill.

"I think it will be fine, and I'm only here for as long as I am needed."

"You are going to retire soon. Do you have any plans?" asked Jill.

"No, not really, I just want to go to some place that is laid back and warm."

The three walked downstairs. Eva was sleeping in Linda's arms. "Jase, Eva loves Linda! Just look at her. She smiled and went right to sleep. Linda has been holding her the whole time we were upstairs."

Ann could not take much more. "Dr. Brick, this house is beautiful. Did they have to do much renovating?"

"Yes, as a matter of fact they did. Michael had his people work nonstop."

Linda could not pass this one up. She started to say something, but Ann interrupted her.
"Well, I think that you should give the baby back to her Mother. It is time we go. Jill, we will see you first thing in the morning."

As both of the women leave, they walked past the Professor. He tipped his captain's hat at them.

"And who might you be?" asked Linda."

"People call me Professor." Linda looked him as she walked by.

They watched as Linda and Ann walked to the car. Linda turned and waved.

"Jase, I like Linda, don't you?"

Before he could answer the Professor said, "I like her too, but the younger one is a bitch."

Chapter 21

As they head back, Ann is livid.

"What's the matter Ann? The Bricks like me. This will be an easy job."

"Linda, I don't know what you are trying to pull. Just do your job and keep your mouth shut."

"What the hell is your problem, Ann? They are a nice family, and that little girl is the cutest thing I have ever seen."

"That little girl's mother was terminated for this project. The Bricks think she died in a car wreck. They are a hundred times better parents then she was. The mother was so high, that she didn't even know she was in a wreck."

"Ann, I thought you said she died in the wreck?"

"No, she died at the hospital. Michael wanted her terminated. With all her drug problems and no family, it was not hard."

"So you killed her! Ann, you have crossed the line. For the rest of your life, you will see that woman with her little girl. Believe me, Ann, because I know it's true. I hope you can live with yourself. Some agents never get over their first kill."

Tears were running down Ann's face. "Ann, pull over at that restaurant on the right," Linda commanded. Ann pulled over and stopped.

"How about some coffee, I am buying. Anyway, you are in no shape to drive."

Ann followed Linda into the restaurant. They order coffee and rolls, and then they sat down in a far corner away from everyone.

"Ann, you look like shit."

"Thanks, Linda, I really needed that." Ann was still trying to hide the fact that she was crying. She sat there wiping away her tears.

"Ann, this is a rough life. Not everyone can do it. You have no friends, you cannot trust anyone and most of the time you are all along. I spent almost thirty years in this shit, and I'm tired of it. From what you have told me, you probably saved that little girl's life. She is better off with the Bricks. Yes, you had to play God. It sucks, doesn't it?"

Ann nodded.

"So get over it and drink your coffee. You are in too deep to turn back. Sometimes the bitch has to cry, but don't let anyone see you, and one more thing."

"What is that?" Ann asked.

"Don't turn into Michael. He made a pact with devil and gave up his soul."

"Linda, I didn't think that you knew Michael."

"Yes, I am familiar with him. I have worked on some of his projects. As you have found out, he will stop at nothing to get the job done. I didn't think he was that bad at first, but he has changed, we all do. Michael is the best in the business, and he is pure evil. I have heard that he has a family somewhere. I feel sorry for them. He only answers directly to Richard. Richard, now there is a piece of work. He makes Michael look like an angel. Stay away from him. At least Michael tries to act nice in public. Richard is a true asshole all of the time."

"Linda, will you miss it?"

"I'm glad I am getting out, and not anytime too soon, if you asked me. Are you about ready to go?"

"Yes."

"This time, I will drive. You can watch the cornfields."

They arrived back at the adoption agency just as it was time to close. Martha Woods was leaving.

"Martha, would you mind coming back inside for a moment," asked Ann. She turned around and followed them back into the building.

"The Bricks will be here first thing in the morning. Why don't you take the day off? Also, how would you and your son like to take a trip on us for the next thirty days? Someplace far away, you can leave next week. It is our way of thanking you for your help."

"Ann, who the hell are you, and what do you want with the Bricks?"

Ann put her finger on her lips. "Martha, let's not go there, OK?"

"I'll be glad when you are gone, and I suppose that nurse is one of you too?"

"Goodbye Martha, see you in two days."

Ann and Linda walked into the office.

"Linda, sometimes I hate my job, but at other times, I love it."

"Good, there is still hope for you. Now you should call Michael. Maybe the asshole has left already."

Ann pulled out her phone, took a deep breath and then called.

A voice came on. "This is Michael, please leave a message."

"I got Michael's voice mail, that's a first. I wonder why he didn't answer."

Chapter 22

Jase watched the two women leave. "Professor, this has been a very fast couple of weeks. What are you doing?"

"I'm calling the airport. What time did Michael say he was leaving, a little after 6:00?"

"Yes, with a layover in Chicago."

The Professor called the airport. "Information please, the Professor waited, and then a voice came on. "Are there any flights to Chicago at 6:00? Really, thanks." He hung up.

"Hell Brick, there is one. It leaves at ten after six. Maybe he did leave, let me try something else. Do you have a phone book?"

"Yes, somewhere let me look. Here it is. What are you looking up?"

"Michael's motel, give them a call and see if he has left."

Jase laughed, "If it will make you feel better, I will."

Jase entered the numbers. "Motel front desk, how can I help you?"

"May I have Mr. Greyger's room? This is Dr. Brick."

The girl at the desk answered. "Mr. Greyger left this afternoon. He said that if anyone called for him, to give them his cell number. Would you like it, Dr. Brick?"

"No, I already have it, thank you." He ended the call.

The girl at the desk looked up. "How was that, Mr. Greyger?"

"You did just fine. I will call him later. I have a plane to catch."

Michael walked out to his car and drove away. He turned to the right. The sign pointed left for the airport. He drove to an empty office trailer next to the highway. It belonged to the State Highway Department, and it had not been used in some time. When he arrived, there was a car with state plates on it sitting in front. Michael pulled into the lot, parked next to the white state car and walked in.

"Good afternoon, Michael. How are you?"

"Fine, but I did not expect to see you here." Michael sat down.

Across the desk sat a short fat man, in an expensive suit with pants that were too short.

Michael watched as the man went through his laptop for a moment, then he stopped to speak. "Michael, this is taking way to long and costing way too much. What have you found out?"

"Richard, everything is under control."

"If everything was under control, I would not be here. Have you seen the laser? Does it work?"

"Yes, I have seen it work."

"So why don't I have it?"

"The day of the demonstration, Dr. Brick removed all the records of the cancer project and the laser. He also removed the CPU. Without it, we don't know how the laser works."

"I don't give a damn about the cancer bullshit. I want that laser, and I don't care how you get it."

"Yes sir," Michael answered. "We searched the lab and his house. We even searched his van."

"Well, you have missed something. I don't want this to fall into some other hands, if you know what I mean. What happened at the Brick's apartment? Who found the bugs, and why have you stopped surveillance of the van?"

"A professor from the university found the bugs, and he also stopped the car that was following the Bricks."

"Michael, does this professor have a name?"

"Professor William Williams. He is about fifty something and very sloppy. He likes his booze, has a loud voice and he looks like he does not have a pot to piss in."

Richard started hitting keys on his laptop. He stopped and turned the computer around toward Michael. "Is this the professor?"

Michael scanned the screen. The picture and information on the screen was the Professor, but the photo was taken over ten years ago. He was younger and was dressed in a suit and tie. His hair was cut short and he looked professional."

"Yes, that's him," Michael replied.

Richard sat back in his chair. "Michael, here is your problem. The Professor was one of us. He has been out of circulation for quite some time, but he knows how we think and how we work. We need to get the Brick's out of here. I want them in Virginia away from the Professor."

"Ok, but it will not happen overnight. The Brick's are adopting a child tomorrow. If you try to stop the adoption, they will stop work on the project, believe me I know. I tried it once before. Let's get them settled in the new place on campus. Then I will convince them it would be in their best interest to go to a new location, and I will tell them about the lab in Virginia."

"Go on," said Richard.

"I already have a plan. Do you want me to search the Professor's house?"

"No, if he sees any of your people again, he will know something is up. He probably already thinks you are involved. Don't let him fool you, Michael, he is not the man you want to fuck with."

"Can we confront the Professor?"

"No Michael, I think that he has ties too deep to the Bricks. It is not worth the chance. Now do I still have time to use the plane ticket?"

Michael gave Richard the ticket, and they exchanged car keys. Both men left the trailer.

"I will call you in about a week. By then, the Bricks should be settled in. We also have an agent posing as a nurse and staying with them."

"Good, I want to know everything. What did you do with the two men who took the video of the Bricks in their home?"

"They should be in your office when you get back. There is no room for them in my projects, so do whatever you want with them. I don't want to ever see them again."

Michael watched as Richard got into his car, his socks showing as he walked. "You would think with all the money he makes, he could dress a little better. His pants are so short he looks like a circus clown." Michael walked around to the back of the car. He bent over and pulled the thin layer of plastic from the license plate with the state numbers on it, revealing a local plate number. Now he could drive around unnoticed.

"Tinted glass, Richard thinks of everything." Michael got in and drove off.

118

Chapter 23

Jase and Jill were up early. "Jase, when do you think we can get Rex?"

"For right now, let's get this adoption under control. Rex is fine at the lab. Plus he gets a lot of attention there. Everyone loves him."

Jill smiled at Eva. "This week you get a brother and a dog. Not bad for one week."

"Jill, as soon as you get done feeding Eva, we will be ready to go. It will be good to talk to Martha. I have some questions for her."

Jase's phone rang. He glanced at the caller ID.

"Good morning, Professor."

"Brick, do you need me to go over to the lab? I'm not doing anything right now, and I know that you are all tied up with the baby thing."

"Yes, that would be great. Rex needs to go for a walk, do you mind?"

"You owe me. Call when you get back. I might need a ride. I think I've found another car just like the last one. The insurance company gave me almost $2,000 for the last one, and the new one is $650. Hell Brick, I made almost $1,400 on this deal."

"Only you could pull it off, Professor. As soon as Jill and I get back, I will call you."

"Is the nurse coming too?"

"Yes, as far as I know."

"Well hell, I might come over to see my new niece and nephew."

"That would be nice. I'll call you when we get settled in."

Jase was grinning. "Jill, I think that the Professor likes our nurse."

Jill looked at Jase. "That should be interesting. We are almost ready to go. Do we have everything?"

"I think so," Jase was a little nervous. "You know, in two weeks we have gone from being us two, to being us four. And now we have a dog. I'm glad we are getting some help. I hope Linda works out."

"I'm sure she will, otherwise Martha would not have sent her. Now let's go, we have a son to pick up."

The trip to the adoption agency seemed to take forever. Eva was sleeping, and Jill was watching the endless fields of corn. Jase was preoccupied with the thought of the lab project, the babies and the new house.

Suddenly, he heard the steel drums. He handed the phone to Jill. "Here, see who it is."

"It's Michael," she answered. "Hi Michael, guess where we are going?"

"I hope that you are going to pick up your new son."

"That's right, and we are so excited. How can we ever thank you enough?"

"Jill, just keep your husband working on his project, and keep me informed of his progress. Above all, take care of those kids. You are a very lucky couple. I'm sorry that I cannot be there. I just called to wish you the best."

"We are sorry you can't be here also. Jase is driving, so he will have to call you later. Is that all right?"

"He does not have to call back. I just wanted to say hello, and to tell you to keep up the good work. You have my number, so please call if you need anything. And Jill, as I told your husband, if you ever want to come to Virginia, let me know. I have a place right on the water that would be perfect for your family. It is located off RT. 10 in the Chesapeake area. Have you ever been to the Chesapeake, Jill?"

"No, we haven't. It sounds very nice, maybe someday."

"I know you two are on a mission, so I will not keep you. Tell Jase I said good luck, and I will be talking to you soon."

"Ok Michael, it was good to hear from you."

She hung up. "What a nice man." Jase nodded and kept driving.

They were almost there. Traffic was light, which was normal for this road. A white car followed a short distance from the van. The driver was careful not to get too close.

Michael smiled as he watched the Bricks.

Chapter 24

Jase pulled up to the adoption agency, and they looked at each other. "This is it, Jill." They gently retrieved Eva from her car seat. Jill looked at the other empty car seat and smiled. She pictured her new son sitting in it.

They walked in the door expecting to see Martha. "Hello," Ann said. "Martha had something come up and could not be here today. She said to tell you hello. Come this way, someone is waiting to see you."

Jill grabbed Jase's arm as they walked to the nursery. Linda Peach was already there.

"Mr. And Mrs. Brick, may I introduce your new son. Do you have a name yet?"

Jill spoke. "No, not yet, but I was thinking of Michael, what do you think, Jase?"

Linda could not hold back. Before he could answer, she said, "You don't have to make up your mind now, take your time. Now, come over here and hold your little boy."

He was only a few weeks old, but he smiled up at Jill and Jase. Jill gave Eva to Jase and then took the baby boy from Linda. "Look Jase, he is watching you. Eva, this is your new brother."

Jase was so overwhelmed, he couldn't speak.

"Is the mother here?" asked Jill.

Ann spoke. "No, she had to go back home. She was glad that you two were the ones to adopt her child, and she asked that you not tell him about her."

"That's odd, isn't it?" Jase asked.

Ann answered, "No, not really, but you must respect her wishes."

"Now, Dr. Brick, would you please come this way. I have some papers for you to sign."

As they left the room, Linda was holding Eva. "Jill, I am looking forward to helping you with your family."

"We are also looking forward to that. Will you be riding back with us?"

"No, I will follow you back in my car."

"Linda, I'm sorry we did not get to see Martha. Maybe I can call and thank her."

"She had something come up. I don't think she will be back for at least thirty days. She had some kind of family emergency to take care of."

"Well, I hope that everything is all right."

When they walked out of the nursery, Linda handed Jill a check list. "The baby is in good health. Ann is giving Jase all his records. We should be about ready to go."

As they walked into Ann's office, Ann and Jase were just finishing.

"Ann, it has been a pleasure. Please tell Martha we are sorry we missed her." Jase looked at Linda. "Can we give you a ride?"

"No thanks, Dr. Brick. I have my car out back, so I will follow you to your house."

Linda left to get her car, while Ann walked out with the Bricks. "Call if you need anything. It is nice to see the children get a good home. So many times that is not the case. Good luck."

They put the children in their seats and drove away. Linda followed behind in her car.

As the cars reached the edge of town, Michael watched from a distance.

They pulled up to the house, and Linda pulled in behind them. "Where do you want me to park?" she asked.

"Right there is fine," Jase answered. They all help get the family into the new house.

"Linda, is your car unlocked?" Jase asked. "I will go and get your things."

"No, Dr. Brick, wait and I will go out with you." She did not want Jase looking around in her car. "Let's get the kids in first."

Jill said, "You know, Linda, I do have my hands full. I'm glad that you are here. I already feel that you are part of the family."

"I guess I will go and check the lab. It looks like you two have everything under control."

Not receiving any arguments, Jase said, "Goodbye," and left.

"Jase seems like a good person. You are very lucky. What kind of work does he do for the university?" Linda asked.

"Research mostly. When he was younger, he almost died from cancer. Since that time, he has devoted his life to finding a cure."

Linda was taken off guard. "I had no idea. So this research is personal."

Jill nodded. "Now he has his research and his family. And if I can help him, he will succeed in both. He is a very caring man."

Linda thought, "Michael, you bastard, you better not hurt these people."

"Jill, do you have any other names for your son? There are a lot of Michaels out there."

"I don't know. We will see." Jill answered.

Chapter   25

As Jase started to drive away, his phone rang. "Hello Professor."

"Brick, are you coming my way? I need a ride."

"Sure, are you at home?"

"Hell yes, where else would I be? I don't have a car yet. Let's go look at one."

"I'm almost there. Meet me out front."

When he arrived, the Professor was waiting next to the curb. "Brick, you can't beat the service."

Once in the van, the Professor voice changed. "I think that someone has been watching my house."

"Normally I would think you are paranoid. But after everything that has happened the last few days, I don't know anymore."

"I know. Let's go look at a car." The Professor gave Jase the address.

"How is your new boy, and when do I get to see him?"

"As soon we look at the car. It would not be red, would it?"

"That's it, pull over." An elderly man was walking out of the house.

The Professor waved at him. "I just talked to you on the phone." They shook hands. "Is this the car you wanted $500 for?"

The owner of the car smiled. "No, this is the one I wanted $650 for."

"Well hell, let's look at it."

The car was very clean and in good shape. When Jase looked at the odometer, it only had forty thousand miles on it.

"Professor, look at the mileage. Even the inside looks like new."

"Go ahead and start it, I left the key in the ignition."

The Professor started the car. "Can we take it for a ride?"

"Sure," the owner said.

"Jase, this car is just like new." They drove around the block. "I have seen enough. I wonder why he is selling it. I'll bet he is too old to drive, and he had no choice."

The owner was waiting right where they left him. "Well, how do you like the car?" he asked.

"It is in good shape. Why are you selling it?"

The man answered, "Well, every twenty five years I buy a new car, and they won't give you anything for the old one. I find someone who looks like they need a car and give them a good price. You look like you could use one. Can you afford it?"

The Professor was insulted and was going to say something, when Jase gave him a dirty look, he answered, "Yes I can afford it." They shook hands.

"What type of car did you get this time?" The Professor asked.

"Come on, I will show it to you." They walked to a garage behind the house. He pushed the key pad, and the door started to rise.

Jase started to laugh. They were looking at a new red Corvette, with the sticker still in the window.

"For over fifty years of my life, my wife would not let me buy a sports car. This time, I put my foot down. What do you think?"

"That is about the nicest car that I have ever seen." answered Jase.

As they were walking back, the man said, "I like you fellows. Why don't you to come back in twenty five years, and I might have a car for you."

Jase started to leave, "When you get the title done for the car, come over to the house. Jill will want to see this one." When he left, Jase went straight to the lab.

"Good afternoon, Doctor." said the girl in the office. "It has been really quiet all day. Allan Smith called and left you a message. He would like to have you call him back if you would. How is the new baby? Do you have a name yet?"

"No, not yet. Did Mr. Smith leave a"--- Before he could finish, the girl handed him the phone number.

"Thank you, I will call him from my office."

Jase went straight to his phone. He had not talked with Allan Smith since the presentation at the lab. He called the number and got Allan's voice mail.

"Hello, you have reached the voice mail of Allan Smith. Please leave a message." Jase left his message and then hung up. Before he could take his hand off the phone, it started to ring.

"Hello, this is Dr. Brick."

"Dr. Brick, this is Allan Smith. Is this a good time to talk? If not, I can call later."

"This is fine, what can I do for you? I should tell you that the government is very interested in my work."

"Dr. Brick, I must meet with you as soon as possible. My employer is also very interested in your work. I can come this week. Would that be alright?"

"Yes, but a lot has happen since I talked to you."

"Like what, Doctor?"

"Well for starters, my lab was ransacked, my apartment was bugged and I have adopted two children."

"You did all that in two weeks?"

"Yes, when would you like to meet?"

"My jet is ready to take off right now. Is that too soon?"

"Probably, give me a couple of days. We just brought home our second child. Things are a little crazy right now, if you know what I mean."

"I understand, how about this Wednesday?"

"That would be fine. Would you like to come to the lab?"

"That will work. I'll call when I get in. And Dr. Brick, please don't tell the government people that I am coming."

"Why is that?" Jase asked.

"I'll explain when I get there. See you soon."

Jase put the phone down. "Well that was interesting," he thought.

As soon as he walked into the lab, he was greeted with a bark from Rex. He walked over to the cage and opened the door. "Rex, how would you like to go home? Boy have I got a family for you."

Rex was excited to see Jase. After some hugging and petting, Jase took Rex to the van.

Rex did not get to ride in the van very often, because he would jump and bark at every car that they passed. "I see that we need to get you out a little more, Rex," Jase said as he drove.

When he pulled up at the house, the Professor was getting out of his car. As soon as Rex saw the Professor, he ran to meet him. They were like two old friends.

"Well, he knows who feeds him when everyone else is too busy. How are you doing, Rex?" The Professor asked.

Jase pulled a leash out of the van. "We had better put this on him. We don't know how he will act with all these people in the house."

The Professor took the leash and put it on Rex. The dog's tail was still going strong as they walked in.

"Anyone home?" Jase yelled.

Jill came to the top of the steps. She had a finger on her lips. "Please be a little quieter. You act as if you are new at this father stuff." She smiled.

"Look what I brought you," he pointed to Rex.

"I'll be down in a little bit." Jill said in a soft voice.

The two men and the dog went into the living room and sat down.

"Professor, I had a very interesting phone call a little while ago."

The Professor raised his head and quit smiling. "I'm listening."

"You know who Blake Canon is, don't you?"

"Sure, who doesn't?"

"Well, Allan Smith, who works for him, is flying in Wednesday to talk with me. Would you like to be there?"

"No Brick, I don't think that is a good idea until we find out who we are dealing with. But I have a gift for you."

The Professor reached into his pocket and pulled out what looked like a pen. He pushed the side of it.

The pen played back their conversation. "You put this in your pocket from now on. Don't you love these little toys?"

Jase took the pen. "This might not be a bad idea." He put it in his pocket.

"Now, here is the second thing." The Professor showed Jase another scanner. Jase watched as the Professor turned on the unit. "This is called a frequency finder. All you have to do is turn it on, and it will scan the area that you are in. It does not make any mistakes. Try it."

Jase took the finder. He turned it on, and it started to scan the room. "I don't think it found anything. Am I doing it right?"

The Professor took one of the bugs out that he removed from their old apartment.

"Watch the meter while I energize this bug." The meter went off the chart.

"Brick, put it on your belt. Let everyone know you have it. Turn up the sound so everyone can hear it. One more thing, they can bug your cell, so watch what you say."

Jill and Linda came down the steps. Rex got excited when he saw Jill. When he saw Linda, he his tail stopped wagging, and he did not move.

Linda walked over to the dog. "You must be Rex. How are you?" She got down on her knees in front of the dog and put both hands out. "Come here. We are going to spend a lot of time together, so we should get to know each other."

Rex walked over to Linda, smelled her hand, then his tail started to wag a little.

"I have never met a dog that I could not get along with. Now cats, they are another story. They have a mind of their own."

Linda looked at the Professor. "Well I remember you. I was meaning to ask, what kind of sailor hat is that? I don't think I have ever seen one like that."

The Professor was quick to answer. "I'm not sure, but I liked it, so I bought it."

"Professor, have you been introduced to Linda yet?" asked Jill. "She will be helping us out for a while."

"Hi Linda, you sure look like someone I used to know. Have you travelled much?"

"No Professor, how about you?"

"Way too much. Now how would you ladies like to see my new car?" He took them outside to see it as Jase went up to check on the babies.

"Professor, I don't know if I had ever seen you in a car this nice," said Jill.

"I know, do you think it will ruin my image?"

"No, I think you are safe," Jill laughed.

As they talked and checked out the car, Michael watched.

Chapter 26

Jase climbed up the steps and very carefully went into the nursery. Eva and her new brother were sleeping. "We really need to give you a name," he said. "What will it be?"

He sat in the rocker and watched as they slept. He thought of how he would make life good for the two of them. When he turned around, Jill and Linda were at the door watching him. Jill motioned for him to come out into the hall. The proud father rose and walked out of the room. With a happy sigh, he went down the steps with Rex close behind.

"What are we going to do with Rex tonight? We don't have a cage for him."

"We will see how he does here tonight. If it doesn't work out, I will drive him back to the lab and then pick up a cage tomorrow. Do we have anything to feed him?"

"Yes, I all ready took care of that." Jill showed Jase where the dog food was stored. "Looks like Rex is ready for some now. Come on Rex, let's get you some dinner."

Jill was feeding Rex as the other three sat around the kitchen table. Jill asked, "Would everyone like some ice tea?" She was already getting glasses out. She opened the wrong door at first, and then she found the right one.

The Professor was looking at Linda. "How long have you been a nurse?"

"Professor, what an odd name. Why does everyone call you Professor?" She quickly changed the subject.

"My name is William Bill Williams, what would you do?"

"I think that Professor will do just fine. Do you teach here?"

"No, I dabble in electronics, nothing to serious. I'm trying to slow down a little and have fun."

"I don't think that I have met anyone quite like you, Professor?"

Jase spoke up. "And I don't think that you will, no matter how hard you try."

This time Jill spoke. "What are you going to do now, Jase? Are you in for the night or do you have to go back to the lab?"

"No, Jill, tomorrow will be a big day. I think that I will get an early start. Would you like me to take Rex or leave him here?"

"Ask me in the morning," Jill answered. "Linda, do you need anything?"

"No, not right now, but I'm sure that there will be something later. Tomorrow we can work on a schedule, and then we can go from there."

Suddenly, the baby monitor went off and Jill and Linda jumped up. They looked at each other and then went up the steps.

"What do you think, Professor? Do you like her?"

"I do, but I think I will check her out just to be sure. But first, I have to go to the VFW. Do you want to come?"

"No, not this time, but I will walk out with you."

They walked out to the car. "There is some work we need to do on the laser, so let me know when you think it will be safe for you to come and help."

"Not for a while, Brick, we need to sit back and watch. Let's see what happens next. What if whoever is doing all this is only interested in the laser?"

Jase answered, "You never know. Now that you have wheels again, drop into the lab tomorrow."

"Ok Brick, but I don't get up very early."

Jase went back inside the house. As he retrieved his case and started going over his work, Linda came down and sat in the living room. "Dr. Brick, how far along is this cancer project you are working on?"

"Right now, I think I can cure almost every type of cancer unless it is in the final stage."

"Won't that scare the shit out of the people that get rich by treating cancers?"

"Yes, I'm sure it will. Right now, it cost thousands of dollars to treat breast and lung cancer. In some cases, that only gives the patient an additional three or four months of life. And the quality of the life in the last few months, in most cases, is not very pretty. Then after the patient dies, the family owes their life savings to the hospital or cancer center. I hope I can change all that in the near future."

"You know that the drug companies will try to stop you."

"That's why I have been talking to the government. I don't trust the private sector. Linda, I am ready to start now, but I need to make sure that I can trust the people I am dealing with."

"Dr. Brick, if there is anything that I can do to help, let me know."

"Thank you, Linda. That means a lot to me, and I'm sure it does to Jill also. So Linda, have you been a nurse all your life? Have you ever been married?"

"Well, I studied and taught self defense, but that was a long time ago. I never married, and I don't have a family. By the time I thought I was ready, I was too old to have children, and for that I am sorry. You and Jill are so lucky. Don't let your job take that away from you like I did."

"Linda, you know you are welcome here, and I hope that you stay for a while."

Linda could not speak, because she was fighting back the tears in her eyes. Thank you, Dr. Brick, you have no idea what that means to me."

"Linda, it's Jase."

"Alright Jase, I will try not to forget."

Jill called down. "Linda, would you come up here. Both of the children are awake."

Linda smiled, "I think I better go up and help Jill out." She went up to the nursery.

Rex came over and laid down at Jase's feet. "I think everything will be alright, Rex, don't you?" Jase rubbed the dog's ears and went back to work.

By this time, the Professor was at the VFW. He sat at the bar with his gin and squirt, trying to put this puzzle together.

The bartender came over. "Where is your sail boat docked these days?"

"Over in the Chesapeake, but I really need to get it to Florida before winter. I need another hand, do you want to go?"

"Sorry, I get seasick going over a bridge. That is why I moved to the plains."

"Well hell, you're no fun."

Chapter 27

Jase was thinking about the past. When he was eleven, he spent the summer on an island in Lake Michigan. His uncle was a retired yacht builder, and he owned a marina on the island. One time his uncle had come up to him and said, "Jase, how would you like to go for a ride on my last yacht?"

"Uncle Jack, that would be great."

As they walked down the pier, Jase's uncle put his arm around his shoulder, "Jase, this is my last boat. I have built some fine ships in my day, but this one is just for me. Shall we take her out?"

Jase had never been on a sailboat before and he was a little scared. As they sat down in the boat, Jase was in front and Uncle Jack at the rudder. The first thing his uncle did was lower the keel. The keel was only about twenty four inches from forward to aft. It was a polished piece of wood that went down through the raised slot in the floor.

"Uncle Jack, what is that for?"

"It keeps the boat from turning over when the wind gets a hold of us. Now, let's put the sail up."

Jase helped Uncle Jack raise the sail. As soon as the sail was up, the boat began to move. Jase remembered how clear the water was and the blue sky. He watched his uncle's face as they sailed. It was the face of a happy man, who was thinking of the times he had turned over forty foot yachts to their new owners.

"Uncle Jack, did you make a lot of boats?" Jase asked.

"I made just enough. This is the last one and it is for me. Do you like it?"

Jase smiled and nodded, "Yes." The island was far behind them now. The waves were getting choppy. "We should be getting back," said Uncle Jack. "We are in the shipping lanes, and we don't want to be run over by the cargo ships."

Jase watched his uncle turn the craft around. His uncle's thinning hair was blowing in the wind, and he was smiling proudly. Jase would never forget his trip in the last sailing boat of Uncle Jack. As they came closer to the island, the water became calm. There was a natural bay where Uncle Jack had his marina. Two small yachts were docked at the pier.

"Looks like we should get back. They might need some help at the marina."

When the two arrived at the marina, Jase helped his uncle tie up at the pier. Inside the marina, Uncle Jack sat him down and gave him a hamburger and a bottle of soda pop. It was a day that Jase would never forget, a day with Uncle Jack. That was the last summer Jase saw Uncle Jack, but he never forgot his kindness and his smile.

Jase came out of his daydream. "That's it. Jill!" he yelled, as he ran up the steps. "Do you remember when I was little, and I spend the summers at the island?"

"Yes, I remember." Jill knew something was on his mind.

"Uncle Jack was just about the nicest person I have ever met. I think that we should call our son Jack. Uncle Jack would have liked that."

Jill did not have to think twice about it. She looked at the baby, "Hi Jack, welcome to the family."

Linda said, as she was holding the baby, "Well Jack, I am pleased to meet you."

Jase smiled at Jack. "Now Jack, when you get older, I will tell you about your Great Uncle Jack, the ship builder."

After Jack and Eva went to sleep, everyone came down to the living room. Linda said, "We can take care of things around here tomorrow, so why don't you try to go to work?"

"Maybe I will. It will be good to get back in the swing of things. Alright, it is settled, I will put in a full day. You two will have to do without me. Somehow, I don't think that will be a problem. Tomorrow night, I would like to take everyone out to dinner, if it is all right with you two?"

Jill and Linda looked at each other. "That would be fine, but it will depend on how the children are doing. Where would you like to go?"

"How about the little steak house outside of town? It's not very fancy, but the food is good and it's family friendly?"

Jill looked at Linda. "Sounds good to me, how about you, Linda?"

"Why not, we deserve a break. We have been at this for over two days now."

"Good, I will call from the lab. If everything is a go, I will call ahead for a table."

Linda stood up. "Well, I have the feeling that I might be up a little tonight. Jill, I will take the first shift. I might knock at your door, if I need help. I think that I will get some sleep."

"Linda, if one cries the other one will too, so I will be there. These first few nights will be something, I'm sure."

Linda smiled and went upstairs. When she got to her room, she made sure that no one else could hear her as she made her first call.

"Ann, this is Linda. Everything is fine. The doctor is going to work in the morning. Jill and I will watch the children all day, and then we are going out tomorrow night for dinner. I will let you know if anything turns up."

"Sounds good, I will call Michael and let him know."

A block away from the doctor's house, a phone rang in a car. "This is Michael."

"This is Ann, Linda is on location and operation Brick is a go."

"Thank you, keep me updated." Michael hung up.

The next day started off pleasantly enough. After watching Jill and Linda feed the children, Jase was ready to leave. "Goodbye Eva, goodbye Jack," he said with a smile. "Goodbye ladies," he said as he walked out the door.

The Professor was waiting for him at the lab. "Hell Brick, you're late. We have a lot to do today."

"What do we have to do?" he asked.

"First thing, we have to be ready for your visitor tomorrow. Second, have you checked the lab for bugs lately?"

Jase reached for the bug finder on his belt. "Let's check." After scanning the lab and the office, the Professor was satisfied.

"Now, what can I do to help. Are you going to work on the laser?"

"Not today. I thought that you didn't want me working on it until we know who we are up against."

"Just testing you, Brick. We don't want them to know everything yet."

The two men agreed that for now, they needed to get ready for the visit with Allan Smith.

"Are you going to be here?" asked Jase.

"Let me know when he arrives. I might drop in. And Brick, how is the new recruit doing?"

"Linda is doing fine. I don't know what we would do without her. We are all going out to eat tonight, if the babies are up to it. We are going to your favorite place."

"The VFW?"

"No, the steak house. Would you like to meet us there?"

"Just let me know when, Brick."

They worked nonstop all day. The Professor was in the lab with the laser cleaning up, and Jase was in his office checking his notes.

The Professor walked into the office. "Are you buying dinner tonight? You have worked me all day without a break."

"You never know, I might. Are you ready to take off? I am just wrapping up here."

"Yeah, just give me a call when you find out what you are doing."

"Will do, and thanks for the help, Professor."

They both left the lab. Jase watched the Professor get in his new used car and drive away. Then he went home to his family.

"Well, the house is still there. That is a good sign," Jase said to himself. He walked into see Jill and Linda sitting at the table. "How was your day?" he asked.

Jill said, "Nonstop, but it was great. You should have seen Jack. He smiled all day. How could anyone ever give him up?"

Linda spoke up, "Well, no one will again. He sure has found a loving home here."

Jill turned toward Jase. "Are we still on for tonight? This will be our first outing together. I can taste the steak already, how about you, Linda?"

"I would love to go. I don't eat red meat, but I'm looking forward to being with all of you."

"Good, it is settled then. I invited the Professor, if that is all right?"

"Eva and Jack will like that. And you never know, we might need a sitter someday."

Jase answered, "Not right away, I hope. When would you two like to go?"

"After we feed the kids, which should give us a little more time to eat.

"But not much," Linda laughed.

"I will call the steak house."

Before long, one of the children woke up, and soon the other was also awake. Jill and Linda went into action. When Jase heard the commotion, he was on the phone to the steak house.

"Hi, I would like to reserve a table for dinner. There will be four adults and two babies. We will be there in about forty five minute."

The host from the restaurant answered. "That should be fine. What is the name of your party?"

"The Brick family," Jase answered.

"Dr. Brick, we haven't seen you in a while. Sounds like you have been busy. We will look forward to seeing you."

"Thank you," Jase said.

Next, he called the Professor. "Professor, we will see you in about forty five minutes at the steak house."

"Jase, did you call the Professor?" Jill asked.

"I left a message for him. He will be there, I have never seen him miss a free dinner. Linda, you might as well ride with Jill and me. No sense in taking two cars."

"That sounds good to me."

The steak house sat right outside of town. It was long brick building with a very cozy atmosphere, and always had a good crowd. Before the Bricks arrived, four men walked into the restaurant. They were greeted at the door by the owner.

"Good evening, gentlemen, do you have a reservation?"

The large man standing in front of the rest answered, "No, we just need to have a little dinner."

"I'm sorry, but there will be a slight wait before we can seat you."

The man answered. "That table over there is empty, we will take it."

"That table is reserved and the party should be here anytime. Sorry, but you will have to wait. Can I seat you at the bar until we have a table for you?"

The man was getting louder and was starting to make a scene. People in the restaurant were beginning to watch.

"If that is the best you can do in this chicken shit place." The men started to go over to the bar and take a seat.

Dom, the owner, stopped the men. "Gentlemen, I have reconsidered. This is a family restaurant, and I don't want any trouble. I think that you should leave. Maybe someday if you can behave yourselves, you can come back, but not tonight."

The men started to mumble.

Dom said, "Do I have to call the police?"

The men started to walk to the door.

Jase and his family were just arriving, unaware of what was going on in the steak house. They pulled into the parking lot and parked. Jase was carrying Jack and Jill had Eva. Linda was right behind them.

"Jase, I forgot my purse in the van, can I have your keys?"

Jase smiled and handed Linda his keys. "Do you want us to wait?"

"No, go get the table. I will be right there."

Jill was about to the door, when it opened sharply. Out came the four men who were asked to leave. When they saw Jill and Eva, they tipped there ball hats. But when they saw Jase carrying Jack, their attitude changed. Linda turned and watched.

"What is wrong with this picture?" The man in front of the others said, and he pointed to Jack.

Jase ignored them and walked by. Dom came over to meet them. "Did those men give you any problem? I just asked them to leave."

"No, but Linda is still outside. Would you mind checking on her?"

Linda kept a close watch on the men, as they came over to the car next to the van.

"Hey there sweet thing," one of the men said.

Linda did not turn around. This made the man angry.

He reached over and touched her on the shoulder, which turned out was the wrong thing to do.

Just as the man reached out for Linda, a red car pulled up. Before the Professor could turn off his motor, Linda had the man's arm and pinned him against the van.

"I don't think that I like you, so the best thing you can do is get in your car when I let you go. Do you understand?"

Linda did not even work up sweat. The Professor watched with his his hand on the door handle.

"Do you understand?" Linda asked again.

This time the man nodded his head yes.

As soon as she let him go, he came at her with the others right behind. Before the Professor could open his door, Linda hit the first man in his neck. The next one she kicked in the side of the head. With two men down, the other two came at her.

"Well hell, Linda, you can't have all the fun." The Professor went low and took the feet out from under the third man. He went down with the other two. All that was left was the big man with the loud mouth.

Linda pushed his fist away and hit him in the nose with her palm. Then when he bent over, she hit both of his ears with her palms at the same time. He went down with blood coming out of his ears and nose.

Linda retrieved her purse from the van, "Why Professor, you have a little dirt on your leg."

One of the men started to get up and he reached for Linda. She turned his hand over and bent it backward, holding his upper arm with one finger. "Now, do I have to break your arm or are you going to be nice?"

He called her a bitch.

"Wrong answer," Linda ran the man's head into a light pole. All of the men lay on the ground.

The Professor was watching Linda. "I think that you are more than just a babysitter."

With her cover blown, Linda took out her cell phone. "This is Linda, I need a clean up in the parking lot of Dom's Steakhouse, four white trash on the ground." She brushed herself off and looked at the Professor.

"I think that you and I need to talk, Professor, but not tonight. I don't want to spoil the night for the Bricks."

The Professor put his arm out and he and Linda walked across the parking lot and into the restaurant.

Dom was coming out the door. "Did you see where those men went that just came out?" he asked.

"I didn't, how about you, Professor?"

"Sorry, I just pulled up." They all went inside.

"We thought we were going to have to send a search party for you," Jill said.

"No, the Professor pulled up and I waited for him." Linda winked at the Professor.

"Jase, this is going to cost you," the Professor laughed. "Linda, how would you like to see where I work, if you ever have a chance to get away from the Bricks for a while?"

Jill and Jase raised their heads at the same time.

"I would like that. Would you like to go for lunch first?" she answered. "How about it, Jill, could I borrow Linda for a little while tomorrow?"

"Sure, I think that would be great."

Outside in the parking lot, a van was loading up the men. Michael was watching from across the street and shaking his head in disappointment.

Chapter 28

This had turned out to be one of the best nights Linda could remember in years. "I feel like I'm part of the family, she told the dinner party."

Jill responded, "Linda, you you are part of the family." The Professor watched Linda for the rest of the night.

Jack was the first to start to cry, then Eva. They had finished eating, so they called it a night. No one mentioned the little incident that happened outside. Jase paid the bill, and then they went out to the van.

"Jase," Jill said, "This looks like blood on the ground next to the van."

Jase came over to the side of the van. "Yes, it does. I hope that no one was hurt." Then he went back to the driver side and got in.

The Professor smiled at Linda and closed the back door for her. Jase and Jill were surprised, but they did not say anything.

"See you people tomorrow." The Professor grinned at Linda. She waved at him and smiled.

They pulled away, and he watched the van fade into the distance. He walked over to his car mumbling and trying to figure out what had happened tonight. Then he drove back to the VFW for his nightcap.

As he sat down at the bar, the bartender asked, "Professor, you have the look of the curious cat, and you know what happened to that cat?"

"That is exactly how I feel," he said and ordered a drink.

Back at the house, Linda and Jill were putting the children to bed. Jase was happy to sit and read a book. For now, all was good at the Brick's home.

Across town, Ann's phone started to ring. "Where do you want the white trash?"

"How bad are they hurt?" Ann said in a calm voice.

"Pretty bad, they will never be the same after tonight. What do you want done with them?"

Ann sighed, "Make it look like they were on drugs and got in to a fight. Leave them somewhere outside of town, maybe at a road side park. If they die, they die. Michael would be proud of me," she thought. She ended the call and went about her business.

After Jill and Linda got the children in bed for the night, Linda called to check in with Ann. Ann picked up the phone and said, "What the hell happened tonight, Linda?"

"Wrong place at the wrong time, did I kill anyone?"

"Doesn't look like it, but damn girl, you sure altered the rest of their lives. What did they do anyway?"

"They crossed the line. They thought I would be their date for the night. It did not work out in their favor."

"Linda, did anyone see it?"

After a short pause, she said, "The Professor did. He even took one of the men down himself."

"What did he say?"

"Nothing, but he would like to have lunch with me tomorrow. I told him that would be fine."

"What are you going to tell him?"

"Nothing, I happen to know a little self defense and it sure came in handy for me."

"Well Linda, I hope that he buys it. Let me know how that goes for you."

"I will, talk to you tomorrow."

The next morning everything seemed normal. Fall was around the corner, and some of the fields were almost ready to be harvested. Students were starting to arrive for check-in on the campus. Everyone at the Brick's house was up early. Jase had left for the lab, and the women had their hands full with the children. No one had time to think about what happened at the steakhouse last night except for the Professor.

He started running Linda's name through channels that he had not used in years. There were not many of his old friends left at the agency, but he found one. He called that old friend using one of the phones he bought from the mart.

"Professor, how are you? I didn't know if you were still around. What can I do for you?"

"I want you to check on a name for me, Linda Peach. I think she might be working with the agency. Can you check it out without anyone finding out about it?"

"That is a big order, Professor. You know I am not supposed to give that information out. I could lose my job."

'Well hell, are you going to do it or not?"

"What is the name?" he said with a sigh.

"Linda Peach, she is a nurse. Be careful, and when you get something, call me at this number. It will be good for a week. If I don't hear from you by then it won't matter anyway."

"Professor, this sounds big time."

"It is, watch your step. And thanks."

When the Professor got to the lab, he found Jase deep in his work.

"Well hell, are you going to sleep all day?"

Jase looked up. "Hi Professor, hey, what is going on with you and Linda? You two sure hit it off last night."

"Hit it off is a good way to put it, Jase. Is this the day when the guy is coming to meet you?"

"Allan Smith, yes, he will call when he gets in. He has his own jet."

"Never met anyone with their own jet," answered the Professor.

"He should be calling anytime. I'll keep you posted."

"Good, but if you have to call, use the unlisted phone. I used it this morning, so by the end of the week, I will get new number."

Jase was just about to say something back, when his phone rang.

"Dr. Brick this is Allan Smith. I'm at the airport. I have arranged for a car to pick you up, and it should arrive at any minute. It will bring you back here, if that will be all right."

Surprised, Jase answered, "That's fine, and how long will our meeting last?"

"That is up to you. I have just been informed the car is outside of your lab. See you soon." He hung up.

"Professor, look outside the front of the lab. Do you see anything?"

"Yeah, a limo, is he coming in?"

"No, I'm going to the airport. I'll call you when I know something."

"Be careful, Jase. Hell, you're the only one who buys me steak. Linda is going to have lunch with me. It should prove to be a very interesting day."

Jase nodded. "Yes, this day should prove interesting, to say the least."

"I'll wait in here until you leave. Good luck."

Jase walked outside. The driver was waiting with the door open. "Good morning, Dr. Brick. Mr. Smith is waiting for you."

Jase got in, and the door closed behind him. The driver seated himself behind the wheel. Not another word was spoken for the entire trip. When they arrived at the airport, they were escorted through the VIP entrance and pulled up to a small Leer jet. The driver got out and opened the door. "Mr. Smith is waiting for you in the jet."

As he entered the jet, he saw Allan Smith standing next to the door. "Glad you could make it, Dr. Brick. There is someone I would like you to meet. They walk back to the seats in the rear of the jet.

"Dr. Brick, this is Blake Canond."

Chapter 29

Jase offered his hand in a greeting. "Dr. Brick, Mr. Canond does not touch anyone," said Allan.

"Have a seat, Dr. Brick." Blake Canond pointed to a chair. "I think that we have a lot to talk about. Allan has told me about your research, and I'm very impressed. Does your research also involve melanoma?"

Jase was star stuck, but he got an answer out. "Yes, it does."

"Good, let me tell you a little about myself. Two weeks before your demonstration at your lab, I had surgery to remove a mole. This mole turned out to be stage three cancer. My personal doctor has been reading your papers, and he is also very impressed. He said that I have about four to six months to live. Dr. Brick, I'm only fifty one years old, with a young family. I will not accept my doctor's prognosis. Have you ever cured melanoma?"

"Only on paper, Mr. Canond, but I'm sure that I can. Is the cancer in your lymph nodes, and did they remove them?"

"My lymph nodes were not showing any signs of contamination at the time of my surgery, and I would not let the surgeons remove them."

Jase said, "Good, can I see where the melanoma was located? And, from this time forward, I will be touching you."

"Agreed, go ahead. The area is on my right flank."

"I need you to stand up and remove or pull up your shirt."

Jase looked at the scar, and then he checked under his arm pit for anything that looked suspicious "Do you have the lab report?"

Allan Smith handed the report to him. Jase sat back and started to read it.

"Now, Dr. Brick, no one knows about this. If word was to get out, my company stock would collapse. There are literally billions of dollars at stake."

Jase kept reading the report. "Blake, from now on, we are on a first name basis, all right?"

"That would be fine, Jase. I like that better anyway. There are not many people that I call by their first names. You and Allan are two. Can you help me, and what are you going to do next?"

"Well, I cannot treat you here. You need to be in a hospital."

Allan spoke up, "That won't do. The public must not know anything about this. We cannot afford any leaks."

"You are making this hard for me, Blake. This is a very fast moving cancer, and we need to address this right away. So, where are we going to do this?"

Allan spoke up again. "Many times a year, Mr. Canon's jet is parked at one of two airports. It is at one of them now, with a complete surgical suite and full staff."

Jase looked at Allan, "Is that normal?"

"Yes, even now it is about one hour away parked in Chicago."

This time Blake spoke. "As you know, Jase, I'm one of the richest people in the world, If I die, not only will I be gone, but my empire will be in shambles. My family does not know about my cancer. My children are young, and they will be taken care of. But the thousands of people who work for me and their families will suffer. Now, what is our next step?"

"First, I must go back to my lab. I need to prepare a chelation compound that should work for your cancer. Allan, have your car outside my lab in the morning. We are going to Chicago. I will need a small amount of money to get started."

"Jase, Mr. Canond is prepared to give you a cash advance today. We don't want any checks to be traced back to him. The less the public knows, the better. Whatever you need, we will give you before you leave."

Blake raised his hand. "Jase, if you can do what you say you can, this is my offer, because you are going to need some help. There are people in the medical profession that will try to stop you. I have a small island off the gulf coast that is at your disposal for your research. And, I will give you one half of everything that I own. This is a deal of a life time, mine."

"I want copies of all the scans, x-rays and anything else that you have that I can use. Is your personal doctor going to be there? I would like to consult with him."

Allan answered, "We have everything you need right here." Allan handed Jase a folder.

Jase looked at Allan. "I will be ready to go first thing in the morning. And please, if you have to call me, be very careful what you say. My home was bugged and my phones probably are also."

Jase stood and offered his hand to Blake. This time Blake reached out and took it. "I have a lot of work to do tonight, so I must be going. The sooner we get you started, the better. Were you joking about the island and the money?"

"I don't think that Mr. Canond jokes very much about money," replied Allan.

Allan and Jase left Blake, and Allan walked Jase to the limo. "This briefcase should be enough to get you started. I will see you tomorrow. And thank you, Blake is a good friend. Please take good care of him."

"Until tomorrow," Jase said. He sat back quietly in his seat as he was whisked away and back to the lab. The jet was starting to move before the car was out of sight.

Jase arrived back at the lab as the phone was ringing. "Hello, this is Dr. Brick."

"Well hell, Brick, I thought you were never going to call."

"Professor, meet me at the lab ASAP."

"Right after Linda and I have lunch, is that all right?"

"It will have to be. And bring me a sandwich, this is going to be a long day."

"What the hell is going on Brick?"

"I can't say yet. Don't forget the sandwich." Jase hung up. He didn't want to say anything to Blake, but the clock was ticking fast and it was not in his favor. He had a lot to do.

He picked up his cell phone and called Jill. "How is your day going?"

"Jase, what is wrong? I can tell by your voice that something has changed."

"Jill, is there any chance that Linda can watch the kids? I am going to need some help this afternoon."

"I'm sure she can, but what is going on, Jase?"

"I will explain when you get here. Linda and the Professor are having lunch today. When he brings her back, have him bring you to the lab. I will explain everything then."

On the other side of town a phone rang. "This is Michael."

"Michael, Dr. Brick was taken to the airport, and he boarded a private jet. He was there for over an hour. A limo brought him back to the lab, and he called his wife shortly after that. He told her that he was going to need some help today and to let the nurse keep the kids."

"Thanks, let me know if you hear anything else."

Michael called Ann. "Ann, this is Michael, I will be coming in this afternoon. We are going to have a meeting. I will call you when I get there."

"I look forward to seeing you, Michael." Michael hung up before she was done talking.

The Professor pulled up outside Brick's house. He started to get out, but Linda was all ready coming down the walk.

"This is going to be a quick lunch. Jase called Jill, and said that he needed her to come to the lab as soon as we are done. He also asked if you could bring her back to the lab."

The Professor turned toward Linda. "You know, Linda, I really like you, but you are not who you say you are. I think that the Brick's are in over their head, and they are going to need some help, so why don't you come clean? Are you working for the agency? I will find out soon enough, with your help or without it."

"Professor, what are you hungry for? I am buying."

"That's more like it. We are going to the best place in town. Have you ever been to the VFW?"

"No, I have not, is it nice?"

"It's nice and quiet. We need to talk."

They walked into the club, and the bartender waved at the Professor. They sat at one of the tables away from the rest of the customers.

The bartender came over. "None of my business, but there are only four people in here. Why do I have to walk clear over here to take your order?"

The Professor was quick with his reply. "Right, you are not very busy and we are hungry. Give us two specials and put a rush on it." The bartender left. "Now Linda, tell me what the hell is going on?"

"Professor, up until this week I did work for the agency. I don't know what they want with the Brick's research, but it must be very important. Hear me out, Professor, I love those children, and I will not let anything happen to the Brick family."

"I believe you, Linda. For now, let's keep this from the Bricks, agreed?"

"Agreed, now what is going on at the lab? Jill said that Jase was really stressed with some project. Do you have any idea what it is?"

"Not yet, but when I take Jill back after lunch, I will try to find out what the emergency is."

The bartender came with the food. "Two specials and two gin and Squirts."

"This is what you eat for lunch every day?"

"Hell Linda, you pulled the corned beef off your Rueben." She washed what was left of the sandwich down with the gin and squirt.

"Professor, this thing is going to get worse. There are a lot of companies out there who are making money treating cancer, and they don't want anyone screwing that up. We have not even seen them get into the picture yet."

"I know, and I know the agency. They could not give a shit about Brick's compound. What are we missing?" they finished their lunch.

"Are you ready to go back? Wasn't that about the best lunch you have ever had?"

"I'm not even going to answer that ridiculous question, Professor. How you can eat like this each day and still be alive is beyond me."

"I have all the food groups. Alcohol kills any germs, meat provides protein that makes me strong and bread for carbohydrates. I forget what the last one is."

Linda shook her head in amazement. "I think we had better go back now."

They walked up to the bar. "This one is on me," said the Professor.

"I would hope so," Linda replied.

When they came into the house, Jill was in the kitchen. "How was your lunch?"

"I have never had a lunch like it. It was truly one of a kind."

Jill turned and looked at the Professor. "You didn't take her to the club, did you?"

He smiled back.

"Oh Professor, how could you. Linda, there are some sandwiches made in the fridge. The kids are asleep in their bedroom. They should be good for awhile. Call me if you need anything."

Jill gave the Professor a dirty look. "How could you?" she asked again. "Come on let's go." She handed the Professor a lunch for Jase. "He might need this."

The Professor grinned at Linda. "See you later."

"Not if I can help it." Jill said. She was reading him the riot act as they walked out the door.

Linda was giggling as she went up the steps to check on the children. They were both fast asleep. Her phone starts to vibrate, and it was Michael. "Yes Michael?" She said as she walked down the steps.

"Linda, what is going on at the lab?"

"I don't know yet, but it must be important. You mean you didn't cause it, Michael? That must be a first."

"Linda, find out."

"Sorry Michael, I have two little children to take care of. I'm sure when the Bricks get back, they will let me know. And remember Michael, I retire at the end of this week, don't forget."

"Linda, you retire when I say you retire. This is one of the most important assignments you have ever been on."

"Michael, what on earth can the agency want with Brick's chelating research?"

"Who said we wanted that? Now keep your eyes open and let me know when you find something out."

"Got to go Michael, the babies are crying. See you later."

The babies were still asleep. "Those little kids are great. That is the first time I could ever hang up on Michael and get away with it."

Jill and the Professor pulled up in front of the building and went into the lab. "Good, you two are here. I can't say too much, but I have a client that will die if he doesn't get treated. I need you two to help me prepare a chelation compound. I'm leaving first thing in the morning, and it all is top secret. You can't tell anyone."

"Jase, did you run a scan in the lab today?" Jase handed the scanner to the Professor.

"What is that, Jase?" asked Jill.

"Just a little precaution to make sure that no one else is ease dropping in on us."

"How long have you been doing this, Jase?"

"Ever since our home was bugged. I have been scanning the new house too. Right Professor?"

Jill turned sharply and looked at the Professor. "You two knew about this and did not bother to tell me?"

"Jill, it is not the Professor's fault. I did not want to worry you. You have enough going on with the children and the new house."

The Professor said, "Jill, we didn't find anything. There is nothing to worry about, but we are not taking any chances. You have your hands full, that is all."

Jill was still a little pissed. "Alright Jase, if you want my help, then no more secrets."

"Today, I met with Blake Canond."

"The billionaire, Blake Canond?" Both the Professor and Jill said at the same time.

"Yes and what I am going to tell you has to stay here. There are billions of dollars at risk."

"Go on," Jill said.

"He has stage three melanoma. If any one finds out about it, his companies will fall apart overnight. This could affect the world, not just him. There is a lot at stake here. Can I count on both of you?"

"How about Linda, she knows something is going on?" asked Jill

"We can't tell her yet, but I think that we can trust her. Professor, would you mind staying close to the house for a few days? I will be flying out in the morning to treat Mr. Canond."

"Jase, how are you going to buy everything that you need? This is going to cost a lot of money," asked Jill.

"Professor, in that brief case on the desk there should be some money. Will you open it and count it for me?"

The Professor walked over to the desk, "This brief case, Brick?"

"Yes, is it locked? I never checked."

"Doesn't look like it." The Professor opened the case. "Jill, could you come over here a minute?"

Jill walked over to the case. "Jase, honey, didn't you look inside of the case?"

Alarmed, Jase looked up and then slowly walked over to the desk. "They didn't leave me a check did they? They were supposed to put a little cash in there."

The Professor turned the case around and pulled the lid back. "How much money did they say they were going to give you?"

Jase looked into the briefcase. It contained more money than he had ever seen in his life.

"Oh my God, I was carrying all that money around? How much do you think is in there?"

The Professor reached over and pulled out a sheet of paper. "If you go by this sheet of paper, and I see no reason that we should not, $500,000."

"I left it set on the desk all day, even when I was out of the room. Do you realize what could have happened? Do you…"

Jill stopped him. "Settle down, nothing happened. Would it be all right if I put this in the safe for you?"

Jase just nodded. They had a small fire safe at the back of the lab. Jase used it for samples and sometimes things that were a fire hazard.

"Jase, do you think that we could take a chance and remove some of the solvents out of the safe for now?"

Jase smiled and said, "I think that might be all right."

"Professor, I will need coolers, plastic bags and ice. I also need you to pick up a few things at the pharmacy. I have already called them, and everything should be ready within the hour."

"Jill, could you help me mix some of the compounds. I need enough for a sixty day supply."

"Well Brick, I guess I will be off," said the Professor.

"Thanks Pro," Jase replied.

"Pro, what the hell is Pro? No one calls me Pro." The Professor started to walk out waving his hands. He stopped dead in his tracks and turned.

"Hell Brick, do you have any money?"

Chapter 30

At 5:00 pm, Jill called Linda. "Linda, I'm so sorry, how is it going?"

"Don't worry about a thing. The two little ones are fine. I can't remember when I have had so much fun. So how is the emergency coming?"

"We are almost done. I will explain when I get back. Jase can finish up, and then the Professor can drop him off at the house. He has to leave early in the morning. You are a life saver Linda, thank you." Jill hung up.

Jase said, "Jill, we can't tell Linda what we are doing, so keep that in mind. Let's get Mr. Canond back on his feet."

"Jase, I think that we can trust Linda."

"Right now no one else can know except you, me and the Professor."

Within the hour, Jill wrapped up. "Jase, I'm going home and give Linda a break. Try to get home as soon as you can."

When she left for home, Jase called the campus security. "This is Dr. Brick, could you keep an extra watch on the lab tonight? I have some research that is almost ready. If anyone broke into the lab, it would take me weeks to replace it."

"Sure thing doc, but I will need to call Dean Charles and clear it."

"I will call him for you. If you see any one around here, call me at once." Then Jase dialed the Dean's number. "Hi Dean Charles, this is Jase. I have a favor to ask."

"Anything I can do, Jase."

"Tonight, I have a very important project going on. I have asked the security to keep an extra watch on the building, if that is all right with you?"

"No problem, Jase. By the way, Mr. Greyger called to say hello and said that he would be in town the next few days. Can we stop by tomorrow to see you?"

"Tomorrow will be bad. In the morning, I have to fly out to see a sick friend, how about the next day?"

"I will ask Mr. Greyger and get back with you."

"Sounds good, I look forward to seeing both of you." Jase hung up.

"Hey Professor, how is it going out there?"

"Hell Brick, today is going to cost you." He walked into the lab.

"I'm glad you don't need the laser. That would be a bitch right now."

"It is good that we don't. If I'm right, his cancer is already starting to spread. I need to get it stopped before it is too late. But have the laser ready. If it has spread, we will need everything we have to stop it."

"Are we done here, Brick?"

"I think so, let's pack up. Will you drop me off on your way to the club?"

They exchange grins. "Why I would be happy to, but don't ever call me Pro again, agreed?"

"I promise."

As they walked out of the lab, a security guard stood outside the building. "Good night, Dr. Brick," he said. Jase and the Professor waved. "Good night."

When they pulled up in front of the Brick's home, the Professor said, "I think that I will come in and say hello."

"Why Professor, do you have something going on with Linda?"

"You never know Brick."

It was about dark when they entered, and the house was quiet. They could hear noise coming from upstairs. Jill and Linda came down the steps holding the babies.

"You know, after a rough day, just seeing this bunch makes me feel good," said Jase.

Jase took Jack from Linda. "How are you son? We need to talk. Why don't we go over here and sit down." The little boy watched Jase as he sat down. When Jack saw the Professor standing there, he let out a scream and kept screaming.

"Here Dad," Linda said as she took the baby back. "Did that mean old Professor scare you? Sometimes he scares me."

Jack soon settled down. Jase went over to Jill and reached for Eva. "Don't worry we won't look at the scary man." The Professor rubbed his beard and grinned.

"Jill, I talked to Dean Charles. He said that Michael was back in town. Maybe we could hook up while he is here."

"That would be nice."

The Professor and Linda watched each other, afraid to say anything.

"Linda, you have had a big day. Do you two want to go out or anything?" asked Jill.

"Jill, the Professor and I are…" before she could finish, the Professor answered. "That would be nice. Are you sure you can do without her for an hour?"

Jase answered this time. "After the day we have put in, I think you two should go out for a drink."

"Let me go up to my room. I will be right back." Linda walked up to her room and opened the door without turning the light on. She closed the door and went over to the window. She looked to see if there was any one keeping tabs on the house. Two blocks down and facing the house, a white car was parked? She could see the light of a cell phone, and someone was talking, "Michael, you bastard."

Linda pulled her phone out of her pocket and dialed Michael's number, then watched.

"Hi Linda, how are you. Is that you at the upstairs window?"

"Michael, what are you doing here? How long have you watching us?"

"What was Dr. Brick doing in the jet today at the airport?"

"You have all the connections, and I'm sure that you know who the jet belongs to."

"We are looking into it, and I should know shortly. I thought maybe you would know what Jase was doing. He is your assignment, remember."

"What do you really want, Michael?"

"I want the God damn laser."

Linda was shocked. "That is what this is about, the laser? You could not give a shit about the cancer cure. You just want the laser. What is so damned important about the laser?"

"Linda, this is a national security issue. For you everything it is on a need-to- know basis, and right now, you don't need to know."

"Michael, if you don't tell me the truth about this operation, you can count me out. I will retire."

"Settle down, Linda. Don't do anything you will be sorry for."

"I'm leaving with Professor Williams in a little while. Don't have me followed. I will try to find out what is going on, and I will call you tomorrow."

"I will call Richard tonight. If he agrees, I will bring you up to speed on the project."

"These are nice people, so don't fuck with me."

The line went dead and Linda realized what she had done. Michael had people eliminated for less than she had said. She got her purse and went down the steps.

"Are you ready, Professor," she asked?

As they walked out, she could see that Michael was on his cell phone again. The Professor saw her looking in the direction of the parked car.

"Is that a friend of yours?"

"Keep walking Professor, and let's get into the car."

When they were in the car, the Professor turned to look at Linda. "Linda, you're shaking."

"Drive, Professor."

"Where would you like to go?"

"How about the VFW, I could use a drink. Do you think it will be busy tonight?"

"No, shouldn't be too bad. Who was in the car?"

"Michael, he has been watching us all night."

"That is not exactly true. I have seen that car around for over a week, and it is pretty hard to miss. I used to have one about like it. It is a standard government issue."

Linda started to laugh, "Professor, we have got to talk. I think the VFW is the perfect place. They won't let Michael in."

Michael slammed his phone down. "No one talks to me like that," he said. He called Richard. "We have a problem. Linda is getting attached to the Bricks, and now she wants to know about the project. Should I let her in or get rid of her."

There was a pause. "Michael, she is an important part of this project, so we can't get rid of her because you want to. What happened, did she say something that upset you? You are lucky she wasn't with you."

"How did you know I talked to her on the phone?"

"Michael, if you had pissed her off in person, she would have ripped you apart. She has more black belts then you have brains. I don't see why we can't tell her about the project. Maybe that would speed up the process."

"Alright, I will call to her tomorrow. Good night."

Linda and the Professor walked into the club. Everyone was at the bar, so they headed for the back tables.

The bartender came over. "I see that you are going to make me work tonight Professor. What can I get for you two?"

Linda held up her hand. "This time, Professor, I think that I can order for myself. Do you have any thing that does not have meat in it? And I would like two gin & Squirts."

The bartender answered, "Cheese plate and a salad."

"Put some ranch dressing on it, and we have a deal."

He looked at the Professor. Give me two gin & Squirts and a burger with mustard and pickle."

"Professor, you dumbass, one of the drinks I ordered is for you."

"That's all right, we can handle them."

The bartender shook his head, grinned and walked away.

The Professor's phone started to vibrate. "Professor, can you talk? Do you know how hard it is to find a pay phone these days?"

"Yes, what did you find out about Miss Peach?"

Linda was listening, but didn't say a word.

"She does work for the agency. She is ready to retire, but they brought her back for one more project, real top secret stuff. She has three black belts, and she could snap you in half in a heartbeat. Oh, one more thing. Richard is calling the shots on this one, so don't call me again unless it is for my birthday or something."

"Three black belts, you don't say. Thanks, I owe you."

Linda was pissed. "You had me checked out?"

"Well hell, you had me checked out."

"No, I did not! It must have been Michael."

"Ok Linda, what are they after? It can't be Brick's cancer research, but when the medical industry finds out that he has a cancer cure, they may want to kill him. He will put the cancer centers out of business overnight."

"No, Michael wants the laser. Why, I don't know. He is the one who ransacked the lab. Don't tell Jase and Jill. They would not believe you anyway. That's all I know. Michael is going to meet me tomorrow, and he will either tell me everything, or kill me. If you don't see me tomorrow, you will know what happened. Professor, what is Dr. Brick doing tomorrow?"

"He has a friend that has cancer, and he is trying to save his life. That is all I know. Brick and Jill were mixing stuff up all day. A plane will pick him up in the morning, and if all goes well, he should be back tomorrow night. Tell Michael, that Jase has a sick friend with cancer, but he does not need the laser for this one. That should slow Michael down."

"Why is the laser so important? Why does Michael want it so bad?" asked Linda.

"Don't know, Jase is all wrapped up in his chelating stuff. He does not talk about the laser."

174

"Professor, the laser does not belong to Jase does it, it's yours. It's no wonder Michael couldn't find it. You have it."

"Linda, you can't say anything, do you hear me? If Michael gets his hands on the laser, he will destroy everyone who has anything to do with it. You know I'm right. See what you can find out tomorrow. We can't let him win this one. I will talk to you more tomorrow, right now your salad and cheese plate are on the way." The two were quietly thinking the rest of the night.

"Linda, I think I know how to fix this thing. You find out all you can, and I will take care of the laser. They hold up their drinks and make a toast to their newly formed friendship.

"Professor, you and the Bricks are the only friends that I have."

Chapter   31

The Professor dropped Linda off.

"Looks like Michael moved his car. I like it better when I can see him. Thanks Professor, see you tomorrow." Linda walked into house.

"How did your evening go?" asked Jill.

Linda looked at Jill and Jase. "Well hell, I don't know. See you two in the morning." She went up the stairs. Jase and Jill grinned at each other.

The morning arrived quickly. When Jase was ready to leave, Jill said. "You need to take a few things in case you have to stay for a day or so." She handed him a small bag.

"Even though I am only going for the day, I will miss you."
He kissed her goodbye and walked out the door.

When Jase arrived at the lab, Allan Smith was already there.

"Good morning, Dr. Brick."

"Allan, everything is ready. We need to load up. Can your driver help me?"

Allan motioned to the driver. He got out of the limo and opened the trunk. "Good morning, Dr. Brick."

As the driver finished loading the limo, Jase asked Allan, "Last night I looked into the briefcase. Why did you put so much money in it?"

"Blake wanted you to know he was serious, and Dr. Brick, he is scared."

"He has a right to be. Let's get going."

They drove to the airport, where a small jet was waiting. Jase and Allan walked up to entrance door. "Don't worry about your equipment, it is being loaded as we speak."

Only the staff was aboard, and soon the jet was in the air. Jase watched out the window as the airport disappeared and was replaced with blue sky. When the jet started to descend, Allan said, "Dr. Brick, Blake's personal doctor will be waiting on the plane. I thought that I would give you a heads up."

"Alright, he doesn't think I can do it, does he?"

"Something like that. Mr. Canond wants you to be in charge, so if Dr. Aunser wants to change anything you do, it is your call. Dr. Aunser has some of the best credentials in the world, but he goes by the book. Mr. Canond thinks that you are writing the book."

"So I should watch my back?" asked Jase.

Allan nodded, "Yes that would be a good thing to do. Now, Dr. Brick, you asked about the money. It is yours to use as you see fit, but please do not tell anyone that it came from Mr. Canond. His medical staff would walk off the job, if they knew of our offer to you."

"Last, but not least, Mr. Canond would like to offer you protection when you need it. It is only a matter of time, before your breakthrough is made public. At that time, you will have a target on your back. You will put the cancer treatment people out of business. We believe they will stop at nothing to keep your breakthrough from getting out. The general population won't know you ever existed. Jase, you need Blake as much as he needs you."

Allan glanced out the window, "Looks like we are coming in for a landing." The flight attendant came by to check seat belts and then disappeared.

As they departed from the jet, Jase saw a 747 sitting next to them on the tarmac. They walked from one jet to the other. As they entered the 747, they were met by Dr. Aunser. "Good morning, Dr. Brick. Let me show you our facility."

Jase had never seen a custom jet before. The ceiling had multi levels with indirect lighting throughout. All of the plush furniture had seat belts, and there was a fully stocked bar next to a staircase. Jase felt like he was walking into the lobby of a grand hotel.

"If you would follow me, Dr. Brick, I will show you our medical area." Jase followed the doctor down the steps.

"Because of the weight of the medical equipment and the possibility of interference with navigation, I had the area put in the center of the plane. It has its own air filtration system and operating room. We can perform about any kind of procedure right here. Mr. Canond is a very important man, and it is my job to make sure that nothing happens to him."

Jase watched the doctor as he spoke. "Now tell me, Dr. Brick, how do you plan to proceed?"

"First, I want to see all of his records including MRIs, CTs and x-rays, everything."

"Then what, Dr. Brick?"

"Then I will start the IV."

"What is in this IV?"

"It is a chelating compound that will help his body destroy cancer by removing toxins, metals and anything else that advances cancer cells. This, in turn, will strengthen Mr. Canond's own immune system."

"How can you stop this chelating compound from taking out what the body needs at the same time?" asked Dr. Aunser.

"That is why I need to review his records. Will you get them for me?"

Dr. Aunser did not like taking orders from some research doctor. He turned and went into the next room. "So this is Dr. Brick," he said to himself.

Allan Smith had come down to the Medical area. "How are you two getting along? Is there anything that I can do for you?"

Dr. Aunser answered, "No, go away."

Allan looked at Jase. "Dr. Brick, how about you?"

"Could you have Mr. Canond come down, we are about ready to start."

"I believe that Mr. Canond will be right down. He is looking forward to talking to you again, Dr. Brick."

Blake Canond had a Spanish accent. His tall frame and dark hair made him stand out. There was no doubt that he was in charge, when he walked into a room. Although he had a commanding demeanor, his smile was warm.

Blake Canond walked in. "Well, Dr. Brick, how do you like my jet? The good doctor here helped me design it. We had a mess getting all his equipment in, but we did it."

"I'm very impressed, but we need to get started as soon as we can. Now, can we fly somewhere?"

"Yes, I guess we can, but why?"

"My chelating compound has not been approved in the United States, and it could take years to be approved. But if we were over another country, I would not be breaking the law."

"Allan, would you tell the pilot that we would like to go to Canada, and then return when Dr. Brick is ready."

"I'll get right on it sir."

"Now, the first thing we are going to do is start the IV," Jase said.

"You haven't told me what is in the IV, Dr. Brick." Dr. Aunser was staring at Jase.

"That is right, I haven't. Other than me, there is only one person in the world that knows what is in it, and that is my wife."

Blake started to laugh, "I can see that you two have some issues. Just remember, we are all on the same team. Dr. Brick, Dr. Aunser will help you with anything that you need, so let's get started."

After that point, things went smoothly. Jase administered Blake's first IV. While Blake was sitting there, Jase went over the procedure with him.

"Blake, I'm going to change your diet. First, you cannot eat red meat."

"Oh my God, I did not expect that."

Jase smiled, "There are a lot of things in red meat, chemicals, hormones and who knows what else. Your body can fight cancer if you let it. Here is your new diet for the next two months. Your lymph nodes are a little swollen, but this IV should take of that. Any cancer in your body should attach itself to the chelating compound in the IV, and the body will dispose of it through your bowels. Now for the good stuff, Dr. Aunser, Blake will need a weekly enema."

"And Dr. Aunser, this is crucial. He must follow this diet to the letter, because the IV is taking some of the good stuff out along with the bad. If Mr. Canond does not follow this exactly, he will starve to death. Also, this will be a workout for the kidneys, so please keep a close watch on them."

Jase turned to Blake. "I think that you are going to be all right. Would you have Allan pick me up for the next few weeks on Mondays?"

Allan spoke up, "Dr. Brick, it would be my pleasure."

Jase turned to Dr. Aunser. "Is there anything else that you need?"

"No, Dr. Brick."

"Good, please call me day or night. Oh, and Blake, you might not want to go far from the restroom for a while."

Blake reached out to Jase, "Thank you, Jase." Dr. Aunser almost tried to stop Jase from shaking Mr. Canond's hand.

"Jase, how would you like to go home?" said Allan.

"That would be fine."

After the 747 landed, Allan and Jase walked to the smaller jet. Jase looked up, "Looks like we missed the sunset."

"Maybe not, we'll see." When they walked into the door of the smaller jet, Allan said, "Tell the pilot we are ready for immediate take off. We need to get this man home."

They already had clearance to take off. As the jet climbed high above the clouds, Allan said, "Come this way, Jase."

The door to the cockpit was opened. He was greeted by the pilot and the co-pilot. The pilot said, "Allan thought that you would like to see the sunset. Since we are going west it should be a good one."

Chapter 32

The small jet landed after dark. "Allan, will you call me tomorrow? Blake's cancer is picking up speed. I think we started the treatment in time, but we need to watch him very closely. Do you think Dr. Aunser will follow my instructions?"

"Yes, I know he will. I could tell he was impressed with you. I'll call you around lunchtime."

They shook hands, and Jase got into the waiting limo. The driver took Jase to the lab. When Jase got out of the car, he handed him his bag. "Goodnight doctor," he said.

The guard at the lab waved, and Jase waved back. Exhausted, he got into his van and went home. "I wonder how Jill and Linda got along today?" he said to himself.

After Jase left the next morning, everything was quiet. At lunch, Linda helped feed the babies and get them down for a nap.

"I need a few things at the store. Do you need anything while I'm out, Jill?"

"No. When Jase gets back I might go out and get a few things, but I'm good for now."

Linda went up to her room and peeked out the window. "No Michael, I don't know if that is good or bad," she thought.

She walked down the steps and said, "I'm leaving Jill." As soon as she was in her car, her phone rang.

"I didn't think you were ever going to leave."

"Where are you, Michael? Have you been watching me again?"

"Settle down and meet me over at the park. I have a white Ford, but you know that."

"I'm on my way," she answered.

Linda had no problem finding Michael. She pulled up next to his car and got out. Michael was sitting on a bench not far away. Linda walked over slowly and sat down.

"Well, Linda, what did you find out? Where is Dr. Brick going in the limo?"

"There is someone he knows personally that has cancer. He is trying to save his life, and that is all I know. No one is saying who he is. What did you find out?"

"Richard said to bring you up to speed. We need that laser to take out a target. Richard thinks that if we can use this new laser, we can take out our target right in front of everyone. It will look like a heart attack."

"You are still playing God, aren't you?"

"Call it what you want, but we will get that laser."

"How about Jase and Jill, what will happen to them?"

Michael paused, "I don't think Dr. Brick will survive long after he tells the world he has the cure for cancer. There is too much at stake, and too much money at risk. If he is smart, he will let someone buy him out, then he can go to an island somewhere and retire. He should have a good life."

"Alright Michael, I will see if I can get you the laser, but you leave the Brick family along."

"Linda, you seem to be getting attached to them. Are you?"

"If I get you the laser, you leave me and the Bricks along, agreed?"

Michael smiled, "Agreed. I guess we should have brought you in at the start. I see that now. You are doing a good job, Linda, thank you."

Linda got up from the bench and walked over to her car. Michael sat there as she drove away. She made a quick stop and picked up some flowers, then went back to the house.
She walked in with the flowers. "Do you think we could put this somewhere, Jill?"

"I think there is a vase under the sink, let's see."

"How long will Jase be gone?"

"I don't know, I hope he makes it back tonight. When he gets wrapped up in something like this, he will not stop until it is done."

"Jill, I don't understand what he doing?"

"I can't tell you details yet, but a good friend of Jase's has cancer. He was told that he has a short time to live. Jase is doing everything that he can to change that. He doesn't want anyone to know about it for now, because this is a very important person. Also, if Jase has to use his new compound, it has not been approved yet."

"Well, I hope that it all goes well for him."

"Once Jase gets his work approved, it could change the way we treat many diseases, not just cancer."

In her mind, Linda could here Michael voice, "I don't know if Dr. Brick will survive when his cancer cure gets out."

"Linda," Jill waved her hand in front of her. "You look like you are in a daze."

"Just daydreaming, now what are we doing next. I was only gone a short time, but I miss those two already."

The Professor was driving past Jase's lab. There were two cars out front. One belonged to Dean Charles, and the other was a white Ford.

"Michael!" he said. He turned in and parked next to the cars.

As the Professor entered the lab, he could hear Michael talking to the Dean. "Hell Michael, when did you get back?"

Michael turned around. "We were just talking about you. Are your ears burning?"

"Well maybe, what are you two up to? Jase is with a sick friend, and he won't be here today. If there is anything I can help you with, let me know." The Professor started to walk out.

Dean Charles said, "Do you know anything about the laser?"

The Professor's eyes opened wide, he smiled and he stopped and turned, "Not very much. What did you want to know?"

"Well, Michael was interested in how it works."

"I have heard Jase talk about it enough. It should not be that hard, but there are a few things he would not tell me. He had some crazy notion that it might be used as a weapon. How stupid is that?" He watched Michael's face as he talked. Dean Charles laughed, but Michael did not.

"How could it be used as a weapon, Professor?" asked Michael.

"Search me, but you know how seriously these researchers take their work. So what can I tell you?"

'What is the power source and how is it implemented?" Dean Charles continued to ask questions.

"Slow down, Dean, all I did was help Jase calibrate a few things. He should be back tomorrow. Michael, if you are here tomorrow, maybe he will tell you. I know just enough to be dangerous."

"I might stop tomorrow, Professor."

The Professor tried to look overwhelmed. "All right then, maybe I will see you tomorrow." The Professor turned and walked out.

"Come on Michael, let me show you the rest of the school," said Dean Charles.

Michael's heart was not in the tour, but he started to go along anyway. Then his phone rang. "Excuse me, Dean, but I have to take this."

Dean Charles said, "No problem."

"This is Michael. Hello Richard, right now I'm taking a tour of the lab with the Dean Charles. Sure, can I call you right back. Good. I'll talk to you in a short while."

Michael turned toward Dean Charles. "Something has come up, so the tour will have to wait, sorry."

"That's all right, Michael, maybe next time."

"Yes, next time. Right now I have to take a conference call in a couple minutes." Michael shook the Dean's hand and left the lab.

"I owe Richard one for getting me out of there." Michael thought as he called Richard.

Richard's phone rang. "Michael, I hope that you have good news for me."

"Not really, the key parts of the laser are missing. Brick hid them, because he thought that someone might use them as a weapon. He will be back tomorrow."

Richard paused for a minute. "Michael, we ran the number on the jet that Dr. Brick's was on. The plane is owned by Blake Canond. We don't know who is in the jet, but whoever it is, must be very important. Our window of opportunity is about to close. Do I make myself clear?"

"Yes Richard, you are very clear. I will do everything possible to get this wrapped up."

"No more excuses. I need it done now."

"Yes sir," Michael hung up. He would have to wait for Dr. Brick to come back tomorrow.

Michael drove back to the motel that he had stayed at before, and he was greeted with a warm welcome. He smiled and went to his room. He needed time to think. "How could he move things faster? Time was running out."

Richard also had to report in. As soon as he was done talking to Michael, he called Robert Lee Seaban.

Richard went out in front of his Washington office and used a pay phone. He called the number that he had memorized. The phone was answered with a standard recording. "The number that you have reached is not in working order. Please try again later."

After the phone beeped, Richard dialed 1861. A person on the other end of the phone answered. "My I help you?"

"Is your line secure?" asked Richard.

"Please enter your code number." Richard punched in 1776.

"Richard, how are you? How is our project coming?"

"Mr. Seaban, we have not acquired the project at this time. We need only to retrieve one small part for the project to be completed."

"Richard, must I remind you that I have pumped millions of dollars into this project. I have bought the media and have supported the far right ultras. These people are easy to manipulate, but we need the laser. These puppets can only do so much, and if this president is allowed to stay in office, she will complete everything that she said she would. If she gets the medical bill passed, it will hurt the medical insurance industry. We must finish this project. She must not be allowed to succeed. In forty five days, we will have our opportunity to complete the project. Money is not the problem, you are. Get it done!

"Yes sir." Richard slowly hung up the phone.

Robert Lee Seaban owned communication companies throughout the world. It is rumored that he had controlled the governments in many small countries, and now he has his eyes on the United States. But the first thing he had to do was win over the middle class, and so far, it has not been too hard. His organization has infiltrated the schools. He also controlled the press and broadcasting media. He was rumored to own at least three of the most powerful judges in the country, and many in the lower courts.

The Seaban family lost everything during the Civil War. They did not have to fight, because they owned slaves. While the poor were fighting for the South, the Seaban's family lived the good life until General Sherman arrived and took it all away.

For this act, the Seaban family took an oath of revenge. After the war, the family stayed in the cotton business. The Seaban family replaced their slaves with sharecroppers. Seaban's grandfather became even richer at the expense of someone else. He taught his family how to use capitalism to their advantage.

Five generations later, Robert Lee Seaban still carried on his family's oath for revenge.

He knew how to control the media to keep the country in a constant state of unrest. Robert Lee Seaban was a man who liked to be in control.

Richard knew not to cross Mr. Seaban. He had enough power to destroy him and his family, even death was an option. His latest project was to take out the first black woman President of the United States. Even Michael had no idea of the magnitude of the project. Michael was a good soldier, and he did what he was told without question.

Chapter   33

After his long day, Jase was glad to be home. He walked in to see Jill and Linda rocking the babies. They were almost asleep, so he knew better than say too much. He went upstairs to change out of his clothes and take a shower. By the time he came back downstairs, the children were in bed. Both Jill and Linda were ready to hear about his day.

First he described the huge jet. He told them that he thought that he might have been over Canada, but was not sure.

When they asked the condition of his friend, Jase could only say this would be a good trial for his procedure. He told them that his friend's lymph nodes were already swollen, and he would not know anything for a day or two. When they finished talking, they all retired for the night.

The next morning, before Jase had left for the lab, a call came in. He did not recognize the number. When he answered the phone, it was Dr. Aunser. "This is Dr. Brick."

"Dr. Brick, Mr. Canon's lymph nodes have shrunk. If I had not seen this with my own eyes, I would not have believed it. I thought you should know."

"That is the best news I could have heard today. Thank you for the call. If anything else changes, please call. We are not out of the woods yet, but this is a good first step."

Before he could put his phone back in his pocket, Jill and Linda were standing in front of him. Jill put her hands on her hips and said, "Well?"

"He is already showing signs of improvement. The treatment is working."

Jill was so proud that she had tears in her eyes, and Linda was as excited as Jill.

Jase said, "I can't wait to talk to the Professor. I don't think I can eat right now, I will have to take an early lunch."

"I don't think so, Dr. Brick. You sit down, your meal is ready." Following Jill's orders, Jase sat down.

Jill and Linda knew they were watching Jase make history. Even though Jase thought he was too excited to eat, he did so anyway. As soon as he finished eating, he left for lab.

"I will call you if I find out anything new," he yelled as he walked out the door.

The Professor was waiting for him when he arrived, and they walked in together. "Jase, Michael is in town, and he wants to know more about the laser. He will probably show up anytime."

Jase looked surprised. "Don't you think we can trust him? So far, Michael has been there for us."

"Jase, at this point, we cannot trust anyone, especially Michael."

The two sat down and started to come up with a plan. The Professor still had not told Jase about Linda. He was afraid of the reaction Jase might have.

"Jase, the first thing we have to know is how many players we are dealing with. I have the feeling we haven't seen all of them yet. If Michael really wants the laser, we should give him one."

"Professor, are you serious?"

"Settle down, Jase. What we give Michael will be just enough of a laser to get him off our backs. By the time he finds out it doesn't work, we will know where he stands."

Jase looked puzzled, so the Professor explained. "I have the main part of the laser hidden. What if I made another unit that can't be tampered with? And it can only be used three times, and then it would destroy itself. By then, we should know what Michael is up to."

Jase was still thinking about what the Professor had said, when Michael walked in. "Good morning, gentlemen. How is the new Brick family?"

"Michael, good to see you, and the family is fine."

It was like a playing game of chess when they began to talk. "The Professor said you had some questions about the laser. Is there anything I can answer for you?"

Michael tried not to come on too strong, so he started with, "I was very impressed with your chelating compound that first day. With everything that was going on with the children and all, I did not even think about the laser and how it works. Could you tell me more about it?"

Jase knew Michael was falling into his trap, and he felt guilty for setting it. If it wasn't for Michael, he would not have two children, a new house and more funding for the school. But he went on with the plan.

"Michael, do you think that there are people who would try to steal the laser, and should we make it public yet?"

Michael paused, "I'm sure there are people who would like to acquire the laser, and yes, I think you should go public."

Jase was watching the Professor and could tell he was enjoying the conversation. He was ready to set the trap. "I guess I could put together one for back up, but where would we store it?"

Michael jumped at the chance to answer. "Jase, do you remember that place I told you about in the Chesapeake Bay area? It would be perfect. I could fly you there long enough to finish the laser. You are not going to find a more secure place than that."

Jase turned to the Professor. "Do you think that is an option, Professor?"

Michael was surprised by the question to the Professor. "Jase, what part does the Professor have in this?"

"The Professor could put together most of the unit here in the lab, and then we could take everything to your location for the final assembly. Would that be all right with you, Professor?"

"If you think that I can do it without you, Jase. But you will have to ask Dean Charles. You know how he is about taking off unexpectedly. Maybe Michael could talk to him. He seems to really like Michael."

"I would be happy to talk to Dean Charles for you."

"Good, now we have a lot of work to do. Michael, as soon as I have everything ready, I will give you a call."

Michael was ready to relay the good news. "Well, if there is anything else I can do, please let me know. I will call Dean Charles right now," and he left.

Jase and the Professor sat down at the desk. "The plot thickens. What is next?"

"Well Professor, now we have to give him a laser. Can you do it?"

"I have already started, and you will love it. I need to use some of your money."

"I had almost forgotten about the money," answered Jase.

"Only you could forget about the $500,000 setting in your lab."

"We must keep track of everything we spend. Let's put a notebook in the safe, so we can write down each time we take some out. We should not tell anyone about the money."

"Don't worry, Jase, I won't tell anyone where I got the money. I will have the laser ready to roll this week."

"Good, now I have to check in on Blake Canond."

Jase used the phone at the desk. He got the recording as before, and as soon as the he hung up, the phone rang.

"Dr. Brick, this is Allan. I'm returning your call."

"How is Mr. Canond?"

"Dr. Aunser is very pleased. I think he almost likes you."

"Is Dr. Aunser with you? I would like to talk to him."

"Yes, and I think he would like to talk to you also."

Allan gave the phone to Dr. Aunser. "Dr. Brick, Mr. Canond is responding very well. I think we are ahead of your projected schedule."

"Good, now we have to watch for a couple of things. First, we might damage some of his smaller veins and arteries, so it is very important that we watch his blood pressure. Second, we have to keep giving him the protein and minerals plus the basic vitamins. Watch for fungus around his toe nails or a change in his hair color. These are all signs of deficiencies of one kind or the other.

The cancer cells are attaching themselves to the chelating compound and are being removed from his body through his urine, so watch for kidney stress. Not only are we taking out the cancer cells, but we are also taking out some of the nutrients that he needs. We must provide what the body needs to manufacture new healthy cells.

Thank you Dr. Aunser, you have been very helpful. Now could you please put Allan back on the line?" Dr. Aunser handed the phone to Allan Smith.

"Jase, this is Allan."

"Allan, could you pick me up again. Monday would be fine."

"Of course, Jase, the limo will be at your lab first thing Monday morning."

"Good, I will see you then." Jase hung up.

Jase worked on the compounds, and the Professor worked on the laser. At that same time, Michael was talking on the phone.

"Richard, this is Michael. I should have a working laser in about a week. Dr. Brick is putting one together as we speak."

"I will have a team ready to modify the laser. The plan is to put one laser in each of two TV cameras. Do you know how far the range is on the laser?"

Michael answered, "No, but I don't think that will be a problem. Can you tell me more about the target?"

"Not yet.

Right now it is on need to know basis. As soon as I can tell you, I will. You might say this project involves the White House, so the less you know, the better."

Michael was satisfied with Richard's answer. He gave his regards and terminated the conversation.

"I wonder who the target is at the White House?" he thought. Michael was pleased and thought he could relax for a few days. Then he remembered that he had to talk to Dean Charles. Michael didn't care for the Dean. He was just a pawn in this game. When he left for the Dean's office, he knew that this time Dean Charles would insist on a tour of the school.

For the rest of the week, everyone was busy. The Professor was finishing the copy of the laser, and Jase was preparing for his Monday visit with Blake Canond. Jill and Linda were taking care of the family and becoming good friends.

Linda knew she could not keep the truth from Jill forever. It was harder and harder not to say anything. Jill adored Michael so much for the help he given them. How could she ever tell her that Michael was the one that caused all of their problems? She had no idea how to get away with this lie. On other operations in the past, she would just finish the project and leave, never to see any of the people involved again. This time, she had let herself become involved, and she truly cared about the children. She thought of herself as Aunt Linda and wanted to watch the children as they grew up. But until the Professor and she could find out what Michael was up to, she would not dare say anything.

The rest of the week passed very quickly, and soon it was Monday morning.

Chapter 34

Jase was at the lab early. The smell of fall was in the air, although officially fall was weeks away. Jase hoped it was a good sign. The winters were harsh in the Midwest, and he did not like what came after fall.

Jase had everything he needed in a bag. "I look like the doctor from the Norman Rockwell picture," he thought.

He walked out the door as the limo was arriving. The driver jumped out and opened the door for Jase. "Good morning, sir, the jet is waiting. The jet was sitting quietly at the airfield. As soon as the pilot saw them approaching, he started his final check.

The limo pulled up next to the steps, and Jase was greeted at the door by the flight attendant. "Good morning, Dr. Brick. Please take your seat. The pilot is ready for takeoff. As soon as we are in the air and reach cruising speed, breakfast will be served. Mr. Canond's jet will meet us in about an hour."

Jase sat back and looked out the window. The sun was just coming up. When he looked to the north, he could see a little fall color on the ground. But when he looked to the south, it was still green as far as he could see. "I could get used to this," he thought.

The attendant came back to Jase's seat. "Please feel free to move around the plane, the restrooms are front and aft. I will bring your breakfast out as soon as you are ready. Would you like bacon with your eggs?"

Jase answered, "I would like to wash up first, and bacon will be fine."

He found that the restroom were much nicer than he had expected. It reminded him of something you see at a hotel, not in a jet. When he came out of the restroom, his breakfast was sitting on the table. As he sat down, the attendant brought him a newspaper.

"I'm sorry, but you will not have much time to read. We are half way to Chicago." She smiled and was gone.

Jase was almost finished eating, when the pilot came back to his seat. "Dr. Brick, how is your meal?"

"Perfect, couldn't be better."

"Good, we have to make a little change in our plan. The press has found out about the arrival of Mr. Canond's jet, so there might be some reporters waiting on the ground. We have requested that security keep them away. There is no way that they actually know Mr. Canond is aboard one of the jets, but for your safety and his, we will make the transfer as fast as possible. Please be ready to disembark as soon as we land."

Jase was surprised. "Whatever I can do to help, let me know."

The pilot smiled, "We will get you delivered as fast as we can. Thanks for your help." He returned to the cockpit.

The attendant came and took his tray. "Dr. Brick, please buckle your seat belt. We are approaching our destination." She turned and disappeared.

The jet came in for a smooth landing. As soon as they stopped, he was up and waiting at the door. The pilot came back to say goodbye. "We will be here whenever you are ready to go back. When I open the door, you will see some press over at the fence. They will try to find out who you are, and the less they know the better. Here is a hat. Make sure that you pull it down over your face."

Jase took the flight crew hat and put it on. Then he smiled at the captain.

The captain shook his hand. "Are you ready?" He opened the door for Jase.

Jase was down the steps and was almost to the waiting van, when the windy city lived up to its name. A gust of wind blew the hat off his head. There was no way to catch it, and it blew half way across the tarmac. He briefly turned toward the fence, and then ducked into the van. The van whisked him to Canond's jet. Upon arrival, he rushed up the steps.

"Have a seat, Jase," came the voice from the interior of the plane.

Jase turned to see Allan Smith and Blake Canond sitting in a cluster of chairs facing each other.

"I hope that your trip was good," said Allan.

Jase promptly went over and sat down, silently staring at Mr. Canond.

"Dr. Aunser will be up in a minute," Blake Canond said as he motioned to the co-pilot to take off. The man nodded and left. After the door shut, the engines start to roar. Within a matter of minutes, the large jet was moving.

"What is our next step, Dr. Brick?" Blake seemed very pleased.

"When Dr. Aunser gets here, I would like to give you a quick exam."

"As soon as we are airborne, he will be up. I hear you two are getting along very well."

Jase didn't answer right away. Blake waved his hand in front of Jase's face and repeated the question.

"Sorry, but I cannot get over the way you look. Your color and your energy are so much improved, and it has only been a week."

"Dr. Brick, how long will it be until I know if your treatment is working?"

"I can tell you now. Normally with cancer as advanced as yours, you would be gone in about six months or less. Right now, I am more worried about your circulatory system and your kidneys. Do you have trouble using the restroom?"

"No."

"What color is your urine? Is there any blood in it?"

"No."

"Is there any odor?"

Blake laughed, "My piss looks like a fountain drink, bright yellow, almost florescent. You will have to ask Dr. Aunser about the blood and smell of it."

The jet was getting ready to takeoff, as they settled back in their seats.

Blake was watching Jase. "Doctor, you are creeping me out. You keep staring at me."

"Sorry, but I am just so happy. You look great. You have a healthy look about you that you did not have before. How do you feel?"

"I have more energy now than I have had in years. Whatever you put in that stuff is helping my energy level, that's for sure."

After waiting in line for clearance, they took off.

"Jase, would your wife mind if you are gone all day? There is someplace that I would like to show you. By any chance, do you have your passport?"

"After our last trip, I should have it with me. But no, I do not."

"Maybe next time, do you like palm trees, Jase?" asked Allan.

"Why do you ask?"

"Mr. Canond has a small island off the gulf coast near Costa Rica. We can't land because the jet is too large, but he would like to show it to you from the air."

Blake reached over and put his hand on Jase's shoulder. "I think it would be the perfect place for you to advance your work."

"We have a lot to do today, but I would like to see it sometime. Could Jill come along too? She would love it."

"You can bring anyone that you want to, just tell me when."

"Can we go on a weekend?"

Allan spoke, "I will make all the arrangements and call you."

"Good morning, Dr. Brick." Dr. Aunser came over to sit with the group. "What is your plan for us today?"

"We are going to do another IV."

Blake roared, "I knew that this was going to be a fun day."

"Blake, have you been staying on the diet I gave you?"

"That is the hardest part. As you know, I love my steak."

"For right now, you must not eat red meat."

"Dr. Aunser has been trying to get me to eat better for years."

Aunser nodded, "It is true."

"Well, let's get started." Jase stood up.

They all walked down to the medical area. Blake sat down in his chair, and Dr. Aunser started the IV.

"Jase, have a seat. The IV is going to take about two hours, so now would be a good time to talk." Allan and Jase sat down next to Blake. Dr. Aunser checked Blake's vital signs and watched the IV drip.

"You know, Jase, as soon as the world finds out about your cancer cure, your life will change, hopefully for the better. But if you do not sell out to the big corporations, your life could be in danger."

"What do you mean, Blake?" Jase asked.

"How would you like it if you had billions invested in a cancer treatment, and some unknown doctor comes up with an inexpensive cure? You could lose your shirt overnight. This is big business. What would you do? First, you would try to buy out the rights to the cure and then bury it. I think that I know you well enough to say, that is not going to happen. Second, if you cannot get rid of the cure, you get rid of the person who has it. No one said capitalism is perfect."

Jase asked, "Do you really think that people would go to those lengths to stop me?"

"Do you remember a few years ago when someone came out with a shot that would stop you from getting cavities? It was all over the news for a few days, and then you never heard about it again. I have no idea what happened to it. Maybe it never existed. But if it did, think what it would have done to the dentistry industry. Are you willing to take the chance? Is your family willing to take the chance? Please think about it."

Jase, you must have two things to succeed in this world. One is money, and the other is power. If I live, you are going to be a very rich man. I will keep my word and give you half of everything I own. If I die, it really doesn't matter, does it?"

"Blake, you are not going to die on my watch."

"That is what I want to hear, so let me help you. Tell Allan about everyone that you are working with, and who is this Professor person? Is he a friend of yours? How much do you know about him?"

"Stop right there. Yes, he is a friend of mine, and he has been instrumental in the development of the laser. All I know about him is that he retired from the government a few years ago."

"Would it be alright if I had Allan run a background check on him, just for my benefit?"

"Sure, knock yourself out. While you're at it, check out Michael Greyger. The Professor doesn't trust him, and lately he has been very interested in the laser. He is also the one who is funding my work."

Allan was writing everything down. "I will get started on this right now." Allan got up and left.

"I don't know what I would have done without Allan. He is a life saver, and he is the one that found you, Dr. Brick. I trust him with my life."

Jase and Blake talked for an hour. Allan came back into the room, and handed Blake a copy of a news report. Blake read it and handed it to Jase. "It would seem that you are quite famous today, Jase."

Jase took the report. He could not believe what he was looking at. "University doctor helps billionaire with Cancer."

"Someone this morning must have taken your picture and found out who you are."

"Blake, what will we do?" asked Jase.

"Nothing, this kind of thing happens all the time. Would you like to have some fun with it?"

"I guess so, but how?"

"By the time our jet gets you back on the ground, Canond Industries' stock will have taken a hit. Just a mention of the word cancer will make the stocks dive. Allan will give you a receipt for the money that I gave you for services rendered. When Allan notifies you, I want you to put all of the money in stocks for my company. I will do the same. By tomorrow, the press will be at your door, and Allan will help you with a press release. Do not talk to anyone until Allan tells you to. Allan will be with you when you make the press release."

Blake looked at Allan. "You know where I'm going with this?"

"Yes sir and I like it. Jase, your life is going to make a major change. Please let Mr. Canond and I help you. This is big."

Chapter 35

By now, the jet was heading back to Chicago. The three men were sitting in the lobby of the jet having dinner. Jase and Allan were having steak while Blake was eating his vegetables. Blake was bitching a little about watching them eat their steak. Jase said, "Blake, when the time is right, I will get you the best steak money can buy."

"You have a deal, Jase. Now, what are you going to do with your money?"

"I don't know."

It was about dark when they landed. This time more people were watching from the fence, and there were flashes from all the cameras. "I think it would be a good idea for the driver to take you to your house tonight. He can pick you up in the morning, and drive you around for as long as necessary. Until we make our statement to the press, we must not say anything to anyone."

"Boy, Jill will be surprised." Jase could hardly wait to tell her.

"I would imagine that she all ready knows, Jase," said Allan. "Remember, don't talk to anyone. You and Jill will have to be very careful for a little while. If you would like, I could have security sent to your house."

"I don't know if that will be necessary yet, but thank you."

The jet stopped and the door opened. "See you next Monday." said Blake.

Blake stopped in the exit doorway and shook hands with Jase.

Camera flashes were going off. "You will see that one in the paper in the morning. Remember, Jase, don't say anything to anyone until Allan gets back with you."

Jase walked down to the waiting van and was promptly taken to the smaller jet. As before, as soon as he arrived, the jet was ready for takeoff. He walked up the steps and in a few minutes, the jet was in the air.

The attendant came over to see if he needed anything. "I see that you have had a big day, Dr. Brick."

Jase answered, "Yes," with a smile.

Upon arrival at the university airport, there were more people waiting. The captain had the limo come as close to the jet as he could. Jase went down the ramp and jumped into the limo. "Dr. Brick, I have instructions to take you to your home and not to stop anywhere."

"That would be fine with me," Jase answered.

"Dr. Brick, you might call home and have them open the back door for you."

Jase did as he was asked and called Jill. "Hello, by any chance is there anyone around looking for me?"

Jill laughed. "The back door is opened dear, and we are way ahead of you. You can explain when you get here."

"Thank you, I owe you one. Is Linda there, and have you heard from the Professor?"

"They are both here. All we need is you."

"I'm leaving the airport now, see you soon."

A block away from the house, the driver turned the lights off. "You have done this before, haven't you? Thank you very much. Let me out in the back, and I will see you in the morning."

The driver handed him a card with his number on it. Give me a call ten minutes before you are ready to leave and tell me what door you would like to use."

"I will, and thanks again." The car stopped and Jase ran for the door before anyone knew he was there.

Jill was at the door. "Welcome home, stranger. You made the news tonight. I don't know whether to ask for your autograph or kiss you."

"Close the door and then lock it. Got anything to drink?"

Jase walked into the living room. "Well hell, Jase, and I said you were no fun."

"Let me sit down and catch my breath." Jill handed Jase an ice tea.

"As soon as you catch your breath, we want to know everything." Jill sat down next to him. "And where is our van?"

"I could not get close to it, so the driver brought me here. He is going to pick me up in the morning."

"Dean Charles and Michael have been calling. They both want you to call them back."

"That is not going to happen. Mr. Canond is checking out Michael for me. By tomorrow, I should know everything about him. I was told not to talk to anyone until Mr. Canond's man calls me."

"Sorry, Professor, you will have to stay the night. I don't think it is safe even for you to leave. Could you call Dean Charles for me? Tell him we need security to get rid of the press around here, and as soon as I can say anything, he will be the first one I call."

The Professor was immediately on it. Jase waited until he was back, and then he started his story about the day.

"First things first, Linda, how much time before you retire? Would you like to work for us fulltime?

Linda looked at the Professor and he looked back her. "Jase, there are a few things you and Jill must know before I answer. The Professor and I both worked for the same agency that Michael works for. The Professor retired years ago, and I retired this morning. I have not told them yet. The only thing I care about is this family. All I know is that Michael wants something you have very badly, and it is the laser. He doesn't care about the cancer cure. He only wants the laser."

Jill was shocked and almost in tears. "You moved into our house just to use us. I thought you cared about us and the children."

"Jill, I do. I was told that you needed a nurse and a bodyguard for the children and that is what I am. I had no idea what Michael wanted until a couple of days ago. Ask the Professor."

Jill turned to the Professor. "You knew all about this! How could you not tell us?"

"Jill, I have been watching Michael from the first day I met him. I didn't know for sure until Linda and I talked at the steak house after she took out the men who didn't like Jack."

Now Jase was mad. "Professor, you didn't tell me anything about that."

"Look, Jase, all we know is that the government wants the laser, and I don't think Michael will stop at anything to get it. We need to go along with our plan."

"Plan, what plan? Jase, you have been holding out on me too!" Jill was upset.

"Jill, I didn't know about all this until right now. All I knew was that the Professor and I were checking out everyone. The Professor is building a mock laser for Michael, and he will give it to him next week. By then, he will be out of here."

Linda spoke up. "We cannot let Michael know that we are on to him. From what little I know about him, he is dangerous. We must play along with him for now. I have been looking out for you and the children, and I will not let anything happen to them. You have to believe me." Both of the women started to cry and then embraced.

"I was so worried about how I was going to tell you. You might not know it, Jill, but you are my best friend. I'm closer to you than I have been to anyone in my life."

"Back to my question, Linda, will you work for us? We need your help." Jase looked right at her.

"Yes, I would consider it an honor, and you don't have to pay me. I have a good retirement."

Everyone was watching Jase. He started to smile.

Chapter 36

"Mr. Canond believes that my life is in danger. He thinks that my research will bankrupt the cancer treatment industry. Personally, I don't think so, but he has offered us some protection."

"What kind of protection, Jase?" asked Linda.

"He is letting us use his limo for starters. He also has offered his island somewhere in Central America for a lab. And one more little thing...."

Jill was becoming impatient. "Jase, keep the story moving."

"Mr. Canond was going to die. I don't think there was any question about it. He offered me one half of everything he has, if I can pull him through. After what I saw this week, I think he will completely recover." No one was said a word.

"So for right now, we do whatever Mr. Canond says."

"Well hell, Brick, how much is that guy worth?"

"I don't know and I didn't ask, but he is one of the richest people in the world. It looks like we will be seeing a lot of him. Professor, how would you like to sleep on the sofa tonight?"

"I think that would be fine, and then I will go to work with you in the morning."

"The limo will drop you off at the airport. Will you drive the van back for Jill? And Jill, can you take the Professor to get his car? Now let's try to get some sleep. I may have to make a statement for the press tomorrow. Mr. Canond will let me know in the morning."

Linda's cell phone started to buzz. She took it out of her pocket. "It might be Michael, so please be quiet." Then she answered the phone.

"This is Linda."

"Linda, can you talk?"

Linda nodded to her friends, who were watching her every move. "Yes Michael, I can talk. What can I do for you?"

"It looks like I'm getting the laser next week. I would like to thank you for your help. If you could stay on until we have the laser in our possession, I would appreciate it"

"Michael, that is good news."

"One more thing, Linda, do you know what Dr. Brick is doing with Blake Canond?"

"All I know is it has nothing to do with the laser. Blake Canond is interested in the cancer treatment or something." Linda looked at Jase and made a face. Jase nodded that what she said was alright.

"Well Michael, I'm glad it is over and we can all get back to normal."

"Linda, I will be talking to you in a couple of days." The call ended.

"Did he buy it?" asked the Professor."

"You never know about Michael. If it was not for the reporters outside, he would have been on the porch listening to our every word."

Suddenly the door bell rang and everyone jumped. Jill went over to the door and slowly opened it.

"Hi Jill, we asked all those people out front to leave. The campus security will watch the house tonight. So if you hear someone on your porch, don't worry, it will be me. Goodnight."

They retired for the night. Tomorrow would come soon enough. Jill made sure that all the blinds were drawn.

Jase's cell phone rang early the next morning. The sound of steel drums on his ring tone reminded him of the offer he had received the day before.

"This is Dr. Brick," he answered.

"Jase, Allan Smith, what time do you think you will be at the lab?"

"Within the hour, what do you have in mind?"

"Canond Industries took a big hit this morning on the stock market. I think we will need to make a statement to the press this afternoon. I will be at your lab later this morning to go over the details. After today, I think your secret will be out about your cancer treatment. We can discuss that when I arrive."

"Ok Allan, I will see you when you get here."

Jase hung up. "Well, it looks like the day is already off to a big start."

"What is going on?" asked Jill.

"Allan Smith is coming to the lab this morning to talk about the press release today."

The Professor walked out to the kitchen where everyone was sitting. Linda and Jill were feeding the children, and Jase was having a cup of coffee.

Linda took a close look at the Professor. "You look the same in the morning as you do look before you go to sleep."

The Professor gave her a dirty look. "It is all part of my disguise. You got any more of that coffee?"

Jase handed him a cup. "Did you hear the phone conversation?"

"Yes, and we have a lot of work to do. The place will be overrun by this afternoon, so I won't be able to work on the laser."

"Jase, There is a limo out front, time to go," said Jill.

"Let's go, Professor." Jase opened the door and then looked in each direction. "The coast is clear."

Before they could get to the car, the driver had the door opened for them. "Good morning, Dr. Brick." After a glance at the Professor, he said, "Good morning sir. Will you be riding with us this morning?"

The Professor answered, "Hell yes."

Inside the limo, the driver asked, "Will you both be going to the lab?"

Jase answered. "No, the Professor would like to go to the airport. He is going to pick up my van."

"Very good, Dr. Brick," answered the driver.

The Professor tilted his head left and right, "Very good, Dr. Brick."

Jase was watching the driver in the mirror. He smiled when he heard the Professor's comment.

"Would you drop me off first at the lab?"

"Yes sir, no problem. Mr. Smith will be arriving shortly, so I will have to go to the airport to pick him up."

As the limo reached the lab, Jase could see the campus security out front. The limo pulled up and stopped. Jase got out, thanked the driver and went inside.

"Good morning Jase," said the guard.

"Did you have any visitors last night?"

"No sir, pretty quiet," answered the guard.

"Good, that is the way I like it. I will put coffee on, if you want some?"

"That would be great. I will be there in a few minutes."

Jase started wondering to himself, "What did I get myself into? One day you have nothing but a dream and now who knows what the future will bring."

He started the coffee just as the guard was coming in.

"In a little while, I will have a visitor. The driver is going to pick him up now. Let me know when you see the car coming back." He handed the guard a cup of coffee, and he took it outside.

The phone at the desk rang. "This is Dr. Brick."

"Jase, this is Dean Charles, can you tell me what is going on? My phone has been ringing off the hook."

"Glad you called, Dean Charles. I think we will be holding a press conference this afternoon. As soon as I know what time, I will call you. If I were you, I would expect a big crowd. Can you to be there?"

Dean Charles was excited. "Jase, I knew that you would put this university on the map.

Call me as soon as you know anything."

"I will Dean Charles, you can count on it."

The guard stuck his head inside the door. "Dr. Brick, I think your visitor is here."

"Good." They both walked outside. Allan Smith got out of the limo, said something to the driver, and then walked over to where they were standing.

"Jase, it's good to see you." He said hello to the guard and walked inside with Jase. They sat down at the desk.

"A lot has happened since yesterday. As soon as the press found out who you are and what you are working on, our stocks started to fall. As of nine o'clock this morning, they were down about twenty percent. After we give our press release, who knows what will happen. I have a statement all ready for you to read."

Allan handed it to Jase and he read it slowly. "You want me to tell the press that Mr. Canond has stage three melanoma, and I have been monitoring his progress?"

"That's right. We can't tell them that you have treated him with something that has not been approved. The government would be all over you."

"But Allan, if I say what you want me to, they will think that Blake is about to die and that's not right."

"Jase, after you make your statement, I will make mine. I will tell everyone that Mr. Canond is in good hands and expected to pull through. But we cannot give details about your treatment, no matter what. Now, how much of the money do you have left?"

"We still have almost all of it, why do you ask?"

"Be ready to spend it. I think that Canond Industries will bottom out by tomorrow morning?"

"How could it not?" answer Jase.

"Blake has given me permission to tell the press that he expects a full recovery, and if any one decides to sell their Canond stock, he will buy it at market price. You are going to purchase the stock also."

"So you are going to be honest about everything, and still make a lot of money?"

"Yes Jase, we trust that you are going to pull him through, but we are taking a chance.

This is not insider information. If Blake would happen to die, we all would lose everything."

Jase was starting to sweat. "Allan, what time would you like to make the announcement?"

"Two o'clock this afternoon," replied Allan.

"I will call Dean Charles." Jase went over to the phone and called the Dean's office.

"Dean Charles, would 2:00 this afternoon be good for you?'

"Yes Jase, I will alert the press. We could have it at the auditorium."

"That would be fine. I will be there a few minutes before 2:00."

"Jas, how is Mr. Canond doing?"

"He is doing much better. His personal doctor is very pleased. I will see you at 2:00."

"Jase, you are in the headlines now. You will be watched twenty four hours a day. Blake wants you to use the driver for a while until things cool down."

Someone was coming. Jase and Allan looked up to see who was there. "Hello, Dr. Brick," said Michael. Neither Jase nor Allan said anything.

Michael walked up to them. "Hi, I'm Michael Greyger. You must be Mr. Smith." Michael reached out to shake Allan's hand. "We are very proud of Dr. Brick. We think his research will change the world of cancer as we know it."

Allan still did not say anything.

Michael stepped back for a moment. "I'm sorry, Mr. Smith, here is my card."

"Michael, I'm sorry but I have never heard of this agency. Who runs it, and who do you work for? You don't by any chance work for a man called Richard, do you?"

This was the first time Jase had seen Michael look startled. "Well yes, the man I work for is Richard. Do you know him?'

"I know of him. Why is he interested in Dr. Brick's procedures?"

"Mr. Smith, you have me at a disadvantage. You seem to know more about me than I know about you."

Jase watched as Allan cornered Michael. "This is really kind of fun," he thought.

"Michael, Allan and I are going to give a press conference at 2:00. I would like for you to be there."

"I would like that very much. I see that you two have a lot to do, so I will be going. I hope that I can talk to you after the press release, Allan. I think we both have a lot in common."

"We will see, Michael. It was nice to meet you." Michael left as fast as he came.

Allan started to say something, but Jase stopped him, and pulled out the frequency finder that the professor had given him. As soon as Jase turned on the unit, the needle went off the chart. He walked around to where Michael had been standing and reached under the side of the desk. Very slowly he rubbed his hand under the desk, and he stopped about half way in. He motioned for Allan to bring over the glass of water next to the sink. Carefully, Jase pulled the bug off and put it into the glass. The meter needle went back to zero.

"Michael planted a bug?" Allan asked.

"It sure looks like it. Let me give the Professor a call."

"Who is the Professor?"

"The Professor is the one who said I needed a bug detector, and it looks like he was right."

As soon as the Professor answered, Jase said, "Can you come over to the lab and bring the CPU?" The Professor said he would be right there.

"Allan, when he gets here, I will bring you up to date on everything. This is getting more interesting by the day. Let me show you something while we wait." Jase walked into the other part of the lab. Both of the lasers were set up. They only needed the CPU to operate.

"I did not believe it at first, but I think that Michael wants the laser. Why, I don't know."

The Professor came in the front door. "Where are you, Brick?'

"Back here in the lab. Did you bring the CPU?"

"I have it right here. What are we going to do with it?'

"Professor, this is Allan Smith. Give him the CPU."

"It's your show, Jase."

"Allan, will you take the CPU, and put it in a safe place?"

"Professor, there is a present over there in the glass of water for you."

The Professor turned and walked over to the glass. "Where did you find it?"

"I found it under the desk, right after Michael left."

"Brick, I have his laser about ready. I wish I could see his face when he tries to use it."

Now Allan was getting a little curious. "Tell me more about this laser."

"By the way where did you have it hidden?"

"Well Brick, you were right next to it. You know that room full of what you called trash; no one would go into that room."

Jase smiled, "Allan, do you think that Michael is after the laser?"

"I don't know, let me think about it. So who made this laser, you Jase or the Professor?"

"It was my idea, but the Professor put it together. I could not have done it without him."

"How much range does the laser have?"

The Professor was quick with a reply. "The more power the more range. If you had enough power, you could put this thing on the moon. It is very quiet and most of the time you don't know it is on. You could do surgery on someone, and no one would know it. We still need to hook it up with a scanner of some kind, so we can see what we are doing."

Allan was thinking. "So if you had a contract on someone, you could take that person out right in front of a crowd and no one would know. They would think the person died of natural causes."

Jase and the Professor turned and watched each other's face. "That is what he wants. He is going to kill someone. Professor, we can never give him or anyone else the laser."

Allan came over to the laser, and walked around it. "This laser could be the ultimate weapon. You could kill anyone at any time in any place. What will stop this thing?"

"Lead," answered Jase. "Allan, so you think we are in danger?"

"There is no question about it. You and your family have been in danger since you revealed this machine to the world. This could turn into an international event, when the word gets out."

"So, let me hear your plan. Do you have an exit strategy, because you are going to need it," asked Allan. Professor, I'm afraid that since you are also involved, you life is in danger too."

"Hell Brick, I knew you were trouble." Then the Professor smiled, "I really did know you were trouble."

"So what is your plan, boys? You have my attention," said Allan.

Jase spoke first. "We needed some more time. The Professor is going to make another laser, but this one won't work quite like the original one. The new one will work only three times and then destroy itself. We should be able to show Michael a working model, and then leave before he finds out he has a dud."

"Jase, I have the other laser about ready. The CPU is the key. We can set it to work up to three times. After that, the sealed unit will flood with acid. Within seconds, everything that's in it will be destroyed. There is a small sensor on the outside of the unit. If we need to get rid of it sooner, I just push a button."

Allan turned toward Jase. "I have one more question. What makes you think that Michael will not make you look like the one who pulled the trigger? Especially if you and your family take off about the same time as the attempted assassination takes place. And you too, Professor, since you assisted."

"Allan, I think that I will accept Mr. Canon's offer for help. Would you please let him know? I think that as sooner I can get my family out of here, the better. That island in the gulf is looking better all the time."

"Shall we get ready for the press conference? But first, do you have a good place to eat around here?"

"Oh hell, yes," answered the Professor. "And I bet we will have the only limo in the parking lot. Have you ever heard of the VFW."

As they go for lunch, Richard is already on the phone with Robert Lee Seaban.

"Mr. Seaban, we have the laser coming. My people will incorporate it into two TV cameras. You can tell your network that there will be two new people behind the cameras, when the President makes her speech."

"Richard, do the cameras work?"

"Yes sir, you will have recorded history in the making. Just keep them on the President, and the cameramen will do the rest."

Chapter   37

The men returned to the lab after lunch. They only had about 30 minutes until the press conference. The Professor asked Allan, "When have you had a lunch like that?"

"I am happy to say maybe never, but the experience was well worth my time. Jase, is your wife coming?" asked Allan.

"I don't know. I will give her a call."

Jase picked up the phone on the desk, and Jill answered on the first ring. "Well about time, Dr. Brick. We were wondering what became of you."

"Would you and Linda like to come to the press release? It is at 2:00pm in the auditorium. I will call Joyce at the Dean's office to get your seats reserved."

"Yes, we are already to go. We were waiting for you to call."

"Good, I will see you at 2:00. Allan, the Professor and I will be there about 1:45."

"Ok Jase, we are on our way."

"Allan, they will meet us at the press conference. Now, I think that we should be getting over to the auditorium."

The men got into the waiting limo. As they approach the auditorium, they could see the news vans out front. The limo stopped in front of the building. When the driver let them out, the cameras were clicking. Finally, the campus security led the way past the crowd. The lobby was packed with people.

They were escorted to the stage. The Professor saw Jill and Linda sitting to the right of the stage, and each one of them was holding a baby. "I think I will go over with them," he said. "You two can do this without me."

"Dr. Brick, your friend the Professor is a very unusual person."

"Don't be fooled by his appearance. He is a very capable person, but he likes to act just the opposite. He would do anything for you."

"That's good to know, he might have to," answered Allan.

Dean Charles was walking up to the stage. As he stopped in front of the two men, they stood up.

Jase introduced Allan, "Dean Charles, this is Allan Smith. He works for Mr. Canond. We both will be making a statement."

The Dean shook Allan's hand. "Thank you for coming, Allan. Who wants to be first?"

"Dr. Brick will make the first statement, and then I will take over. We will not answer any questions at this time."

"All right then, it is 2:00pm, so I will get this started."

The Dean walked up to the microphone. He raised his hands and said, "Please take your seats." The auditorium became quiet.

"Thank you all for coming. As you all know from watching the news, one of our own staff has been working with Canond Industries. At this time, I would like to introduce Dr. Jase Brick."

Jase got up and walked over to the mic. This was a new challenge for him, but he was ready.

"A short time ago, Mr. Blake Canond was diagnosed with, stage three melanoma. He underwent surgery to remove the mole. I was invited to see Mr. Canond and recommend any additional treatments. It is my opinion, that Mr. Canond's prognosis is good. I will be watching Mr. Canond very closely in the future. Now, I would like to introduce Mr. Smith. He works very closely with Mr. Canond, and he can give you additional information."

As Jase finished, he glanced over at the girls. Both Jill and Linda were smiling as they waved. He turned toward Allan, "It is all yours."

Allan stepped up. "Thank you, Dr. Brick. I feel that this university is very lucky to have a man like Dr. Brick on the staff. He has been very instrumental in Mr. Canond's battle with cancer. With his help, we feel that Mr. Canond will have a fast and complete recovery in the near future. I was not going to take any questions, but maybe I can answer a few."

A reporter in the first row stood up, and Allan pointed at him. "Yes, what is your question?"

"How do you think his stage three cancer will affect Canond Industries?"

Allan was pleased to answer. "First, I don't think that it should affect Canond Industries. We have already seen our stock go down. Mr. Canond is recovering and still in charge. And I might say, he should be in charge for a long time to come. Canond Industries will be more than happy to purchase any stocks at market price, but we strongly urge everyone not to sell. You would be taking a very risky chance. We have time for one more question."

Another man in the front row stood. "This question is for Dr. Brick."

Jase walked over to the mic with Allan. "Yes, what is your question?"

The man answered. "Dr. Brick, are you a betting man? Would you buy stock in Canond Industries?"

Jase smiled, "As of today, I have invested some of my savings in Canond Industries, and I have no intention of changing it." The auditorium was buzzing.

Allan was quick to finish. "That is all the time we have today. As soon as we have more information, we will make it available. Thank you for coming."

Allan looked at Jase. "Whatever you do, don't stop. Now let's go."

They walked out of the building and straight to the limo. Once in the car, Allan said, "Airport please."

"Jase, could you call your wife and have her meet us at the airport. I think that we should all sit down and talk before I leave."

"That would be good, Allan." He called Jill.

"Hi Jill, will you meet us at the airport? Allan would like to talk to the family."

"We will be right behind you," answered Jill.

"Allan, they are on the way."

The limo approached the airport. They waited inside the fence until Jill's van arrived, and then proceeded to the jet waiting near the hanger. "Let's all go into the jet," said Allan.

Jill and Linda were the first to go up the steps. Both of the babies were quiet at this point.

They were met at the door by the attendant. She pointed in the direction of the seats. After everyone was seated, Allan walked over and sat with them.

"Thank you all for coming. But first, who is this little fellow?"

Linda was holding Jack. She said, "This is Jack, and as you can see, he is very happy."

"And you must be Jill?" asked Allan.

"No," Linda laughed. "I'm Linda, and I help with the babies."

"Well Linda, I'm pleased to meet you. Then you must be Jill, and who is this little lady?"

Jill proudly answered, "This is Eva."

Allan continued talking. "Here is where we stand. We think that the government wants your laser. This Michael person really doesn't care one way or the other about your cancer research."

Jill asked, "Are you sure about Michael? He has been so much help to us."

"At this point, Jill, we have no other choice but to believe Michael has only his own interest in mind."

"Now, here is the second problem. As soon as the media releases the news about Dr. Brick's cancer cure, you will be bombarded with offers. I really don't think that the medical industry wants a cure just yet. These people have too much to lose. We must be very careful how we play it."

Allan turned toward Linda. "Linda, I hope that I don't offend you, but I know very little about you and I am reluctant to say anything more in front of you."

"Allan, Linda is part of our family. You can say anything in front of her. We trust her with our lives," said Jase.

"Sorry Linda, I meant no disrespect."

"None taken," Linda answered.

"Jase, have you given any thought as to where you will go after Michael finds out that he does not have the laser?"

"No, not yet, we told Michael that the Professor and I will go to his place in Virginia to set up the new laser. After that, we have no plan."

"Jill, are you going too?"

Jase started to say no, but was interrupted by Jill. "We are a family now. Where Jase goes, we all go."

"Are you interested in Mr. Canond offer?"

Jase said, "Yes, I think we are, but how do we get away from Michael?"

"Let me work on that, Jase. Do you have any back up of your records?"

"Yes, they are in two places. We sent it to a friend in Ohio and a friend in Key West."

"Key West, I like that place, and it is in the gulf. Before you all go to Virginia, I think you should destroy everything that you have here, unless you want something to go with me. Don't take anything of importance with you to Michael's place. Does Michael know that you have backups?"

"I think that I might have told him something about it, but even Jill does not know where they are."

"Good, you might have to give your friend in the Keys a heads up. You are going to need your backup. And if his cover is not compromised, you can continue to use him. Now, I think I will report to Mr. Canond. It has been a long and interesting day. Dr. Brick, I recommend that you get some help with your investments tomorrow."

"Yes, I never had the money to invest before."

"I will have the driver pick you up in the morning and my broker will be in the limo. You can talk to him about the next step. As soon as Blake has the green light that he is cancer free, I think you should double or triple your investment."

The Professor had been quiet all this time. "Can anyone come? I have a little to invest."

"Yes, I don't see a problem. How about you, Linda? Are you interested?"

"Let me think about it."

Now the babies needed some attention. "Can we use the restrooms? Diaper time." Both of the women headed for the restroom.

"Jase, I will be in contact," said Allan.

"Until Monday then," said Jase. The men waited for the rest of the family, and then they all went down the steps together.

"Professor, would you mind taking the van home for the night? We will get it tomorrow."

The driver opened the door, and the five of them entered the limo.

The jet was already warming up its engines. By the time the limo was on the other side of the fence, the jet was moving. They watched as it took off.

Jill reached for Jase's hand. "What next, Jase? I'm really scared."

As they arrived at the house, Rex was barking. "I guess I know what I am doing. You two go on ahead. Rex and I need some walking time."

Jase and Rex took a long walk around the campus. Each time there was any kind of noise Jase would catch himself looking over his shoulder. After about forty five minutes, they returned home. He could smell the meal that Jill was cooking. It reminded him of days in the past, when he was little and going to his grandmother's. That was a happy time for him, and he wanted no less for his children.

When he walked in from the calm, he realized that he was home. He could hear the babies crying in the kitchen.

Jase's phone rang. It was the Professor. "Jase, have you read the paper?"

"No, I just got in."

"Go get it, I'll wait."

Jase asked if they had the paper yet. "It's on the end table next to the door," replied Jill.

He went over and picked it up. There was a picture of him on the front page. The headlines read, "Who is Dr. Brick? Can he really cure cancer?"

"Professor, I will call you back."

"No you won't, Brick, I'm coming over."

Without saying another word, Jase hung up the phone. "Jill, you might want to see this."

Jill came in holding Jack. Jase held up the paper. She handed him the baby and sat down with it.

"It says here that Dr. Brick is on the brink of curing all kinds of cancer, and according to Dean Charles, you have secured funding from the U.S. Government. Also, Dean Charles is proud to say that you are directly involved in the treatment of Blake Canond of Canond Industries. He expects your cancer cure to make history."

Linda was listening. "The fool does not know what he has done. He will bring people from all over the world, from the big corporations to every family that has someone who has cancer. They will all be at your door."

The second she finished talking, the front door opened startling everyone. The Professor entered.

"I did not hear you knock," said Jase.

"I didn't, but I will knock twice the next time. What the hell does Dean Charles think he is doing? Did you tell him any of that shit?"

"No, he came up with all that by himself," Jase answered. "Maybe it won't be so bad."

"Look Brick, all I can tell you is start packing. This dream of yours is getting out of hand."

Linda's phone rang. "I think it is Michael. That is all we need."

She let it go to voice mail. "I'll here about that one. I will call him back in a little while."

Linda turned toward Jill. "Could you excuse me for a moment? I will find out what he wants, as if we did not know." Linda went upstairs to make the call.

"Yes Michael," she said.

A loud voice at the other end was shouting. Linda pulled the phone away from her ear.

"Michael, do you want me to talk or just listen?"

The phone was quiet. Then Michael came back on.

"Sorry, I guess when I read the news, I was a little upset. Did Jase know anything about this?"

"No Michael, that much I know. He is as upset as you are or more."

Michael was still on edge. "We don't need any attention right now."

Linda could hear another phone ringing in the background. "Linda, I will call you back. I have to take another call."

Linda was glad that was over, but she knew he would be calling back. She opened the door and went down to the rest of the gang.

"That was Michael," she said. "And he is not happy. We will have to see what he does next."

Sitting in a mansion on the west side of the James River, a very irritated short man was calling Michael.

"Michael, this is Richard. I thought that you had Dr. Brick under control."

"Richard, I told Dean Charles what to say. The Dean is helping us get the Bricks out of the MidWest. Now they will have to come to Virginia."

"Don't do anything stupid. I want the laser here ASAP, even if you have to bring the entire Brick family. I also have people to answer to. Your job is on the line, Michael. Do I make myself clear?" The line went dead.

"That went well." Michael sat back in his chair deep in thought.

By now, Jase had read the entire article in the paper. "Linda, you are right. This is bad. We will be overrun with people from everywhere."

The phone on the end table rang with the sounds of steel drums. "You might hear those drums sooner that you thought," said Jill.

Jase raised the phone to his ear. "This is Joyce at Dean Charles' office. I have been getting a lot of strange calls. At 5:00 I turned the answering service on. I think you should come over to the office in the morning to pick up your messages."

"I will get there as soon as I can, but I have a meeting first thing in the morning."

"Thanks Jase, I think we have epidemic starting."

Jase looked at the rest of the crew, "Looks like it's started. Joyce said she can't keep up with phone calls."

Jill turned on the TV. The six o'clock news was beginning. When Jill hit the news channel, Jase's picture was on the screen. The attractive blond newscaster was interviewing a person from one of the largest non-profit cancer research groups in the country.

"For over thirty years, your organization has raised money to help end cancer. How is it possible that one man from a small university can have a cure that will end cancer, and he has had little or no budget? Can this be true in your opinion?"

The women answered, "We have funded hundreds of millions of dollars for cancer research. To think that an unknown doctor can do what we have not been able to is ludicrous. It is not that we haven't made progress, we have. If this Dr. Brick was on the up and up, we would have known about it before now."

The newscaster went on, "Dean Charles at the university said, and I quote, "He has received funding from the government." She waited for a response from the woman.

"We will talk to Dr. Brick, and if he has anything to report, we will let you know."

The newscaster then asked, "But this would be good news for your organization, wouldn't it?"

"Absolutely, nothing would make me happier than to have to look for another job. But I don't see that happening."

The newscaster turned toward the camera. "Well there you have it. Is the battle for cancer over? More news when we have it, now for the weather."

Jill turned the TV off. "They have already started to make you look bad, Jase."

"I'm glad my name is not on any of this crap," said the Professor.

"It's not over yet, Professor. What are we going to do about Michael?" said Jase. "I will talk to Allan tomorrow. Maybe he can help. I'm sure he will have some ideas, but for right now, are we going to invest in Canond stock?"

"Jase, do you think Mr. Canond will make it?"

"Yes Linda, I do."

"Well, I have some money saved. It is not doing very well in the bank, so I think I would like to take a chance."

Jase turned to the Professor. "Hell yes, I will put some in. I think this is the best opportunity I've seen for a while."

"Tomorrow is our chance. Jill, how much should we put in?"

"Can we get it out if we need it, Jase?"

"I think so. We will have to ask in the morning."

"Then keep a little out, and put the rest in. We did not have anything a month ago. If we lose it, we will be like we were before, happy."

"Professor, how close are you to making the laser for Michael? Can you finish the laser at Michael's facility?" asked Jase.

"Yes, but what do you have in mind?"

"I think we are going to need to leave. Linda, how do we find out more about this place? We have to have freedom in coming and going, and I need to be close to an airport."

"Jase, I don't know, but Michael is going to call me back. I will tell him you are very nervous about staying here with all the attention you are getting."

"My mind is going in every direction. What is next?" Jase was stressed.

The Professor raised an eyebrow. "I think I know what you need, Jase. I'll be right back."

He left and went out to his car. When he came back, he had a thermos in his hand. "Ok Brick, get the glasses out. It's margarita time."

They salted four glasses. Jill insisted they fill two of them only half way for the ladies. Jase and the Professor indulged in the rest.

Chapter 38

Morning arrived too quickly for the four. The limo arrived promptly at the sidewalk out front. Jase walked out to the car. The driver opened the door, and Jase could see someone sitting in the back as he got into the limo.

"Good morning, Dr. Brick. My name is Nelson Shay. I represent Mr. Canond on financial transactions. He said that I might be of service to you and your friends."

Jase shook hands with Nelson. "I do have some questions."

"Good, that is what I'm here for."

"Would you like to come into the house? There are two other people that want to talk to you."

Nelson smiled and made a gesture with his hand, "Lead the way."

The driver opened the door for the two of them, and they started to walk to the house.

When they reached the porch, Jill opened the door. "Good morning, my name is Jill."

"Good morning, Jill. I'm Nelson Shay."

Jase introduced the others. "Nelson, this is Bill Williams, aka the Professor, and this is Linda Peach. She is helping with the family. Let's all sit down, shall we?"

Nelson was the first to speak. "As you know, Mr. Canond's stock is taking a hit. But as soon as the world knows he will be alright, it should rebound."

The Professor was next to speak. "How much has the stock gone down?"

"Almost half of its value, but I think that it should level out by tonight. In my opinion, this time tomorrow would be the perfect time to invest in this stock." Nelson gave each one a paper explaining his fees and how he would take care of the transaction.

"If you are interested in purchasing this or any other stocks, I need you to sign this release." He then gave each one another copy to look over.

"Dr. Brick, Allan Smith told me you might want to purchase stock with cash. Is that true?"

"Yes, Jill and I would like to put in $450,000."

Linda's head snapped around and she looked over at Jill. "Where did you get that kind of money?"

"Long story Linda. As soon as Mr. Shay leaves, we will have a talk."

The Professor handed Nelson a check.

Nelson glanced at it, "Thank you, Mr. Professor."

Then Nelson turned to Linda. "Would you like to invest? There is no pressure."

"Easy for you to say." She reached into her pocket and pulled out a check. "Who do I make this out to?"

Nelson pointed to the paper he gave her. "Make it out to the firm at the top of the letter."

"How long will it take for the stocks to go back up?" asked Linda.

"As with any stock, no one knows. But if I were to make an educated guess, it will rebound as soon as the world knows Mr. Canond is OK. And, a lot of that depends on Dr. Brick."

"You know, a month ago our life was pretty simple. Now, Jill and I are doing things that we never would have dreamed of."

Nelson finished the paperwork and closed his briefcase. "Shall we go and get your money, Dr. Brick? Oh, and Allan Smith will meet us at your lab."

Nelson thanked everyone for their time, and he left his card with each one. "When I think it is time to sell, I will call you. Normally, I don't get into small transactions like this. But when Mr. Canond asked me to help you, I said I would be happy to. And Dr. Brick, thank you. Without your research, the world would have lost a very good person."

Jase and Nelson said their goodbyes and walked out of the house. The driver opened the door for them, and they stepped into the limo. The limo glided away as the leaves were starting to fall from the trees.

Inside the house, Linda corners Jill. "Where did you guys get that kind of money?"

When the Professor heard the question, he started for the door. "Professor, did you know about the money?" asked Linda.

He turned and nodded. "I have to go and build a laser for your old boss, see ya," and he was gone.

As Linda and Jill were going to sit down, Jack started to cry and then Eva followed.

"Come on Linda, I will tell you as we get the kids."

As they pulled into the airport, Allan Smith was waiting at the jet. The limo stopped next to the plane. "Good morning, Dr. Brick," Allan said as he entered the limo.

Jase greeted Allan with a smile. "Allan, did you have any idea that my life would change on so many levels?" he asked.

Allan nodded. "I don't think that you have seen anything yet. You are dealing with forces that you did not know existed. Before you were a pawn, now, my friend, you are a major player."

Jase did not realize the limo was moving, because it was so quiet. In a short time, they were at the lab.

There was already a small crowd out in front of the building. Security was there trying to control the crowd. "I didn't expect this," said Jase.

Allan reached over and touched Jase. "Let's bring the money out here and take care of our little transaction. I will go in with you. Nelson, if you would stay here, I think it would be best."

Nelson grinned, "As much as I want to walk through the crowd, I will be happy to stay here."

"Jase, may I do the talking?"

"By all means, please do. Is that the news people over there to the right?"

Allan turned his head, "Yes, I do believe it is."

"May I open the door for you now?" asked the driver.

"Thank you, John," said Allan.

"I never knew his name was John," said Jase.

Allan answered, "John has been with us for years, since he lost his wife. Sometime you two must talk. He really likes you."

As the door opened they were met with a rush of questions.

"Dr. Brick, is it true, can you cure cancer?"

"Dr. Brick, what kind of cancer can you cure?"

There was no organization to the questions. Even if he wanted to, no one would stop talking long enough to let him answer.

Allan raised his hand. "Dr. Brick is working on the cure for all cancers. He is close to a cure, but he has not reached that point yet. I'm sure he would like to answer your questions, but you will have to ask them one at a time."

Now Allan pointed at a man to his right. "Sir, do you have a question?"

A small man trying to fight his emotions in front of the crowd answered. "My wife has breast cancer. Can you cure her?"

Allan started to answer, but was cut off by the man. "I want to talk to Dr. Brick."

Jase stepped up to the man. "I am very close to the cure, but I am not there yet."

"How much longer do you need, my wife is dying. Can you help her?" Jase tried to answer the question, but he was interrupted before he could say anything.

"Dr. Brick, my name is Diane Worth. I am the CEO of the Cancer Research Environment. Have you ever heard of us?"

Jase answered, "Yes I have, and I have seen you on TV. I believe your work is very commendable."

Diane quickly came back with a question. "Dr. Brick, you seem to know about us, how is it we don't know about you?"

"Ms. Worth, my research is my life. It is the only thing that I know. I almost died of cancer a few years ago. After seeing what it did not only to me, but also what it did to my family, I decided to dedicate my life to finding a cure. And with a little luck, your organization will not be needed in the near future. I know that is the same goal you are striving for, isn't that right, Ms. Worth?"

Diane Worth paused for a moment. "So you think that you can do what years of research and millions of dollars have not?"

Now that there were TV cameras running, Allan went into action. "Your organization has helped countless numbers of people. No one can take that away from you. Dr. Brick is trying to find a cure for cancer, not treat it. How can you justify $13,000 for one shot of chemo, or $65,000 or more to treat a person, only to extend their life for a short time? Dr. Brick is trying to come up with a procedure that will not bankrupt the family, and instead of prolonging a very painful illness, provides a cure for it. He is trying to change the way we think about cancer treatment. I don't know if you can relate to that, but I hope you can. Now he has research to do. If we have any news for you, we will let you know."

Allan motioned for Jase to go into the lab. But before Jase would leave, he said, "Allan, I would like to talk to the man whose wife has breast cancer."

"I will see what I can do," said Allan.

As Jase went into the building, the crowd was already thinning out. The only ones left were Diane Worth and the man Jase wanted to talk to.

"This is not over yet," Diane yelled at Allan. "You will be hearing from me." She turned and went to her van.

Allan walked over to the man who asked the question about his wife. "Could you come back in a few minutes after the crowd leaves? Dr. Brick would like to talk with you."

The man's face lit up, and he had tears in his eyes. "I will be back."

"Come into the building, we will be expecting you." Allan smiled and went inside.

Diane walked up to the man. "What did he say to you?"

The man answered, "He said he could not help me." Then he turned and walked away.

Diane was furious. She got into her van and drove away. "I will ruin you, Dr. Brick."

"That went well," said Jase. "Who knew trying to help was going to be so hard."

"Let's get the money before anything else happens," said Allan.

Jase went over to the safe and took out the case. He opened it, took out a little and left $450,000 in it. Then he closed and locked the case.

"Hello, Dr. Brick, are you in here?" Came a voice from the hall. The sad little man walked in.

Jase met him at the door. "Thanks for coming back. I wanted to talk to you."

"Dr. Brick, I know that I'm asking a lot, but can you help me? I think my wife is dying and the doctors have taken everything I have."

Jase offered him a chair. "I'm afraid that I didn't get your name."

"My name is Larry Stone," he answered.

Jase sat down. "Larry, has your wife had surgery? If she did, how drastic was it?"

"Yes. The doctor at the local cancer clinic said he could do everything that the big cancer hospitals do. I turned my wife over to him because I trusted him."

"Did they remove the lymph nodes?"

"Yes, but when I asked how many and why, the doctor got mad and refused to answer me."

"Larry, here is what I can do. Has your wife taken any chemo or radiation?"

"She is supposed to start this week."

"First of all, there is no room in medicine for a doctor who is that arrogant. Sometimes a doctor's ego becomes more important than the welfare of the patient being treated. When this happens, it might be time to look around for a new doctor. I will give you the name of a doctor who deals with nothing but breast cancer. I know that she will treat your wife as a person, not a number. Take your wife to her. I will call and set things up. What number can they call to reach you?"

The man handed Jase a card. "This has all my information on it. How far away is this doctor?"

"She is about eighty miles from here. Check with some of the local cancer help groups. They might be able to help with mileage expense. That is about all I can do at this time. I'm sorry that I could not do more. Remember, you are in charge. If your doctor does not have time to talk to you, find one that does."

Larry got up. "Dr. Brick, you have given me more information in five minutes than my wife's doctor has given me since this thing started. Thank you."

"Larry, I think with you in charge now, things will be better. At least you know that you are doing everything that you can. There are a lot of people out there that simply turned over their loved ones to a doctor with no questions asked. You must ask questions and learn all you can quickly. Your wife's life depends on it. Coming here today is a start. I wish you and your wife the best."

Jase walked Larry to the door. "I don't know where I will be in the near future, so it might be almost impossible to reach me. I have to finish my research. Good luck, my friend. I will try to keep tabs on your wife."

Jase and Allan watched as the man walked out of the door. "You know Jase, when he came in, he didn't have a prayer. You put him back in charge again, and his wife now has a fighting chance. Let's get the money. I think Nelson might be ready to go."

The limo was still waiting out in front of the lab. When they reached it, Nelson asked, "I take it you had complications, Dr. Brick?"

"Nelson, you would have been very proud of Jase in there. I know I am. John, let's go back to the airport. I think that Mr. Shay would like to get back."

246

On the way to the airport Jase filled out all the paperwork needed for the purchase of the stocks.

"Nelson, you fly ahead. I will have the pilot come back and pick me up later."

The limo stopped at the jet, and Nelson got out. "Thank you, Dr. Brick, it has been a pleasure."

They watched Nelson walk up the steps to the jet, and then they pulled away.

"How long before he deposit's the money?" Jase asked Allan.

Allan opens his laptop. He turns it around to Jase. "How does it feel to have $450,000 of stock in Canond Industries?"

"That was quick. How did he do it that fast?"

"Let's go back to the house. Are you hungry?" Allan asked.

"Yes, but I don't have any money with me."

"I think that I can take care of the meal today. You still have not adjusted to the jet set yet, have you?" Allan laughed.

"There is a restaurant ahead on the left. Michael took Jill and me there."

"Sounds good to me," Allan said. "John, pull in at that restaurant ahead of us. Would you like to come in with us?" asked Allan.

The limo pulled up to the front, and John opened the door for Allan and Jase. The three of them walked in.

"Three?" asked the waiter.

Allan asked if they could sit in a private area if possible. They were seated at the same table that Jase sat at with Michael.

"Is this table all right?" asked the waiter.

"Perfect, and thank you," said Allan.

The waiter came back. "Dr. Brick, the gentleman sitting over there would like to join your party."

On the other side of the room sat Michael.

"It's Michael," Jase said.

"Please, by all means have him join us," answered Allan.

Chapter   39

"Keep your cool Jase," said Allan. "This was going to happen sooner or later."

Michael and the waiter came back to the table. The waiter sat one more place for him and walked away.

"Thank you, Dr. Brick. It is good to see you."

"Michael, you remember Allan Smith, and this is John. He also works for Mr. Canond. I'm sorry John, but I don't know your last name."

"Allan, how is Mr. Canond? I have been watching the news," asked Michael.

"Michael, thanks to Jase, I think he is on the road to recovery. Jase is a very gifted man."

"I'm glad to hear it, and yes, Jase is very gifted. We have had our eye on him."

Allan looked directly at Michael. "What does the agency want with Jase? I fail to see the connection."

Michael, in a cool voice said, "We think he has the potential for big things, and we would like to be a part of it."

Now Jase spoke, "I have told Allan all about you, Michael, and how you helped us when we needed it."

"Michael, what do you think of all the news about Jase? Mr. Canond and I feel he might not be safe here any longer. What do you think?"

"I think you are exactly right. Jase, the offer still stands if you want to go to Virginia. By the way, how is the other project coming?"

"The Professor is putting the final touches on the laser this week. We should be able to go then. You know, this is just a rough prototype and it will only work up to three times?" Jase watched Michael's face twitch when he told him.

"No, I did not know that. I'm glad that you told me."

"What are you going to use the laser for, Michael?" asked Allan.

"As of yet we don't have a plan, but I want to show it to some other interested people. Will you be able to come and set up the laser for us, Jase?"

"I think so. Maybe all of us will come. It is getting pretty hot around here for us, but you must know that if you have been watching the news."

"Let me know, and I will set things up."

The waiter was back. "It is time to order," Allan said. The laser was not mentioned for the rest of the meal.

Michael's phone rang. "This is Michael," he answered. After a minute, he said that he would not be able to finish lunch with them because something had come up. Michael pushed his chair back and stood up.

"It was good to see you again, Allan, and nice to meet you John. And Jase, give me a call."

"Sounds good, Michael," Jase replied. "Sorry you can't stay longer."

They watched as Michael left the restaurant. "That was awkward. I have never seen him act like that. Did you notice, Allan, that he did not even ask about the cancer treatment?"

"Yes, I noticed. I don't know what he is up to, but you can bet it is not good. Are you going to give him the laser, Jase?"

"He will only have it for a short time, just long enough to get in trouble. Now, how are we going to get away from him?"

"Good question. When we are done eating, we should go back to the house. Will the Professor be there?"

"I'll call him and find out." Jase called the Professor. "Are you still at the house?"

"No, do you want me to go back?"

"Yes, we will meet you there."

Jase put his phone back in his pocket. "I would like to know what Michael is up to. One thing is for sure, we will find out soon."

Allan put his drink down. "I hope that it is not too late when we do."

By this time Michael was already on the phone to Virginia. Richard was talking on the phone in his office at the south end of the compound.

"That is good news, Michael. So we should have the laser here by next week?"

"Yes, Dr. Brick said that he might also come with his family to help set up the laser."

"Give him anything he wants, but get him here."

"I will." Michael hung up.

Chapter 40

The compound looked like any other mansion on the river, but the south wing housed all the offices of the agency. Richard was in his office overlooking the river, trying to get the nerve up to make a call.

He never liked to call Robert Lee Seaban. Each time he had to talk to him, he felt intimidated. Mr. Seaban controlled the media. It is rumored that he even has influence with at least two Supreme Court Judges. He was very successfully at brainwashing the middle class.

Richard got up his nerve and made the call. A voice answered on the other end of the line.

"Is this a secure line?"

"Yes," Richard paused.

The line was silent for a moment, then a voice said, "Richard, how are you? I hope that you have good news for me."

Richard answered, "Robert, we should have the laser here within the week, and Dr. Brick is coming also."

"Good, our window will be open in about two to three weeks. My network has requested to have two TV cameras inside of the correspondence room. We need to have the lasers put into the cameras before they are delivered. When the president speaks, we will aim both the lasers at her heart. It will look like she had a heart attack, and we will have the coverage of her death. It is a win/win situation."

Richard interrupted, "Robert, we have done a lot of things in the past, but we have never taken out a president, at least not in this country."

"Richard, don't get all patriotic on me. This is for America, don't forget it."

"Yes Robert, but if we mess this one up, it could take down the agency."

"That's easy Richard, don't mess up."

"We won't. I'll keep you updated." The phone went dead. Richard was starting to sweat as he hung up the phone. He turned and stared out the window.

Back at the restaurant, they had just finished lunch. John was first to get up. "I will go get the limo," he said.

Jase turned to Allan, "John seems like a nice person. I like him."

Allan agreed, "He is."

The two men walked to the checkout, and Allan paid for the meal. "Now let's get back to the house."

When they walked out to the limo, John was waiting with the limo door open. "Thank you for the meal, and Dr. Brick, I enjoyed talking with you."

"Please call me Jase from now on."

John smiled and closed the door after the men entered the car.

Once inside the limo, Allan spoke, "Back to the Brick's house, John."

When they arrived at the house, the Professor's car was already there. John stopped the limo in front and opened the door for the men. "I will park the car out back for now."

By the time they were on the porch, Jill had opened the door.

"You guys must have a sixth sense or something, the babies are asleep. Come on in. We were just wondering what happened to you."

"John is out back. Would you like to see if he wants to come in?" Jase asked.

Allan went over to the Professor. "How close is the laser to being finished?"

"Hell, it's been ready for days, but I didn't want the world to know about it yet."

Jill walked back into the house. "Jase, John does not like to leave the limo alone. He said if he needs anything, he will be in."

They all sat in the living room. Allan was the first to speak. "Linda, will you go with the Bricks if they leave?" Everyone watched Linda for her answer.

"Yes, I don't know anywhere else I would rather be. This was my last job for the agency, and you guys are like family to me."

Allan watched Jill as she reached for Linda's hand. Linda was almost in tears.

"Professor, how are we going to keep the laser from getting into the wrong hands?"

"Well hell, that is easy. Each laser has a closed CPU that contains all the working parts of the laser. The CPU box is lead lined, and it cannot be scanned. It will work only two times. When they try to energies the third time, they will self destruct. Just don't be sitting between them. The only thing left will be two empty boxes because everything in the lasers will have been destroyed. There will be nothing left to be traced."

Jase was surprised. "Professor, you had this worked out a long time ago, didn't you?" The Professor smiled. Allan was pleased with the Professor. "You know, Professor, if you ever want a job, I am sure Blake would have something for you."

"Hell, it took me too long to break Brick in. I don't think I could do it again with someone else."

"Does anyone know where this place is in Virginia?" asked Allan.

"All I know is that it is off Rt. 10 on the west side of the river," said the Professor.

Linda spoke up. "I have been there two times. There is a long gravel drive off the main road. About the time you think you are on the wrong road, this mansion appears. There are three parts of the buildings. First is the main house, and it is in the center. Next is the research area that is located in the west wing. And last is the office area located in the south wing. That is where Richard's office is located. Between each wing are enclosed walkways. Then between the main house and the office area is a communication center."

Allan asked, "Where are all the cars?"

Linda answered, "Underground, I have no idea how many levels there are or what is in them."

Jase asked before anyone else could. "Who is Richard?"

"I don't know what his last name is, but he runs the agency. You mention his name and people jump."

"How many people are there?" asked Allan.

"You would never know it, but about a hundred. The land has sensors about every thirty feet, so no one comes or goes without notice."

"Sounds like a prison to me," said the Professor.

"It looks like a resort. It has pools and tennis courts. It is beautiful, but you can't do anything without Richard knowing it."

Allan was quietly thinking. Everyone was watching him. "The first weekend you are there, you need to take a family outing."

Linda spoke up. "There is nothing around there but government land, fishing boats and yacht clubs."

Allan paused, then asked, "Have you ever been to Gettysburg?"

Jase said with a puzzled look, "No."

By this time, Allan was grinning. "Just south of Gettysburg is the Eisenhower Inn. Make reservations for the weekend, and I will pick you up there. Can you have your demonstration ready for Richard the first week, Professor?"

"Hell, it is ready now."

"As soon as they have the laser, you need to leave. These people don't like to have people hanging around that know too much. I think that you will need to disappear as soon as possible." Allan continued, "Jase, you said that you have backup for everything. Can you get it?"

"Yes, I have a cousin in Key West. She is a dancer and she works in a little place down there. She has everything that I have."

Jill was surprised and a little angry. "I think that is a good way to put it, Jase."

Linda reached over to touch Jill's arm. "What is going on Jill, I don't understand."

"Jase's cousin is a male. He just looks like a girl."

Linda let out a laugh, but caught herself half way into it. She put her hand over her mouth to try to keep from laughing.

"Jase, if you can get to Gettysburg on Friday morning, we could have you in Key West Friday night. Professor, you said that you have a boat in the Chesapeake area. Where is it docked?"

"My boat is at Sting Ray Point right on the ocean. South of Deltaville there is a marina."

"Do you want to go with Dr. Brick and the family?"

"Hell yes."

"Make sure you are out of there by Thursday. Go right to your boat, and I will have someone pick you up."

Jill was still mad. "You sent everything to your cousin in Key West?"

"Now Jill, I didn't tell you for two reasons. One, no one would suspect her of anything other than a party. Two, I knew you would not like it."

Linda jerked Jill's arm. "I have to ask, what is this cousin's name?"

Jill tried not to laugh, "Peanut, they just call her Peanut. It is short for Peanut Butter."

Linda was starting to breathe funny because she was trying to hold it in. Then it was no use. She spit all over Jill trying not to laugh. "I'm sorry Jill, but I can't help it." Jill was trying hard not to laugh, but when she saw Linda's face they both lost it.

"What is going on, Jase?" asked Allan.

"I'll tell you later."

"You will have to destroy all your papers here before you leave. That goes for you too, Professor."

Allan reached for his phone. "This is Allan."

Someone on the phone told him to turn the TV on. "Jill, could you turn the TV on?"

Everyone waited to see what was going on. Jill turned on the news channel.

"That's the woman that gave me a hard time. Turn it up," said Jase.

The woman on the TV went on talking. "This Dr. Brick says he is close to changing the way we deal with cancer. He also said that he was going to put the Cancer Research Environment out of business. I take it for what it is worth. We have seen nothing that shows even the smallest part of research from Dr, Brick. Like so many people before him, he is trying to make money from people who are down and scared. He will probably get rich, and people will get hurt. If I'm wrong, I'm sorry. But I don't care for anyone using sick people to make a profit. Until we meet again, Dr. Brick. This is Diane Worth saying we are watching you."

"Who does that bitch think she is?" said Jill.

"Jill, she is just doing her job," said Jase.

"More like she is trying to keep her job," answered Jill.

Allan stood. "Jase, I must go now. You have my number."

"Allan, I need to see Blake on Monday."

"All right, then you leave on Tuesday."

Allan reached for his phone, "Bring the limo up front, please."

Jase walked out front with Allan. "I don't think we could have done this without you, thank you."

"It's not over yet, Jase. See you on Monday."

The limo was in front of the house and John had the door open. "Goodbye Allan," yelled Jill from the front door.

Allan waved and climbed into the car.

Jase watched the limo go down the street. He turned and walked back to the porch. Then he asked, "Jill, when is the Fantasy Festival in Key West this year? It should be coming up soon."

"That is all we need," Jill said. "You better call your cousin and find out if she is going to be there."

"Good idea, I will call her right now." Jase pulled out his phone and dialed a number with a 305 area code.

The phone rang but went right to voice mail. "You guys have to hear this. Jase put it on speaker phone. A deep voice came on. "You have reached Peanut Butter. I'm sorry I cannot come to the phone right now, but leave me a message and I will call you back. You won't be disappointed."

"Peanut, this is Jase, you have this number. Call me back on a secure phone line."

"So you two played together when you were little? What did you two play with, dolls?"

"Jill quit, he just had other interests. He is one of the happiest people in the world, and Peanut really likes you. So be nice."

"Ok Jase, I was just having a little fun. Are you going to ask her to be the godmother or godfather to our children?" Both of the girls were laughing.

Jase smiled, "I was going to ask you about that." Out of nowhere, came the cry of two babies. "See, it even woke the children." The girls went up stairs to get the children.

"We have a lot to do Professor, and only a short time to do it. I guess I should call Michael and get this show on the road." Jase used his other phone. He went to Michael's number on speed dial.

"This is Michael."

"Michael, this is Jase. Can we go to your place next week?"

"I don't know why not, has something happened?"

"Yes, Jill and I can't go out for anything without being put on TV. I don't think I am ready for this."

"Jase, let me make a few calls. Are your wife and the kids coming?"

"Yes Michael, all of us. The Professor will come with the laser. Jill and I will be there next week. Tuesday would be good. How are you going to move the equipment?"

"I can have a plane there Tuesday. The Professor can ride with the equipment if he wants."

"Good, I will start getting everything packed. And Michael, thanks for your help."

Jase hung up. "How was that Professor, do you think he believed me?"

"I don't think it makes any difference as long as he gets his laser."

Jase yelled to the Professor before he left. "Don't destroy anything yet, not until I hear from Peanut." The Professor acknowledged with a wave.

Jase walked up the steps to the nursery. The girls were taking care of the kids.

"Looks like we are going to be moving again. Let's take only what we need and the things that we cannot replace."

Jill nodded, "We are already ahead of you. Linda, do you have anything that you need to do?"

"No, not really, I don't have any family. All my banking is done on the net, and I would not miss meeting Peanut for anything."

They all went down the steps to the kitchen. The children were hungry. Jill looked puzzled. "Jase, we are not going to send all our stuff to Michael's place, are we? Where are we going to send the rest?"

"I will talk to Allan and see what he says. I hope that Dean Charles is not to upset. Should I give him a call?"

"Not yet Jase, I think that the less people know, the better," said Linda.

"You are probably right."

Jill bent over the children as she was feeding them. "You two sure are going to have an exciting life if this is any indication of how it is going to be."

Jase was sitting in the chair thinking of what he was going to do next, when his phone rang.

A deep husky voice said, "Hi Jase, this is Peanut."

Chapter 41

"I don't know what a secure phone is, so I called from a pay phone. There are not many around anymore."

"Peanut, how are you?"

"Jase Honey, I know you didn't call me to ask how I am, so what is up? And how are those kids?"

"Peanut, the kids are fine. We thought that we might come down to see you a week from next Friday. Do you have the papers that I sent to you?"

"Sure do Honey, and no one knows about them, just like you said. Am I going to get to see the kids?"

"Yes, we should be there on Friday night."

"Oh good, you will be here in time for the Fantasy Festival. Are you coming by car or plane?" Peanut was getting excited.

"We don't know yet. Are you sure that you have all the things that I sent you?"

"Jase, everything is locked up in the safe."

"Peanut, be careful, and don't tell anyone that you have talked to me. See you in a few days."

"Ok Jase, I'm so happy that you are coming. Tell Jill hello for me."

Jase looked at Jill. "Peanut said to tell you hello, and she cannot wait to see you."

Jill said, "That's nice, I really would like to see her too." She turned to Linda and grinned.

The rest of the week there were a lot of things going on. Michael's people had already started to move some of the lab equipment out. The Professor had the laser almost ready to ship.

Early Friday morning, Jase's phone rang. "Hello, this is Dr. Brick. Allan, good to hear from you."

"Jase, I saw where you called. What can I do for you?"

"We have some things that we need to move, but we don't want them to go to Virginia. Where can we store them?"

"Do you have one of the companies locally that have the portable storage units?"

"I think so, but I will have to check."

"I will have our people find one for you and try to have it at your house by Monday. They can put the storage unit in back where no one can see it. And Jase, I won't put it in your name. That way no one will know where it is going when we are ready to move it. Does that sound all right to you?"

"It sounds good to me. Are we still on for Monday? I need to see Blake."

"The jet will be there first thing Monday morning."

"Allan, I will see you then."

The phone went silent. Jase turned toward Jill and told her everything that Allan had said.

"And Jill, Peanut said she could not wait to see the children."

That night the Professor came by. "Well hell Brick, I am ready to go. I think that I will take my car down to Virginia. That way, I can drive over to my boat and no one will know. Everything is packed, and all the records that I had are history. I hope that you have a backup."

"My cousin has the backup. She will be waiting for us. By the way, where did you have your copies?"

The Professor grinned. "You know where all that stuff was in my back bedroom? It was there in plain sight. No one in their right mind would go into that room."

Jill and Linda overheard the Professor comment. "You can say that again. I would not go into that room for anything," said Jill.

"See, there is a method to my madness. When are you going to take off? And, I need to know where I'm going, Jase?"

Jase got his phone out and dialed Michael.

"This is Michael."

"Michael, this is Jase. We are just about packed. The Professor is going to drive out. It should take him a couple of days. Can you give me an address for him?"

"Is the laser ready to ship?"

"I think so. I should be completely packed by Tuesday morning."

"Tell the Professor that we will ship his car, and he can ride with the rest of you. My people will be at your house on Tuesday."

"That sounds good, Michael." Jase hung up.

"Looks like we are leaving on Tuesday. Allan will have the rest of the things out of here by Monday."

They spent the rest of the weekend getting ready. Monday morning the limo was waiting outside for Jase.

"Jill, I have to go and check on Blake. I will be back here as soon as I can. If you need anything, call me. This next week will change our lives forever." Jase said goodbye to the family and rushed out the door.

John was waiting by the open door of the limo. "Good morning Dr. Brick. The jet is ready to take off as soon as we get to the airport."

Jase sat in the back not saying a word. A million things were going though his mind. "Why does Michael want the laser? Would they be able to get away from Michael without him knowing it? And, will the laser self destruct before they get to use it?"

They drove up to the jet where everyone was waiting for him. As soon as he sat down, the seatbelt sign came on.

The attendant came up to Jase. "Dr. Brick, we will serve breakfast as soon as we are airborne."

He smiled and said, "Thank you. Are we going to Chicago this time?"

"Yes, Mr. Canond's jet will be waiting for you there."

When they landed at Midway, the larger jet was waiting. They pulled up as close as they could to it.

As soon as the door opened, Jase was out. He went up the steps and Allan greeted him as he entered.

"Allan, I am so nervous. Can we pull all this off?"

Before he could answer, Blake called out. "Dr. Brick come and sit down. We are about to take off. Allan tells me that you have a full plate these days. How do you like the jet set?"

Jase sat down across from Blake. "If you had told me that all this was going to happen in a few short weeks, I never would have believed it. Mr. Canond, how do you feel?"

"I feel fine, but you need to call me Blake."

Dr. Aunser was also there. Jase turned toward him and asked, "Are there any infections, temperature spikes or anything out of the ordinary?"

Dr. Aunser answered, "The only thing that I have noticed is that his kidneys are working overtime. I think that it is quite a strain on them."

"It can't be helped. He has a lot of cancer cells floating around that his body is flushing out. We must keep the colon cleaned out."

Blake spoke up, "How long do I have to continue the colon cleansing? I think that is the worst thing about all this mess."

Jase responded, "I think that you could go from every week to every other week now."
Jase went on, "How is your stomach? Are you tolerating my compound?"

"Yes, I even crave it. Whatever is in it has given me more energy than I have had for a long time."

"Now Blake, I would like to have you keep this routine for three months, and then we can taper it off. I want you to stay on the diet I gave you and don't eat junk food or red meat."

"Jase, do you know how bad I want a good steak?"

"When it is time, I will have one with you."

They did not even notice that the jet was in the air.

"I would like to examine you, if that would be all right," Jase said.

They went down to the medical area. "As soon as we are done, I have something to show you, Jase," said Blake.

The exam only took fifteen minutes. "It looks like you are right on track. You said that you have something to show me?"

Blake was putting his shirt back on. "Come this way." Blake took Jase and Allan to a room that Jase had never seen before. There was a large conference table in the room. On the table was a model of an island.

"Jase, this is my island, and it is part of the deal. I think that right here would be a good location for your research facility." Blake pointed to the model. "You can stay at my house until yours is built."

Blake went on. He had given this a lot of thought. "As soon as you are ready, I will take you to the island and show you around. I will have my yacht waiting at Key West. Your family can stay on board while you are there. It should arrive there in a couple of days."

Jase didn't know what to say. "How can I ever thank you, Blake."

"Just keep me alive. My family will be at the Island, and they would like to meet you and your family."

"Speaking of Key West, will you be there?" asked Jase.

"No, I am going to the Island to meet with my family."

268

Jase turned to Allan, "Did you have any luck with the moving company?"

"It should be at your home already with some help for the ladies. Jase, does Dean Charles know you are moving?"

"Not yet, but I will have to tell him before we go."

Blake spoke up. "Allan, I think we should put the university on our donation list, don't you?"

"I will take care of it as soon as the Bricks have left. Jase, why don't you let me tell the Dean that you are moving."

"All right, if you think that is best."

The jet was starting to descend. "Are we going in?" asked Jase.

"Yes, unless you have some other business to take care of," Allan said.

Jase looked at his watch. "No, I guess we have been up here for a while."

The seat belt sign came on and they all took a seat.

"Jase, we will see you in a couple of days." Blake reached out and offered Jase his hand.

Their handshake had formed a bond of trust. Blake looked into Jase's eyes. "Thank you, we will help you get through this."

When the jet came to a stop, Jase was at the door. Allan put his hand on Jase's shoulder. "We are all in this together. We have your back."

Jase nodded, and then quickly headed down the ramp and onto the waiting jet. The door opened before he got to the steps. He rushed up the steps and took a seat.

"How was your visit, Dr. Brick?" asked the attendant.

Jase answered, "Fine, thank you. You know I don't even know your name, and I have been on your flight many times."

"My name is Marie. I have been with Mr. Canond for seven years. I hear that you are a very good friend of his."

"I think so. He is not the man I thought he was going to be. I believe that he really cares about other people. Is that the way you feel?"

"Yes, Dr. Brick, that is the way we all feel. He has handpicked all of us. And I might add, he has changed our lives. Now sit back and relax. We will have you home in a few minutes."

Jase closed his eyes. The next thing he knew, Marie was tapping him on the shoulder. "Dr. Brick, we have landed. I didn't want to wake you. You were sleeping so peacefully."

Jase stood up, a little refreshed from the short nap. He could see the limo waiting as he walked through the door. John was smiling as Jase walked over to the car. "How was your nap?"

Jase looked at him and thought, "They must know everything about me."

"John, it will be good to get home. I have a big schedule in front of me."

John answered, "Mr. Canond has asked if I would stay close for the next few days in case you need me."

"John, you are always welcome at my home."

They arrived a little before sunset. "The trees look so beautiful this time of year. It is like the fourth of July in the fall, but we know what is just around the corner," said Jase. His eyes were on the trees, but his mind was somewhere else.

John pulled up in front and they walked up the sidewalk. As soon as they walked in, he knew he was home when he could hear the children crying. Jase looked at John, "Now I know that I'm at home. Would you like to stay here tonight, John, we have room?"

"I already have a room at the University Inn here on campus. Call me if you need anything. I will be here in the morning. Would you like to see if your wife needs anything before I go?"

The house was suddenly quiet. Jill was coming down the steps. "Hi John, hi Jase how was your day?'

"Good, do you need anything? John was asking before he goes."

"Not really, but you might want some of Linda's home cooked dinner before you leave."

"That would be nice," replied John.

Linda was on her way down and they all walked to the kitchen.

Jase's phone rang as soon as they sat down.

"Dr. Brick, this is Michael."

Chapter 42

Jase held up his hand and everyone was quiet. "Michael, how are you?"

"Fine Jase, I have arranged for two planes to pick you up tomorrow. What time will you be able to leave?"

"We have not unpacked from the last move yet. We should be ready in the morning. Who is moving us?"

"I can have people at your house by 8:00 am, if that is all right."

"Would you hold on? Jill, Michael can have his movers here at 8:00. Is that all right?"

Jill gave Jase a stupid look.

"Michael, make it 8:30."

"Good, I will have a private plane for you and your family waiting at the airport when you get there. Ask the Professor to meet us at the lab, and we will help him load the equipment. Also, the plane can hold his car. He should like that."

"I will tell him. We will see you tomorrow, thanks Michael." Jase put the phone down. "I better call the Professor."

Before Jase could call, the front door opened. "Well hell, I didn't know you were having a party."

"Are you hungry, Professor?" Jill asked.

"Well sure, this might be our last meal together."

"Don't even joke like that," scolded Linda. "You know how we feel."

"Sorry, I thought I would cheer you all up."

"Well it didn't work," said Linda.

"Have a seat Professor. Tomorrow should be quite a day for us." Jase continued, "Michael will have a crew at the lab first thing in the morning. You need to be there. He said that they will haul your car with the lab equipment, and you can ride with it. The rest of us will be in a private plane. I guess we will see you in Virginia. Do you have any questions?"

"Hell yes, Jase, how will I find you Friday night in Key West?"

"Do you remember the number of the cell phone you gave me?" Jase asked.

"Yes, but what happens if that does not work?"

"There is a club on Duval Street where they do female impersonations. Just ask for Peanut."

The Professor stared at Jase. "Does Peanut have a last name?"

Jase took a deep breath and then answered. "Her last name is Butter, Peanut Butter."

The two girls howled until they had tears going down their cheeks.

"Professor, Peanut is my cousin. She is a little different, but a very nice person."

"Alright then, I will see you in the morning. Thanks for the supper." John stood up. "I will call in the morning to see if you need anything, best of luck."

Everyone told John goodbye. Jase walked out to the limo with him. Before they got to the limo, a buzzer went off on Jase's belt. "John, stay here, I will be right back." Jase walked back into the house. He grabbed the Professor and showed him the frequency finder.

The Professor asked, "The limo?"

Jase nodded as they walk out to the limo. The Professor walked around the limo watching the finder as he moved. He stopped at the back of the car and reached under the bumper. "Do you have a flashlight, John?"

"Yes, in the trunk."

"Very slowly open the trunk and hand me the light." John handed the light to the Professor.

"Hell Brick, I don't think I have ever seen this one before. It looks like a multi-use-thing-of-a-bob."

"What does that mean?"

"Well, it looks like a tracking service and an explosive device. You and John might want to go back in the house until I can get this thing off the car. I don't think it should be too hard, but I have been wrong before."

Jase and John started to walk away.

"Jase," yelled the Professor.

Jase stopped in his tracks. "What Professor?"

"See if any cars pull away. Look for one with the lights off."

Jase and John walked up to the porch. They stood there watching.

"Jase, look down the street to your left. A car with no lights was pulling away. Walk out a little and look at the car. I don't think it will move as long as he thinks you're looking at him. I will go back into the house and out the back door. I will try to get the plate number and call it in."

"Don't take any chances, John," said Jase.

John walked through the house. Linda asked, "What is going on, John?" John pulled a gun from under his jacket.

Now Linda was on the move. "Jill, stay here with the children." Linda grabbed her purse as she followed John out the door.

John said, "What are you doing, Linda?"

"I have been training for this for the last thirty years and you need back up."

The two move like the wind, using only hand signals. John stopped to pick up a small red ball in the yard near the bushes next to the car. The windows were tinted, and they could not tell if anyone was sitting the car. Linda wondered why John had picked up the ball.

By now, both of them had their guns drawn. Sneaking up on a dark car and not knowing if anyone was in it, was not a good situation and both of them knew it.

"Linda, I am going to take out one of the tires. Cover me." Linda didn't say a word but John knew she understood.

John came up from behind the car in its blind spot. He took out his knife and cut the valve stem on the back tire. Then he took the rubber ball that he had found in the yard, and very gently pushed it into the tail pipe. Linda watched John. She could not believe what she saw next.

275

John motioned for her to stay down. He put his gun in the holster and stood up. He started to walk by the car, then stopped. He tapped on the hood. The passenger window came down a little.

John smiled, "It looks like you might have a tire going flat." Then he started walking back to where Jase was standing.

Linda didn't move. The car tried to start, but could not. The motor turned over and over, then there was a small explosion and the ball shot out of the tailpipe. There was a heavy smell of gas in the air. The car finally started. Then riding on three good tires and one flat, the car moved slowly and turned down the first street it could.

Linda stood up, looked around and then she caught up with John. "That was very impressive, John. I don't think that I ever have seen that one before."

"Since no one was hurt, I didn't think we should push it. Professor, how is it going?"

"Not bad, this is a nice piece of hardware and very high tech. It is not looking very good for the agency."

John looked puzzled. "Why a tracker and a bomb?"

"They didn't want to take Jase or me out until they got the laser. But you John, it seems are expendable."

John smiled, "So it would seem. Would you mind if I take your little toy and make sure that I don't have any more surprises."

"You are good to go," said the Professor.

John turned, "I think I will have to get one of these."

The Professor walked over to John. "Here, I will make another one by morning. This one is too big anyway."

John waved, stepped into the limo and drove away.

"You know, Jase, I am getting to the place that I don't like Michael."

Jase puts his arm around the Professor. Come on old friend, we still have supper to eat."

Linda was already on the porch with Jill. As the two men came closer to Jill, they could tell she was upset. "Not out here, Jill, let's go inside," said Jase. They all sat down at the table.

"Jase, what have we gotten ourselves into?" asked Jill.

Linda took out her phone, and everyone was quiet. She pushed the call button. Then she put it on speaker.

"This is Michael, I'm not here right now. Please leave a name and number."

"Michael, this is Linda. You told me that you could trace any license plate number in the world. Well trace this one." She left Michael the plate number and then hung up.

Not too far from the Brick's home, a black Ford sat on the side of the road with a flat tire. The driver was on the phone.

"This is Michael. I need a car now, and get this one picked up. There is a restaurant right outside where the car is parked. I will be in there."

Michael put his phone down and started inside. Before he could enter, the phone went off again. It was Linda's call. He did not answer. He walked in and sat down.

"Just coffee thank you, he told the waitress in a friendly voice. There should be someone coming to pick me up in a few minutes."

"I see that you have a flat tire. Can I call someone for you?" asked the girl.

Michael responded, "That's not my car."

The girl smiled and went to get him the coffee. She told the cook, "Keep your eye on that one. I saw him get out of that car, but he said it is not his." They both nodded and went about their work.

Ann walked in. She saw Michael sitting at the corner table, and she joined him. "How is it going, Michael," she said.

Before he could answer, the girl brought Michael his coffee. "Can I get you something?" she asked Ann.

"Some sweet tea, if you have it in a to-go cup." The waitress smiled and left.

"Well, what have you been up to Michael or should I ask?"

"Don't start Ann," Michael raised his hand a little.

"It must have been good. I wish I could have seen it." Michael gave Ann a cold stare.

"Ok, I'll quit. So what are we doing next?" Ann asked. She knew when she had pushed Michael enough.

"The first thing we do is have my plane brought here in the morning. The Brick's and company are going to Virginia. So you stay away until I tell you different. I don't want them to know you work for me."

"Fine Michael, I need to clean up this mess around here anyway. Is Linda's last mission complete then?"

Michael's cell phone beeped, and he picked it up. The voice mail from Linda was on it. Michael stared at Ann as he replayed the message.

He handed the phone to Ann. "Just push repeat." Ann did as she was told and listened. "She is a very good agent. How was she to know it was you? You can't blame her for that."

Michael cooled down. "I guess you are right. Call her in the morning and tell her that the car was stolen and we are checking on it. Also, tell her that I will be arriving in the morning in my plane to personally escort them back to the safe house in Virginia."

"Now that is the Michael that I know," said Ann.

"Send that car somewhere far away from here. You are stuck with me for the night."

Ann responded, "It would be my pleasure, Michael."

While they were talking, a tow truck pulled up, put Michael's car inside and was gone.

"Sure beats AAA," said Ann. "Are you ready? My tea is on the way."

They got up and left in Ann's car. After they went out the door, the waitress turned to the cook. "There is something not right about those two."

At the house, Jill and Jase were doing the last of the packing and Linda was watching the children. "Jill, how did the moving go with Allan today?"

"Fine, they parked in the back and had everything loaded by noon. The man in charge said, "Thank you, Mrs. Smith. He must have thought I was Allan's wife."

Jase stopped what he was doing and looked at her. "Oh, that's nice."

"Jase, are you jealous?" Jill grinned.

"No, but I do have to admit you took me off guard."

"I think we are done. Everything that we could pack is packed. The rest we will have to do in the morning, after the kids are ready," said Jill.

The Professor walked in. "I am going home. I hope to see you again tomorrow night. Remember, from here on out everything that we say or do will be watched."

Jill ran over and gave the Professor a hug and softly said, "Thank you," in his ear. As soon as she lets go of him, Linda did the same.

After the Professor left, Linda said, "Jase, where did you find him? He is truly a friend."

"It is a long story. When he came to the university after he retired from the government, he looked normal. Then something happened. I really don't know what, but he puts on this act like he has nothing. He said it is so his friends and family won't bother him, and I think it is working. But he would do anything for me, and I would do anything for him."

Jill spoke up. "I think we all should try and get some rest." They all agreed and went up to the bedrooms.

None of them could sleep. Jill told Jase, "This has been the best house we ever had. Too bad it didn't last."

Chapter   43

Jill was up first with Linda right behind. They both sat in the babies' room waiting for them to wake. Linda said, "Are they not the most precious children you ever seen?"

"Yes," answered Jill. "I am so happy, but I have a feeling that they are going to have a bumpy ride for a while."

Jase was awakened by his phone. "This is Dr. Brick," he answered.

"Jase, this is John. Is there anything I can do for you?"

"No," answered Jase. "Will I see you again?"

"I'm sure of it. But for now, I will be watching until your plane takes off. Call if you need me."

"Will do, and again, thank you." Jase put the phone down and got up. He could smell breakfast cooking. By the time he arrived downstairs, the food was on the table.

"What is all this?" he asked.

"We have a lot of food here. So eat up, Dr. Brick, but don't expect it every day," Jill grinned.

The phone started to ring. "It's Michael," he said. "Good morning, Michael, how are you?"

"Fine Jase, do you need transportation?"

"If you don't mind, that would be great. We are all ready to go. Do you remember Rex? He is going with us."

"That's no problem. I will have someone at your door as soon as I can. See you at my plane."

Jill and Linda were staring at Jase. "Michael is sending someone to pick us up."

At the same time, the Professor was loading the last of the equipment into the van. One of the men asked him, "We were told that we are taking a car. Where is it?"

The Professor pointed at his red car. "It will cost more to move that old car than it is worth."

The Professor looked him right in the eye. "If my car does not go, nothing else goes. Got it?"

"Yes sir, will it make it to the airport or do I have to tow it?"

Upon seeing the Professor's face, the man said, "I was just joking. Would you please follow us in your car?"

"That's more like it, yes I will."

When the Professor arrived at the airport, there was a military plane waiting. They drove past the gates and up to the plane. The Professor got out. "I have not seen one of these for a while."

Someone was yelling to the Professor. When the Professor turned around, he could see Michael. "Professor, good morning."

Michael put his hand out to the Professor. "Would you like to ride with the equipment or with us in my plane?" Michael pointed at a twin engine Beech Craft sitting by itself.

"We can hold twelve people, and I can guarantee it will be a lot more comfortable than the military cargo plane."

"Well hell, are there free drinks?"

"Only if you like gin and squirt Professor, you know it is still morning don't you?"

"It's five o'clock somewhere," the Professor grinned. They walked over to the plane. "How old is this thing anyway?" asked the Professor.

"It is at least thirty years old. It used to belong to a man I did business with in South America. We did not see eye to eye on a few things, so now all that is left of his empire is this plane."

"What kind of business Michael or should I ask?"

"You probably should not ask," answered Michael

."Anyway, back to the plane, this is a Super King Air. I think it is about the quietest plane around. It has been maintained very well and is in excellent shape. I see your friends coming. Will you be flying with us?"

"Hell yes, but first, I have to get Jase's case from my car." The Professor walked back to the red car, picked up the case from the back seat and started back.

Jase could see the Professor as they drove up. "Jill, do you see what the Professor is carrying?"

"Oh my God, we forgot all about the money that was left in the safe." Jill answered.

The Professor and Michael watched as the van drove up. Jase was the first to get out. Michael met him at the plane. "It is a good day for a plane ride."

"Michael, where are we going?" asked Jase.

Before Michael could answer, a short fat man walked down the steps from the plane. Michael was very surprised, but he did not let it show.

"Dr. Brick, this is Richard. He is in charge of the agency that I work for."

Everyone stared at Richard. "His suit must of cost a lot of money, too bad it doesn't fit," thought Jill.

Richard stood at the entrance of the plane. "Dr. Brick, It is good to finally meet you, and this must be your wife," he said as he stared Linda.

"No, this is Linda Peach. She is helping us with the children. This is my wife, Jill," replied Jase.

Richard greeted everyone. "And who is this?" he asked.

Linda answered, "This is Rex. Be careful, he is a very good judge of character, and he might bite."

Richard pulled his hand back, "Welcome Rex, I hope you are house broken." Richard looked toward Jase.

"I think he will be alright, but this is the first time he has ever been on a plane," smiled Jase.

"Good for you, Jase," thought Linda. "You don't have to take his shit."

They were all on the plane except for Michael and Richard.

"Richard, I did not expect to see you here. So why are you here?"

"I don't get a chance to fly in your plane very often, and it is a good day to fly. You and I can talk later. But for now, let's take our guests to Virginia."

As soon as the two were inside, the plane started to move. "Michael has told me so much about all of you. He had the plane completely renovated. He is very proud of his plane. We should be landing in Virginia in a few hours, so please make yourselves comfortable. If you need anything, please ask."

Richard went up front. "Anytime you are ready. Let's get this show on the road."

The seats were facing each other. Jill and Linda sat in the back. Jase and the Professor faced Richard and Michael.

"Where are we going in Virginia?" asked the Professor.

"We will fly into a private airfield close to the James River. The other plane will land at a nearby naval air station. Professor, you will have your car tonight. Michael will see to it that you have everything you need."

Richard continued to talk. "You can come and go anytime. All we ask is that you give us some time to arrange your travel for you."

Jase spoke up, "Michael, how far are we from Gettysburg?"

"Not that far, why would you like to go there?"

"Yes, if it's not much trouble."

Richard spoke up. "Dr. Brick, we would like to have a demonstration of your laser. How long would that take?"

"We should have everything up and running in the morning. Is that all right?"

"That would be great. I run the house like a resort. I think that you will be very happy during your stay," replied Richard.

Jill was ease dropping. "Jase, can we go to Gettysburg this weekend?"

"Well I guess so. Would that work for you, Michael?"

By now, Jill was with the guys. She crouched down between the seats. "I want to pick out the motel. The last time I let you pick out the rooms…"

Jase cut her off. "You can pick out the rooms. I was going to ask you to anyway." Jase rolled his eyes.

Jill lightly punched him. "We have two children and Linda now. What are we going to do with Rex?"

Jase turned to Michael, "What can we do with Rex?"

Michael answered, "If worse comes to worse, we can always find a place in Gettysburg to board him. Professor, will you be going to Gettysburg also?"

"Hell no, I have my boat at Sting Ray Point, and I have not checked on it for a while."

"Well, it sounds like you have your first weekend planned. See, I told you that you would like it here," Michael smiled.

Jill said she was going back and try and to take a nap while she could, and the rest decided to do the same.

They landed at a small airstrip west of the James River. The plane taxied to the terminal. Everyone was in a rush to get off of the plane.

"What a great ride, but it sure is nice to stand up again," said the Professor.

"Where to next, Michael?" asked Jase.

"The van is waiting over here." Michael pointed to the side of the terminal where a van sat with the doors open. The driver was coming over with a cart for the bags.

It was early afternoon, and the trees were still very green here. It was quite a change from the Midwest fall that they had left behind. Both of the babies had been awake for some time. Everyone was aware that they were on the flight, but no one complained.

Richard's car pulled up. "Michael would you like to ride with me? There are a few things that we need to go over."

Upon hearing Richards's friendly command, Michael turned to the group. "The driver will take you all to the resort. I will see you there as soon as I can." Michael walked over and got into the car with Richard.

"Hey Jase, I would like to give you my first impression of Richard. He is a little arrogant asshole, watch out for him. That's all I'm going to say." The Professor grabbed Jase's case and went in the direction of the van. "Oh, I thought that I might carry this in case you forget it again."

Jase picked up Jack, and Jill carried Eva. Soon they were all on the way.

"All the land looks the same around here," said Jase. He sat up front with the driver.

"There is a lots of marsh land here and the government owns most of it. There are a few homes, but most are owned by fishermen who can't afford to live any closer to the ocean," replied the driver. "You can drive for miles around here and everything looks the same. Then out of nowhere there is a mansion. We have the working class and the super rich. It has always been that way." The driver stayed silent after that.

After a few minutes they turned onto a gravel road. The driver remarked, "Almost there."

They drove down a long gravel road. Then, like Linda had said, "As soon as you think that you are lost, you are there."

Jase said, "Well look at that." Everyone looked up to see a beautiful landscaped clearing. As soon as they passed through the clearing, they could see the mansion. It was a stately white house with a red tile roof sitting next to the river. They drove up to the center of the mansion and under a large portico used for loading and unloading passengers. As soon as the van stopped, there were people opening the doors and helping them out.

"Welcome to Virginia," said the young man who opened the van door. "My name is Thomas. If you need anything, let me know."

Jill smiled at Linda. "I think I might like this place."

Linda responded, "Be careful what you wish for."

Thomas said, "We have been expecting you. Would please follow me, and I will show you to your rooms."

They followed Thomas into the elevator and up to the second floor. He opened the door into a suite. As they walked into the room, they could see the river.

"This suite has three bedrooms. Ms Peach, I will have your things put in the room on the left, and Dr. Brick, you are on the right. This way everyone has access the baby's room in the center. The main sitting area of the suite has a fully stocked wet bar. If there is something else that you need, let me know. Each of the masters has a hot tub on the balcony, and we have a very nice dining room on the lower level. Please look around and enjoy."

Thomas turned to the Professor. "If you follow me, I will show you to your room."

The Professor winked at the rest and followed Thomas out of the room.

"This is really nice, Jase," said Jill. "I don't think I have ever been in anything as beautiful as this."

The door was still open when the Professor came back in. "Well hell, you can't beat the rooms."

"What do you say we take a look around, Professor, if that is all right with Jill," said Jase.

"Go ahead, we have to get the kids settled in."

Jase and the Professor walked down to the first floor where the dining area and the front desk were located. "This place is massive," said Jase.

They started to go toward the south wing of the compound, when they were stopped by a man at the doorway. "I'm sorry, Dr. Brick, but you do not have clearance for this part of the building."

The Professor remarked, "Is this place a resort or a prison?"

The man at the doorway responded again. "I'm truly sorry, but you cannot enter this part of the building."

"Let's go Professor," said Jase. They started to walk to the west part of the building and as before, they were stopped at the doorway.

"I don't like this Jase. It doesn't feel right. We can't go anywhere."

Jase told the Professor to follow him. They walked up to the desk. "What's going on here? We can't walk anywhere without being told we can't enter."

The girl behind the desk answered. "Almost every place around here you need to have a security clearance to enter. Our staff is getting yours approved as we speak. Why don't you have a seat in the dining area, and someone will be with you shortly."

They walked over to the dining area and sat down. "May I get something for you?" asked the waitress.

The Professor responded, "Gin and squirt."

"And for you, sir?"

"I'll have the same."

She walked away with the order.

"The only thing you can do here is drink," said the Professor.

It was not long before they had their drinks. "Is there anything else I can get you, Dr. Brick?"

"No thank you."

"How about you, Mr. Williams?"

The Professor was a little surprised, but answered, "Not right now. How much do I owe you?"

"Nothing, you are our guest."

The waitress left as the girl from the front desk was walking up to the table. "Dr. Brick, Michael said he will be right with you," then she went back to the desk.

"What do you think of this place?" asked Jase.

"Scares the shit out of me, how about you?"

"The same, let's sit here and see what happens next."

They sat and watched people come and go until they heard Michael walking up behind them.

"I see you found the restaurant. They did not have any squirt, so I had some brought in. Can I give you a tour of the place?"

"Yes, I feel like I'm in a prison." said the Professor.

"No, not even close, but you are in one of the highest security areas in the country. Almost everything here is top secret, so please bear with us. I am getting you clearances for the areas that you will need to be in. Would you like to see your lab? Please follow me." Michael walked to the west part of the building and this time no one stopped them. They went to the elevator and Michael pushed the down button.

"This place has a basement? How do you keep it dry with all the marshes and the river next door? It must be wet all the time."

Before Michael could answer, the Professor spotted the down buttons on the elevator panel. There were ten levels of buttons.

"This I have to see. You have more levels below the ground than you have above it," said the Professor.

"We are only going down one level, Professor, but I think that you will be impressed. As soon as I get your ID cards, you will be free to come down here anytime that you want."

"Michael, what is in the other side of the compound? We were not permitted to enter there either," said Jase.

"Administration and communication are restrictive areas. The only time you can be in that area is with someone who has a clearance. My office is in that area and so is Richard's."

The Professor spoke up. "Richard sure seems like an asshole."

"Sometimes in this business, you need an asshole, Professor." Michael replied.

The door opened to a brightly lit large room. "I think everything that you need is here. Your equipment should be arriving soon. Professor, your car is already in the parking garage. Thomas will be glad to take you there."

"Now Dr. Brick, when you arrived, our scan showed that you have a large sum of money with you. Would you like to put it in the safe?"

Jase was shocked, "You scanned my money?"

"Everyone that comes into the compound is screened for all kinds of things, so do you need to use our safe?"

"No, for right now, I will keep my money with me. And Michael, you are starting to creep me out a little."

"Oh, you will get used to it. We are here to help you, but we must keep our defenses up." Michael walked back to the elevator. "If you have seen enough, let me show you back to the main area."

When they arrive at the first floor, the door opened and Thomas was standing there waiting.

"Mr. Williams, if you will come this way, I will take you to your car."

"See you later, Jase. I want to check the car out and see if they scratched it or something. Oh, and I made you something." The Professor gave a new detector to Jase. "This one is a little smaller than the last one."

"What is that, Dr. Brick?" asked Michael.

"Just a little toy the Professor made me," Jase replied.

"Professor, I will be in my room, come up whenever you ready. Michael, when should everything be here?"

Michael answered, "Within the hour, I will have the staff let you know when everything is here."

"Thanks, that would be helpful. Michael, is this entire place bugged?" Jase was looking at the detector.

"Yes," answered Michael.

"How about our rooms?" asked Jase.

"We have every room in the compound wired, except the rooms for the guest. But as soon as you walk into the hall, we know it."

"Well, thanks for letting me know." Jase shook Michael's hand and went up to their suite. Jill and Linda were waiting for him.

Chapter   44

As Jase walked to the elevator, Michael headed for the communication area. He walked in and went straight to a man sitting at a monitor. "Shut the Brick's room down, now!"

The man at the desk hit some keys on his computer. "Done Michael, what's going on?"

"They are running a test for bugs. Keep the ones on outside of the rooms until I tell you different."

"Yes sir, it's all shut down and I will tag it."

Michael patted him on the back and started to go to his office. Before he got to his office, he was stopped by a staff member.

"Michael, Richard would like to see you in his office."

Michael turned around. He got into the elevator and went up to the next floor. The entire floor was Richard's office. As soon as the door opened, he stopped at the desk right in front of the elevator.

"Hello Michael, Richard is waiting for you. Go right in," said Richard's secretary.

Michael thanked her as he went in. Richard's desk was at the far end of the room. Large windows offering a panoramic view of the river wrapped around the room. A wood burning fireplace and a leather couch and chair added a feeling of warmth to the office. Richard loved the feeling of power his intimating office gave him

"Michael, come in. How is the laser coming?" Richard asked.

"We should have it here at anytime."

"Sit down, Michael." Richard waited until Michael had taken a seat.

"Michael, we have been through many operations together, have we not?"

"What have you got on your mind, Richard?"

"This is the most important mission we have ever attempted. The future of our country is at stake."

Michael started to say something. "Let me finish, Michael. We have silenced a few leaders in our day, haven't we?"

"I guess so," replied Michael.

"We have been asked to take out one more."

"Who wants this, Richard?"

"That does not matter. Michael, how do you feel about the way this country is headed?"

"I don't understand, what are you getting at?"

"What do you think of the new President? Do you think that she is taking us down the wrong path?"

"Yes, but why are you asking me?"

"We have been asked to remove her."

"Richard, this agency has never taken out one of our own. If anyone found about it, they would shut us down."

"Michael, slow down. Even the CIA doesn't know that we exist. Hell, there are a lot more sleeper agencies just like us out there. If we don't do it, one of the other ones will."

"Richard, think what you are doing. I have always backed you one hundred percent. But to take out the President of the United States? The repercussions would last a lifetime and beyond. They still have not forgotten JFK."

"We are better at it now," answered Richard. "Listen Michael, in a few days there will be a press conference from the White House. One of Seaban's networks will be there."

"Seaban, Richard you know he is crazy!"

"Maybe so, but he has been backing us for years with both money and support of our missions on SBN."

"Ok Richard, how is the agency going to take out the President?"

"We will have TV cameras on both the left and right side of the room behind the reporters. Each one of the cameras will have one of Dr. Brick's lasers in it. They will be aimed at the President's heart. When she dies, it will look like she had a heart attack, and Mr. Seaban will have the best scoop ever. The headlines will read 'The President dies of natural causes'. We can't mess this one up."

"I need to think about this one, Richard."

"No you don't. You have no choice. The agency would not react very well if you did not support the mission. Do I make myself clear?"

"Yes Richard, perfectly clear."

"Now go and get the lasers ready, and let me know when I can see a demo. And Michael, this will happen with or without you."

Michael got up and walked out of Richard's office. For the first time, he did not know what to do. If he failed to complete this assignment, Richard was capable of taking him and his family out.

Michael walked to the elevator and waited for the door to open. He rode down to the next floor. He didn't want the door to open, but it did. He walked slowly to his office and he told his secretary he didn't want to be bothered unless it was about the Bricks. He sat looking at a picture of his family.

Jase walked into his suite. Jill was the first to ask, "Well, what did you find out?"

Jase pulled out the new monitor that the Professor had given him. "Looks like the room is clean, no bugs."

"That's good," Jill said.

The Professor walked in behind Jase. "How does the room look, any bugs?"

"No, the hall outside is bugged, but the room looks clean." Jase handed the scanner to the Professor.

"They must have de-energized the rooms," said the Professor.

"Why do you say that Professor?" asked Jill.

"I checked the rooms before I went down to the lab. This entire building is bugged, but at least they turned the circuits off for our rooms."

"So we are in a prison, Richard's prison," said Jill.

Someone knocked at the door and Jase opened it. "Dr. Brick, I have all of your security badges. Just clip them onto your shirts, and no one will stop you. You can go to the lab anytime you need to."

"Thank you, Thomas, has our equipment arrived yet?"

"Yes, Dr. Brick, they are unloading it now."

"Good, the Professor and I will be down shortly."

Thomas turned to leave and as he started to say, "If you need any…"

Everyone cut him off. "Yes we know, call Thomas."

Linda asked the Professor to check the balcony for bugs. He did and came back in. "Looks clean."

Linda waved her hand for everyone to go out on the balcony. "Everything is bugged, the yard, the dining area, the lab and the parking area. So make sure that you don't say anything that you don't want Michael or Richard to know."

Both of the babies were awake. "Why don't you take the babies down to the dining area and get some food for yourself," said Jase. "The Professor and I are going back to the lab."

The Professor and Jase put on their ID badges and headed for the lab. This time no one stopped them. When they arrived at the lab, all the equipment was there.

"Professor, let's get the demo ready for Michael." In less than an hour, they had the lasers online.

"Jase, here come Richard and Michael. They must have been watching us."

"Are we ready for the demo?" asked Richard.

All we have ready is the laser. We should have the rest by tomorrow morning." The Professor was toying with them, to see what they would say.

"That's fine, but I would like to see the laser work. Michael has told me so much about it," replied Richard.

"Alright then," Jase said. He had set up the plywood and the pea hanging from a string.

The Professor closed the blinds as Jase energized both of the lasers.

"Richard, would you come over here while we wait for the lasers to warm up?" Richard walked over.

"Now, put your hand in front of the green laser beam." Richard was a little reluctant, so Jase put his hand in the beam.

"See, nothing to fear. Now put your hand in front of the red beam." This time Richard did. He smiled.

"Now, watch this." Jase put the first beam on the plywood. And then he put the second beam on it. "See the pea that is hanging on the other side of the wood? Watch what happens when I put both beams on the pea at the same time."

"Should I move back?" asked Richard.

"No, you are fine." Jase brought both beams together on the side of the pea. The pea turned black. "Now watch what happens when I turn up the power." The pea exploded.

"Think of it Richard, performing surgery without making an incision."
Jase waved at the Professor to open the blinds as he powered down
the lasers.

"Now, the lasers will only work three times, and this counts as
number one. After the third time, we have to rebuild it. It can't be
tampered with or it will self destruct. That is a little safety factor that
the Professor built in."

"That is a great idea, Dr. Brick," said Richard. "You never know who
you can trust."

Jase asked, "Now, can we store the lasers somewhere out of sight until
we are ready? I would hate to have someone turn them on when we
are not here."

"Good idea, Dr. Brick. Michael, can you find room for them on the
next level?" Richard was very excited.

"If that is all right with you, Dr. Brick." said Michael.

"Will I have access to the next level?"

Richard responded, "Michael, see if you can get them clearance on
the next level."

Michael hesitated, but after Richard gave him a dirty look, he said,
"Yes."

"I think we are off to a good start, Dr. Brick," Michael said. "You
said that you might want to take a weekend trip. Will you go this
weekend?"

"I think that would be nice. Jill and Linda could use an outing. Jill
was on the net, and she said there is a hotel just south of Gettysburg.
Do you know anything about it?"

"Must be the Eisenhower Inn, good choice. Would you go Friday, Saturday and Sunday?" asked Richard.

"Do you think that we could get a reservation this late?" asked Jase.

Richard answered, "If I know Michael, he probably has all ready made reservations."

Michael said, "No, but I will get right on it. Professor, will you be going with Dr Brick?"

"Hell no, my boat is not far from here, and I have not seen her in almost a year. If I can get out of here, I will be sailing by Thursday."

Jase turned toward Michael. "Don't forget Rex, we will take him with us. I'm sure that someone at the Inn can find a place for him to stay."

Michael and Richard were pleased at how easy it was to get the lasers under their control.

Richard was first to speak. "Well, I have a hundred things to do, so I will talk to all of you later."

Michael was next. He grabbed two men who were walking by. "I need you two to move some equipment to the next level for storage."

"For storage, all that is on the next level is…"

Michael interrupted him. "I know what's on the next level. Now will you please move this equipment down to the next level? Dr. Brick will check on it later."

"Yes sir." This time there were no questions.

"Michael, what is on the next level?" asked the Professor.

"Let me get your security clearance for that level, and then I will show you."

"That sounds good to me. Come on Professor, let's take some of the work up to our rooms. We can tell the girls about this weekend." They walked out leaving Michael behind.

Michael talked to the two men in charge of moving the laser. "Do you think you can get the lasers into the cameras?"

"As soon as we get them down to our lab, we will start on it."

"Remember, do not energize them. We will find out how they work later. For right now, get them into the cameras."

"Yes sir, we are on it."

As they walked back to the suite carrying two brief cases containing only blank papers, Jase asked, "Do you think they can figure out how to get into them?"

"Not a chance. I can't do it, and I hope that they do not try or we will be here all weekend building new ones."

"That would not be good, Professor."

The door unlocked automatically when they got close. "Must be the ID badges," said the Professor.

Jase closed the door behind them. He had his poker face on. Jill and Linda were watching his every move. Then he smiled.

"Would you like to go to Gettysburg?"

"You did it, Jase. We were so scared. Now, tell us everything."

"Tomorrow we work here in the room all day."

"But Jase, we don't have anything to work with. We destroyed everything before we left," said Jill.

"I know that, and you know that, but Michael doesn't know that. And anytime we leave the room, the brief cases must be locked up. They will find out soon enough that they do not have anything in them but blank papers. So after while, let's all go down to the restaurant and have a meal on Michael."

Linda reached over to touch Jase on the arm. "Jase, we are on very deadly ground here.

When Richard finds out what we have done, he will put a price on our heads."

"Linda, if we did anything other than what we are doing, do you think we would still be alive?"

"What scares me is that six months ago I was working for the agency not against it."

"We must all relax," said Jase. "See, be more like Rex." Rex was over in the corner sleeping in the sunlight and snoring.

It rained all night. No one felt like getting out of bed, but the two children had other ideas. This was the first time Jase had time to play with them. Linda and Jill watched as the new Dad worked his fatherly magic. Life was good for now, and the new family enjoyed every minute of it.

Suddenly, there was a knock at the door. "Well, it has to be ether the Professor or Thomas," said Jill.

Jase opened the door. There stood the Professor holding his case.

LASER
By A.W.STRAWSBURG

"Jase, I have been going over these papers all night, and I can't seem to make out what you meant."

"Get in here, sometimes Professor," Jase did not finish, he just let him in.

"Jase, I have been watching the scanner. Sometimes it will come on long enough to see what we are doing. So we need to make it look like we are working on something."

"Alright, but for now, put your brief case on the table and make sure it is locked," said Jase.

"Then we all can go and get some breakfast?" asked Jill.

"Professor, do you have that steel tape measure in your pocket?" asked Jase. The Professor promptly took out a six inch ruler from his shirt pocket.

Jase put both of the cases on the table exactly six inches from the edge and six inches from each other. Linda pulled out one of her blond hairs and placed it on the table and the cases.

"If any one tries to open the cases, we will know it," Linda said.

"Now, let's go and eat." Jill was hungry.

They went to the dining room and sat at a table overlooking the river. The waiter came over. "It is really very pretty out, but I think it is supposed to rain all day." He handed everyone a menu. "I will be back to take your orders."

"That was odd," said the Professor. "He did not take our drink orders."

The waiter went to the phone. "They are all here eating." Then he hung up.

Linda said, "I know what they are doing. I will be right back." She got up and almost ran back to the room. When she got there, Thomas was about to enter the room.

"Hi Thomas, is there something I can help you with?"

"No, Ms. Peach, I always check the rooms to see if they need anything and make the beds. It is what I do."

"Well don't let me be in your way," she said.

They both walked into the room together. Thomas looked through the rooms very quickly. "Everything looks good for now. I will check back later." Thomas started to leave.

"Thomas," Linda said.

"Yes, Ms. Peach."

"Don't worry about the beds. If we need anything, we will call you." Thomas had already forgotten about the beds.

"And Thomas, please don't enter the rooms unless we are here."

"Yes, Ms. Peach."

Thomas couldn't get out of the room fast enough. He went straight to Michael's office.

"What did you find, Thomas?"

"Before I could look, Ms. Peach was on me like a dirty shirt. But everything looked alright. She asked me to not go into the rooms unless they were there."

"Did you see any papers that they were working on?"

"No, all I saw was two brief cases on the table, and I think that they were locked."

"That is alright, they will be gone all weekend. We will have plenty of time to see what is in the cases. Go back and do what you do."

"Yes Michael." Thomas left the office.

Linda walked back to the dining area. "Our good friend, Thomas, was about to enter the room when I got there. We are going to have to be very careful."

Everyone ordered their breakfast and watched the rain. As they were dining, Jase's phone rang. It was Dean Charles.

"This Dr. Brick, may I help you?"

"Jase, where are you and what is going on? Everyone is looking for you. That Diane Worth has been calling all day. What do I tell her? And Michael Greyger called and pledged enough money to build a new lab for you. I have everything, except you."

"Michael thought that we would be safer at a government facility than at the school for now. That is all I can tell you. As soon as I can say more, I will call you. And to be perfectly honest with you, I don't know what is going on myself."

"Jase, you have left me in a tight spot. As soon as you can tell me something, please let me know."

"I will Dean." Jase hung up.

"I feel bad that I could not tell him anything. He has been very good to us. He said that Michael had called him and made a large pledge to the university." Everyone was silent. They all had something to say, but knew that they could not say anything until they got up to the rooms.

Very quietly, Michael walked up to the table. "So Professor, are you going to your boat if it continues to rain tomorrow?"

"Hell yes, I'm sure there is a lot to do rain or shine, and it will be good to sleep on the ship for a few nights. After this is over, I think I will take a long trip in the gulf."

"That sounds great Professor, I wish I could go with you," answered Michael.

"I think that tomorrow will be fine. I would like to leave early, that is if Jase will let me."

"Anytime Professor, I could never have gotten this far without you. Enjoy your long weekend. Will I see you in the morning?" asked Jase.

"I don't know. If the weather is good, I will start out at daybreak. If not, I will see you before I leave. Would you like to go, Michael? I have a very good supply of gin on board," said the Professor.

"Sounds great, but I have a lot going on right now. I will have to work all weekend. Maybe next time, thanks for the invite though."

Michael walked over to Linda. "So you are retired now? What are you going to do?"

"The Brick family has asked me to stay on, so I think that I will for now."

Michael didn't like that answer. "Really, I thought that you wanted to get out on your own for a little R&R?"

"I will. But for now, I love helping out with the kids."

Jase spoke, "Well, I have to get back to work. If the rest of you want to stay here, be my guest. There is not much to do here, but watch the rain or the TV."

Jill said, "It looks awful out. I think I will take the kids back to the room. They are about asleep."

"I think that would be a good idea," said Linda. They started to get up.

"Michael, can we tip here?"

"No, the help is not allowed to take any tips from our guests. If you gave someone a tip, they could lose their job." Jase put his money back in his pocket, and everyone started to walk back to the room.

Michael said, "If you need anything, let me know."

As they walked away from the table, Linda turned and saw Michael stare at her and then hold his hand up to his ear. She could read his lips. "Call me." A cold chill went down her back, but she kept walking.

When they got back to the room, the Professor looked around. "I think it is clear," he said.

Linda spoke, "Michael wants me to call him. I better do it now."

"Call from your room." Jase took the scanner from the Professor. "Here, take this with you."

Linda said, "Wish me luck," and she went into the room.

She still had Michael on the speed dial. He answered, "Linda, how are you? We are very happy with the job that you are doing."

"Stop right there, Michael. You told me that I was finished. I am now retired. These are very nice people. You got your laser, so why don't you leave them alone."

"Linda, are you becoming involved with the Brick family?"

"Michael, just do what you are going to do and leave them alone. And no, I am not getting involved. As soon as I can, I am going someplace alone. I will give you an address to send my retirement to."

"Linda, we are very grateful for your service. If you change your mind, I'm sure I can find a place for you."

"Thanks Michael, I will keep it in mind." Linda answered sharply. "Is there anything else?"

"No, I think after this weekend we should be in good shape. Thanks again, Linda."

"You are welcome, Michael." Linda put her phone down. She walked out into the main room. "Well, whatever they are doing, it is going to happen very quickly. I think that we should leave as soon as possible."

Chapter 45

By the next day, the rain had eased up a little. Instead of coming down in buckets, it was a drizzle. The Professor was on his way to his boat. He had installed a scanner under his dash before the car had left the university. He turned it on, and the car was bugged. All he could do was hope that it was not a bomb. They probably wanted to know where he was going.

In about an hour, he was close to Stingray Point. He had heard a rumor that Capt. John Smith was stung by a stingray while fishing, and that is why it was called Stingray Point.

When he saw the sign for Deltaville, he knew that he was getting close. Deltaville was a sleepy little town that came alive in the summer. He passed through the town in just a few minutes. His next stop was the Point. He pulled into the marina that was on the left. His 32 foot yacht seemed small next to some of the ships, but he was glad to see her. It had been too long.

The Professor parked his car next to the fence and stared out at the bay. The ocean was a little choppy with small white caps. He grabbed one of the carts used for taking items to and from your ship and went to check her out. The ship was sitting fine, but was a little dirty from the weather. Maybe if he had time, he could give her a once over.

He kept looking over his shoulder to see if anyone was following him. He crossed the wood pier until he arrived at his docking space. Walking fore and aft, he checked the outside of the ship. He pulled on the mooring line until the ship came close enough to board. Once aboard, he saw an envelope stuck on the hatch. It read, "Professor, go to the lighthouse on the other side of the marina. We will pick you up. Bring your gear. Glad you could make it, Allan."

The Professor did not unlock his hatch. Instead, he returned his cart and walked past his car on his way to the lighthouse.

"This is great. How long am I supposed to stand here? What if someone sees me?" It started to rain harder, so he walked under the light house. He wondered if he had made the right move.

Then he heard a chopper. As it came closer, he could see Canond Industries on the side of it. "I guess this is my ride," he said to himself. The chopper landed not far from the lighthouse. The Professor walked over to the open door.

"Professor Williams, please get in. We haven't much time." The man in the chopper grabbed the Professor's hand. "Have a seat sir."

Even with the door shut, the chopper was noisy. The pilot handed the Professor some noise suppressors. "Is that better?" asked the pilot.

"Yes," yelled the Professor. "Now, where are we going?"

"We have a boat to catch," answered the pilot as they headed out over the ocean. As soon as they left the coast, they flew south. The farther south they went, the more sunshine they saw.

"The ship is already on its way to the Keys, so we will meet it in route," said the pilot. "This is going to be a fast trip. I will get you there as quick as I can. We did not know if you were going to make it."

"I know the feeling, but we aren't there yet. Did I mention that I hate choppers?" The pilot smiled. He hardly said another word the rest of the trip.

The Professor was getting a little airsick, when the pilot pointed to a ship on the horizon. As they came closer, the ship slowed down. On the back of the ship, the landing pad lights turned on.

"What the hell! Are you going to land on that?"

Again the pilot smiled. Before the Professor knew it, they were on the landing pad.

The deck crew was strapping down the chopper, even before the door was opened.

The Professor did not move. The door opened from the outside, and the Professor turned to see who opened it.

"Welcome aboard Professor, how was your trip?" Allan Smith was standing at the door. "You look pretty pale, Professor. Come on, and let's go inside."

The Professor had to pry his hand from the door. He was cold and sweaty. Allan helped him out of the chopper and showed him to the main deck. They sat down in the lobby of the yacht. Soon the Professor started to come around.

One of the crew handed the Professor a drink. "Is gin and squirt all right?"

The Professor could not answer the girl, but she knew it was all right. The first thing that he could say was, "Another please."

Allan waited for the Professor to regain his composure before he asked him anything. "Are you all right Professor?" asked Allan.

"Yes, I am now. I hate choppers. Give me a boat in forty foot waves anytime. At least you don't have far to fall."

Now, Allan was serious. "Are the Bricks going to make it to Gettysburg?"

"That is the plan. By the way, are we going to Key West?"

"Yes, we will be there tomorrow. We should be past the rough weather in a few hours, and then it will be smooth sailing the rest of the trip."

The Professor sat back and looked around. "Hell, you know a person could get used to a little boat like this."

Allan smiled. "Let's hope that Dr. Brick does not have any trouble."

The stewardess came over. "Can the chef put something together for you, Mr. Williams?"

"That would be nice. What are the options?"

Allan said, "Come on Professor, let's go to the dining area."

Chapter   46

Jase was up early. He went to the lobby desk. "Did the Professor leave yet?"

The man behind the desk answered, "Yes, Dr Brick, he was out of here very early. He is very proud of that car of his, isn't he?"

Jase grinned, "You have no idea."

Jase walked over to the dining area and sat down. Thomas walked over to him. "Dr. Brick, it seems that you are on the news this morning. Would you like to see?"

"Sure, why not, I bet I know who is talking about me." Thomas put the news on. It did not take long for them to get to Jase.

"This is the founder and CEO of the Cancer Research Environment, Diane Worth." The news reporter went on. "Since you discovered Dr. Brick and his cancer project, what has happened?"

"Thank you," she said. "This industry is involved in a lot of very costly research. All we are trying to do is find a way to treat cancer and save lives."

The news reporter stopped her. "But are you not trying to end cancer as well?"

"This has been my life's dream. I don't like it when someone comes in for a profit and takes the life savings of victims of cancer."

"But Diane, when you treat a person, it is a very heavy financial burden on that person's family as well. One injection for chemo could run over $10,000."

"This is true, but the research that got us here was very expensive, and might I point out, we are still here. At the first sign of trouble, we did not pull up and leave like Dr. Brick. No one knows where he is."

"Diane, do you think that this is because you confronted him on TV?"

The waiter brought some coffee over to the table, and Michael was right behind him.

"Have a seat, Michael. This woman is afraid of me, and I have not done anything to her."

Michael watched the news show. "Would you like me to do anything, Dr. Brick?"

"What could you do, Michael?"

"Well, I don't want to add fuel to the fire, but I'm sure we could get you some positive coverage on the air."

"Michael, do you know what she is afraid of?"

"Tell me, Jase."

"I am so close to curing cancer that I will put her and every other cancer clinic out of business. Think about it, no more chemo or radiation. Do you know how many people it would put out of business?"

"I never thought of it like that, Jase. I think that it is a good thing that you are here with us where it is safe."

Jase turned and looked at Michael's face. "Michael, do you think that someone would try to kill me or my family because of my research?"

"Anything is possible, Jase. Just be glad you are here."

Michael thought he would change the subject. "I heard that the Professor left early this morning."

Jase answered, "That's what I heard too. His life is his sailboat. That is what makes him happy."

"Oh, by the way, the car will pick you up when you are ready, and the driver will be back to pick you up Sunday. I hope that you all have a wonderful weekend."

"You too, Michael, we are looking forward to getting away. I'm leaving all my work here. We asked Thomas to keep everyone out of our rooms unless we are there. Would you please insure that he honors our request?"

"You don't have to worry about Thomas, you can trust him."

"I am glad to hear that." Jase said as he was getting up. "I think I will go back to the room. I have a lot of things to do today."

When Jase arrived back at the room, Jill and Linda were watching the news. He could tell they were both upset.

"Jase," said Jill, "Can we do anything about her? She is trouble."

"Not right now, but we will have our day. Michael asked me if there was anything he could do."

Linda was holding Jack. She raised her head to speak, never taking the smile off her face. "That's scary, if Michael offered to help." Then she turned her attention back to Jack. He was smiling back at her.

"Let's talk about something else," Jase said. "We need to take everything tomorrow. I will leave behind the two briefcases on the table. Everything else goes. What time do you want to leave?"

"Between 8:00 and 9:00 am, would be fine. But Jase, don't you think we should leave some things behind? Maybe we could leave some things that we do not need. It would make it look more like we are coming back."

"Maybe, but if we leave it, it is gone forever. The Professor left his case here. I will put it on the table with mine. I hope that will slow them down some."

Linda was still making faces at Jack. She never took her eyes off him. "Jase, Michael will have the cases opened as soon as we are gone."

"What should I do, Linda?"

"They have a safety deposit box in the safe. Have them give you the key. That should slow Michael down until the first of the week."

"Good idea, Linda, I will do that right before we go."

Jill was holding Eva, who was asleep. "You have no idea what you are in for. Do you think Peanut will want to hold her?"

Jase smiled, "Wouldn't you?"

The rest of the morning dragged on. "I hope that the Professor is all right," Jill said.

"Don't underestimate him," said Jase. "I'm sure he is fine." For the rest of the day they concentrated on the children.

Morning came with sunshine and a little wind. Thomas knocked on the door and Jase opened it.

"Dr. Brick, whenever you are ready, the van is parked outside of the lobby."

"Thank you, Thomas, we will eat first. Do you have a safety deposit box that I can put our work in?"

"Yes sir, behind the main desk. Would you like me to take something to the desk for you?"

"No, not yet, we will do that when we leave this morning. We will have some bags and baby things to be taken down when you are ready."

"I can take some of it right now, if you want."

Jill waved at him and pointed at a stack of luggage. "You could take these if you want, and we can bring the rest after we eat."

"That sounds good. I will get these in the van, and I will be waiting for you when you are ready," said Thomas. "You will probably arrive at the inn before check-in time. Would you like me to take you any place until then?" asked Thomas.

"We will have to see, but thanks for asking." Jase did not want him standing around.

Thomas had the cart with the luggage and was going out to the van, when he was stopped by Michael. Michael put a small electronic device in Thomas's hand.

"Would you put this in a place where they won't find it? I would hate to lose track of Dr. Brick and company."

"Yes sir, I think I know just where to put it."

Michael gave Thomas a pat on the back. "I can always count on you."

When the family came down to the dining room, Jase was carrying the case with the money. They were shown to a table next to the window. Michael came over to the table.

"May I sit with you?" he asked.

"Of course, Michael, it is a good thing we did not go yesterday. Today is perfect," said Jase.

"Now, if you need anything, please call me. I will send Thomas right away. If not, he will see you on Sunday. What time would you like to be picked up?"

Jase answered, "Can we call you? If things are going good, it might be later. You never know with the children."

"That sounds like a plan." The waiter was there to take orders. After they had finished, Michael excused himself. "I will talk to all of you the first of the week. Have a good trip."

They all answered, "Thank you." Then Michael left and went straight to his office. He told his secretary to send Thomas in. Thomas came in before Michael could sit down. "Where did you put the transmitter?"

"I put it under the collar of the dog. Everywhere they go the dog goes."

"That would not be my first choice, but I think that will be all right." Michael sat down in his chair. As Thomas left the room, Michael's phone rang. "This is Michael."

"Can you come down to the lab? We have the lasers mounted in the cameras."

"I will be right there." He did not waste any time getting to lower level 3. This level was not like the level that Jase and the Professor had seen. On this level was one new weapon after another.

One of the research people came up to Michael. "Michael, look at this." He handed Michael what looked like a baseball.

"What the hell is this?"

The researcher smiled, "This ball is a small nuclear device. If you throw it into a room, it will take out anything that is carbon based. And there is no radiation residue. We need a place to test it. Do I have your permission to go out west to the Yucca test sites and use one of the underground test units?"

"I will call the first of the week to see what I can do for you. You know, those ten by ten test bunkers are for bomb testing only."

The researcher responded, "This is a nuclear bomb. I don't think that we should test it here, do you?"

Michael said, "Get that thing away from me. You make me nervous. Is that thing armed?"

"Yes, would you like to see how to detonate it?"

"Put it somewhere safe. I don't want to see it again." The researcher smiled and left.

Finally, Michael was looking at the cameras. "Tell me how this thing works."

One of the two lab technicians pointed at the laser. "We calibrated the laser to the lens of the cameras, so while you are taking the picture, you are also aiming at the target. You cannot see the laser beams with all the lights on. What do you think?"

"Are you sure that it will work?"

The other lab technician said, "As much as we can be. The Professor put most of the lasers in a lead lined container. We could not get into it without breaking the seal."

"All right, I will have someone pick them up and get them to the site. Thank you, and remember this is top secret."

Both men nodded. "We will have them ready to ship."

"Good, I'm going up and tell Richard that everything is a go." Michael left.

"I wonder who they are going to rub out this time?"

The other man said, "Keep your mouth shut or it will be you." They both agreed and went about their work.

Michael went to Richard's office. "Well?" Richard asked.

"It's ready to ship," Michael answered.

"Monday is the big day. I will call Robert and tell him to pick up the cameras." Michael sat while Richard was on the phone.

"Robert, we have the items that you need, and they are available for pick up."

There was a delay in the response, and then Seaban answered. "I will have the items picked up in thirty minutes." The phone line went dead.

Richard looked at Michael. "They will be here in thirty minutes."

Michael stood up. Before he walked out, he asked, "Are you sure about this, Richard?"

"We are in too deep to back out now, Michael."

Michael left the room. He was walking back, as Jase and family were going to the front desk.

"Well, Jase, are you ready to go?"

"Almost, I would like to have these two brief cases put into the safety deposit boxes."

Michael was surprised a little. "Do you think that is necessary?"

"You can't be too safe. You have taught me that, Michael." He handed the cases to the desk clerk.

The man at the desk handed Jase the keys. "Here you are, Dr. Brick. Is there anything else I can do for you? Would you like to put that case in with the rest?"

Jase answered, "No," and thanked him.

"I will see you in a few days, Michael." He put out his hand and Michael shook it. Jase walked out to the waiting van.

Michael looked at his hand, and it was wet. Jase was sweating. Michael promptly walked out to the van. "Dr. Brick, are you all right? You don't look so good."

Jase was sweating more. "Yes, I'm all right. I just need to get away for a couple of days."

Michael watched as they all got into the van and drove away. As soon as they were gone he went to the communication room. "Are the tracers working?"

The young man at the desk answered, "Yes. The Professor's car is at Stingray Point. Looks like some kind of yacht club."

"How about the transmitter on the dog?"

The young man punched up the screen. "They are headed for Gettysburg."

Michael said, "Call me if anything changes. They are up to something."

Michael went back to the front desk. "Did you give Dr. Brick the right key for the deposit boxes?"

"Yes sir, that is what he asked for. Is there something wrong, Michael?"

"I don't know. How long will it take you to get into the boxes?"

"We don't have anyone here this weekend that can crack the safe."

"Get on the phone and find someone, and get them in here now."

Michael started to go to Richard's office. But there was nothing he could do for now, so went back to his own office.

Chapter 47

The van made good time, even though there was a lot of traffic on the small road. The two babies were asleep almost as soon as the van moved. Linda could see Jase was nervous. She put her hand on his arm. "It will all work out," she whispered. The trip was very quiet.

Jase thought he would check the monitor that the Professor had given him. He turned it on, and the red light flashed.

He motioned for Jill and Linda to watch the screen. Whatever it was, it was up front with them. Jase moved the monitor around each of them. When it came closer to Rex it locked in on his collar. Jase quickly hid the monitor. Then he said to the dog, "How are you doing, Rex. You are being really good." Jase put his hand under the collar, and he could feel the tracer attached to the bottom side.

Thomas was watching in the mirror, but he could not see anything. "How is your dog doing, Dr. Brick?"

"Fine, I don't think he has moved an inch."

"We are almost there. As soon as we get on RT 15, the Inn will be up ahead on the right. There are a lot of battle grounds to see and shops too. Thomas stopped himself. "I am starting to sound like a tour guide, sorry."

Jill was quick to answer, "That's all right, Thomas. The more we know about this place, the better,"

Thomas pointed to the right just ahead. "We are here. I will take you to the front desk."

The parking lot was a maze of parking spaces and cars. Thomas took them to the door and retrieved one of the carts for their clothes and bags.

"What are you going to do with your dog?" Thomas asked.

Jase answered, "I will go to the front desk and find out." He walked into the lobby.

"May I help you?" asked the clerk behind the desk.

"Do you have rooms for Dr. Brick?"

"Yes sir, but the rooms are not ready yet. You can leave your bags here and have a seat in the bar area. We will come and get you when the rooms are ready."

"That will be fine. We have a dog. What can we do with him?"

"I will have to check. For now, there is a large lot in the back."

"Good, I think we both could use a walk." Jase turned toward Jill and Linda. "I will take Rex out back for a walk."

"No," said Linda. "I will take Rex. You need to be with your family. I will be all right."

Thomas brought the cart in to Jase. "We are going to have to wait for our rooms, so there is little that you can do for us. Thank you, Thomas, we will see you Sunday."

"You are welcome." He went out the door to the van, and they watched him pull out of the parking lot.

"Let's leave the cart here at the desk and go into the bar area. Keep a look out for our ride, Jill."

"Who am I looking for?"

"I won't know until I see him."

Jase and Jill took their children and went into the bar area. They sat along the edge of the room, so they could see everyone coming in. Across the room in the corner someone stood up.

"Jase, is that who I think it is?" said Jill.

John walked over to the table. "Glad that you made it. We did not know if you would be able to get away. The Professor is on his way, and we are going to meet him. How much longer before you get your rooms?"

"They said we should have them soon," Jase answered.

"Good, we want you to check into the rooms. I have some bags that we will put in the rooms to make it look as if you are there. For now, I will go and check to see if you were followed. I will check back with you in a little bit."

"John, we feel better all ready. How are we leaving this place?"

"I have a car out back, and I will take you to a nearby airport. From there you will fly right into Key West. We should beat the Professor there. When you get your rooms, I will follow you to them. I will leave my bags in the rooms, and we will take yours with us."

"John," said Jase, "We bought Rex. He is part of the family too, and he has a tracking device on his collar."

"Where is the dog now?"

"Linda has him out back."

"I will put him in the car, remove the collar and bring it to the room. Stay here, I will be right back."

They sat for about ten minutes, and then John walked by the table. He gave them a thumbs up. The desk clerk came over to the table. "Your rooms are ready. Can I help you take your bags up to the rooms?"

"Yes, thank you."

"Will you please follow me?" Jase and Jill followed the man to the back wing of the Inn. Jase watched as John followed with another cart, being very careful not to get to close.

"I have you on the first floor. There is a master bedroom on the right. Will there be anything else?" he asked.

"No, and thank you." Jase handed him a tip.

After he had gone, there was a knock at the door. Jase opened it, and John was standing there. He brought in the other cart. "The sooner we leave the better. We must get out of here. Linda is with the dog, and I put his collar on one of the tour busses."

They walked into the hall. John said, "Follow me." He pushed the cart, and Jase and Jill carried the two babies.

The car was in the first row. As soon as Linda saw them coming, she opened the door. John opened the trunk, quickly put the luggage in and drove off.

John took them to a small airport. Jase and Jill had no idea where they were, but they recognized the small jet waiting in the sideline. John drove up to the jet. The door opened even before the car had stopped. Jill and Linda took the babies up to the entry door and Rex followed them.

Jase helped John get the bags into the jet. John stopped at the door before he left, "It has been a pleasure, Dr. Brick." He shook Jase's hand and was gone.

The jet was warming up as Jase sat down. "Welcome, Dr. Brick, it is good to see you again," said the attendant. "We should be airborne in a moment. Please buckle your seat belts. As soon as we are in the air, I will be back."

Eva and Jack did not like the take off. First Eva cried then Jack. The stewardess came back. "Crying is good. It will help them adjust to the air pressure. Next stop is Key West, can I get you anything?"

The girls had already pulled out the bottles and the diapers. "I would like to have a drink," said Jase.

"Would you like to have the Professor's special?"

"That would be fine. How did you know about that?"

"We try to stay on top of things. We should be in Key West about 4:00pm, so try to relax."

Michael's hair was standing up on the back of his neck. He knew something was wrong, but he could not put his finger on it. He called down to the communications area. "Where are they now?"

"The Professor's car is still in the same place, and the Bricks are moving all over Gettysburg. It looks like they are at the battlefields."

"Call me if anything changes."

"Yes Michael."

Chapter   48

It was a good day to fly. The ocean was blue and green, and when they were up above the clouds, they saw nothing but sun. The small jet glided gracefully south. Jase tried to watch outside the window, but was soon fast asleep.

Jill and Linda let him rest. They talked mostly of the journey. The more they talked, the closer they became. The children were quiet, until it was time to eat or have a diaper changed. Both were model passengers.

Jase awoke when the jet started its descent though the clouds. The sun was shining down hard from the west. He could see the crystal clear water surrounding the Florida Keys. He did not see any large ships, only private boats. Jill came over to him, "Is this what the doctor ordered?"

"Oh, I hope so," he replied. Jase pointed to the Keys. "We are almost there."

The attendant came back to the seat next to Jase and Jill. "We will be landing soon. Mr. Canond has asked me to give you some instructions. When you arrive in Key West, you should first retrieve your back up copies. Mr. Canond has reserved rooms for you at a historic hotel on Duval St. He reserves the same rooms every year, although sometimes he is not able to use them."

"I know exactly where the hotel is, and I have been in it many times. I have been told it is haunted," Jase exclaimed.

"Good," said the attendant. "Mr. Canond also said not use your personal cell phones. Turn them off or throw them away. If you want to, you can leave them here, and I will see that they are sent to you at Mr. Canond's Island. Do you have any questions?"

"Yes, I do," said Jill. "Where is the Professor?"

"He is on Mr. Canond's yacht. He should be in Key West first thing in the morning. There is no where the yacht can dock, so he will have to come ashore by helicopter."

Jase started to laugh. "He hates choppers. He will turn as white as this table top."

The attendant smiled, "From what I have heard, maybe whiter. He was not at all happy when he had to take the ride out of the yacht club."

"I wish that I could have seen that," Jase said.

"Do you have Allan Smith's number?" asked the attendant.

"Yes, I have it on my phone," Jase answered.

"Now remember, your phones stay here. I will get you new ones. We don't want anyone locating you."

The attendant left for a minute and came back with three phones. "These phones have all of your numbers on them, plus Allan's. We are about to land, so I will take my seat. One more thing, Dr. Brick."

"Yes, what is that?"

"How much money are you caring with you?"

"Why do you ask?" Jase said.

'Mr. Canond does not want you to open a bank account or anything that could be traced to you."

"What does he want me to do with the money?"

"I'm glad you asked. I have some more information for you. Nelson Shay left a message. He said that all of you have more than doubled you investments, so I think that you should go and have a good time in Key West. It would seem that you have all come into some money."

"Jase," said Jill, "You put $450,000 in the stock." Jill sat there looking at Jase and both of them were grinning.

Linda asked the attendant, "Did you say more than doubled?"

"Yes, that is what Nelson Shay said."

The two girls looked at each other, and then said at the same time, "Oh my God."

"Jase," asked Jill, "How much do we have in the case?"

"I think close to $50,000."

"What are you going to do with that kind of money?" asked Jill.

"I have a friend who runs an art gallery for a local artist. We might have to invest in some art," Jase was grinning. "He said that we are always invited to the Fantasy Fest party on Saturday night. Linda, have you ever been to the Key West Fantasy Fest?" asked Jase.

"No, what is it like?"

Jill grabbed her arm, "It is the friendliest place in the world. There are no words to express this week in Key West. If you don't have fun this weekend, you never will."

The jet was coming around for the landing. The small airport was quiet, and they came straight in.

As the group was preparing to get off, Jase handed his cell phone to the attendant. Jill surrendered hers also. Linda said, "I think that I will keep mine, but I will turn it off."

They walked down the steps not far from the terminal. "For an international airport, this is the perfect size. Every time I come here, it is like coming home," said Jase.

They walked in and waited at the baggage claim. They loaded all of their bags on a cart and went outside for a taxi.

A driver was waiting for the next fare. He shot right up to the sidewalk. The small van was a perfect size, and they all climbed in.

"Where to?" asked the driver as he put the bags in the back.

Jase answered, "Duval Street, but first we have to take the dog somewhere."

The driver nodded, pulled out of the airport and turned right. They followed the ocean for a short time before turning toward Old Town Key West. The driver took them to a private pet sitter that he knew, and he went in to see if they would take Rex for the weekend. After getting Rex settled in, they went to the hotel.

In no time they were on Duval Street. The front of the hotel was blocked off because of Fantasy Fest, so the driver let them off at the rear entrance. The parking lot was full, but that was no surprise. One of the hotel staff ran out to meet them with a cart.

"Are you staying with us at the hotel?"

"Yes, could you help us with our bags?" asked Jase.

Before Jase was finished speaking, the young man was loading the bags on the cart. "Will you follow me to the lobby?"

They walked through the parking lot to the main door.

"I will stay here, until you have checked in."

Jase walked over to the desk as the girls got some punch from a table that was set up inside of the door.

The clerk behind the desk asked, "May I help you?"

Jase handed her the conformation sheet that the attendant had given him. She looked at the paper. "We have been expecting your party. We have two rooms ready for you. Do you have any request or needs?"

"Yes, we have two small children," Jase answered.

"One of the rooms already has two baby beds. Is there anything else?"

"Not right now." Jase thanked her.

"Here are your room cards. Everything has been prepaid, so you are ready to go."

Jase walked back to the group and Jill handed him some punch. He showed the room numbers to the young man. "Right this way," he said. They went down a hall to the elevators. They were on the right and the dining room and the coffee shop on the left.

When they arrived at their floor, they walked to their room and opened the door. The room was nicely remodeled with the charm of Key West. The windows overlooked Duval Street.

After the attendant set the bags on the floor and hung up the clothes that were on hangers, Jase opened his brief case and handed the man generous tip.

"Thank you," the attendant said, as he tried to look inside the case.

Jase smiled and closed the case. The attendant left the room and took Linda's luggage next door.

Linda and Jill checked out the baby's cribs. Both of the children were asleep. "Let's try and put them down without waking them," said Jill. They carefully lowered them into their beds without a sound.

Linda said, "I think that I will go and check out my room."

"Linda, if you want to take a break, I think you deserve one."

"I think I will, Jase, but don't you dare leave me when you go see Peanut."

"Don't worry, we will all go see her together," Jill answered. "What are you going to do, Jase?"

"I'm going to see if I can spend some of our money."

"Are you going to the gallery?"

"Yes, this should be a busy weekend for them. I hope that George has time to talk. I know he will ask if we are interested in going to the party tomorrow night."

"Yes," Jill answered. "But how can we go now that the children are with us?"

"Let me check and see what I can come up with. It sure is good getting back to Key West. I feel like I'm home. I need to call Peanut, but I don't have her number. It was on the old phones. I will have to walk down Duval Street and see if I can find her."

Jase went down the elevator to the ground floor. To save time, he walked through the coffee shop to Duval Street. The street was closed off for the venders. On the street, the party was already getting started. It was like walking into another world. There were women of all ages in body paint and costumes. Men were dressed in their fantasy costumes as well. Everyone was having a good time smiling and laughing.

Jase watched as two older men driving their electric wheelchairs were looking at some of the younger women in body paint. "Isn't this a hoot?" one of the men said to the other.

"Yes, this is the best I have felt in years," he answered as they drove past Jase.

On the other side of the street was the gallery. With so much to look at, before he knew it he was there.

The gallery was busy with the Fantasy Fest celebration. Jase walked in and looked for a familiar face. It did not take long.

"Jase," a voice called from the back of the gallery. It was George, an old Buckeye friend from Ohio. "What brings you to Key West, are you going to be here for the party tomorrow night?"

"Yes, if we can find a sitter for the kids."

"Kids, how many do you have?"

"We have two, a little boy and a little girl."

"You must have done this very quickly. A year ago you didn't have any."

Jase replied, "We adopted both, and I would like you to meet them. But first, I would like to make an investment, maybe an original painting. Do you have anything that you consider to be a better than average investment?"

George was silent for a moment as he thought about it. "Come this way, Jase," George said as they went into his office. Behind his desk was an original painting.

"This painting was one of the first action paintings produced by a local artist and has not been published yet. You could buy this one for a good price. And when it is published, it could go for as much as ten times your purchase price. We have no idea when a piece will be published, only the artist knows that."

Jase started to look at the painting. "Let's take it to the viewing room where you can see it better," said George. He carried the painting into one of the viewing rooms and sat it under the lights. The artwork came alive. The black frame set off the painting of whales swimming just below the ocean surface. The three whales and the blue ocean were in perfect balance with each other.

Jase was thinking. "George, I will bring Jill in later tonight. If I buy this, can you keep it here for a little while? I don't know where I am going to put it yet."

"It can stay in my office until you are ready."

"Good, will you be working tonight, and what is the name of the painting?"

"Yes, I will be here. The name of the painting is BELOW THE SURFACE."

Jase got up and started to walk out. He turned and said, "It is good to see you again, George."

"And you too, Jase, see you tonight."

"One more thing, can I look at your phone book?"

George walked over, reached under the desk and pulled out a local phone book.

Jase went though the book until he found the number for Peanut, and he wrote it down.

"Thanks George, see you later." Jase walked past the fountain and out the door.

Once he was outside, he stopped at the ice cream shop near the gallery and called the number.

"This is Peanut, leave a message. You won't be sorry."

Jase ordered some key lime ice cream and sat down to watch people walk by. He saw some things that were unbelievable. Jase laughed. Everyone was having a great time.

As he walked down Duval St, he saw a parade of people led by a policeman on a motorcycle. Everyone was smiling. It was good to see people so happy.

On the corner there was a small group of people carrying signs saying "Repent." The only one not carrying a sign, had a movie camera and was taking pictures of all the girls in their body paint.

A man next to Jase asked him, "Do you think that he is going to take all the movies back and show them to his church members?"

"I don't know, but I would like to hear the sermon after that show."

"Amen brother," the man chuckled and walked away.

By now, Jase was back in front of the hotel. He walked in the main door and grabbed some punch. Then he went into the lobby and sat down to read the newspaper.

Suddenly his phone rang. "Hello Jase, are you here yet?"

"Peanut, yes we are at the hotel."

"How did you get a room there? They fill up fast?"

"It's a long story. When would you like to see the kids?"

"Why not have breakfast with me in the morning. Do you remember where to go?"

"Sure, on the other side of the street, a few blocks down on the left."

"How many, honey?" Peanut asked.

"There will be three adults and the two children."

"Good, I will get a table for us. Is 8:30am OK?"

"We will be there, thanks Peanut."

By now the girls should have had their nap. He walked back to the main lobby, turned right then went to the elevator. The restaurant and coffee shop were busy when he walked by. He walked to the elevator and pushed the up button.

When he got off the elevator he could hear the housekeepers speaking in Spanish. They were wondering how they were going to get everything done. Then one of them said, "We say this everyday, but we always seem to get done." She put her hands up in the air and walked away. As Jase approached them, they both said hello and asked, "Is your room alright?"

Jase answered, "Everything is fine, and you are doing a great job."

As soon as he passed, he heard them say in Spanish, "I wish all the people were like that." He smiled to himself as he opened the door to the room. Jill and Linda were sitting and talking very quietly.

"Well, how did it go? Did you find out anything?" Jill asked.

"Yes, I did. First, there is a picture at the gallery that I would like you to see, and we are all having breakfast with Peanut."

Linda clapped her hands and said, "Oh good." When Linda clapped her hands, Eva started to wake up. Then Jack was awake.

Linda picked up Eva. "Sorry little one, but you need to get up anyway." She hugged her and then started to check if she was wet. Jill did the same with Jack.

"They really are good children," said Linda. "Jase, where are we going next? Where is this Island?"

"I really don't know, Linda, somewhere in the Gulf. We will find out very soon. I wonder how the Professor is doing?"

"Why don't you call Allan and find out?"

"Good idea, Jill." Jase pulled his new phone out. Allan Smith's number was on the speed dial. He made the call.

"This is Allan."

"Allan, Jase here. We were just checking. How is the Professor doing?"

Allan laughed. "Well, he has all the color back in his face from the ride to the ship. Now, he is taking a little nap. He can put the gin away."

"Yes he can. Don't try to compete with him. You would lose."

"Jase, when do you think that we should pick you up?"

"We don't have the back-up yet, but we should have it tomorrow. I think that it would be better if we left on Sunday. This place will be a nightmare to get out of tomorrow."

"I agree. The helicopter can only carry half of you at a time, so we will need to make two trips. I will call you in the morning as soon as we drop anchor."

"Sounds good Allan, until then." Jase put the phone in his pocket.

He turned to Jill and Linda. They will be here in the morning. If everything goes right, we will be out of here on Sunday.

"Jase, where will the boat dock?" asked Linda.

"It is a too risky to come to the island, so the helicopter will pick us up."

"Linda, would you like to take a walk with us? We have to go to a gallery."

Jill grabbed Jase. "First call down to the desk and find out if they can tell us where we can borrow two strollers."

Jase made the call and asked the person at the desk about strollers. Jase hung up. "He said that they have two strollers. Someone left them here about a month ago, and we can use them."

340

"What are we waiting for?" Jill asked.

When the elevator doors opened, they could smell the food from the restaurant. "We might want to eat here tonight. It smells very good," Jase said.

They got to the end of the hall and turned left. The strollers were already in front of the desk. Jase pointed at the strollers. The desk clerk said, "Dr. Brick, will that work for you?" Jase nodded.

They were soon on Duval Street. The street was blocked off, so there was no traffic. Linda and Jill were laughing.

"Jill," said Linda, "I will if you will."

"I don't think that I'm ready for some stranger to put paint all over me and walk around with nothing on." Jase looked relieved.

When Jill saw his face, she said, "At least not today." Jase acted like he did not hear her.

At the gallery, the cold air felt good as they walked into a dream world of art. The walls were covered with colorful paintings, and the center of the gallery was filled with unique sculptures.

"Jase, you made it back. Come over here, I want to show you something." As they got closer, George said, "Jill, it looks like your family has grown a little. How are you?"

"Fine George, this is Linda. She is helping us for a while."

"Nice to meet you, Linda, how do you like Key West?"

"So far so good, I have never seen anything like it."

George took them into the viewing room. "What do you think Jill, do you like it?"

"Yes, it is beautiful. I don't think that I have ever seen anything quite like it."

Jase asked Jill, "What do you think, should we buy it? George said that he would keep it here until we were ready for it."

"Buy it Jase, if we have enough to get it."

"George, can we go into your office, or somewhere with a little more privacy? I'll be right back, Jill."

Jase followed George into the office. "I don't know how much I have. Can I use your desk?"

"Of course, do you need to call you bank?" George asked.

Jase opened the case that he was carrying. "What is your best price for the painting, and will the artist sign the back to Jill?"

George's mouth fell open. "How much money have you been carrying around?"

"I don't know, close to $50,000. I can't spend it all. We have to have enough to live on while we are here."

Jill looked at her watch. Jase has been there for a long time.

Soon Jase walked out of the office without the case. He handed Jill a receipt marked paid in full.

When Jase put out his hand to George, he put a band on it. "You can't get into the party without this." Jill and Linda received one also. "See you tomorrow night," said George.

It was almost time for sunset. "Jase, I am too tired to walk to Mallory Square," Jill said. "Let's go back to the hotel, get something to eat and then call it a night. I wonder if Michael has missed us yet?"

Linda spoke up. "The sooner we get out of here the better. When Michael finds out we are missing, he will be really pissed."

Chapter   49

On Friday night in Virginia, Michael got a call. "Michael, this is communications, can you come down here?"

"I will be right there." Michael has been uneasy all day. As soon as he got there he asked, "Where are they?"

"The Professor car has not moved. Dr. Brick's party has not moved for some time, and they are not at the hotel. All we can figure out is that the dog lost his collar sometime during the day."

"Or they are not there at all. Get someone out there and find out where they are. Also, get someone to Stingray Bay and see if the Professor is where he is supposed to be."

"Yes sir."

"I knew this was all too good to be true." Michael walked out to the desk. "Do you have that safe opened yet?"

"No sir, we just found our man. He is on the way."

"Let me know when it is opened."

"Thomas," yelled Michael, "Go upstairs to their room and tell me what you see." Thomas left for their rooms.

Michael went back to his office. The phone rang. "Michael, this is Thomas."

"I know who it is. What did you find?"

"It looks like they took everything with them except for a few odds and ends they left laying around."

Michael slammed the phone down, and then immediately picked it up again. "Richard, we may have a problem. Are you close to your office? I will be right there."

Michael went to Richard's office. "We might have lost the Bricks."

Richard showed his true colors. "Michael, you stupid son of a bitch, how could you lose the Bricks?

Michael calmly answered. "We don't know for sure that they are gone. I have someone checking the hotel, and someone checking the marina. And we should have the Doctor's papers soon."

"This is our most important operation yet. Tell me that the lasers are ready to roll?" bellowed Richard.

"Yes sir, they are at the white house now. They went right past the security."

"You screw this one up, Michael," Richard didn't finish what he was going to say. He was so mad, his face was red and he was shaking.

"Don't get upset yet, we don't even know if they are missing."

Michael's phone rang and he lifted it up to his ear, then he slowly took it down. "Dr. Brick's papers are in the safe."

"Yes, go on. What kind of shape are they in?" demanded Richard.

"It would seem that they are blank. There is nothing on them."

Richard sat there with his face getting redder by the minute. Then in a controlled voice, as he glared at Michael, he said, "You find the Bricks, and you find your Linda Peach. I don't care how you do it, but I want them here, now."

Michael stood up and walked out of Richard's office. He could feel Richard staring at his back. He went back to his office, and as soon as he sat down his phone rang.

"Michael, they checked into their rooms. The bags are still setting here, but they have not been opened."

Michael was trying to stay calm, "Do you think that you could open the bags?"

After a few moments, the man came back on the line. "They are full of rags. There are no clothes in any of the bags."

Michael hung up the phone, and then he raised it again and made another call. "Yes Michael, what can I do for you?"

"I'm only going to say this once, so listen. I don't know where the Brick family went, but I want them found. Someone has to be helping them. And, one more thing, I want to know where Linda Peach is. When you find her, come straight to me. Don't talk to anyone else. Is that understood?"

"Yes Sir, Is this a red alert?"

Michael paused, "Hell yes," then he hung up.

It looked like a war zone inside the communication room. A few minutes ago there was only one man working in the communication area, and now there were five people. One man was checking the airports, and a woman was checking taxis. They had people at the Eisenhower Inn asking if anyone had seen the Bricks. At first there was nothing to report, and then Michael got a call.

"This is Michael."

"Michael, so far the airports are clear, and transportation has not come up with anything. No one at the Inn remembers anything about the Bricks. The clerk said he helped them take their bags to the room this morning, but that's all he knew."

Michael slowly responded. "Keep on it, and let me know if you come up with anything."

Now he had to go tell Richard. When Michael walked into Richard's office, Richard was staring out the window at the river.

"You lost them didn't you?" He slowly turned around. "Monday we are going forward on our operation at the White House. Will the lasers work?"

"We saw them work in the test, and I don't have any reason to believe that they wouldn't work now."

"Well Michael, we can't test them now. They are already setup at the White House. I had better call Mr. Seaban. Stick around, and I will put it on speaker."

Richard put the number in, waited for the recording and then he hung up. Michael watched as Richard waited.

When the phone rang, Richard put it on speaker.

"Richard, I hope you have good news for me."

"Not bad, we just wanted to keep you informed. We have temporarily lost track of Dr. Brick, but it should not stop our operation. We still have a go on it."

Robert Lee Seaban paused, then answered. "You know Richard, I have a lot riding on this here laser. If y'all can't do the job, maybe I should move on. There is a lot of other agencies that would love to have my support."

"Robert, we have been doing business for a long time, haven't we?"

"Why yes, Richard, we have."

"Have I ever let you down?"

"Well, not that I can remember."

"You trusted me this far, so trust me a little farther."

"Alright Richard, but if you blow this one, you will be the one holding the bag. I don't look kindly on someone who can't hold up his end of the deal."

"Robert, I will call you when I find out more."

"Richard, is Michael there?"

"Yes Robert, he is listening to our conversation."

"That's good. Michael, up to now you have always been one of the good old boys. You have a real nice family, and I hope that nothing ever happens to them. Do you think that you could help Richard clear this little matter up for us?"

Michael was staring at Richard. "Robert, are you threatening me and my family?"

"Why no, Michael, I just wanted you to know I would think very highly of you, if you could spend a little more time on this matter and clear it up as soon as possible. I would certainly appreciate it."

Michael responded, "Robert, I am already on it with everything I have."

"Just make sure that you do it. Now gentleman, I have some other pressing matters to attend to. Good night." Seaban smiled and hung up his phone. Then he turned to a very lovely young woman beside him in his hot tub, "Now young lady, why don't you tell me more about yourself."

Richard and Michael were quiet. Finally Richard said. "Don't let Seaban get you riled."

"Richard, he threatened me and my family. I think that we should revaluate this operation and shut it down, while we still can."

"No, that's not going to happen. Who do you think is trying to help Dr. Brick?"

"It could be any number of people or corporations. He has the key to curing cancer. For good or bad, he has the potential to change the cancer industry. With his new methods to treat cancer, he could put most of the cancer clinics out of business. On the other hand, one of the big medical companies would pay highly for his information, and then bury it. The list goes on and on."

"Michael, check on the guy that picked him up in his jet, that Canond fellow. Call him and ask if he has seen Dr. Brick, and then monitor all his communications after that. He might know what is going on."

Michael got up and started to leave, when Richard said, "Michael, this operation will go forward with or without Brick. I have another idea. Call that woman that has been a pain in Brick's ass. What is her name?"

"Do you mean Diane Worth?"

"Yes, she could probably find him all by herself. She sounds like a real bitch."

Michael nodded and left. He went to the communications area. "Get in touch with the head of the Cancer Research Environment. The person in charge is Diane Worth. Tell her I want to have a talk with her tonight. I'll be in my office."

Michael was in his zone. He worked best when he was under pressure. It was getting late, so he went straight to his office.

Michael's phone rang. "Michael, Diane Worth is at her home, but whoever answered the phone said that Miss Worth has retired for the night."

"Bull shit, get her up!"

"Yes sir, hold on and I will patch it through."

Michael waited for the call. Soon the phone rang. "Michael, when I hang up, Miss Worth will be on the line."

"Hello, this is Michael."

"Michael who? Who do you think you are calling me at this hour?"

"I am sorry Miss Worth, but this is very important. We have been looking for Dr. Jase Brick."

Diane calmed down. "So what did that quack do now? I haven't been able to find out where he is."

"Nor have we. I thought that maybe you could help us, since you have been looking for him also."

"What did you say your name is?"

"Michael. I work for the government, but I can't tell you much more than that. We are aggressively looking for him. Maybe we can help each other?"

"Maybe, call me in the morning, and then we will talk."

"Thank you, Miss Worth. Would 8:30 am work for you?"

"That will be fine. Good night." She hung the phone up with a smile on her face. "I got you, Dr. Brick," she said.

Michael called the communication room, "Anything new?"

"No sir, we will call you if we find out anything else."

Chapter 50

Blake Canond's yacht was heading south toward Key West. The Professor was sitting on the deck watching the porpoises swim with the ship. They played with the bow as if to show the ship that they could out swim her at anytime. Allan Smith came up and sat down. "So far so good, the Bricks are in Key West. All we have to do is pick them up when they get the back-up, and then head for Blake's Island."

The Professor asked Allan, "This is a big ship. How are you going to dock?"

"This is a busy weekend in Key West. On a normal day, we would have a hard time docking there. But it would be impossible to get a dock this weekend, so we will have to drop anchor out at sea."

"How do I get to the island?"

"The same way you got on the ship, by helicopter."

"Bull shit, I don't want to see Key West that much."

"I thought that you might say that," laughed Allan. "Why don't you just enjoy the trip? Everything you need is here. If you change your mind, we will fly you over to the Key West."

The Professor looked around the ship. "I have been on worse ships. I might give it a little more time."

"Professor, have you given any thought to where you would like to store your car?"

"No, not really, do you have any place in mind?"

"Not yet. There is a chance that Michael will pick it up or he will be watching to see what we do with it. For right now, let's leave it at the marina."

"Under the circumstances, I think that is best," said the Professor.

"Professor, what will happen if they try to use the laser three times?"

The Professor smiled, "They already used the laser once for the demonstration. I told them it was only good for three times, but now that I think about it, maybe it is good for only one time."

'Then what will happen?"

Instead of hitting the target, they will focus on each other and destroy themselves. You wouldn't want to caught between them."

Allan started to laugh. "I like it Professor, I really like it. Does Dr. Brick know about it?"

"Well hell, I think I forgot to tell him." The Professor was grinning. "You know, I didn't like that Michael character from the beginning."

Allan and the Professor sat back and took in the view.

Chapter 51

Saturday morning came early for Jase and Jill. The two babies were dressed and fed, when Jase knocked on the door between his room and Linda's. The door opened, and Linda was dressed and ready. "I wouldn't miss this breakfast for anything."

They went down in the elevator and out onto Duval Street. Jase was pushing one of the strollers. They crossed the street, and walked until they arrived at a charming little restaurant with steps up to the main door.

"I forgot about the steps," Jase said. Inside of the small dining area Jase heard a scream. "Oh, look at the babies!"

Linda and Jill were speechless. Jase smiled, "Peanut, how are you?"

Peanut stood up. He was over six foot tall and still had eye makeup on from his show last night. He was smiling. "Come over here let me give you a hug. Peanut grabbed Jill. Linda watched Jill's face as Peanut squeezed her. Linda could tell that Jill was overwhelmed.

"Now, tell me who these children are?" Eva and Jack did not know what to think of Peanut. Jase introduced the children. "Peanut, this is Eva and Jack."

"And who is this? She is a tall one?"

"This is Linda, she is helping us with the children," answered Jase.

"Well come on and sit down. This place fills up fast. Tell me Jase, what have you been up to?"

"I can't say yet, at least not here. Did you bring the package I sent to you?" asked Jase.

Peanut had a shoulder bag. "Are you sure that you want it now?"

"Yes, I wish that I could tell you more right now, but I can't."

"Jase, you be careful, I worry about all of you."

"Thanks Peanut. Maybe when we get settled you can come for a visit," said Jase. Then he felt a kick in the side of his leg.

"Jill, how do you like being a mother? Has it been exciting?"

"Peanut, all I can say is this has been the most excitement I have ever had. You have no idea how much I love being a mother."

Then Peanut looked at Linda. "What is it you really do, when you are not helping Jase and Jill?"

Linda looked around as if to see if anyone was listening, then she whispered, "I'm a secret agent."

Peanut put his hand over his mouth. "Oh, that's sounds so exciting. Do you ever get to shoot the bad guys?"

Linda did not know how to take Peanut, so she played along with him. "Sometimes I do. How about you Peanut, what do you do?"

"I'm in show business. Didn't Jase tell you? I impersonate other people. The moneys good, and I have a great time. Tonight I will be on one of the floats. I have been putting feathers together for weeks. You have to see the parade. It will go all night."

"We will be at the gallery," said Jase.

"I'll look for you. Linda, I will throw you some beads. You can't leave Key West without some beads."

Linda was starting to laugh. They ordered some food and talked. Then Peanut reached into his bag pulled and out an envelope.

"Jase, it's never been opened." Peanut handed it to Jase.

"You are a life safer, Peanut. You have no idea how important this is."

Peanut dropped the fancy talk for a minute. "Jase, you know that you can always count on me. I don't know what you are up to, but you are one of the most honest people I know. So when you can tell me what's going on, that will be fine."

"Peanut, I have a question for you?"

"What is that Jill?"

"Do you like to be called he or she?"

"Oh honey, it don't matter. I will answer to about anything."

Jase put the envelope in the large a pocket in his shorts. "This is the result of years of work and research. What will you do for the rest of the day?"

"I have so much to do to get ready for the parade. I sure hope I have enough feathers to finish my dress. If you see one of these chickens running around here without any feathers on her back, you will know it was me."

They talked for a while, and then Peanut said, "Well, we had better give up our table to someone else. They are lined up at the door."

Jase paid for the meal, and they all walked out to the sidewalk. "Peanut, as soon as I can I will let you know where we are."

Peanut hugged Jase. "I don't know what you have gotten yourself into, but if there is anything I can do, let me know."

Jase said in a low voice, "Peanut, I can't breathe."

"Oh, you softy."

They started to walk back to the hotel. "This is where I live." Peanut pointed to a white building behind some of the shops. "It's close to work, and I'm on the second floor. I love it."

Jill said, "It is good to see you again. We will look for you tonight." They waved at Peanut as he went up to his apartment.

Jase said, "Who is up for the beach?"

Jill and Linda looked at each other, "Why not."

"Good, let's go back to the hotel and change. I'll call for a taxi, and we can get lunch at the beach. I used to go there every day when I lived here," Jase said. They walked back to the hotel.

Jase's phone rang. "Hello," Jase answered.

"Well hell Brick, where are you?"

"Professor, are you in Key West?"

"Are you kidding? One ride in that thing was enough for me. I will wait for you here. Besides, Allan and I are bonding. Allan wants to talk to you, so here he is."

"Hello Jase, did you get everything you need?"

"Yes, I have the back-up in my pocket."

"When do you want to be picked up?"

"First thing in the morning, if that is all right."

"I will have the chopper on standby. Just give us a call when you are ready."

"Will do, Allan. We have a little business to take care of tonight, and then we are ready."

"I'll wait for your call."

They went back to the hotel and changed into their swim suits. Jase asked the desk to call for a taxi. When the taxi arrived, they went to the beach next to the old fort. They found a spot with some shade, and then took turns swimming in the ocean. Jase and Jill picked up some rental snorkeling gear at the beach hut, and then swam out to some of the man made rock piles. They swam with the schools of small fish. Then they spotted a large ray as it swam under them. After a while, they went back to the beach, and Linda took her turn. She did not spend much time in the water. When she got out, the family went over to the showers to rinse off. They got a bite to eat at the food hut and set on the deck to eat. They spent the rest of the afternoon relaxing in the sun.

In the late afternoon they called for a ride back to the hotel. The taxi must have been close because he was there in a few minutes.

Once back at the hotel, they all took hot showers and relaxed for a while. "What are we going to do with the children, Jase?" asked Jill.

Linda spoke up, "You to go to the party, and I will watch the kids. When you get back, I will go."

Before sunset, Jase and Jill went to the gallery. Everything in the center of the gallery had been removed, and replaced with food and drink. Chairs were set up if you wanted to rest and talk.

The parade was about to start. "The parade will go until early morning," Jase and Jill turned to see who was talking. They were surprised to see a woman dressed as a cat. Other than her ears and tail, she was covered completely with body paint.

Jase asked, "How long did it take to get all that done?"

"About two hours, do you like it?" she asked.

Jase and Jill both said yes.

"What do you do if it rains?" asked Jill.

"Run, it took too long to get this right. Rain would not be good."

There was a large crowd in the gallery. As soon as one left another would come in. Everyone was enjoying the party. Many of the local people were there.

Jase and Jill watched the parade and had some wine. No one went away hungry. Many of gallery's artists were there to show off their art.

"Are you having a good time?" asked George?"

Jill answered, "Yes, but we are going to have to leave soon. I have never seen so many people in one place."

"It is always the same great party each year, maybe a little larger at times, but always great."

It was time to go. Jase and Jill said good night and worked their way to the door. On the sidewalk, you had to turn sideways to get through.

Somehow they made it across the street, but getting through the last twenty feet to the hotel was a challenge. Just before Jill got to the hotel, a man came up to her and put some beads around her neck.

Jill laughed and thanked him. Even at the hotel, there was friendly chaos every place they went. They finally made it to the elevator. When the door opened, there was more body paint and laughter. Finally, they made it back to the room.

"Well how was it?" asked Linda.

Jill laughed, "You are much too over dressed to go down there."

Linda had to see for herself. "I think that I will go down for a little while. It can't be that good."

Jill smiled and said, "You were warned."

"I will see you two in the morning." Linda went down to the festival.

They did not see Linda for the rest of the night. The noise from the street kept going on and on. The hall was full of people partying until about 3:00am in the morning, then things started to quiet down.

Jase was up early Sunday morning. He walked down to the street. It was quiet. You could not tell that thousands of people were standing there a few hours ago. The streets were spotless, and all the trash cans were empty. There was no trash anywhere. He went back to the room.

By now, everyone was up and packing. Jill and Linda were still laughing about what they had seen the night before.

Jase walked into the room. "You would not believe it," he said. "The streets are cleaned up all ready. You can't even tell that there was a party out there last night. Are we ready?" he asked.

"I think so. You had better call Allan and tell him that we are ready to leave the hotel."

"All right, I think I will walk down to the desk and have them send up someone to take the bags down. I will be right back." As he went down to the desk, Jase checked out his pocket to make sure that he had the back-up.

"Good morning, Dr. Brick. How was your night?"

"Great, could you please send someone up to get our bags and also call a taxi to take us to the airport."

Jase stopped in the lobby and pulled out his phone to call Allan. "Good morning, Jase, are you ready to go?" asked Allan.

"We are calling the cab now to take us to the airport, and we will pick up Rex on the way."

"That will be fine. The pilot said he could take all of you at one time. I will make the arrangements. See you in a little while."

"Thanks Allan." Jase put his phone in his pocket.

When he arrived back at the room, the boy was already there with the cart. Jase gave the room a once over to see if they had missed anything. "Looks good," he said. "Let's go."

By the time they were on the ground floor, the taxi was waiting. Jase walked over to the desk. "Do I have to sign something?" he asked.

"It has already been taken care of." answered the clerk.

The rest of the crew was already waiting in the van. Jase tipped and got in the van.

"Airport sir?" asked the driver.

"Yes, but first we have to pick up our dog. Do you know what the weather report is for the day?"

"Should be a perfect day, where are you heading?" he asked.

"This is going to sound funny, but I don't know," replied Jase.

"Well no matter, you have a nice day wherever you go."

Their first stop was at the dog sitter. Someone was waiting out front with Rex.

The taxi drove along the ocean. The airport was on the left side of the road as they drove up to the entrance. While the driver was unloading the van, a man came up to Jase.

"Dr. Brick?" he asked.

"Yes."

"I am Mr. Canond's pilot. I will be taking you to the ship."

They walked into the airport, quickly passed through security and then went out to the helicopter.

"I think that this is the fastest that I have ever gone through an airport," Linda was impressed.

Once in the helicopter, they had clearance to take off. They quickly shot out over the ocean and headed to the yacht. Once in the air, they could see all the boats that came for the festival. The water was clear, and they could see the reefs under the sea. In less than ten minutes, they were about to land on the ship.

The babies did not like the ride. Rex, on the other hand, laid and waited for the ride to be over. They made a perfect landing. The crew on the ship was strapping the chopper down before the pilot could shut down the engine. When they climbed out of the helicopter, Allan was there to meet them.

"Come this way. Have you had anything to eat yet?" asked Allan.

"No, not yet," replied Jase.

They followed Allan into the main dining area. "Have a seat," Allan pointed to the table that was big enough to seat twenty people. One of the crew came over to the table. "What can I get for you?"

Jase answered, "What do you have? Do you have a menu?"

"I think that we can offer you just about anything. Do you want a meal or a sandwich?"

Before anyone could answer, they heard a loud voice. "Well hell, now the party can start."

"Professor," Jase stood up as he came in from the deck.

"Get the Ruben sandwich, it is the best I have ever had."

"That sounds good," Jase and Jill agreed.

"That will be three Professor Specials. Would you also like a gin and squirt?"

"Sure, why not. Jill, how about you," asked Jase.

"That's fine for me, but Linda is a vegetarian."

"Can I have a fruit salad and some yogurt with wheat toast?" Linda asked.

"Yes, coming right up." The steward turned and left the room.

"Allan, how big is this ship?" Jase was checking out the dining area.

"It is one hundred and fifty feet. If you get any bigger, it is harder to get into some of the ports."

"Allan," asked Linda, "How long will it take to get to this Island?"

"It will take two days, and the weather is supposed to be perfect. I hope that everyone enjoys themselves, you all deserve it. Mr. Canond and his family will be meeting you on the island."

Linda asked Allan, "Where is Blake's Island?"

"Come with me, and I will show you."

"I will be right back, don't let the Professor get my drink." She followed Allan onto the bridge of the ship, and he rolled out some maps. "We are right here, and this is where we are going."

"I don't think that I knew there was an island there."

"It took some doing, but Mr. Canond convinced the locals that his help would be a good thing for them."

"Has it been?" Linda asked.

"Yes, but this is considered a third world country. Most of the island is very primitive. Blake has built schools and is trying to do what he can for the local people."

"Does it have any mountains?" asked Linda.

"Yes, and there is one in particular that Blake wants to show Dr. Brick."

"Why is that?" asked Linda.

"During World War II, there was a top secret base there where they stored nerve gas. That is all gone now, but Mr. Canond thinks it would be the perfect place to put a research lab."

"Really, whose base was it?"

"We think it was CIA, but we are not sure. The local people don't care much for our government though."

"I can understand that," Linda said.

"Your food should be ready, so let's go back to the dining area."

For the rest of the day, the ship glided through the Caribbean waters. After all that they have been through, it was a welcome trip. The sunset was as beautiful as any they had ever seen. Allan came out to the bow of the ship, where Jase and Jill sat watching some shooting stars. The moonlight rippled across the water, and there was a light warm breeze coming from the southeast.

"The moonlight is a good thing," said Allan. "There is always a chance of pirates, but we have never had a problem in the past."

"Pirates!" said Jill. "Do you think there are any out there now?"

"Anything is possible, so we keep a sharp lookout for anything that looks out of the ordinary. We are making very good time. The Captain said that we should be at the island by Tuesday. So kick back and rest while you can."

Linda was in the cabin watching the children, when Jase and Jill walked in. "How are they doing?" asked Jill.

"The sea does not seem to be bothering them," Linda replied.

"Jase, will you look at this room. It is bigger than the room we had at the house."

Jase walked over to the dresser. "I wonder what this button is for." He pushed it, and a TV screen rose up from the dresser.

"How about that," Jase said as he put the screen down. "Linda, we can take over from here. Go out to the deck, it is a perfect night to watch the moonlight on the ocean."

"I might get a drink and do that. See you two in the morning."

Jase and Jill retired for the night. The children were asleep. "It was a good day, but I wonder what tomorrow will bring?" said Jase.

Chapter   52

The Press Corp was at the White House early. Monday was always a busy start of the week. All the networks were getting their equipment ready. SNN (Seaban News Network) was also making plans. The White House spokes person came out and gave a heads up. "Please take your seats, and the President will be out in five minutes."

Back at the Virginia mansion, Richard and Michael were watching the TV screen. At the same time in Atlanta, Robert Lee Seaban was glued to the broadcast. The cameras were on.

Richard was talking to Michael. "After the President starts talking for one minute, the camera on the left will energize. Then the camera on the right will do the same. We have installed crosshairs in the viewing screens, so there should be no screw ups. The room is so bright, that no one can see the red and green beams from the lasers.

They waited until Madam President walked out. Everyone stood up and applauded. "Please be seated," she said. "Today is the day when our Health Care bill goes into effect. No longer will any American have to fight for health care. Health care is now and will always be accessible for all Americans. Every American will have the same coverage that members of Congress have. Medical insurance will no longer be a privilege, but a right.

Also, we have closed the congressional retirement plan. They will now be on Social Security like the rest of the country. The next time Congress tries to cut Social Security, they will be cutting their own retirement."

Seaban was watching the members of the Press Core as they stood and clapped. Seaban yelled, "Sit down you stupid assholes." In Richard's office, he and Michael were on the edge of their seats.

Finally, the President asked everyone to sit as she continued her speech.

Suddenly, there was a loud screaming sound. It was coming from the back of the room around the SNN cameras. Then they exploded.

The Secret Service grabbed the President and took her out of the room. The Press Core was asked to calmly leave. The two camera operators from Seaban's crew had been knocked to the ground. Meanwhile, the cameras from all the other news networks were filming the major news event. It would seem that everyone had a scoop except SNN.

In Atlanta, Seaban was watching very quietly. He had to switch networks to see what happened. He slowly moved his hand over to the phone and called Richard.

Michael and Richard were also watching the news. As they stared at each other, neither one said anything. Richard put his hand next to the phone. He knew that it would ring, and it did.

"Richard," said Seaban, "It would seem that we have a large problem on our hands. Would it be a whole lot of trouble for you all to tell me what the hell happened?"

"Robert," answered Richard, "I assure you, we have no idea. We are as shocked as you are."

"Richard, may I remind you that you are in this up to your northern eyeballs. Don't you think for one minute that if I go down, you will not go down with me. Michael, I know that you are there, that goes for you too. Do I make myself perfectly clear?"

"Yes Robert, perfectly," Richard hung up. "Michael, I want Dr. Brick." Richard's voice was shaking. "I don't care how, bring me Dr. Brick and that Professor. One more thing, bring me Linda Peach."

Michael walked out of Richards's office. He wanted to say, "I told you so," but he knew better. He stopped at communications. "Have you found them yet?"

"No Michael, whoever is behind this, knew what they were doing."

Michael stopped in his tracts. "Find out where Blake Canond is, and set up a meeting for me. If he asks why, tell him it's a national security issue."

"I'll get right on it, Michael." The communication room was now in a frenzy.

Michael went back to his office. He said to himself, "Dr. Brick is much more on the ball than we gave him credit for. Where are you Brick?"

Michael's phone rang, and he picked it up. "Yes," he said.

"Michael, Dr. Brick's phone, the Professor's phone and Linda Peach's phone are not energized."

"Linda's phone should have an emergency tracking system in it, if she has not taken the battery out. Try to turn her phone on."

"Hold on Michael, I'll check."

Michael waited for a few minutes, and then started to get impatient. He yelled into his phone, "Call me when you have something."

"Michael, hold on, I think we may have something. She is in the Gulf. We are plotting a course now."

Michael leaned forward in his chair. "As soon as you get a fix on her, send up a jet and see where she is. Do not make contact, we don't want anyone to think that we are onto them."

Early the next day at the Key West Naval Air Station, they received orders to locate a craft in the Gulf of Mexico. A jet took off at daybreak, being careful to stay out of Cuban air space. The pilot locked in on the yacht and took pictures. He made a wide turn, so as not to draw attention to the jet. Then he returned to Key West. When the jet landed at the naval air base, the pilot has already sent the photos in. "Who wanted the photos of the yacht? It was a big one, even had a bird on the back."

"I don't know some agency back in Virginia. It was a high priority and ASAP."

The pilot shrugged his shoulders and walked out. "See ya," he said.

Michael was looking at the photos of the yacht. Richard was with him. Thomas had come in and handed Michael an in-tel on the yacht.

"Well," said Richard. "Who the hell is it?"

"The yacht belongs to Blake Canond Industries. Blake Canond is one of the..."

"I know who Blake Canond is." Richard cut Michael off. "See if you can find out where he is going?" Richard stormed out of Michael's office.

By now, it was after 8:30 am. Michael told Diane Worth that he would call her first thing in the morning. He called the communication room. "Patch me through to Diane Worth." Then he hung up.

In a moment, his phone rang. "Michael, when I hang up, Ms. Worth will be on the line."

"Good morning, this is Michael."

"Before we go any further, I want to know who you are and what part of the government you are calling from."

370

In a pleasant voice Michael answered. "My name is Michael Greyger. I work for an agency of the government that deals with security. I would hope that you will not repeat anything that I have told you or I am going to tell you. We have reason to believe that Dr. Brick is in the Gulf of Mexico, so it would seem that I have bothered you for no reason. We do not know why he left the country. He was working on a project for us, so we hope that he was on the up and up with us."

"I knew it. He is a scam artist, just like I thought."

"Now Ms. Worth, we don't know that for sure, so please don't speculate yet."

"Michael, I cannot promise that. He has caused a lot of trouble for me by telling people that he has a cure for cancer."

"Yes, we know that, but we don't know that he does not have a cure. Let's give him a little time."

"Are you ordering me not to say anything, Mr. Greyger?"

"I can't order you not to, but I wish that you would not."

"We will see. All I want for him to do is prove what he says he can do. Good day, Mr. Greyger."

"Good day, Ms Worth, and thank you for your time."

Thomas was standing in Michael's office while he was talking to Diane Worth. "Do you think she will say anything?"

"That was the whole point of me calling her. That bitch will stop at nothing to make a name for herself."

Thomas smiled, "Michael, you never cease to amaze me."

Chapter   53

Monday morning Linda was in her cabin when she happened to pick up her phone. It was on. She quickly turned it off, put it in her pocket and went up to the dining area. Jase and Jill were already there, and each of them was feeding a baby. The Professor and Allan came up at the same time.

"By this time tomorrow, we should be at the Island," Allan said.

Linda said to Jase, "When we got to Key West, I'm sure I turned my phone off."

"I know you did, I saw you. Why do you ask?" replied Jase.

"Well, this morning I picked it up, and it was on."

"Let me see your phone, Linda," said the Professor.

He started to analyze it. "Is this the phone that the agency gave you?"

"Yes, it is the newest model," Linda replied.

The Professor was studying the phone. "I would say that this unit can be energized from an outside source. We are being tracked. Allan, ask the Captain if there are any boats close to us."

Allan jumped up, and he was only gone for a moment. "Professor, there are two boats. The captain thinks they are small craft, probably fishing boats."

"Can we intercept one of them? Maybe one of them is Cuban." The Professor was hopeful.

Allan went to ask the Captain to intercept one of the boats. The Professor got up and went with him.

The Captain pointed at the radar. "We should have a visual on this one anytime."

They all watched the port side of the ship, as they turned into the east.

"Do you have anyone that can speak Spanish?" asked the Professor

"Yes, three of the deck crew are from Cuba," said the Captain.

"Good, have them come up here."

"What do you have in mind, Professor?" asked Allan.

"Have one of your crew ask someone on the fishing boat if they will return the cell phone to a friend in Cuba. Tell them that the friend left it onboard. Give them some money and tell them that the owner might give them a reward also. Just make up a name."

They waved at the small fishing boat as it came along side. The Cubans were more than happy to help. They told them that if they couldn't find the owner of the cell phone, they could keep it. They all waved as they cast off.

Linda came to the bridge. "You might want to come back and see the news, Professor."

He followed her back to the dining area.

Jase said, "Have a seat, Professor, I think that you might find this interesting."

Jase had picked up a news broadcast from the United States. "At a press conference at the White House a few minutes ago, the President had to be removed from the press room. We don't have all the facts yet, but two of the cameras from SNN exploded. No one was hurt, but it took everyone by surprise. Here is a clip of what happened."

"The President was giving her speech, when there was two loud high pitch sounds, each coming from the two SNN news cameras. Then they exploded."

"Professor, look at the cameras."

"They were trying to kill the President. They were using our laser to kill the President," the Professor was shocked.

Allan said, "Professor, I think that when you changed the amount of times they could use the lasers, you probably saved the life of the President of the United States."

"We are the only people that know what they tried to do. Richard will be coming for us." Linda was putting two and two together. "This whole thing was a plot to kill the President."

Everyone sat and stared for a moment. Then the Professor spoke. "How far are we from the Island, Allan?"

"Around 300 miles," Allan replied.

"What is the range of the bird?"

"The chopper has a range of close to a thousand miles."

"Even if we have to go in two groups, I think we should take the bird. And you know I do not like anything that has to do with helicopters."

Allan spoke next. "We will change course to Mexico, and hit one of the resort areas. That should throw them off for a while. I need to call Blake and see what he thinks." Allan left for the bridge.

Jill sat there for a moment, and then she asked Linda, "What do you think Michael and Richard will do?"

"Clean up loose ends," replied Linda.

"What does that mean?" Jill asked.

"Cover their asses, and get rid of anyone one who has information that can hurt them."

Allan came back. "Blake wants everyone to fly in, and then he will fly back to the ship with his family. They are going on a vacation in Cancun. He will wait for you before he leaves."

"So get ready, here we go again. Don't leave anything on the ship that belongs to us," said the Professor.

Allan said, "One good thing is that not many people know Blake has a house on the Island. If we can give them the slip, it will take them a long time to find us. By then, I hope that we have this thing under control. This agency has a lot of people in high places. Linda, I think that you are in the most danger of all. You could shut the agency down."

The Professor said, "Alright we have a plan. Let's stay calm and keep our heads. Let's start to pack. The sooner we can get off this ship the better."

Jase and Jill took the children on the first trip. The Professor, Allan, Linda and Rex were on the second.

By 1:00 pm, Allan said, "The Island is coming up on the horizon." Rex settled down at the Professor's feet. "Why Professor, I think that Rex has kept you from getting airsick."

"Well hell, I have to stay strong for the dog. I wouldn't let him think I was scared."

Allan smiled and turned back to look at the Island.

There was a landing pad at the mansion next to the beach. There was also a large dock close by.

"That is a pretty nice dock even for Blake," said the Professor.

"It was left over from the CIA, when they were here. It did not take much to get it back into shape. There seems to be a lot of people at the landing pad," Allan said.

The pilot said, "Allan, some of the people have guns. What do you want me to do?"

"Do you see Blake or Dr. Brick anywhere?"

"Over there, next to the main house. Blake is waving for us to come in."

Then the radio came on. "Allan, everything is fine. Come on in."

"Let's go," said Allan.

They came in for a smooth landing. As soon as they landed, twenty men with guns walked closer to the chopper.

"Be calm," said Allan. "Let's see what this is all about. At least we know they are not Michael's people."

Chapter   54

Back at the agency headquarters, it was getting very hot. The security at the White House had taken the cameras and was in the process of tearing them apart. The two camera men were in custody, and the Secret Service was interrogating them. One of the things that they questioned was the crosshairs in the camera viewing area.

In Atlanta, Robert Lee Seaban was waiting for someone to call, and it didn't take long. He answered the phone. "Mr. Seaban, you have some people here to see you. They are from the FBI."

He paused for a moment, then answered, "I have been expecting them, send them in."

The two men were standing in front of the secretary's desk. "Gentleman, he was expecting you. Go right in."

They walked into the office. One of the men showed Seaban his identification. "We have a few questions for you."

"Gentlemen, have a seat."

"We would prefer that you came with us, sir."

Seaban pushed his chair back. He stood up and put his jacket on. "Will this take long, I have a meeting at 2:30?"

One of the men answered, "You might want to cancel that." Then they all walked out of the office together.

As he walked past the secretary, he said, "Cancel everything for the afternoon." Then he left with the two FBI agents.

Word travels fast. Outside of the Seaban building, the Press was everywhere.

"Mr. Seaban, do you have any idea what caused the explosion at the White House?" one reporter asked.

"Why no sir, I don't. But I will say this, if there is anything that I or my news network can do to help, we will do it. The White House has the full support of SNN."

"Another question, Mr. Seaban, you have repeatedly said that this liberal President was the worst thing that could happen to this country. Do you think that any of your employees would try to harm her?"

"No sir, that would be grounds for termination. If I ever even heard of one of my people hinting anything like that, I would call these people right here," and he pointed to the men he was walking with.

There was a black SUV waiting at the sidewalk. They escorted Seaban into it and the motorcade left. Richard was watching the broadcast. "Get Michael in here." Richard knew if Seaban was cornered, he would take them down too.

Michael walked into the office. "Have you seen the news, Michael?" asked Richard.

"Yes, what are you going to do?"

"Michael, you were right. We should not have got into bed with Seaban. Now, this is how we are going to clean this mess up."

"Richard, it's over," said Michael.

"Bullshit, I'll tell you when it's over. I want Dr. Brick and his friends erased. Then I want Seaban taken out."

"And how do you think you are going to do that? Seaban is probably spilling his guts right now. He will try to make it look like you are the one who should be in jail, not him."

Richard pointed his finger at Michael. "You are in this too Michael, so get Brick."

Michael turned and walked out of the room. Richard was yelling at him as he left. "Don't you walk out on me when I'm talking to you, do you hear me?"

Michael did not turn around. He walked out of the outer office and kept going. He walked around the compound for some time and then came back inside. He had to make a decision on whether to follow Richard or put a stop to all of it. The Secret Service probably did not know the agency existed, so why push it. Seaban was a slippery person, and he had enough money and connections to get out of about anything.

He walked back into Richard's office. "I think we should ride this one out. Seaban can take care of himself. I think we should stay calm for right now, and sit back to see what happens."

Richard sat looking at Michael. "If you are wrong, Michael, we all hang."

"I know, but we can't stir up any more than we already have. I will be in my office." He walked out.

Seaban did just what Michael said he would. By the end of the day, he was back at his office. The Secret Service sent the cameras out to be tested. For the next few days, SNN was all over the news. Seaban even used it to promote himself.

Michael called the communication room. "Where is the ship now?"

"It is headed toward Mexico, and Linda Peach's cell phone is almost to Cuba."

"Do we have enough time to intercept the boat to Cuba?"

"I don't think so, Michael, they are almost in Cuban waters now."

"Well let me know where the yacht puts into port."

"Will do, Michael."

Michael hung up the phone. "It would seem that Dr. Brick was not as naive as they had thought. He has been one step ahead of them almost the entire time." Michael sat in deep thought.

Chapter   55

Allan watched as the helicopter came in for a landing. The men that were standing around the landing pad were chased away by the Canond Security Team as Blake came out of the mansion.

As soon as they touched down, one of Blake's men opened the door. Jase was with Blake as he approached the chopper.

Allan was first to ask, "What is going on, Blake?"

"It seems that these people have heard that Dr. Brick can cure cancer, and Rico here has asked Dr. Brick for help. He thinks that the mother of his boss, Juan Valdez, has cancer." Rico was a swarthy Central American dressed in camouflage.

Blake continued, "He said money is no object. When I told him how much I am paying, I thought that he was going to faint."

"Rico," called Blake, "Come over to the pool. Allan, the Professor and Jase also walked over to the pool area, and they all sat down.

"Rico is in the drug business. That is all I know. We share this island with his people. They were here first, and they have always been good to us. There is a little village on the other side of the island, and that is where the woman lives. Dr. Brick, what can you do to help her?"

"Blake, is there an air strip on the island?" asked Jase.

"Yes, but it's only for small planes."

"How can we get her to your jet, so I can check her out? I don't have any equipment here."

"Rico," asked Blake, "Will you bring the woman here to my house?"

"I will have her here tomorrow. Will you help her, Dr. Brick?"

"I hope so." Jase answered.

"I will be back tomorrow with Mrs. Valdez."

Rico went over to his jeep, jumped in and drove into the jungle. The rest of his men disappeared back into the jungle too.

"How do you feel Blake? I should give you a checkup while you are here."

"Better than I have in years. But first, I want to show you something. Let's take a walk. Do you see that mountain? I would like to show it to you. Professor, I think you will like to see it as well."

Blake raised his hand. Two open jeeps rolled up to where they were standing. As they got closer to the mountain, an entrance appeared. The jeeps they were riding in stopped, and they walked the rest of the way to the entrance.

"It's big enough to drive a tank into it," said the Professor.

"I have already started to clean this place up. It's a fortress in the mountain. How would you like to have your research facility here?"

Jase didn't answer. As soon as they were inside of the entrance, Blake hit a switch and the inside came alive. It was big. More room than he would ever need, or so he thought.

"It has its own power. The compound draws its power from here too. Believe me, Jase, we probably could power the entire island from this mountain."

"Have you checked this place for air quality?" asked the Professor.

Blake motioned for the Professor to walk with him and the rest followed. Blake answered, "It would be easier to show you."

He took them to a large steel door. He handed everyone noise suppressors. "You will need to put these on and don't touch anything."

The door was over eight inches thick, but Blake opened it easily. "The noise that you hear comes from all the systems running at their lowest setting. But even when everything is running at maximum, no noise is detected outside the steel door."

Blake motioned for everyone to go back outside the room. "Now Professor, as for air quality, it is good enough for a surgical area. I think it must have been made for a bomb shelter."

Jase had not spoken a word up until now. "Blake, do you know how much this will cost and how much time it will take?"

"Jase, do you know how much money you have? Unless I die of cancer, you are one of the richest men in the world."

"Blake, we need to talk about that. I cannot expect you to give me half of your money. That is ludicrous."

"Jase, we will talk about it later. Right now, I need for you and the Professor to do something for me."

"Of course, name it." said Jase.

"Will you give me a material list, so I can get your project started?"

Jase looked at Blake, and he was grinning with excitement.

"I would like to go into partnership with you, and put the cancer centers out of business. Don't answer now, think about it. Now come on, I want to introduce you to my family."

Blake was headed for the outside.

As they started to walk out, Jase said, "I think this might work for my lab. Blake, why did the CIA build this place?"

"The locals think that they stored nerve gas here and maybe even produced it. All that is left now is an empty bunker in the mountain. The CIA claim they know nothing about it."

"Blake, what country has control of the island?" asked the Professor.

"This island is its own country. They have no military and they believe in protecting their environment here on the island. In the near future, this might be one of the hot spots in the world, but their biggest challenge is the drug cartel. It has no respect for anything except money. Jase, if we could turn this island into a cancer clinic, it would change it forever. And you would not have to answer to anyone again."

"Blake, it seems that you have been doing a lot of research. How much room is in the mountain?" asked the Professor.

"It is huge, Professor. I think that you could put a football field in it. Now, let's head back." They headed down the mountain, arrived back at the mansion and pulled up in front of the main house.

The front of the house was facing the east. The house had a two story atrium with glass walls from floor to ceiling. Tropical flowers of all varieties covered the sides of the entrance. The modern white architecture blended perfectly with the view of the ocean and the mountain behind them. Between the main house and the ocean was a stunning infinity pool. Four Caribbean guest cottages separated by a flower covered pergola set next to the pool overlooking the ocean.

"How safe is the island, Blake?" asked Jase.

"Very, my compound is a lot larger than it looks, and I have security a detail that keeps a close watch on everything. They are in the process of bringing their families here to live. By the time that we are done, we will have a small city. I don't do anything unless the locals approve it. For every house I put up here, I put up one for the people on the other side of the island. I see Jill has already met my family. Let's go up and join them."

As they walked to the house, Blake pointed to the guest area. "That is where you will be staying. There are four cottages for you and your friends to stay and they all have a view of the ocean. Do you like it, Jase?" asked Blake.

"How could I not like it?"

"Good, now come in and meet my family."

Across the entire front of the house was a large balcony. All of the windows and the doors to the balcony had hurricane shutters. When they walked in, Jase and the Professor were speechless.

The sliding glass doors to the entrance of the atrium were open. Inside the living area, Linda was playing with Jack. "Jase, have you ever seen anything like this before?"

"No," he laughed. "Where is Jill? Is she lost in here?"

"Keep walking and you will see her," said Linda.

When they walked to the other side of the living area, they passed through another set of doors into a garden. The mansion wrapped around the open garden. In the center of the garden, Jill and Eva were sitting with some other people. Jase could not speak. He was too busy trying to take in the sights.

"What do you think?" asked Blake. "This house has been my dream since I was a child. I think everyone should realize their dream, don't you? I designed it myself."

The Professor said, "I don't think I have ever had a dream like this. Hell, if I had, I would have remembered it."

"Professor, on the left side of the garden is where my family resides. On the right side is where the staff resides and food is prepared. On the end of the garden is a clear acrylic wall that keeps the jungle out but does not block the view of the mountains. Do you like it?"

"Hell yes, I like it," answered the Professor.

"Gentlemen, allow me to introduce my family. I see your wife has already been introduced.

When they approach the others, a woman in her forties stood up. "Jill, this must be your husband, and this must be the famous Professor I have been hearing so much about. My name is Aine (Annie)."

Jase reached out to shake Aine's hand. "I am very glad to meet you."

The Professor came up. "Well hell, this is about the nicest dump I have ever seen."

Aine smiled, "I was warned about you, Professor, welcome."

As soon as Eva saw Jase, she started to smile. Jase reached out to pick her up.

"Alright Jase, hold out your other arm, Jack saw you too." Jase turned around. Linda was holding Jack. As soon as he saw his Dad, he smiled too.

They all sat down. "Now, who are these two?" asked Jase.

Jill said, "This young fellow is Cian (Keen), and this is his younger sister Chloe. Cian is thirteen and Chloe is ten."

"I'm very happy to meet you." said Jase.

Cian walked over to the Professor. "Pleased to meet you, I don't think I have ever met a Professor like you, sir." Everyone got a chuckle from that one.

"I don't think that I have ever been insulted in a nicer way. Cian, it is my pleasure to meet you also," the Professor laughed.

Blake looked at Cian, "Son, would you like to show the Professor to his room?"

"Would you please follow me, sir?" said Cian.

Aine was a little less than six foot tall. She has strawberry blond hair, lovely pale skin and an Irish accent.

"Aine is from Ireland," said Blake. "Can you tell?"

"Well, sometimes I have a wee bit of an accent." she blushed. "Now your wife knows where you will be staying, so go and relax, you have had a long day."

"Jase, that is not a bad idea. After dinner tonight we will talk. You and the Professor need to give me your list of supplies. Also, Nelson will be here tomorrow."

When Jase stood up, he still had both children in his arms. "Give me one of them, before you drop them both." Jill took Eva, and she fell asleep in her arms.

Blake put his arm around Aine, as the Brick's walked away. "What do you think, Aine, do you like them?" asked Blake.

"Now how you could not like them, don't be silly."

"That is good, because I think they will be with us for a very long time. I don't think they realize how much trouble they are in."

"You know, they don't deserve that. We will do as much as we can for them." Aine turned and smiled at Linda.

"I will be going too. Thank you both, I don't think they would have made it, if not for you." Then Linda left for her cottage.

Jill led Jase past the pool and to their cottage on the north side of the house overlooking the ocean. They had one large bedroom, a living area, a small kitchen and patio. Linda's cottage was right next to it facing the pool. There were tall wood ceilings with fans above the white stucco walls and red Spanish tile floors.

Linda knocked on the door. It was open, so she walked in. "I have been all over the world, but I have never seen anything that would compare to this," she said to herself.

Jase and Jill were playing with the children in the living area, and the children were laughing. The Bricks were so occupied with each other, that they did not hear her come in. Linda stood and watched them for a moment. Then she backed out very quietly and went to her cottage. She sat looking out at the mountain. For the first time in her life, she was happy.

Linda could here laughter. She walked out to the pool area. Cian and the Professor were talking. The Professor was trying to show Cian how to call Rex. "Now watch this," he said. "Rex come." Rex did not give the Professor as much as a glance.

"Rex and I go way back, he probably did not hear me." He called again, "Rex, come here boy. Come on."

Cian was laughing very hard now. "Mr. Professor, maybe Rex doesn't speak English." Cian sat down on the deck, still laughing. "Come here Rex," Cian said in French.

Rex stood up, came over to Cian and sat down with him.

The Professor grumbled, "Traitor."

Linda was watching everything. "Why Professor, you have some competition." She smirked.

"Oh hell, I told Rex to go to the boy. It would make the boy feel better."

"Professor, would you like to join me for a drink?" Linda held out her arm.

The Professor turned toward Cian, "While I'm gone, maybe you could teach Rex some other language."

"Would Spanish be alright, sir?"

"Yes that would be fine."

Linda was laughing, and the Professor was mumbling, "Would Spanish be alright, the little smartass."

They walked back into the atrium of the main house. Over to the right they saw one of the staff. "Can we get a drink around here?" asked the Professor.

"I would be more than happy to get that for you. Would both of you like a gin and squirt?" she asked.

"They were warned about you." Linda whispered. "That would be fine, thank you," answered Linda.

"Would you like to go into the bar or go back out to the pool?"

"You have a bar? Why am I not surprised," answered the Professor.

"I believe the Professor and I will go to the bar," said Linda.

They followed the girl to the bar. Inside of the bar area was a pool table, a large TV on the wall and some round pub tables and stools.

Linda pointed to a table and they sat down.

"What are you thinking, Professor?"

"I'm thinking life was a lot simpler before I met Brick, but I would not trade this time for anything."

Linda nodded as the girl brought the drinks to the table.

Linda asked the girl, "Where are you from?"

"I live on the other side of the Island. Most of the staff is from there as well."

"What do think of Mr. Canond?" asked Linda.

"He is a very generous man, and a good person. You will see."

They sat and relaxed for a while, and then the girl came back. "Can I get you anything else?"

"We would like to have one more, please. But I do have a question for you."

"What is that, Professor?"

"Squirt, is that something you normally have here?"

"No, I have never seen it before. Mr. Canond had it brought in.
I will be right back."

"You cannot beat the service. I can't wait for our meeting tonight after
dinner." said the Professor.

At five, one of the staff came to the Brick's cottage. "Mr. and Mrs.
Brick, may I watch the children while you are at dinner?"

Jill answered, "I would like to feed them and get them ready for bed,
but thank you."

Not taking no for an answer, the girl asked again. "Mr. Canond
thought that you could have a nice supper meeting with him, and I
am very good with children. I have four brothers and sisters."

"What is your name?" asked Jill.

"Tania."

"That is a very pretty name. How soon is dinner?"

"Thank you. Dinner will be at sunset. It comes very fast with the
mountain so close."

"Tania, if you would like to help me with the children, I think it is
time for their dinner," said Jill.

With a smile, Tania said, "Yes." Jill started to show Tania where
everything was for the children.

Linda was sitting with Jase. "I think Jill has found another sitter."

"That might be a good thing. You two might have a chance to do
some things together," Jase smiled.

Thirty minutes later, Chloe came to the cottage. "Would you like to come for dinner now?" At the same time, Cian was getting the Professor.

The children loved Tania, she was an instant hit. Jill was giving her last minute instructions to Tania. Jase walked over to Jill. "If she has any problem, she will call you." Chloe took Jill's hand and started to walk out of the room.

They all entered the atrium and went to the right. The dining area was next to the bar. The view was nothing short of fantastic, looking west to the jungle and east to the ocean. The Canond's were just ready to be seated.

Blake sat down at the head of the large wood table. "Everyone, please have a seat. I would like to make a toast." They all raised their glasses, "To a long and prosperous friendship. I have recently talked to Nelson Shay. It would seem that Canond Industries has completely rebounded. At this time, I would like to welcome our newest millionaires, Linda, the Professor, and Jase and Jill. Nelson will give you all the good news when he arrives in the morning."

The dinner went very smoothly. Fresh seafood and fruit were served with a Caribbean flair.

Finally, Blake said, "Now, let's have the staff clear the table. We have a lot to discuss."

"Jase, do you and the Professor have your list of things that you are going to need?"

"Yes, we do. How soon can we get construction moving?"

"I have already had the plans drawn up for the clinic. I want you to look over them, and tell me what needs to be changed."

Then Blake asked, "Now, the first thing I would like to know is how much of this laser is your doing, Professor, and how much of it is Jase's?"

Jase answered, "Blake, the idea was mine, but the Professor is the one who made it work."

"That is what I thought," said Blake. "Here is what I would like to do. I would like to offer you a partnership. I think that we can go into the cancer cure business right here on the Island. We don't have to answer to anyone, and I think we should ask the same price of everyone." Then he paused.

Jase was first to ask. "Do you mean half of everything?"

"Yes, whatever that family has, we charge half."

"Linda, you could be in charge of collections. With your background, it would not be too hard for you to find out about someone's assets."

"Jase and Jill, you will be handling the medical end, and Professor, you could take care of the tech side of the program."

"But there will be people out there that will not be able to afford treatment. We would turn into what we are fighting against," said Jase.

Blake was laughing. "Think about what I said, half of everything. If the family has nothing, what is half of nothing?"

The Professor answered, "Nothing."

"And the family only pays once, no matter how much or how many people get sick. Nelson will be here tomorrow, and he can help set up the corporation. Think about it tonight."

"Now, what are we going to do about the lady who is coming to see you tomorrow?"

Jase asked, "Where is your yacht. Is Dr. Aunser on it?"

"It is off the coast of Mexico, and yes, Dr. Aunser is on the ship."

"Good," said Jase. "How can we get them together?"

"You, the woman and one of her family can take the helicopter to the ship. I will have the ship head south, so the trip won't be so long. It can dock right here. The dock has been made to fit the yacht."

"Jase, you are a very rich man."

"Blake, we need to talk about that. There is only one way that I can accept all that money."

Blake interrupted Jase. "The money has already been put in a bank account in your name in Jamaica. Nelson will fill you in tomorrow. Now, let me see the list of things that you need. Jase, you are in charge of getting everything. What are these 500 gallon tanks for?"

"I will have to show you, but I'm sure you will be impressed. Professor, we are going to need more lasers. But this time they have to be linked to a scanner, so we can see what we are doing."

"Well hell, there goes my beach time."

"One more thing, you are going to need a house of your own here on the Island. I will have one of the architects here this week, so we can get started. Remember, for every building we put up here, we need to put one up on the other side of the island."

Chapter   56

Everything was moving very quickly in Virginia. Michael was at his desk all day Sunday. On the hour, every hour he would get an update. They were all the same, no news. He had been outsmarted by a college professor. Michael did not like to lose, even if he deserved to. He walked to the communication room. As soon as he entered, he was greeted to a "Nothing yet."

"Give me a run down on the President's news conference today. Have they found out anything on the exploding cameras?"

"Sorry Michael, even with our clearance, we can't get any information. It is locked up tight."

"Alright, can you tell me if the yacht is in international waters?"

"Yes it is."

"Tell the coast guard to stop her if she gets in U.S. waters. I want to know if Brick is on that ship."

"Yes Michael."

Next, Michael walked to Richard's office. As soon as he entered, Richard was on his feet. The little fat man came out from behind his desk.

"What in the hell are you doing, Michael? I have not heard anything from anyone. You picked the wrong time to fuckup, I always hear from Seaban at least twice a day and today nothing. You are in this as deep as I am."

"Sometime the best thing to do is nothing, Richard. Seaban will call you when he can. I'm sure his phones are tapped. As soon as he can get a secure line, you will hear from him. Then you will wish you hadn't. I am doing everything I can to locate Dr. Brick. Let us hope that he has not figured out what we tried to do."

Richard turned to Michael, "He has outsmarted you on every turn. What makes you think that he does not know?"

"We have no way of telling. We need to sit tight for now."

"Get out of my office. Come back when you know something."

Richard settled back in his chair, his hands still shaking. Then his private line rang. Slowly he picked up the phone.

"Richard, Seaban here. You know I trusted you and your agency, now it seems that we have a little problem. Those Secret Service people have enlisted the help of some other agencies. You better pray they don't come up with anything. Might I remind you sir, if I go down, your Northern ass goes right down the toilet with me." Then the line went dead.

Richard picked the phone up again. "Michael, would you come to my office, please?" He sat quietly and waited for Michael.

Soon Michael arrived. "Sit down, Michael."

Michael sat down cautiously. "I'm scared to ask, but what now?"

"I think Seaban has become less useful. I would like him to be erased."

"Richard, you could start a war within. Haven't we done enough?"

"Michael, Seaban is going down, and I don't want to go down with him. Make it look like an accident."

"Richard, I don't think this is a good idea."

"End of conversation, Michael. Take care of it and don't fuck it up."

Michael rose from the chair and left the office. As he walked back to his office, he spotted Thomas in the lobby.

"Good, you saved me a phone call. I need the eraser team in my office, as soon as you can do it." Michael kept walking never missing a step.

Thomas disappeared. "He is young and wants to move up. These new kids have no morals," Michael thought. Thomas would do anything he was asked to. He reminded Michael of himself at that age.

Michael decided not to go back to his office. He stopped at the front desk. "I will be going home. Call me if you need to, but make sure that it's important if you call. I will be back tomorrow by noon. Have my car brought out front. I will be waiting."

By the time Michael was out front, his car was pulling up. He thanked the attendant and drove away.

The trip took close to an hour, depending on how much traffic was on the road. This time of year, most of the vacationers were gone. He made it home in less than an hour.

As soon as he walked through the door and barely had his jacket off, he was met by his daughter. She was in her night gown.

"Now why are you not in bed?" he asked.

"Daddy, I was sick again. Mommy said I could stay up until you came home."

She reached out her arms for her Dad to pick her up. He received a hug as only a daughter can give.

She coughed when Michael held her. She whispered in his ear, "I love you," then gave her Dad a kiss.

"Let's go find your Mother."

"She is in the kitchen, Daddy."

"Well, that's where we are going."

Michael walked into the kitchen, as his wife looked up. "Michael, I'm so glad you are home. Let's put this little girl to bed." Cindy was already asleep in Michael's arms.

They walked to the child's bedroom and laid her down in her bed.

"Mary, how long has she been sick?"

"She has had a cold for almost a week. I made an appointment with the doctor in the morning. I knew you were busy, so I didn't call, but I'm glad you are home now."

They walked back to kitchen. "I have some coffee," she said.

"That would be great," Michael answered.

Mary poured a cup for herself and one for Michael. As she handed Michael his cup, she looked at his shirt. "What is that on your shirt, Michael?"

"Where?" Michael asked.

"Here, on your shoulder." Mary came over and touched his shirt, "Michael, its blood."

They both ran to Cindy's room. Right next to the child, was a small amount of blood on her pillow.

"Get dressed, Mary. We are going to the hospital ER."

Michael picked the little girl up, but she did not wake up. Michael called, "Cindy, Cindy," but the little girl did not respond.

Mary was back. "Mary, I can't get her to wake up."

Mary tried, but still with no results. The child did not move.

"Let's go, the car is still in the driveway." Michael carried Cindy out to the car. "Don't worry about the child seat. Get buckled in, and then I will hand her to you."

Once Mary had the child in her arms, Michael ran around the car, got in and pulled out of the drive. Michael was on his phone. "This is Michael, and I need back up. I am headed for the hospital. Call the hospital and tell them my daughter is not responding, and we are on our way in. My ETA is fifteen minutes. Call me back when you get through."

At night the Chesapeake area was sometimes very foggy, and tonight was no exception. But Michael had not slowed down for anything before in his life, and a little fog was not going to stop him now.

Michael's phone rang. "Yes, what did you find out? Good, we are almost there."

"What did they say, Michael?"

"The ER will be waiting at the door."

Michael's precision driving had them at the hospital in record time.

As soon as they pulled up, the ER door opened and the staff was at the car before Michael could open his door.

Mary opened her door, and the staff put Cindy on a cart and had her in the sliding doors before Mary could get out of the car.

"Go with them, Mary. I will park the car and be right in."

Mary followed Cindy into the ER. They could not get the girl to respond.

"How long has the child been like this?"

Mary answered the nurse. "No more than thirty minutes."

"Has she had a fever?"

"Off and on, but not very high," Mary was about in tears.

The ER. doctor came in. "I want this girl on a ventilator, now. Anyone that is not working on the child, please step out to the waiting room."

One of the nurses walked over to Mary. "There is nothing you can do right now. Will you come with me so I can get some more information?

They went into a small office, where an older lady started asking questions about Cindy. Mary was in tears, when Michael walked in. She could feel his strength, as soon as he entered the room.

"Do you have any idea what is going on?" asked Mary.

"It's too early to tell, but you did the right thing getting her in here as quickly as you did. Now both of you take a seat in the waiting room. As soon as they know something, someone will be out to talk to you." Then the lady showed them to the waiting room.

Michael tried to use his cell phone, but there was no signal. The volunteer at the desk in the waiting room spoke up. "I don't think you can get a good signal in here. You will have to go outside or on one of the upper levels."

Michael thanked the woman, and then went outside. He called the agency and left a message that he would be at the hospital if anyone needed him.

They sat in chairs that would let them see a little of what is going on. Every time the door would open they could see people rushing in and out of their daughter's room. After an hour, a doctor came out.

"Mr. Greyger and Mrs. Greyger." The doctor said. Michael and Mary stood up.

"Would you come with me?" They followed the doctor to a room where they could talk in private.

"We have put your daughter on a ventilator. She stopped breathing right after she came in. We are running another blood test. When the first test came back, her white blood count was way down, so now we have to find out why. Have you been on any trips lately or been exposed to anyone who was sick? Anything that you can think of might be helpful."

"No, we haven't been anywhere. Is she awake?" asked Mary.

"No, not yet, as soon as she is, I will come and get you."

Michael put his arm around Mary. On the outside he showed no emotions, but inside he was ready to crack.

Michael had lost track of time, when the doctor finally came back out. "We would like to have permission to run some scans. A cat scan first, if nothing shows, an MRI. We have a few ideas, but we need to do some more test to be sure. One thing we do know, it is not a virus or a cold."

"Of course," said Michael. "Let's find out what we are dealing with."

"Good," said the doctor. "I have another doctor coming in to help. His name is Dr. White. He is one of the best in the country. Have a seat and try to be comfortable. This will take a couple of hours." Then he walked back in to the ER.

"I forgot to ask what type of specialist Dr. White is."

"Ask the volunteer, Michael," said Mary. Michael walked up to the desk.

"Can I help you?" the volunteer asked.

"I hope so, what kind of doctor is Doctor White?"

"Let me check." The volunteer got out his book. Mary was watching, but she could not tell what the volunteer said.

Michael turned and walked back to Mary. He sat down.

"What did he say, Michael?"

At First, Michael could not answer, and he sat fighting his emotions.

Now Mary was getting nervous. "Michael, what did he say?"

Michael turned to Mary. His eyes were full of tears, and his lips were quivering.

Mary was starting to shake. "Michael, you are scaring me."

Michael turned so that Mary could not see the tears that were running down his face. "Dr. White is a children's cancer specialist."

Chapter 57

The sunrise was one of the most beautiful that Jill had ever seen. As if it had no cares, the ball of fire rose ever so slowly on the edge of the gulf, and above the water on its climb for the sky. Seagulls drifted in the wind, only stopping to catch breakfast.

Jill did not want to wake anyone. The children were sleeping very peacefully and Jase was doing the same.

Jill was looking back at the last few months. "We have done more in the last few months, than most people do in a life time."

Then the first cry of reality took her out of thoughts and back into the real world. She walked back into the room. Jase did not stir. She would let him sleep.

She heard a slight knock on the door and then it opened. "Would you like some help?" asked Linda.

Jack was starting to cry, and Eva was not far behind. They changed the two, and took them out into the family room. They both were on the same schedule. Jill held Jack and Linda had Eva.

"What a life, growing up on an island in the gulf. Have you two given any thought to it?" Linda asked Jill.

"No, we haven't, but this has been Jase's dream from day one, that and finding a cure. We were both so naive back then. The world is a scary place. We thought the world would greet us with open arms. We didn't understand the greed that existed."

Jill heard Jase getting up. So she walked in, "Good morning, sunshine."

Jase gave her a little kiss, then he came out and gave one to each of the children. He walked over to Linda and gave her a hug. "Thank you Linda, you have been a life saver."

Linda stood there looking at him as he walked out of the cottage. "I have to get some coffee," Jase said.

Linda was surprised. "Linda, he really appreciates all that you have done for us," said Jill. "He does most of his thinking at night in his sleep. Almost all of his ideas came to him in his sleep. I don't think that his mind ever shuts down."

Jase came back. Would you all like to join me for breakfast?"

"Go ahead Jase, Linda and I will be there shortly."

Jase walked out as fast as he walked in. He went straight for the dining room. Blake was already there talking to the Professor.

"Jase, come over and sit down. What would you like to eat? It is going to be a big day for you?"

"Blake, I have been thinking. How are we to know how much a person is to pay? If the family only has some chickens, how do we charge them?"

"Jase, we can trace most bank accounts. We will have to learn as we go, and if someone only has two chickens, we charge one chicken. I think the rich can pay for the poor."

Take this Reco person, how do we check out his boss?"

"I'm not sure of that yet. Let's see how it goes."

They could hear the sound of jeeps coming down the mountain. One of the staff walked up to the table. Blake nodded to him.

"Just to stay on the safe side, I have asked for security to make themselves visible. Please invite our guest in for something to eat."

Soon two men and a woman walked into the dining area. Everyone stood up to welcome the guests. They could tell the woman was scared.

Rico was the first to speak, "Dr. Brick, this is my boss, Juan."

Jase reached out to shake hands with Juan. "Juan, what is your last name?" he asked.

In a very low voice, the man said, "Valdez."

Jase got a huge smile on his face, "As in the coffee Valdez?"

The little man angered very quickly. "No, I don't think that man ever existed."

Rico held up his hand. "Mr. Valdez does not like to be compared to a poor coffee grower. Please do not mention it again."

Jase could hardly help keep from laughing. "I'm sorry if I insulted you. Is this your mother?"

Juan said, "Yes."

"Please have a seat, Mrs. Valdez, and tell me a little about yourself. Have you seen a doctor, and, if so, what did that doctor say?" She started to sob.

"Blake, is there some place that I can talk to Mrs. Valdez in private?"

"Use one of the guest houses next to yours."

Jill and Linda were just coming in. "Jill, can you help Mrs. Valdez to the empty guest house? I think she would feel better if you were there."

"Mrs. Valdrez, would you follow me?" Jill helped the lady up and talked to her all the way to the guest house.

"Juan, your mother did not speak. Is there anything I should know?"

"She is much scared. There are no doctors in the village, and the other women in the village told her that she has cancer."

"All right, I will take a look at her. I don't have any testing equipment here yet, but we can fly her to a medical facility that does. Is that all right with you?"

"Yes, that is why we came."

"Good, now I would like to say something. I am in the business of healing people, and it would seem you are in the business of killing them. I don't have any use for anything that has to do with your drug world. I will treat your mother no matter what is wrong with her, but I don't want to see any of your guns or drugs on this island. Do you understand me?"

"You cannot order me to do anything."

"But I can, and I did. If she does have cancer, I will charge you for the treatment, but let's not jump to conclusions. Let's cross one bridge at a time. Do you agree?"

"Yes, Dr. Brick, one step at a time."

"Now, I must go and see your mother. Please have a seat, and I will be back as soon as I can." Jase excused himself and left the mansion. When he arrived at the guest house, he knocked on the door.

Jill had the woman sit on the side of the bed. "Mrs. Valdez, may I call you by your first name?"

"Jase, her name is Maria."

Jase smiled, "How are you today, Maria?"

She shrugged her shoulders. "I don't know."

"Maria, I need to look at your breast." Jill helped the woman take off the robe that she had given her.

"Now tell me Maria, why do you think you have something wrong?"

Soon she felt more at ease. Jase was so good with her that she even joked a little with him, as he checked her breast and her lymph nodes.

"Maria, I don't see anything that calls for alarm at this point, but I don't have any testing equipment here. I think it would be a good idea to run some test at a hospital. Will you go?"

Maria smiled and said, "Si."

"Alright, I will go and talk to your son. Jill will help you get dressed, and I will see you in a few minutes." Jase walked out and closed the door softly behind him.

"You have a very nice husband. You are very lucky."

"Well, thank you," Jill answered.

Jase went back to the dining area. When Juan saw him, he jumped up. "What did you find?"

"Have a seat, Juan, your mother will be here in a moment. I did not find anything wrong with her, but I would like her to go to a hospital for some test.?"

"How soon?" asked Juan. Jase looked at Blake.

"I can have a plane here within the next two days."

Jill and Maria walked back to the dining room. "Please sit down, Mrs. Valdez, and have something to eat."

At first Juan was not in favor of her going, but after seeing how happy his mother was, he agreed.

Jase asked, "How can I get in touch with you when the plane is here?"

Maria paused, and then went through her bag. She pulled out her phone. "My son gave me this phone, but I never use it much."

"Does the phone work on the Island?" asked Jase.

Juan spoke up. "There is a tower on top of the mountain. Try it." He gave Jase the number. Jase called the number and Maria's phone started to ring.

"Dr. Brick, I don't text."

Jase smiled, "That will be fine Maria. I will call you when we are ready."

"Dr. Brick, will you be coming also?" Maria asked.

"I don't know yet Maria, but you will not go alone. Do you a have a passport?"

"She does have a passport," her son answered. "What kind of hospital are you going to take her to?"

"Juan, there is a private hospital in San Jose. They can run all the test that she needs there. I will call and set everything up, unless you would like to take her?"

"No, Dr. Brick, I need to stay away from San Jose. If you know what I mean."

Blake stood up. "Juan, if Maria is all right Dr. Brick will not charge you. The plane trip is on the house, but if he finds anything wrong we will charge as we agreed. Maria, it has been a pleasure to meet you. Is there anything else we can do for you today?"

Juan answered, "You do your part and I will keep my word, until we meet again."
Jase and Jill walked Maria and her son to their jeep.

Maria grabbed Jase's hand, "Thank you, Dr. Brick." And then they left.

"Blake, you know as soon as the hospitals discover I'm here, they will not accept any of the people I send. We need to get equipment here as soon as possible."

"You are probably right. Nelson Shay is coming today, and he is bringing an architect with him. This is a number one priority. If I were you, I would rest. We are going to have a long day."

The entire time Jase was talking to Juan Valdez, the Professor sat quietly. After Mrs. Valdez had left, he spoke. "Jase, do you think she has cancer?"

"Let me put it this way, Professor. How soon can we get a good laser online and linked with an imaging device?"

"That is what I thought. Blake, how are we paying for all of this?"

"For right now, find out who has what you need and tell me or Nelson."

"When will he be here?" asked Jase.

"Anytime, I am surprised he is not here already."

"We are going back to check on the children." Jase and Jill went back to the guest house. Linda was talking to the babies, as if they knew what she was saying.

"How did it go, Jase?" Linda asked.

"It went alright. I think there is a good chance she has breast cancer, but there is no reason to get her all shook about it until we know for sure. What do you think, Jill?"

"She let me feel the lump. It was scary. I feel so sorry for her."

"Now both of you sit down with me, I have something I want to ask you."

Linda and Jill looked at each other, and then they sat down.

"Jill, I think we can make a go of it here. What do you think?"

"I think the children would like to grow up here, and this Island is your dream and mine too," said Jill.

Linda, we want you to stay here on the Island. You are part of the family now. What do you say?"

"You are not going to need a nanny forever."

"That is true, but we are going to need a business partner, if you are interested."

"What can I do? I know nothing about what you are doing," Linda answered.

"With your background, we would be foolish not to have you with us. Let me talk to Blake about you. Also, if it was not for the Professor we would be nowhere."

"We agree. Whatever we do, the Professor should be a part of it," Jill said.

Chapter 58

Michael showed up for work the next day. Thomas met him as he entered the building. "How is your daughter sir?" he asked.

"Thomas, I will only say this once. My family is private. Thank you for asking, but don't ever ask again."

"Sorry sir, it won't happen again."

Michael walked over to Thomas. He put his arm on Thomas's shoulder. "No, I'm sorry, I'm a little edgy."

Michael went to the front desk. "Is Richard in?"

"Yes sir, he asked that you come to his office when you get in."

"Tell him I will be right there."

Michael had to walk through the communication room to get to Richard's office. "Please tell me that you have found Dr. Brick."

"No sir, the ship we were tracking turned south and is headed for South America. Miss Peach's phone quit working on the shore of Cuba. Would you like us to do anything else?"

"No, but keep a very close eye on that ship. That's all we have right now."

Michael walked to Richard office. Richard saw Michael coming.

"Michael, come in. Have a seat. I have reconsidered my last order. I have been talking to Seaban. I played the same game he did. I asked him how his wife, children and grandchildren were, and then I wished him the best."

"And how did that go, Richard?"

"Mr. Seaban thinks it would be in both of our interest to work together as we have in the past. I told him that he was making a very intelligent decision."

"So I can call off my eraser team," asked Michael.

"For now, but we may need to erase your good doctor, if he figures out what we were up to."

Michael did not say anything. This was the wrong time to tell Richard that he was losing it. There would be plenty of time to tell him in the future.

"Is there anything else, Richard?"

"No Michael. Thank you for all your help throughout the years."

A cold chill went up Michael's spine. He knew Richard would only say something like that if he was going to, or had already set him up, to protect himself.

Michael walked by the communication room. "Check to see if Blake Canond has any holdings in the gulf between North and South America."

"Michael, do you know what you are asking? That may take days."

"I know, but it is very important, and I would appreciate it very much."

"What is going on?" said one of the men in the communication room. "First Richard is nice, now Michael. What is the world coming to?"

Michael went back to his office. He sat down and stared at a picture of his daughter. He fought the tears coming down his face.

"Where are you, Dr. Brick, where are you?"

Michael's phone rang. "Yes."

"Communications sir, we might have found something."

"I will be right there."

Michael was out of his office and to the communication room. He tried not to run. When he got there, the men were surprised at his fast response.

"What did you find?" demanded Michael.

"Look at this, Canond Industries owns part of an island off the Central America coast."

"Get an aircraft over there and take some pictures ASAP. As soon as you can, confirm that he is there. Make arrangements for me to get there. No, see if they have an airfield. I will fly there myself. Do not tell anyone about this, and that includes Richard. Do you understand?"

"Yes Michael, but what if he asked."

"He won't, unless you let the word out. You will be looking for a new place to work, if that happens."

Michael walked out to the desk. "I have to go now. If anyone needs me, call my cell. And as always, if they don't need me, don't call."

"Yes sir, Michael. We have already called for your car."

He said," Thank you," and he went to get his car.

Michael went straight to the hospital and to his daughter's room. His wife was asleep in the chair. She had been there all night. Cindy was awake, and she looked tired.

"Hi Daddy," she called.

Michael went to her bedside. The hugs were as pure as they could be. Mary opened her eyes.

"Michael, they gave her some blood. She is doing much better. The doctor is supposed to come in anytime."

Mary was tired and worried. She had been in the confines of the hospital room for almost a day.

"Mary, after we talk to the doctor you should go home and rest. I will stay with her until you get back."

"Michael, I don't want to leave her."

"I know, let us take it one step at a time. First we talk to the doctor."

Michael sat on the edge of the bed with Cindy. She had some books on the bed.

"Would you like me to read you one of the books?"

"Oh Daddy, you haven't read me a book since I was a little girl."

"That is all changing right now," Michael said with tears coming down his face.

When Mary saw the tears, she started to weep also.

Cindy saw her dad's tears, and she pulled her dad next to her.

"Don't cry Daddy. It will upset Mommy," Cindy whispered in his ear.

Michael tried to read one of the books. Then there was a knock at the door.

"Hi, I'm Doctor White. You must be Cindy's parents. You sure have a nice little girl here." He walked over to the bed.

"How are you today, Angel. Are you feeling better?"

"Yes sir," Cindy answered.

"Well you look a lot better then you did. Are you eating?"

"Yes sir," Cindy answered.

"Can you say anything other than yes sir?"

"Yes sir," then she started to laugh. "Are you teasing me?"

"Maybe a little," said the doctor. "Can I borrow your Mom and Dad for a little bit? I'll bring them right back."

"I don't want my Daddy to leave. Don't leave me Daddy!"

"I will be right outside the door. And I will not go anywhere."

"Do you promise?" Cindy was crying now.

"I promise." Michael gave her a big hug and a kiss.

Dr. White walked out first with Mary right behind. Michael turned before he walked out.

Cindy was crying and her eyes were full of fear. "I won't leave you, alright?"

Cindy was sitting up in her bed with her arms reaching out for her Dad.

Michael walked back in and gave her another kiss. "I will open the blinds so that you can see us. Is that all right?"

"Yes," replied the fragile little girl.

Michael walked out of the room. He waved to his daughter through the glass window.

Dr. White asked, "Would you like to go to a more private place?"

"No," Michael answered. "I promised that I would stay right here, where she could see me."

"Her red blood cell count was almost nonexistent. We had to give her some blood. I don't know if she would have made it through the night without it. You did the right thing getting her in here."

"So what is going on doctor?" asked Michael.

"We don't know yet. For some reason she does not have enough red blood cells. Until we do some more testing, we will not know if it is a cancer or something else. But for now, she is stable."

Mary put both hands over mouth, and Michael made her put them down. "Cindy is watching everything we do. We have to be strong for her."

Dr. White said, "Sometimes my job is very hard, especially when I don't have good news. As soon as I know anything else, I will let you know."

"Someday, someone will come up with a cure for this crap. Until then, we treat it the best way as we know how."

"Dr. White, do you think that this is some kind of cancer? A simple yes or no is all that I am asking," Michael demanded.

The doctor hesitated, then he said, "Probably, but we cannot be sure yet. As soon as I find something out, you will be the first to know. Now I must go. I will drop in after awhile. You have a very brave little girl."

The doctor gave the two a smile and went down the hall.

"What are we going to do, Michael? What if she has cancer?"

Michael put his finger to his wife's lips. "We will deal with it together. I have to finish one last project at work, and then I'm done. We will take care of Cindy together."

"Do you promise, Michael?"

"Yes, now are you all right to drive?"

"I think so," Mary held out her hands. They were shaking.

"I will call for a ride for you. I want you to go home and rest. I'm going to be very busy in the near future, and I need you to be strong. You call me if you need anything."

Michael thought of how many times he has said that to people, but this was the first time he had meant it.

Michael called the agency. "This is Michael, put Thomas on."

He waited a few minutes, and Thomas answered. "Michael, this is Thomas. What can I do for you?"

"Get a car from the pool. I want you to come here to the hospital. When you get here, come to room 403. I will be waiting."

"I'm on my way, anything else, Michael?"

"Yes, don't tell anyone about this. And I mean anyone."

"Yes sir."

Michael went into Cindy's room. She was smiling now that her Dad was back.

"Now your mom is going to go home for a while and rest. Is that all right?"

"Are you going to stay, Daddy?"

"You could not keep me away."

"Then it is all right. Mommy, Daddy is going to stay with me. You go home and rest, Daddy will take care of everything."

"I know he will Angel."

They both sat with Cindy until Thomas arrived.

There was a knock at the door, and Thomas walked in.

"Mary, this is Thomas. He works for me. He is going to take you home. Would you like him to stop to pick up something to eat, so you will not have to fix anything?"

Mary said, "Hi Thomas, thank you for your help. I am almost ready to go." She put on her coat on and went over to the bed.

"I love you very much. Try to be easy on your Dad. He isn't used to all this rough stuff."

"Don't worry, Mommy, Daddy will make sure everything is alright."

"Thomas," said Michael, "As soon as you drop my wife off, I want you to come back here."

"Yes sir, goodbye Cindy." Thomas waved as he left.

Mary did not want to leave. "She will be all right, Mary. I will call you as soon as I find out anything."

She gave Cindy a kiss, and then she went over to Michael and gave him a kiss.

"Mommy gave you a kiss too, Daddy." She smiled, closed her eyes and drifted back to sleep.

About two hours later, Thomas was back.

He walked in without knocking. "I did not want to wake the child."

Michael rose from his chair. He quietly walked to the door. "Thomas I want my plane fueled and ready to go at a moment's notice. Have communications call me, when they find out anything. They will have to page me through the hospital. My phone will not work in here. Also, have my pilot on call. I want him with me. Tell him we will be flying over water and have two passengers besides me. This is also between you and me."

"Yes sir," Thomas started to leave.

"And Thomas, thank you."

Michael spent the next twenty four hours with his daughter. Each time she would wake the first thing that she would do is make sure her Dad was there.

Dr. White came in a few times to see his little patient. They would draw blood and check her vitals.

Michael stopped Dr. White the last time he was there.

"Dr. White, I will need a copy of everything that goes on with my daughter. Then I will need it updated every day that she is here."

"That is a very unusual request, Mr. Greyger."

"It was not a request. I hope that you understand."

"Mr. Greyger, your daughter is getting the best treatment that is available anywhere."

"Dr. White, I realize that and I have nothing but respect for you. So please honor my wishes."

"The records will be delivered to you at the end of the day."

Dr. White was not happy. He did not like being told what to do, even if it was from a high level government man.

Chapter   59

Jase left the guest house. "Now where did the Professor wander off to?" Jase wondered.

When he saw one of the staff, Jase asked, "Have you seen the Professor?"

"Yes sir, he was headed for the bar."

"That makes sense." Jase went to the bar.

The Professor was sitting at one of the tables. "Come on over Brick and have a seat."

"Professor, are you interested in staying on here as a full partner?" asked Jase.

"Keep talking, Jase."

"The only way that this thing will work is with you."

"What does Blake say about that?"

"We will talk to him this afternoon. I would like Linda to have a part in this also."

They both stop talking. "Sounds like a chopper coming in. Must be Nelson," said Jase. "Let's go and find out."

He was right. A helicopter had landed that was larger than the one on the yacht. As soon as the engine was off, Nelson and two other men got out of the chopper. They started walking up to the main house. As they came closer, Blake walked out right behind Jase and the Professor.

When they walked into the atrium, Blake introduced them. "Jase, Professor you know Nelson and this is Rick Thomas. He is the contractor that is in charge of most of our work. And this is our architect, Larry Fence. He has worked all over the world for us. Shall we go to the conference room?" On the left side of the atrium was the conference room. Three of the walls were glass. The south and east walls had a view of the ocean and beach. From the north wall you could see inside the atrium and on the west wall hung a picture of Blake Canond.

"Please excuse the picture of me, it was a present from my wife. I would have enjoyed a picture of her instead of me."

"How are you, Jase?" asked Nelson. Will your wife and Linda be here? I have some papers for them to sign. I understand that you want them in the new corporation."

"Nelson, I am fine, and I will be glad to go and get them."

Blake called for one of the staff, and she came right in. "Tania, could you go and relieve Mrs. Brick and Miss Peach, and ask them to join us?"

Tania was very happy to do that, and left the conference room. She knocked at the open door of the guest house, and Jill answered. "Mr. Canond would like both of you to join them in the conference room. If you don't mind, I will take care of the babies again for you. If I need anything, I will call you."

Jill and Linda gave Tania some last minute instructions, and then they went to the meeting. They walked in and sat down at the large table. Jill sat down next to Jase, and Linda sat next to the Professor.

Blake spoke first. "The first thing we have to do is take care of your investments. Nelson, would you do the honors?"

Nelson opened his case. "Dr. Brick, you and Jill have made a handsome profit. The stock more than tripled. I would suggest that you diversify some or all of your stock. I have opened an account in Jamaica in your names. With the money from Mr. Canond and the money from your investments, you are going to be very wealthy."

Jase and Jill look at the figures. Jill was in shock. "You mean I am that rich?"

"Yes," answered Nelson. "Not bad for a month's work. Linda, here is where you are with your investment. You also did very well and are now a millionaire. And Professor, now you will not have to buy any more used cars."

Jase spoke up. "I don't think that money has anything to do with it, right Professor?"

"Hell no," he said.

"I have taken the liberty of securing accounts for you two in Jamaica as well. All of you will need to sign these papers to open the accounts. The management of the bank would very much like to meet all of you. Now, are all of you going to stay here and make a go of the Cancer Cure Center?"

Jase and Jill said, "Yes."

The Professor had a question. "Can I get my car on the Island?"

Blake laughed, "You and your car, of course Professor, it's your money."

Linda was a little slower to respond. "What can I do? You are not going to need someone for the children forever."

Nelson asked, "Have you run background checks on people before?"

"Yes," she answered.

"We need someone like you to screen the people when they come in and trace their bank accounts. The price will be the same for everyone. If they don't have anything, our service is free."

"I think I can do that," she replied.

"Now Professor, Jase seems to think that without you, we will not get off the ground. We can offer you all the equipment you need for your lab and research."

"Blake would like to join in this venture. Do any of you have a problem with that?" asked Nelson.

Jase asked, "Equal shares?"

Nelson responded. "Jase and Blake will have equal shares. The Professor, Jill and Linda will split the third share equally. Please think about it. Now let me turn the meeting over to Blake.

Thank you, Nelson. The next thing we need to discuss is a house for you on the island. Rick Thomas is from Canada. He has brought along some sketches of houses. We have the entire beach front to use, so after we finish with the meeting, please get with him."

"Professor, you and Jase need to tell Larry Fence what you want in the center. We don't have a lot of regulations here, but I want to have everything above code. Now, if you will excuse me, I have some other work to be done. One more thing, if we build this together and any one wants out, I will purchase your shares." Blake adjourned the meeting, then got up and walked out, as the rest were busy looking at house plans.

Rick Thomas reminded them, "Blake made a promise to the people on the Island. For every building that we put up here, we will put up one for the people on the other side of the Island."

Jill was overwhelmed. "Jase, you pick out what you think we would like, but don't do anything unless you show it to me first. I'm going back to check on the children."

Linda asked if she could take the drawings back to study them, and she left right after Jill.

"How fast can you have the clinic open?" Jase asked.

"As soon as you can tell me what you want, I will have everything on a fast track. We can build a small temporary unit at first, then take our time and build a super center. That way we will not slow you down. I can have the man power here in a few days after everything has been approved."

"Rick, the Professor and I have made a list of the basics."

Rick glanced over the list. "If this is the basics, I can't wait to see the final blueprints."

Larry Fence said, "Why don't we go up to the mountain and take a look around."

Security brought two jeeps up to the front of the mansion. On the way up to the mountain Rick remarked, "The first thing we have to do is build a better road." Everyone agreed.

Nelson asked Jase, "Do you have any idea what you are going to name the cancer center?"

"I haven't given it much thought, Nelson."

"Well, it needs a name. Since you are the one behind this dream, I suggest we call it The Brick Cancer Center."

Then the Professor put his two cents in. "That sounds too much like every other cancer center in the world."

"What would you call it, Professor?" asked Nelson.

"I would call it, The J. Brick Cancer Cure Center."

"That would sure piss off that woman back in the states. What was her name?" asked Jase.

The Professor replied with a sneer, "Diane Worth."

"I would like to see he face when she first reads it," Jase answered.

Larry Fence asked Nelson, "How good is the air strip?"

"It is all right for small planes. But only one thing at a time, let's concentrate on the center," Nelson reminded everyone.

They pulled up at the front entrance. Larry started by taking pictures of everything, then he and Rick pulled their tape out and determined proper measurements.

Larry stopped everyone. "Here is a thought. The doors are too heavy to take down, so let's leave them functional and build onto the outside of the mountain. It will be nice to have the extra light from the sun. We can hide the doors, but if we ever needed to seal up the mountain, we will have that option. Then we build on the outside of the doors a fully functioning clinic for immediate use. We can build on the inside anytime."

"To the side of the main entrance is a second entrance that goes into the mechanical area," said Nelson.

"That is even better yet," answered Rick. "I have seen enough for now. I have to come back with some more equipment." They all piled into the jeeps. With all the ruts in the road, it was hard to talk on the way back.

Jase asked Rick, "How long before we can get a road to the center?"

"Mr. Canond has already authorized that project. The road will start the first of the week."

"That would be great," the Professor was holding his neck.

"Larry, I would like to go over the list I gave you, so you can incorporate the items that we need in the center."

"That would be good, Jase. I have no idea what you want to do with some of the things you asked for. Why do you need large clear containers?"

"In theory, we will use them in conjunction with the laser. Also, I need some medical equipment."

"Like what, Jase?"

"I will get you a list."

When they reached the mansion, Rick got his transit and tool box and went back to the mountain. The Professor and Jase sat down with Larry Fence.

Jase showed the Professor some rough drawings. "Can you do this?"

"How many sensors do you want on the container?"

"We need as many sensors as possible."

428

"Do you think we should use an ultrasound or something else?" asked the Professor.

"Let's find out where we can look at equipment, and then go from there. You will have to go along, Professor. You are the only one who knows if it will work with your laser. Also, see if you can put sensors on the outside of the tank."

"What the hell for? Are you going to drown then first?"

"Do you remember back in the fifties that someone discovered a liquid that you can breathe in? I think it is called perfluorocarbans. I want to know the effect it has on humans. How long they can stay in it and can it be regenerated for longer use."

"Well hell that should be easy enough," grumbled the Professor.

"Also, see if there are any other products we could use. Check the deep sea divers. They might use something similar."

"Holy shit, Jase, I was only joking."

"And Professor, we are in a hurry. I think our first patient may be coming soon."

"Maria, Jase?"

"Yes, but I hope not"

Larry Fence asked Jase, "So you want to treat people in a liquid?"

Jase responded, "I have given this a lot of thought. If we can have the patient floating in a liquid, that would help them protect against shock. We could even remove tissue on the outside of the body with much less pain than a normal surgery, and keep the patient in the liquid until healed. If the Professor can get the scanners to work in the container, the entire operation would go forward without making an incision."

"I'm impressed, Jase. If you can do this, you will change everything."

"Larry, we found out that the government would like to use our laser as a weapon, and I cannot let that happen. I think that they have already tried to kill the President."

"That was your laser? How did you stop it?"

Jase smiled, "The good Professor was ahead of the game. He rigged it to explode if they used it when we were not there."

"So this branch of the government may think that you know what they tried to do?"

"Kind of scary, isn't it," replied Jase as he changed the subject.

"But listen, if we can incorporate this liquid, we might be able to cure lung cancer using the laser, or remove anything else inside of the body that should not be there. With my laser, the cancer inside of the lymph nodes could be removed leaving the system intact."

"Sorry Larry, I have seen so much. If you are lucky enough to survive the treatment, you may not survive the cost. If you live, you may have lost your home. It is just wrong."

"But according to Nelson, you are going to charge one half of what the family has. How do you justify that?"

"Larry, I don't know what we are going to charge yet. We will not bankrupt anyone. They will not have to sell their house or their car. And that price includes everyone in the family. If you are rich, you pay more. If you are less fortunate, you pay less. If you die, you pay nothing. I better get off my soap box," said Jase.

"I had no idea how you felt, Jase. Now let's get down to business."

The Professor started to leave the meeting. "I have too much to do, so I am going."

"Thanks Professor," said Jase.

After the Professor left, Larry Fence said, "He is a different type of bird."

"Don't sell him short. He has one of the sharpest minds I have ever seen. Without his help with the laser, we would not be as far as we are. Inside his rough exterior, he is soft as a kitten."

Jase and Larry Fence spend most of the night working on the plans for the center. They never even thought about the time until one of the staff asked them if they would care for some breakfast.

Jill came into the conference room. "You two stayed up all night, didn't you?"

"Guilty as charged. I'm afraid your husband dream is contagious. I did not realize it was morning, until I smelled the coffee," answered Larry Fence.

"I don't suppose that you have looked at the house plans yet, have you?"

Jase couldn't even find the papers. He looked up and gave Jill one of the smiles he had for sorry.

Jill smiled, "Try not to be any longer than you have to."

"I think we are about done."

Larry agreed. "Jase is right. This has been one of the quickest nights of my life."

"Shall we get a bite to eat?" asked Jase.

"I think that would be a good idea," Larry answered.

"Will you join us, Jill?" asked Jase.

"That's why I'm here. Linda has the children under control"

The three walked over to the dining area and ordered breakfast. The Professor arrived shortly after they sat down.

"This liquid breathing is very interesting. It looks like you have to filter the liquid and constantly monitor the oxygen in it. The liquid is very expensive, but the good news is I found places that have the tanks."

Jill asked the Professor, "Sounds like you were up all night too."

All the Professor could say was, "I could eat a horse. What is the next step?"

"You are going to have to go and get medical supplies. We need our own drug store, and I think Dr. Aunser can help. It looks like we are in too far now to turn back."

They had breakfast, and then went their separate ways. All Jase wanted to do was take a nap. Jill followed him back to the guest house holding onto the sketches of the houses.

Chapter 60

Michael had been with his daughter for almost 24 hours, when Mary returned. She walked into the room.

"I'm sorry, Michael. I fell asleep and did not get up for over 18 hours. How is she doing?"

"She seems to be holding her own for right now. The doctor is due anytime."

A nurse walked in the room. "Mr. Greyger, you have a phone call at the desk."

Michael went to the desk. "This is Michael."

"Michael, this is Thomas. We think we have found Dr. Brick and I think Richard is going to do something. Can you get back here?"

"I will be there in an hour." Michael hung the phone up and walked back to Cindy's room.

"Mary, I have to go back to work. This is very important, but I will be back as soon as I can."

"Michael, did you get any sleep?"

"No."

Dr. White came into the room. "Here is your daily update on your daughter's condition. What are you going to do with it, if I might ask?"

"I have a hunch, and I am going to check it out. Have you found out what we are up against?"

"Yes, your daughter has a tumor on the right side of her brain. I would like to start treating her as soon as possible. We cannot get to it, so I don't think surgery is an option. The best that we can do is try to shrink it."

"Before we do that, can she be moved?" asked Michael.

"Yes, but I would not wait very long."

"I would like to take her on a vacation before we do anything."

"Mr. Greyger," said Dr. White, "Don't wait to long."

"I won't. Get her ready to leave, and give us all the instructions on what to watch for. I promised my daughter I would take care of her." Mary had to sit down. This was too much for her to bear.

Michael reached out to shake Dr. White's hand. "Thank you for everything you have done for her. How long can I keep her out of the hospital?"

"I would like to see her in a week, so whatever you do, do it quickly."

"I have already called to have my plane on standby."

Dr. White went to fill out the release forms. A nurse was already in the room to help Cindy get ready to leave.

Michael went to get the car. He was waiting outside the front door, when the nurse pushed the wheel chair out. Mary was next to Cindy holding her hand. They loaded her in the car very gently, and then they left for their home.

When the nurse went back to the floor, Dr. White was standing at the nursing desk. "Do you think that was the right thing to do, doctor?" The nurse asked.

He looked up. "I don't think it will make any difference. That little girl is going to go through hell before it is over for her. I hope that wherever he takes her, she has a good time."

Michael drove back to their house. Mary sat quietly next to Cindy in the back seat. When they were almost at the house, Michael said, "Mary, I would like you to pack enough clothes for one week. And dress for the warm weather, we are going to the gulf."

Mary knew that Michael had something in mind. "What are we doing, Michael?"

"We are going to take Cindy to a person that used to be my friend.

Chapter 61

Within the hour, they were packed and getting back into the car. They drove to Michael's office and pulled up in front of the building. Michael told the attendant not to park the car, because he was not going to be there that long.

Michael walked in. Thomas was at the front desk. "Michael, I'm glad you are here. Richard wants to talk to you."

Michael walked right to Richard's office. "Do you need to talk to me?"

"Yes, is your little girl alright? I heard she was sick."

"I think she will be ok. I guess we have located Dr. Brick. I have my plane ready to leave."

"Michael, I don't want you to go. I will send someone else, because Dr. Brick has become a liability. I think it will be in our best interest to erase him and anyone else that might know what we tried to do."

"Richard, I have a plan. I will fly down there and meet with Dr. Brick. If Blake Canond is behind him, we might think about it a little more before we erase him."

Richard was sitting in his chair. He put the chair all the way back, as if he was thinking.

"All right Michael, but don't screw this one up."

"I will leave ASAP. And Richard, I will call you when I find out anything."

Michael left Richard's office, and then he stopped at communications. "Give me the exact location of the island, and set up a flight plan for me. I am leaving for the airport now."

Michael went out to the car. "Is everything alright, Michael?" asked Thomas.

"Just another day, Thomas, I will be back as soon as I can." Michael drove his car out the drive to the main road. The next stop was the airport.

When they arrived at the airport, Michael's Beechcraft was ready for takeoff. The pilot met Michael at the car. "Would you help me load the bags into the plane?" he said to the pilot. "Mary, would you help Cindy get into the plane?"

Michael drove the car over to the parking lot, and then almost ran back. "Are we ready to fly, Roy?" asked Michael.

"Yes, I have the flight plan, and we are good to go as soon as you are ready."

"Good, let's go," said Michael. The plane was stocked with food and drinks. They were in the air quickly and headed south.

"Michael, we will make a stop in Texas to refuel. It is going to be a long trip, so relax."

"I can relieve you anytime you want, let's take shifts."

"Sounds good, I will need a break in a few hours. Do these people know you are coming?"

"No, I think it will be somewhat of a surprise."

They spent the rest of the day in the air, only stopping for fuel at a military airport in Texas. Night came quickly. "Michael, it should be daylight before we land."

"Do you want me to take over?"

"That would be good. I could use some sleep."

Michael took over the plane. "I really miss flying this plane."

He looked over his shoulder. His wife sat with his little girl sleeping in her arms. The moon was bright and there was not a cloud in the sky. The reflection from the ocean below showed the tears going down his face. He raced across the sky to a place he had never been before, and to people that he tried to destroy. How the next twenty four hours would go, only God knew.

The minutes seemed like hours. The twin engine plane hummed as they cruised through the sky. Behind the plane, Michael could see the sun coming up. The orange ball of fire started to light up the horizon. Michael had hours to think of how he was going to ask Jase for help. His stomach was in a knot. Now the sea was bright with the morning sun. He could see the clear water down to the reefs in some places. The pilot started to wake.

"Michael, you flew all night. Why didn't you wake me?"

"Roy, I have a lot on my mind, and I needed time to think. When we land, I don't know what kind of reception we will get. These are nice people that I treated very badly. Now I need them."

"I thought that this was part of a mission."

"It is, please don't make any waves. I will explain everything to you later."

"Michael, let me take over the plane, and you try to relax. We should be over the island soon." Neither man spoke another word until there was land in sight.

Michael had just closed his eyes, when Roy said, "We are coming up on the island. Do you have any idea where we can land?"

"Follow the shore line and hope that we see something."

"So you mean we flew all this way, and you don't know if there is a landing strip?"

"Roy, keep flying." As they flew closer to the island, they could see a mansion with a large dock in front of it. South of the dock was a small airstrip to land. The red sock was blowing in the wind.

"You had me going for a minute, Michael."

"I had me going for a minute too," Michael responded. Roy gave Michael an odd look.

"Fly over a couple of times and let them know we are here."

"I will."

The Professor was out with Rex taking him for a walk. He looked up and saw the plane circle the mansion. "Holy shit, I know that plane."

The Professor and Rex headed back to the house. When he arrived, Jill and Linda were watching the plane too. "Does that plane look familiar, Jill?" asked the Professor.

"No, not really," she answered.

"Oh my God, that's Michael's plane," shouted Linda. "You better go and get Jase, and I will tell the security."

"I don't think you have to tell security, they are already coming." Jill pointed to the men going down to the runway. "I will go get Jase."

This time the plane lowered the landing gear. "Well, it is going to land." The Professor said disappointedly.

By now Jase was awake, and Blake and Nelson were coming over. "Jase, do you know who is in that plane?" Nelson asked.

"I could be wrong, but I think that is Michael's plane."

"Yes, that is Michael's plane, and he is the only one who flies it. He might have a copilot, but you can be sure that Michael is on the plane." Linda was not pleased.

"I think we should let security do their job." Nelson had a radio. "Security, don't let anyone get off the plane. Find out what they want, but don't tell them anything."

"Roger, we copy that."

The plane came in for a smooth landing. As soon as the plane's engine stopped, security was out to meet it.

Michael opened the door, but before he could get off the plane, he was confronted by Blake's men.

"This is private property, and you have no business here."

Michael stepped out anyway. "I want to talk to Dr. Brick." Michael turned to the airplane, and when he turned around, he has Cindy in his arms.

"If Dr. Brick won't see me, please ask him to see my daughter." Michael was crying.

Mary got out of the plane next.

"Nelson, we have a situation here. No weapons, but there is a little girl, and the man requests for Dr. Brick to see her."

"Why?" asked Nelson.

"I don't know. But the man is crying, and I can't understand him."

Blake turned to Jase, "It is your call."

"Bring them up, but make sure no one has any weapons."

As they watched from the front of the mansion, the jeeps brought the visitors to the house. They stopped a few feet from the mansion, and Michael got out. He took his daughter from Mary's arms. "Dr. Brick, I need your help. This is my daughter, Cindy."

Jill walked over to the child and raised her eye lid, but the girl was not responding.
"Jase, something is terribly wrong with her."

Jase grabbed Cindy. "Michael, follow me. Tell me everything you can about her while we walk." Jase listened to Michael's story.

Blake said, "Jase, the yacht has a hospital just like the one on my jet."

"How far is your yacht from here?"

"It should be here within the hour."

"Is Dr. Aunser on the yacht?"

"Yes, what is wrong with the girl?"

"It looks like she is going into a coma. Is the chopper ready?"

Blake nodded to Nelson, and he picked up the radio. "This is Nelson, we have an emergency and we need the chopper on deck now.

"Nelson, the pilot is already on his way," said Blake. They looked down at the helicopter sitting next to the runway. They could see a man running to the chopper.

"Jill, let's see if we can get her awake. After several tries, she opened her eyes. "Daddy, where are we?"

"We are with someone who is going to help you." Michael's eyes were watery and red.

Nelson's radio barked. "We are ready to fly when you are."

Jase was giving orders. "Jill, you go with me. Michael, one of you can go. Make up your mind who is going, but hurry, we don't have much time."

"You go, Michael, I will stay. Take care of our girl." Mary kissed Cindy.

"Don't worry about the children, Jill. I will take good care of them."

"Thank you, Linda," said Jill.

"Let's go, we need to get this little girl to the ship." They were whisked by Jeep down to the chopper. As soon as the door shut, the rotor begins to turn.

The rest watched as the chopper gently rises and shoots out over the water until it was out of sight.

Blake put his arm around Mary. "Walk with me, we have a lot to talk about. How long have you been awake?"

"I don't know," Mary answered.

They walked into the house. "Come into the dining area. Can I get you something to eat?" They sat down, and the chef brought out some cheese and snacks. He held out some coffee.

Mary said, "Please, that would be nice."

"First," said Blake, "I would like to apologize for the welcome you received. But you have to understand, these good people have been running from your husband for some time. He wanted to turn some of Dr. Brick's medical equipment into weapons. We think he might have even tried to assassinate the President. That is why I helped him and his family to get out of the country."

Mary was speechless.

The helicopter was getting close to the yacht, and Dr. Aunser was waiting. The sea was smooth, so landing was not a problem.

As soon as they landed, the deck crew raced to the chopper. When the door opened, Dr. Aunser took the girl and rushed her to the medical room. Jase and the others were right behind him. As they walked into the room, the lights turned on.

"We need to get some blood first," said Jase. "Where are the…"

Before Jase could ask, Dr. Aunser pointed to a tray. Jase grabbed the needle and very gently took a blood sample. He gave it to Dr. Aunser. "I think we need to start an IV."

Cindy would open her eyes and see her Dad, then smile and go back to sleep.

Jase had the IV going. "Let me see those papers you have, Michael." Michael gave the papers from Dr. White to Jase.

"Dr. Aunser, she has a brain tumor, and it has fingers over the side of her brain," Jasc said very quietly.

Dr. Aunser replied, "She is going to need some blood."

"Do you have any blood on the ship?" asked Jase.

"Yes, it seems that she has the same type of blood as Blake."

"It would have helped if we had a disc of the MRI," Jase said.

Dr. Aunser opened the door in the back of the medical room, and waved for Jase to look.

Jase walked over to the door. Inside of the small room was a MRI.

"I should have known. I hope that you know how to use it."

Back at the Island, they could see the yacht coming in. The Captain of the ship glided her to a perfect rest next to the dock.

Blake and Nelson escorted Mary onto the yacht. Normally, she would have been impressed with everything about the yacht. But today with the worry of her daughter being sick, and the conversation she had with Blake, it was the last thing on her mind.
The tears were gone from her face when she entered the medical room. Michael was standing next to the door.

He turned to Mary. "She will be out in a minute. They are giving her an MRI."

Mary confronted Michael, "Is it true, did you try to kill the President?" Michael did not answer.

Mary was getting angrier. "And did you force these people out of the country?" Again, Michael did not say anything.

"Right now Michael, we worry about Cindy. But later, I will deal with you, and what you have done. All of these years you lied to me." Mary was about to slap Michael, when the door opened.

"Mommy!" Cindy was glad to see her Mother.

Jase was listening to the conversation between the two. "So you did try to use the laser as a weapon. I did not think even you would try something like that."

Nelson stepped in. "Michael, do you have a contract out on the Brick family?"

"Michael, how could you?" said Mary.

"The first thing we do is take care of that girl. Nelson have you seen the Professor?" asked Jase.

"The last time I saw him he was trying to get parts for a new laser."

"Michael, come with me. Mary, could you please stay with your daughter. Dr. Aunser is with her now. I have to check on getting a new laser working, because your husband destroyed the last one. Let's go Michael. There is someone I want you to meet." They walked onto the deck and then to the dock. When they got up to the mansion, Jase stopped.

"I would like you to meet our collections person. Michael, meet Linda Peach. She is head of out accounts receivable."

The Professor was walking out of the building as they were walking into it. "Jase, I can't get what I need. We will have to start from scratch."

"Professor, that little girl does not have that much time."

"Would all the equipment you left at the lab help?" Everyone turned to Michael. "I can have it all brought here in twenty four hours."

"How can you do that?" asked the Professor.

"Leave it to me. What else do you need?"

"Well hell," the Professor put his arm around Michael. "Come this way my boy, have I got a list for you." The Professor walked away with Michael.

"Jase, these are very powerful people we are dealing with. Even if Michael tries to help us, the others will not stop until we all are out of the way," said Blake. "Do I have your permission to contact a few friends of my own?"

"Of course, Blake."

"Let me make a few phone calls."

The Professor gave Michael a list. "I don't know if I can get all of this, but I will try," Michael responded. "I need to get to my plane and use the radio."

"You can use the radio here."

"No Professor, my radio has top secret channels. I can get through a lot of red tape in a short time."

The Professor jumped into a jeep and drove Michael to his plane. "I would not want you to take off without your family," said the Professor.

Michael got into the cockpit with the Professor. He picked up the mic and called.

"Michael, is that you?"

"Yes, I need some equipment. Put me in touch with level three."

"Yes sir. Michael, Richard wants to talk to you, hold on."

"Michael, this is Richard. Have you contacted Dr. Brick?"

"Yes," said Michael.

"Does he know anything about what we tried to do?"

"No Richard, he does not have clue."

"Seaban will be glad to hear that. He has been all over me. So, what do you need, Michael?"

"Richard, Dr. Brick said he would make a new laser for me, but he needs everything from his lab. I had to make a deal with him."

"What kind of deal?"

"Well, I have a list for you, and he needs it by tomorrow."

"Who the hell does he think we are, fucking Santa?"

"Richard, he has a patient that is close to death, and he does not have any equipment yet. Now if you want the laser, get this stuff here ASAP. Put it in a Chinook and get it here. He said he would have the new laser ready in a week. I will stay here until it's done. The Chinook can stay here, so I can use it if we need it. Richard, this is the only way you will ever have your laser."

"Alright Michael, I will have everything he wants there by tomorrow. But after I get my laser, it is open season on Brick and Company."

"I understand, Richard. I will call you back at 0:700 tomorrow morning. Michael out."

Michael turned to the Professor. Can you get everything together in time?"

"Let's hope so, for your daughter's sake."

They drove back to the mansion. Michael said to the Professor, "You know that I am a dead man, don't you?"

The Professor answered, "Better you than your daughter."

Blake and Nelson were waiting for the Professor. "How did it go, Professor? Are we getting the equipment?" asked Nelson.

"I think Michael did a real nice job for us, but this Richard fella is going to kill all of us after he gets his laser. Overall though, it was pretty good day."

Blake asked, "Did you hear him say that?"

Michael answered, "Yes, but I can't prove it. I think I can stop him though. You can trust me."

The Professor smiled. "Michael, I've always trusted you. Now let's go tell Jase that his stuff is coming."

They went onboard the yacht. Cindy was up in the lounge. When she saw Michael, she put out her arms for him. Michael grabbed his little girl. She whispered in his ear, "I love you Daddy."

"Jase," said the Professor, "Michael has a lot of pull when he wants to. All your stuff will be here tomorrow."

Dr. Aunser said, "Mr. Greyger, we gave your daughter a blood transfusion. She has her strength for now, but we need to get the rest of Dr. Brick's equipment here, so we can win this battle."

Jill said she was going to check on the children. Jase, Nelson and Blake went to the upper deck. Blake said, "I made some calls, and I think that we should have some company here later on today. It seems that the Secret Service is very interested in the laser also. But Michael was right, how can we prove what Richard said?"

The Professor said, "I'm surprised at you guys. You worry about some of the dumbest things. Oh, I forgot to show you something." The Professor pulled out a mini recorder from his pocket. "I won't play the entire thing, but you might want to hear the last part."

When the Professor played the recording, they all could hear Richard say, "But after I get my laser, it's open season on Brick and Company."

"It gets a lot better," said the Professor. "Blake, do you have a safe I can put this in?"

"Right this way, Professor." Blake took the Professor to his office.

"Jase," said Nelson, "The Professor said that you have a way of attracting excitement. I think he was right."

They were all sitting on the top deck of the yacht. "Has any one seen Michael?" asked Nelson.

The Professor said, "I thought I saw him down by his plane." Everyone started to get up. "Don't worry, you can trust him. He probably wants to know who removed all the wires from the radio and starter. I will fix it for him in the morning, so he can check in with Richard."

Everyone relaxed a little.

By morning, the Professor had the radio working again. As Michael was walking to the plane, the Professor yelled. "Hey Michael, I fixed your radio for you. All it took was a couple of parts and wires."

Michael gave the Professor a dirty look. Then he keyed up the radio and called in.

"Michael, the cargo you ordered has an ETA of 13:30 hours. As soon as the cargo arrives, Richard wants you to call in."

"Roger that, I will call in upon its arrival. Michael out."

The Professor walked up to Michael. "Are you hungry? Let's go and get something to eat. And Michael, you have done the right thing."

When they went back to the yacht, everyone was up. Cindy was eating with her mother. Mary would not look at Michael.

"Michael, what would you like to eat? It's going to be a long day." said Blake.

"Anything will be fine." He sat smiling at Cindy.

"Michael, when you are done. I would like to introduce you to some friends of mine," said Blake. As Michael looked up at Blake, two men in black suits with sunglasses came up from the lower deck.

"These friends of mine are with the Secret Service. They would like to talk to you, after we get your daughter back in good shape."

"All we have to do now is wait," said Jase. "Michael, can you trust Richard to keep his word?"

"I hope so." he answered.

About one o'clock, the Captain called down, "We have three aircraft coming in low. I thought that only one aircraft was coming."

"Don't worry, Captain, two of them are ours. Sometimes a little back up is a good thing."

The Chinook was being escorted by one armed Apache and another Chinook helicopter. When the cargo Chinook touched down, the other two hovered near it. They radioed the Chinook to shut down and prepare for boarding.

The chopper shut down and the cargo doors opened. All of the people on board were ordered to disembark from the aircraft. A small squad of heavily armed Marines left the aircraft.

They could hear the loud speaker from one of the choppers. "Lay down on the ground, by order of the President of the United States."

The squad did so. Then the Chinook landed as the Apache hovered. An armed man jumped out of the Chinook. "Who is in charge of this unit, sound off now."

"I am sir. Sergeant Headwin, Sir!"

"What are you orders?"

"Seek out and destroy all possible terrorist, Sir."

"Have your men stand down. Sergeant, drop your weapon and come over here." The Marine did what he was told.

"Show me your orders, Sergeant."

"My orders were verbal, Sir."

"Who gave you the orders, Marine?"

"A high level government official, Sir."

"Do you have any equipment onboard, Marine?"

"Yes Sir, a ton of medical equipment, Sir."

"Sergeant, have all your men stand down now. Remove all of your weapons and place them over here."

"Yes Sir!"

One by one the Marines put their weapons next to the Lieutenant. After all of the men removed their weapons, they were told to sit down in the sand on the beach. As soon as they were seated, more Marines jumped out of the Lieutenant's chopper.

"Sergeant, show me your cargo."

They walked to the cargo door. All the equipment was in the Chinook. The Lieutenant waved to the Apache to land.

"Is there a fork lift in here, Sergeant?"

"Yes Sir!"

By this time, more Marines were on the ground.

"Sergeant, have your men march in single file to the building in front of you. I would like to introduce you to your terrorist, and I will check out your story."

Blake's security team was out in force as the Marines walked up to the mansion. When they arrived at the pool area, the Lieutenant asked the Sergeant more questions.

"Sergeant, have your men fall in."

"Yes Sir! Fall in." The squad falls in.

"Sergeant, will you tell me and these terrorist who gave the order to remove them."

"Yes Sir! A high level person in the government."

"Sergeant, does this person have a name?"

"Yes sir, his name is Richard Greyger, Sir"

Chapter 62

"Sergeant, have your men stand down. These two men are from the Secret Service. They will be asking you some questions. You better hope you give them the right answers."

"Lieutenant," said Jase, "We need that equipment now. A little girl's life depends on it."

The lieutenant had one Marine watch the men, and the others started to unload the cargo.

"Professor, where do you want the equipment?"

"Right here on the cement next to the guest house. Blake, how much power is available?"

"As much as you need, and I will have the staff right on it."

"Jase, I had them throw in a med tent. We need to set up right here on the pool patio."

Box after box arrived. The Professor was busy getting everything on line. He and Jase had the lasers working in no time. The hard part was combining them with a scanner.

By nightfall, they were almost ready for a test. One of the Secret Service men came over to the Lieutenant. "It would seem that these men were just following orders. They thought they were after some terrorist. They had shoot to kill orders."

"Can we trust them?" asked the Professor. "We could use their help."

"They are just pawns following orders."

"Good," said the Professor.

The Lieutenant walked over to the Marines. How would you Marines like to get off your asses and help us move this equipment?"

They said in unison, "Yes Sir."

"Professor, let's try a test. Put a piece of fruit on the table and covered it with a piece of plywood. Scan it, and put the information into the lasers," said Jase. "Are you ready, Professor?"

"No, but let's try anyway."

They turned on the first laser, and then the second one. The lasers started to burn away the fruit. They continued until there was no fruit left. "We are ready. Let's bring the girl out."

Michael said, "I will get her." He returned shortly with Cindy holding on to him very tightly.

"All right, this is a clean area and no one should be in here except Jill, Dr Aunser and me," Jase said. "Cindy, we are going to make you feel much better. Are you all right with that?"

"Did my Daddy say it is all right?"

"He is right outside, and I think he can hear us."

"Cindy, this is Daddy. Dr. Brick is going to help you."

"All right, Daddy."

"Cindy, Dr.Aunser is going to make you sleepy. Will you tell me when you are asleep?"

"That is silly, how can I do …." She never finished. She was out.

They position her head, so the side with the tumor was on top. Then they put a homemade support structure over her head. They already had the scans, so Jase put all the information into the computer.

"As soon as we start, you will want to up the pain medicine. Watch her blood pressure and use it as a guide. We don't want her waking up at anytime. Are you ready, Dr. Aunser?'

"Yes Jase, I'm ready."

Outside of the tent, Michael and Mary could hear the lasers warming up and see the shadows on the wall of the tent as the procedure continued. Sometimes they could hear one of them speak.

Jill was watching all of Cindy's vital signs. "She is starting to twitch a little, Jase," said Jill.

"Dr. Aunser, would you please give her a little more pain medicine?"

"She has stopped twitching," said Jill.

As Michael and Mary stood on the outside watching and listening, Michael reached over to put his hand on Mary's. It was instantly rejected.

It seemed as if the operation went on forever. "We are almost done. I don't want to go too fast. I think everything looks good, but we need to keep her under longer. I don't know if she could tolerate the pain."

Everyone could hear the lasers shutting down. "I think it would be best if we moved her into the yacht in a little while. How is her blood pressure, Jill?" asked Jase.

"It was high, but now it is starting to come down, and her heart beat is going back to normal too."

"For the first hour, I want to scan her ever twenty minutes. We don't want any bleeding." Jase was pleased with the surgery. "Let's keep her under for a little while, and then wake her up slowly. What a day. Thank you, Dr. Aunser, and thank you dear."

Jase walked out of the tent. "I think everything went very well. We will see in the morning. As soon as she is able, we will start her on some chelative compounds. If she has any cancer left in her system, we can flush it out."

"Michael, Mary, only one of you can stay with her at a time. Don't try to wake her. We are going to leave her under for a while. We don't want her to go into shock. Either Dr. Aunser or I will be there all through the night. The tumor is gone."

Everyone was up all night. The Marines had moved everything up to the tent area.

The Lieutenant came over to Jase. "I didn't want to bother you, but we traced this Richard fellow back to an agency. It has an unlimited budget and no one even knew it existed. We have not been able to reach anyone, but we will continue to look.

I don't think you will need to worry about him any longer."

"I have one more question for Michael. Why do you and Richard have the same last name?" Jase asked.

Michael stopped in his tracts. "Richard is my older brother."

The next day, Jase slowly brought Cindy out of her coma. She did not seem to be in much pain, but they kept her on pain meds anyway. They took a new MRI, and the tumor was completely gone. Jase started her on a chelation IV mixed with vitamins and proteins. She started to pick up more energy each day.

Chapter   63

Michael turned State's evidence against his brother and Mr. Seaban, both of whom disappeared. The agency was shut down. As for Michael, The Secret Service took him underground. But before Michael left, Linda called him into her new office and said, "Michael, I need your Social Security number. You are our first customer. And Michael, it has been a pleasure working for you," Linda smiled. Michael was speechless.

Jill, Jase and Linda, were enjoying their new beach homes. The babies were both crawling. Jack was into everything. Eva thought that she was a princess, and she was. Chloe was now their official baby sitter and loved every minute of it.

The Professor had everything he ever wanted out of life. If he needed something, all he had to do was order it. With his new lab, sometimes he did not come out all day, unless he heard someone say gin and squirt. Then he moved like lightning. When Jase checked all the equipment that the Professor had requested, he could not believe it when he saw the Professor's car. Now he knew that he had seen everything.

Blake's son, Cian, was teaching Rex Spanish. The Professor was at a loss when he tried to call Rex.

The new road to the center was done, and the preliminary Brick Cancer Cure Center was in full operation. Maria Valdez was a volunteer at the new center.

Michael's little girl, Cindy, was doing fine. She was living at her home in Virginia with her mother. Dr. White called Mary and wanted her to bring Cindy into the hospital. When she got there, she showed Dr. White the MRI of Cindy. He took the disc over to compare it to the one that he had taken. "Impossible," he said. He asked Cindy if she had seen another doctor. She answered, "Yes, Dr. Brick." Dr. White could not believe his eyes. He went home early that day.

Robert Lee Seaban was nowhere to be found. His network SNN would give an update every night about him on the news. None of it was true.

Diane Worth was on TV all of the time demanding, "This quack, Dr. Jase Brick, should be forced to come back to the states. He is charging outrageous amounts of money for the treatment of cancer, and I won't stop until this quack is behind bars. Hear me, Dr. Brick, I will force you out and show the world what you are."

In Key West, Peanut Butter was showing everyone the pictures of her darling cousins Jack and his sister Eva.

THE   END